HOKULOA ROAD

BOOKS BY ELIZABETH HAND

CASS NEARY NOVELS

Generation Loss

Available Dark

Hard Light

The Book of Lamps and Banners

The Best of Elizabeth Hand

Curious Toys

Wylding Hall

Errantry: Strange Stories

Radiant Days

Illyria

Saffron and Brimstone: Strange Stories

Chip Crockett's Christmas Carol

Mortal Love

Bibliomancy: Four Novellas

Black Light

Last Summer at Mars Hill and Other Stories

Glimmering

Waking the Moon

Icarus Descending

Aestival Tide

Winterlong

HOKULOA ROAD

ELIZABETH HAND

MULHOLLAND BOOKS

Little, Brown and Company

New York Boston London

Copyright © 2022 by Elizabeth Hand

Hachette Book Group supports the right to free expression and the value of copyright. The purpose of copyright is to encourage writers and artists to produce the creative works that enrich our culture.

The scanning, uploading, and distribution of this book without permission is a theft of the author's intellectual property. If you would like permission to use material from the book (other than for review purposes), please contact permissions@hbgusa.com. Thank you for your support of the author's rights.

Mulholland Books / Little, Brown and Company
Hachette Book Group
1290 Avenue of the Americas, New York, NY 10104
mulhollandbooks
twitter.com/mulhollandbooks
facebook.com/mulhollandbooks

First edition: July 2022

Mulholland Books is an imprint of Little, Brown and Company, a division of Hachette Book Group, Inc. The Mulholland Books name and logo are trademarks of Hachette Book Group, Inc.

The publisher is not responsible for websites (or their content) that are not owned by the publisher.

The Hachette Speakers Bureau provides a wide range of authors for speaking events. To find out more, go to hachettespeakersbureau.com or call (866) 376-6591.

The Kumulipo: A Hawai'ian Creation Chant, translated by Martha Beckwith, copyright © 2000 by University of Hawai'i Press. Used by permission.

ISBN 9780316542043
LCCN 2021950347

Printing 1, 2022

LSC-C

Printed in the United States of America

For Kristabelle Munson,
with love and gratitude

Fear falls upon me on the mountain top
Fear of the passing night
Fear of the night approaching . . .
Dread of the place of offering and the narrow
    trail . . .
Dread of the receding night
Awe of the night approaching
Awe of the dog child of the Night-creeping-away
A dog child of the Night-creeping-hither
   —from *The Kumulipo: A Hawai'ian Creation Chant*,
                translated by Martha Beckwith

"It's so still."
"It's the quietest place on earth. You'll see for yourself. It's so beautiful. There's no one here."
"We're here."
               —from *Stalker*, Andrei Tarkovsky

HOKULOA ROAD

CHAPTER 1

L ate one July morning, Grady's older brother, Donny, texted him
a screenshot of the ad for the caretaker job.

*Caretaker wanted, Hawai'i. Independent & resourceful. Valid driver's
license required. Carpentry skills a plus. Housing provided. Salary
TBD. firemanta@island.net*

Grady laughed. Wtf that Craigs list?

Yeah ima serious dude, Donny replied. email him.

Instead, Grady called his brother. It rolled over into voicemail,
which meant Donny was probably trying to find a place to talk in
private. He was four years older and lived in a halfway house not far
from Portland, Maine, a few hours south of where Grady was on the
Mid Coast. A minute later, Donny rang back.

"Where'd you see that job listing?" Grady asked, voice low so he
wouldn't wake their mother, who worked the hospital night shift
as an LPN.

"Just now, waiting room." Donny was midway through two years'
probation for fentanyl possession and had to take a weekly piss test.
"I'm fucking serious—one of us should live in Hawai'i. And you
need to get out of Mom's house. And—shit, I gotta go—"

The call ended. Grady shoved the phone into his pocket and
walked out onto the back deck. His brother could be a major pain
in the ass, but he had a point. Grady had been living with their
mother since early April, just weeks after the lockdown—almost

3

three months now. Their father was long gone—he'd killed himself when Grady was five. The suicide was like a black drain they'd been circling ever since, though only Donny got sucked down it.

Before the pandemic hit, Grady had worked as a finish carpenter, most recently on a long-term gig for a couple of Masshole plastic surgeons from Marblehead, husband and wife building their dream home on Sennebec Pond. Quartz kitchen countertops, a Japanese toilet with a heated seat that had its own temperature control. Who needed that shit?

The job ended abruptly when the wife got COVID. Grady and the other crew had to isolate for two weeks. Grady definitely felt bad about that. They all needed the work. One guy had just bought a new truck, another had twins on the way. No one got sick, but by the time quarantine ended, all the other building sites had shut down, too. As an independent worker, Grady could collect unemployment, but after his application was bounced twice for no frigging reason, he gave up. His stimulus check went to back rent and two overdue truck payments. So he moved back home.

Now it was July and there was no work other than side jobs. Helping his friend Zeke load his delivery truck with firewood, or taking down trees decimated by venomous browntail moth caterpillars. Clearing brush from the Mic Mac Campground so that rich COVID refugees from Boston and New York could park their RVs and go hiking in the state park while they pretended to quarantine.

Grady scrutinized the screenshot again. *Caretaker wanted, Hawai'i.* The only person he knew who'd ever been to Hawai'i was a heating contractor in Rockland. He'd taken his wife and two young kids and lived on one of the Hawai'ian Islands for a year.

"The kids went barefoot the whole time," he'd told Grady after he returned. "Walked to school barefoot, ate coconuts from our backyard. Me and Lisa surfed every day. It was frigging heaven."

Grady couldn't remember the last time he'd walked barefoot anywhere except indoors. There were no sand beaches in this part of Maine, and the grass was filled with ticks. What would it be like to live someplace he wouldn't have to dig his truck out of a foot of snow—or ice, or mud—for half the year? He didn't know anyone in Hawai'i, but then he'd hardly seen anyone in Maine since the pandemic began. Last time he'd run into his ex-girlfriend Rachel was six months ago. She'd been accepted into the PhD program in archaeology at Boston University. And oh, yeah, she'd gotten married.

After that, he'd dated a girl he met on Bumble, but they'd had nothing in common except the facts they were twenty-eight and single and lived within twenty miles of Rockland. Maine was great if you had money and a partner, but otherwise it was lonely as hell. He sure as shit wasn't going to find money or a girlfriend during a pandemic.

What the fuck, he had nothing to lose. He went to his childhood bedroom and opened his laptop, checked the screenshot again, and emailed firemanta.

CHAPTER 2

The following afternoon, he'd just cracked a PBR and logged into *World of Warcraft* when an email alert flickered in the corner of his laptop screen.

> Hi Grady,
>
> Is there a time we could talk this evening? Also, please send a copy of your résumé.
>
> Best regards,
>
> Wes Minton

"Fuck me." Grady reread the message. Did he even have a résumé? He logged out of WOW, grabbed another beer, and made a list of the carpentry jobs he'd worked on for the last eight years. He found a résumé template online and went to the White Mountains Community College website.

We're training New England's Future Outdoor Leaders!

He'd finished only two years at WMCC before he failed his wilderness solo and his money ran out, but maybe this guy wouldn't bother to check. He cut-and-pasted info from the site.

Studied outdoor recreation and tourism at foremost college, skills in sea kayaking, wilderness medicine, mountaineering, scuba diving, rock climbing. He'd never actually gone scuba diving but figured that might be useful in Hawai'i. He could always learn.

He sat for a minute, then added *Certified EMT*. Which was true—he'd taken EMT classes after he dropped out of WMCC, though he'd only briefly worked as a first responder when he was twenty-two. The local ambulance company had paid for his classes, paid for his textbooks, and offered him a job once he'd completed his training. He'd started a bit nervous, though not much. While the sight of blood bothered him, it didn't make him pass out. Same with protruding bones. He practiced box breathing and other ways of staying calm under pressure and always felt jacked from adrenaline as soon as he stepped into the ambulance. He successfully performed CPR a few times, tended to some rollover accidents. He felt pretty confident that he'd at last found a job he could, if not excel at, at least perform without fucking up. That had ended when he got the call involving Kayla MacIntosh.

He saved his document and got another beer. He hated this kind of stuff, hated thinking about Kayla. He was a terrible liar, unlike Donny, though maybe Donny wasn't so great either, since he always seemed to get caught. But lying came naturally to his brother, whereas it always made Grady anxious, even stupid white lies, like this résumé. Which looked decent, though it would be easy for someone to make a call to WMCC and learn that he'd never graduated. And probably his EMT certification had expired.

But what the hell. He sent the résumé to Wes Minton, logged back into WOW and played for a couple hours. Around midnight, he received a new message from firemanta.

Hi Grady,

Are you free to talk now?

Wes

Cursing, Grady pushed the line of empty beer cans into a waste-basket. He shouldn't have finished the half rack. What time was it in Hawai'i? He went into the bathroom and hurriedly washed his face, slicking back his damp hair. He'd shaved this morning, so he didn't look too derelict. He returned to his room and replied.

I can talk now.

Within seconds, an email with a Zoom link appeared. When Grady clicked on it, a dazzle of light and color filled the screen—green, yellow, red, blue, orange, with a dark blur in the center.

"Grady. Good to meet you."

Grady blinked. The colors were palm trees, gigantic ferns, a trailing vine that looked like a burning pink fuse. In the middle of it all was an older white man's face, tanned and ruggedly youthful, though his dark shaggy hair was mostly gray.

"Hi." Grady adjusted the light on his desk. "Yeah, uh, nice to meet you."

"What time is it there?"

"Almost one a.m."

"Ooof." Minton winced. "Sorry about that. Thanks for taking the time. I'm Wesley Minton. Wes. Okay if we go over a couple things?" Wes leaned forward, his face blotting out the brilliant garden. "You've done a lot of carpentry and construction, right? What about caretaking?"

"Sure. Some of the people I worked for, they're only here a couple months in the summer. I keep an eye on their houses the rest of the year."

"And you're an EMT? Ever performed an appendectomy on yourself?"

"What?"

"Guy I know, a heart surgeon, he had to do that in Alaska. You'll be on your own a lot. You okay with that?"

Grady couldn't tell if this guy was joking, but before he could answer, Wes asked, "Ever been to Hawai'i?"

"No."

"Really?" Wes looked stunned, like Grady had confessed he'd never driven a car. "Well, it's amazing. Different now, because of the pandemic, but that's good. No tourists. I don't see any references here."

Grady flushed. "Oh, yeah, sorry. I can get you those tomorrow morning."

"No worries. I'll run a background check. Maine—what're your numbers like there?"

"Not too bad."

"You'll have to quarantine for two weeks—no screwing around, we don't want to take a chance on you getting sent back home. You okay with that?"

Grady started to reply but stopped. Was this guy actually going to hire him? He nodded cautiously.

"Yeah," Wes continued, "if you violate quarantine, they'll arrest you and send you back to the mainland. Can you handle four-wheel drive?"

"Sure. Would I need to bring my own tools?"

"No, I've got everything here from the last guy. You have any questions, Grady? You travel much?"

"I went to Disneyland once with my family."

"You have a family?"

"I was a kid, I went with my mom and my brother."

"So no significant other? I forgot to mention that. You'll have your own house, but it's compact—it's not really set up for a couple."

Grady's throat grew tight. What the fuck was he doing? Before he could say anything more, Wes clapped his hands.

"Okay, look, you've got my email. After I run the background check, we'll figure out the details of salary and your airfare. Sounds good?"

Grady stared at him. "Sounds good," he said at last.

"Excellent. Talk to you soon," said Minton, and the screen went black.

CHAPTER 3

Grady got himself some water, pulled on his Sea Dogs hoodie, and stepped outside. The air was cool and smelled of balsam fir and rugosa roses. The moon was just past full. Around him stretched woods and fields, the homes of kids he'd grown up with: farmhouses, mobile homes, a few scruffy back-to-the-land DIY homesteads like Zeke's. He slapped a mosquito whining in his ear and tilted his head to stare at the moon, remembering how he and Donny used to camp out here when they were teens, a stolen bottle of Dewar's hidden under their sleeping bags. How they'd do a shot every time they saw a shooting star.

Would you even see the same stars in Hawai'i? Weren't there different constellations in the Southern Hemisphere? But he didn't know if Hawai'i was in the Southern Hemisphere. His only impressions came from old surfing movies. *Jurassic Park* had been shot there, right? And *Lost*? He'd watched that show all during middle and high school, even when it made no sense to him, which was most of the time.

Still, the island setting had been beautiful. He and Zeke and Donny had gotten into arguments over whether it was all real or just CGI. As a young teenager, Grady had wanted it to be real. Not the story or the characters but that place, with its empty beaches and empty sea and air that, even on their crappy little TV screen, seemed to shimmer with something he couldn't put a name to. A threat, maybe, even though that was a weird thing to wish for; the thought that the wider world might be very different from the little he'd seen of it. His rich clients always told him, as an adult, that Maine wasn't the real world. Marblehead was the real world, and places like New York City and Greenwich, Palm Springs and Winter Park and San Francisco. Grady had always thought they were just pissing smoke.

But what if they were right? He didn't believe he was living in the Matrix or some crazy shit like that, like the weird conspiracies Zeke spouted. But what if life was actually different in New York or California?

Here was his chance to find out if all those rich people had been lying, the way they lied about getting him a check end of next week. Donny or Zeke would give their left nut to fly to Hawai'i, especially now. Grady would be crazy not to go.

From somewhere at the edge of the yard, a barred owl called.

Who cooks for you? Who cooks for you?

Grady stared into the oaks, their branches skeletal and leafless from the damn browntail caterpillars. He watched a ghostly shape emerge and then drop to the high grass, before rising like a cloud of smoke to disappear.

CHAPTER 4

The flight to L.A. was barely a third full—solo travelers like himself, a few couples, two families with small kids. Everyone was masked, which made Grady feel like he was trapped in an airborne hospital waiting room. He had the window seat in an otherwise empty row, staring down as Boston gave way to sprawl, the rumpled green of the White Mountains, then nothing as clouds overtook the airplane.

He wadded up his hoodie and tried to sleep. After an hour he gave up, his long legs cramping. There was no food or beverage service. Zeke had picked him up at 2 a.m. and driven him to Logan, but nothing had been open in the airport when Grady arrived. Now he had a frigging caffeine headache.

Rubbing his eyes, he lowered his tray table and pulled down his mask, popped a few ibuprofen. Ate half of the turkey and cheese sandwich he'd made the night before, drank some water. When he checked the moving map on the screen above his tray table, they were only above Pennsylvania.

Groaning, he sank back, knees bucking against the seat in front of him. He took out his cell phone and spent a few minutes reading a guide to the island's wildlife and outdoor activities he'd downloaded. A lot of fishing but also hunting, wild boar and some kind of deer, both introduced by earlier waves of settlers. Maybe he'd get a gun and a gun license.

He closed the brochure and scrolled through the messages he'd received from Wesley Minton in the days before he left. There was no further mention of a background check, so he assumed he'd passed, only a flurry of texts about his flight itinerary, the address of where Grady would be staying—Hokuloa Road, no street number—and the name and cell-phone number of someone named Dalita Nakoa.

> Dalita will pick you up at the airport.

> She will get any groceries you need, text her list when you arrive LAX.

> Be sure to fill out health arrival forms and take ibuprofen before you land on the island.

> They will check your temp at airport.

> Use Dalita's name as your emergency contact.

Was Dalita Wes Minton's wife or girlfriend? Why use her name and not his own? Because she was the one meeting him at the airport? He hadn't mentioned being married, or anything else.

When Grady had Googled Wesley Minton, he didn't find much. Some kind of hedge fund guy who made his nut and moved to Hawai'i. He was involved with a bunch of environmental groups. The Sierra Club, the Nature Conservancy, the Island Nature Trust, and the Hokuloa Wilderness Foundation. The same three images of Minton kept popping up—a generic corporate headshot and two photos of him at charity benefits, one a big environmentalist bash on the island, the other a Planned Parenthood benefit in Honolulu.

In the first photo, Minton wore a Hawai'ian shirt and a very long lei made out of green leaves. He stood beside a tall, beautiful Hawai'ian woman who looked like a model. Grady recognized her name—Maxine Kaiwi.

LOCAL PHILANTHROPIST WESLEY MINTON MAKES LANDMARK DONA-
TION TO PRESERVE ISLAND WILDERNESS

The photo was dated twenty years ago, though Minton looked pretty much the same. He must've been in his mid-thirties when it was taken, not much older than Grady was now. Lucky bastard.

Grady stared at the moving map. They'd only just passed Pittsburgh. How frigging big was Pennsylvania? He closed his eyes and thought of his last conversation with his mom the night before, the two of them sitting on the back porch.

"Are you sure you want to do this?" she'd asked. "You don't know anyone there. You'll be very alone."

"It'll be fine. I'll meet people—"

"You're going to be in quarantine. And you don't know anything about this man."

"I know he's bought my plane ticket and given me a job, which is more than I have here, okay?" He tried to keep his voice level. "I just want to get away for a while. I've never been anywhere. I've never done anything except carpentry. You're always telling me I should aim higher. So I'm doing it. I'll be fine. At least it's the same country."

"It's five thousand miles away." His mother's face tightened, a sign she was fighting tears. "Once you're there, I'll never see you again."

"You will definitely see me again," said Grady, and leaned over to give her a quick hug.

But as he finished packing, he wondered if he'd miss any of this, all of this, when he was gone. He wondered if he'd ever come back.

CHAPTER 5

He woke in the plane's window seat with a crick in his neck and a headache from the citrusy reek of hand sanitizer. As he pulled down his mask to draw a few furtive breaths, the pilot announced they would be landing soon. Across the aisle, a woman grabbed her companion and pointed out the window.

"Those aren't clouds," she exclaimed. "It's smoke from the fires."

Wildfires or not, they landed without a problem. By the time he finally found his gate, the island flight was preboarding. As the line inched toward the Jetway entrance, he felt light-headed with nerves but also a strange relief. He was going to a place where he knew no one, which meant no one knew him except as the person on his résumé: competent and experienced. He felt like he did driving late at night, when his attention would drift then abruptly shift back to the road, and he'd wonder, *Am I dreaming? Am I really here?*

Including the flight attendants, there were thirty-three people on a flight meant for over three hundred. As he waited for takeoff, he texted a grocery list to Dalita Nakoa.

> Tomatoes, ground beef, beer (PBR), chips, salsa, bread, crunchy peanut butter, potatoes. Beer.

Dalita replied with a thumbs-up and an emoji of a brimming beer stein. The cabin crew closed the doors, someone made a terse announcement—five and a half hours flight time, no meal or beverage service, remain masked and seated as much as possible. The plane took off, the coastline receding behind them until all Grady saw was water.

Boredom overwhelmed his anxiety, and he fell asleep. He didn't know what time it was when he woke. His phone still showed Pacific time. The plane had no in-flight entertainment, not even an in-flight magazine. Outside his window was an unbroken field of blue, no hint of where the sky ended and the sea began. There was no turbulence, just the loud background hum from the engines. The few passengers were sleeping or staring at tablets and phones.

Across the aisle from him, a young woman gazed at a laptop, smiling. Long, dark, curly hair framed a round face, half hidden by a blue mask with yellow stars. She had deep-set dark eyes behind oversized glasses and wore dangling earrings. She laughed out loud at something she was watching, glanced aside and saw him looking at her.

Before he could turn away, her eyes crinkled in a smile. He smiled in return, even though he knew she couldn't tell, and she turned back to her laptop.

He stared out his window again. The girl reminded him of Kayla MacIntosh, though this girl was Asian, maybe biracial, and Kayla had been pale-skinned, with gray-green eyes. Still, both had dark, curly hair and a warm gaze, and it felt like years since a girl had looked at him the way Kayla had, the way an old friend might.

They'd been in kindergarten together, the two of them paired up to tend the monarch butterfly eggs they'd collected from the milk-weed patch behind school. After that they were inseparable. Kayla had moved after fifth grade, but in high school they were in the same English class.

By then Kayla was a skinny goth, her dark hair dyed green and her eyebrows stitched with silver rings and safety pins. She didn't seem angry so much as sad: mostly she just listened to angry-sounding music. They'd acknowledge each other in the halls. Sometimes she smiled, sometimes Grady did. A couple of times they hung out in the parking lot after school, sharing a jibbah—a joint—and talking about stuff they'd done as kids: school trips on the ferry to Islesboro, watching seals in Rockport Harbor. Kayla always had good weed. After high school, they fell out of touch. The last time he'd seen her had been when he was an EMT.

The call came in from Rockland, a 911 from a woman who said she was suicidal and had taken an overdose of prescription pain-killers. Grady and Amy and Cameron, his team that night, raced to a run-down single-wide on the south side of town. The door was open, and Grady rushed in first, armed with Narcan, a stomach pump, and a defib. He halted, shocked to recognize Kayla lying on the couch, her eyes slits. Her green-dyed hair had reverted to dark curls, and the piercings were gone, all except a tiny diamond nose ring.

"Kayla," he stammered, fighting panic as he fumbled for the Narcan. "Kayla, can you tell me what medications you took?"

She didn't need to tell him—he saw the bottle of alprazolam on the side table, along with a quart of Gilbey's, nearly empty. Her eyes fluttered closed, her mouth parted so she looked like the girl who'd lain on the floor mats beside him in kindergarten, the two of them refusing to sleep during naptime.

He'd pulled her upright, stuck the nozzle of the Narcan dispenser into one of her nostrils, and pressed the trigger, holding her as he counted off two minutes before administering a second dose. He never stopped chanting her name.

"Kayla, come on, Kayla, hang on, we're here, come back, Kayla, look at me..."

He felt her die, knew the moment she was gone by the way her body relaxed and the sigh that left her mouth, all gin and cough syrup.

He quit the EMS after that, ignored the concerned phone messages and emails from his supervisor.

"It's terrible, but this is part of the job, Grady. I know what happened with your dad, and I know that must make this even harder for you. Take a couple of days off. Call me back when you get this."

Grady never did call back. He gave his notice. He knew he couldn't hack being an EMT, living with the constant replay of Kayla's extinguished eyes. Like those three matches he took on his failed wilderness solo, never catching fire.

CHAPTER 6

Grady angrily yanked down his window shade. This was his chance to start over, leave all that shit behind. He grabbed his phone, scrolling until he found a photo he'd saved of the island. Its eastern section was taken up by a dormant volcano, the west by mountains and a shield volcano. Between them stretched a narrow coastal plain. Hokuloa was on the southeastern coast, a remote, thumb-shaped bulge projecting into the Pacific. The airport was near the island's main city, Liʻulā, nestled on the coastal plain's south shore. He'd shown the photo to Zeke and said, "Doesn't it look kinda like a dog's head?"

"A dog's head?" Zeke laughed. "Dude, you're getting outta here just in time."

Thinking of Zeke made him feel better. Zeke was a prepper who believed you could survive anything, even the apocalypse, with a good knife, good weed, and fresh water. "A knifeless man is a lifeless man," he'd been saying since they were in sixth grade. Grady's was in his checked bag, along with his Leatherman and carpenter's square, a few T-shirts, a white button-down, and a flannel shirt, a pair of heavy-duty work gloves, and his work boots.

He stuck his phone into his pocket. With a yawn, he stood and stepped into the aisle, stretched his legs and raised his arms to see if he could touch the ceiling.

"Does your neck hurt?"

He looked around in surprise. In the row across from his, the young woman stared at him. A thick paperback book was open on her tray. He squinted to read the title: *The Pale King*. It sounded like George R. R. Martin's stuff, which he liked.

He pointed at the book. "Is that any good?"

"Not really. It keeps putting me to sleep."

He wasn't sure if this was a joke or not. "Really?"

She nodded, laughing, and went on. "Yeah. And I always get a headache when I fall asleep on a plane. Do you?"

He hesitated. He could lie and say yeah, that happened every time. Better than admitting this was only the second airplane trip he'd ever taken, right? Still, Grady knew guys who'd never been south of Fenway. He shrugged. "I don't know. I've never fallen asleep on a plane before." The girl laughed again, and he felt his face grow hot. "But, yeah, I do kinda have a crick in my neck."

It felt weird, talking to a stranger for the first time in months, especially a woman. It'd usually take at least two beers before he could begin a conversation this easily at Three Tides or the Rhumb Line.

Now he felt cut off from that version of himself, like he'd rolled a new character in the middle of a WOW raid. He glanced down, saw the girl had on flip-flops with big pink plastic flowers on them. Her toenails were painted silver.

"This is my first time," he said. "To Hawai'i."

"Ohhh..."

She unbuckled her seat belt, scooted into the end seat in her row. After a moment, he did the same, so they could talk across the aisle.

"You will *love* it," she said, lowering her voice as though telling him a secret. "The first time I visited, it was like..." She stopped, staring not at him but at the floor. At last she lifted her head and adjusted her glasses. "It's kind of like the first time you look at the Milky Way through a telescope. Have you ever done that? Or strong binoculars."

Grady nodded. "Binoculars, yeah. It was cool."

"Right. It's like that—I mean, you can actually *see* the Milky Way there. It's clearer than just about anyplace on the planet. That's why they have those massive telescopes on Haleakalā. The air is so clear. On the island, it's like that with everything—the ocean, the mountains, the rain forest." Her expression grew dreamy. "You just . . . see more."

Grady nodded politely. This sounded like the kind of stoned revelation Zeke occasionally shared. "Do you live there now?"

"No. I'm going to stay with my girlfriend, Raina—she lives in Makani. But I've been a few times—I live in Century City, outside L.A., so it's only a five-hour flight. I'm doing postgrad work at UCLA—microbiology—but it's all online now. Why should I be in L.A.? Where are you staying?"

"I'm not sure. I mean, I know where I'll be, but I don't know anything about it. A place on Hokuloa Road."

Her eyes widened. "Really? On the peninsula?" He nodded. "Wow. It's supposed to be incredibly beautiful out there. But hard to get to. It's where that billionaire lives—he owns all that land and made it into a wildlife refuge, so nobody can visit. I didn't think anyone lived there, except him."

"That's where I'm going. I'm the new caretaker."

"Really." Her brow furrowed as she gave him a look he couldn't unpack. "You hear a lot of stories about that place. Ghost stories—you know, like the spirit dog on the Road to Hana. Or choking ghosts, and the Nightmarchers."

"Or Phantom 309," said Grady, playing along, "that trucker with the eighteen-wheeler who picks you up then disappears."

She laughed. "I don't know that one. All I'm saying is, Hokuloa can be really intense. Be careful after dark—there've been a bunch of accidents on that road, and a lot of people say it should never have been built. But there are markers, if you know where to look for them, things to keep you safe. That's what Raina says, anyway."

Ordinarily he'd laugh. But he remembered his survival classes at WMCC, and advice from friends who were experienced hunters: if you're on new ground, pay attention to people who know the land better than you do.

"Yeah, okay," he said. "Thanks."

A voice came over the speakers: forty minutes to landing. The spell broken, Grady waved in farewell before scooting back to his window, and the young woman did the same. "Nice talking to you."

"You too."

CHAPTER 7

Grady felt buoyed by the conversation but also slightly creeped out. Zeke claimed he'd seen his grandfather's ghost rifling through his gun cabinet, but then Zeke also said he'd seen a UFO by the Quoddy Head Light. Grady didn't believe in ghosts, but Hokuloa Road definitely sounded even more remote than he'd imagined, more like Maine's unorganized territories than the blissful place his surfing buddy had described.

He stared out the window and reminded himself that, even if this didn't work out, he'd still be able to tell people he'd been to Hawai'i. Talking with that girl felt like an omen, a good one, he hoped. Now he knew, or sort of knew, at least one person here.

Far below, the blue water was almost purple, dotted with silvery-white specks that must be waves—big ones, if he could see them from this high up. Streamers of cloud flashed past as the plane lost altitude. To the east, a line of rainbow-shaped crescents appeared in the sky: sun dogs. He glanced at the girl across the aisle, to tell her to look outside. But the sun dogs were already gone.

On the horizon, a dark shape emerged from the clouds, then another, and another—the more distant Hawai'ian Islands. Slowly, another, larger island filled the horizon. Grady recognized the long curve that formed its south-facing shore, and, toward its center, a broad flattened plain, dull brown and gray. Tall green hills stretched to the east, their slopes carved with deep ravines, black against the green.

Above them loomed a vast volcano, its fields and forests sloping down to cliffs that dropped hundreds of feet, to tiny white beaches you would need a helicopter or boat to reach. Before the coastal road began to turn north at the eastern edge of the island, a peninsula extended into the ocean, but more a forested cape than a peninsula. A broad ribbon of black cut through the forest—a lava field, Grady realized, a remnant of the last time the volcano had erupted, hundreds of years ago. The tip of the cape appeared slightly concave, as though a giant's thumb had pressed there. Grady opened his phone to the map of the island, enlarging it to read the name of the land formation below.

Hokuloa.

The plane banked sharply, giving him a better glimpse of the dormant volcano. A single wispy cloud hung above its flattened peak, like a torn flag.

The volcano disappeared as the plane dropped. The city of Li'ulā was bigger than he'd expected, the size of Portland. High-rise hotels lined the shore, vast resorts with curated beaches, and wharfs built to accommodate cruise ships, all empty.

Within seconds, a grid of crowded streets replaced the resorts: apartment blocks, acres of tract housing, a hospital. In the near distance, the airport with its ATC tower and a single long runway. No planes save a commuter jet parked in front of a small terminal. Past the runway, dusty brown fields stretched into the haze, packed with thousands of parked cars.

A flight attendant hurried down the aisle, checking seat belts. Grady looked out the window again to see the ocean, alarmingly close. He took a deep breath, his heart beating hard, closed then opened his eyes.

He wasn't dreaming. He was really here.

CHAPTER 8

He grabbed his stuff and waited to deboard. From across the aisle, the girl gave him a quick wave.

"Good luck," she said, and hurried toward the door.

He'd hoped they'd have a chance to talk a little more, exchange names or phone numbers. But frigging COVID seemed to have screwed that up, too.

He joined the passengers straggling into the terminal, a deserted, stiflingly hot building. The AC had been turned off, and the lights. Gray sunlight seeped through windows that hadn't been cleaned. On the wall, a faded photo mural showed people surfing, snorkeling, walking hand in hand along empty beaches, surrounded by palm trees and sea turtles. On the facing wall, photos of native Hawai'ians gazed out past welcoming words, smiling or wise.

ALOHA!

MAHALO

Ā HUI HOU AKU

'A'OLE PILIKIA

PONO

'OHANA

Other than the rattle of suitcase wheels, the terminal was silent. When had the last plane landed? Days ago? A week?

He spotted the dark-haired girl ahead of him, overstuffed back-pack sagging from her shoulders. Eventually he saw a man, masked, wearing a lanyard with an ID card. The man held up a sign that read STOP. Grady halted a good distance behind the girl, who was directed to a table where a health department official stood with a police officer.

After the girl left, the cop waved him over. Grady filled out a form with his reason for visiting and contact info: Dalita Nakoa's name and the address, Hokuloa Road. The cop glanced at the form.

"You're here for a job?" he asked. Grady nodded. "Who's your employer?"

"Wesley Minton. I'm doing some work at his place."

The cop raised an eyebrow. "Minton?"

"Yeah. I'm the new caretaker. I'm a carpenter."

"Right, we don't have any carpenters here," the cop said drily. "We'll call every day to check how you're feeling. If you break quarantine, you'll be arrested and sent back to the mainland. Mahalo. Next."

By the exit, a National Guard officer in combat gear aimed a thermometer gun at Grady's forehead before waving him on. Grady found his way to baggage claim, a gray-walled space that opened onto an access road surrounded by concrete barriers. He grabbed his suitcase from the carousel and walked outside, hoping it would be cooler there.

It wasn't. A hot, steady wind blew, pelting him with grit. Three other people lingered by the baggage carousel, including the girl. They'd all removed their masks, so he did the same, turning as a car stopped on the access road. Maybe this was Dalita Nakoa?

But no one stepped out, and when he looked back at the carousel, only the girl remained, watching a suitcase inch its way to her.

"Hey, I'll get that." Grady walked over and hefted the bag. "Someone picking you up?"

"Thanks." The girl smiled. She was pretty, with freckled, light-brown skin and full cheeks, a slightly crooked front tooth. "My friend's on her way—I just texted her. You?"

"I'm Grady Kendall." He started to stick out his hand, sheepishly dropped it. "From Maine."

"Grady from Maine." She laughed. "That's a long way. I'm Jessica Kiyoko. My friend's in Makani. She says some of the bars have opened up there—maybe we can meet up, once we're out of quarantine? Or someplace else. It's a small island. We can show you around, it'd be fun."

He started to reply, but she looked past him, exclaiming, "Raina!" Turning to him, she added, "Nice meeting you, Grady. Good luck on Hokuloa—I'll probably run into you in a couple weeks."

"That'd be great. Want me to carry that for you?"

"No, I can get it—thanks."

She stumbled from the terminal as a skinny young white woman ran to hug her, their voices shrill with excitement. The other girl grabbed the heavier bag and dragged it to an older Subaru Outback, maroon paint blistered from the sun.

Wistfully, Grady watched the car drive off. He'd texted Dalita when he landed, along with his mom, Donny, Zeke. His brother and mom had responded, Zeke, too, even though back home it was past midnight. Yawning, he leaned against the wall and waited.

CHAPTER 9

Hey! You Grady?" He looked up to see a maskless woman standing on the curb. "Grady Kendall?"

He picked up his bags and hurried to her. "That's me. Are you Dalita?"

"The one and only. This is us, here . . ."

He followed her to a battered white pickup. "You can toss your stuff in the back," she said, pointing to a truck bed crowded with a surfboard, wet suits, kid-sized life jackets, a pink blanket covered with cat or dog hair. He pulled his Sea Dogs cap from his backpack and put it on. Even with sunglasses, it was almost too bright to see. He got into the truck's cab, which was as hot as it was outside.

"Sorry, AC's broken." Grady fumbled in his pocket for his mask, but Dalita waved at it dismissively. "No need worry about that."

The cab smelled of sunscreen, weed, and french fries. He pushed a fast-food wrapper from his seat as she cranked the engine, and they roared down the access road—the muffler was shot. Dalita looked him up and down, taking in his reddish hair and fair skin. "You brought sunscreen, I hope. You gonna need it."

"I did."

"You're younger than I thought."

"I'm twenty-eight."

"For real? You look the same age as my son. No offense."

"None taken."

She didn't look old enough to have a kid close to his age. In her mid-thirties, maybe. Forty, tops. It was hard to tell. No makeup, attractive in a tomboyish way, with smooth, dark skin, a round face, dark eyes. Black eyebrows and short black hair that looked stiffened by salt. On her upper arm, names inked in cursive: Lorelei, Paolo, Tim, Stella. She wore a black sports bra beneath a tank top boasting a faded logo, a hula dancer in a martini glass.

She reached for the console between them, handed him a water bottle. "How was your flight?"

He opened the bottle and drank gratefully. "It was okay. Thanks for getting me."

"No worries."

In the console, a phone pinged, and she picked it up to read an incoming text. The truck veered into the other lane, then back again. Dalita dropped the phone, shaking her head.

"Lor—my wife. Neighbor's fucking dog ate the avos she was saving for lunch." She barely slowed at a red light, turning onto the highway. "You never been here before?"

"Nope. And I've never met Wes Minton. What's he like?"

She groped at the console again, picked up a vape pen and took a hit of cannabis. "Rich as hell, choke money. Nice, though." She held the vape pen out to him.

"No thanks."

"I got your groceries. Except the beer."

She laughed as Grady's face fell. "Jokes! You get plenty. Not enough, let me know. You should be all set at the 'ohana unit—got some staple stuffs left from before."

"Before what?"

"From when the last person lived there."

She coasted through another red light. They were driving through a concrete wasteland of vacant strip malls and fast-food franchises, bars and restaurants and chain hotels whose logos showed palm trees, waves, or dolphins or sea turtles. Past Sacred Fire Tattoos, the Kundalini Nail Spa, Wiki Wiki Fish House, Glorious Gelato, all closed. He saw no vegetation except for a few windblown palm trees and dusty hedges, some desiccated flowering shrubs in concrete planters. The only place open was Blue Island Food, a supermarket.

"That's where you can get groceries," said Dalita, slowing the truck. "Only big one on the island, I used to cashier there. In Makani there's Mak Supe—Makani Superette. That's where the locals go. Get more stuff here."

He counted nineteen vehicles in the sprawling lot. A few masked customers pushed shopping carts toward the store entrance. They all gave wide berth to a middle-aged, leathery-skinned white woman, her long hair wild. She clutched a backpack as she zigzagged through the lot, arguing with herself.

"Ice." Dalita tapped the accelerator. "Lot of tweakers this side. Mostly they live on the beaches or out by the sewage treatment plant, but since lockdown they're all over."

"Where *is* the beach?"

She waved in the direction of a cinder-block church with a marquee that read THOU SHALT WASH THINE HANDS. "Down that side—you could walk from here, ten minutes. But we're going mauka—up the mountain, inland, for a bit—that'll bring us where Hokuloa begins. It's a rough road. You scared of heights?"

Grady blinked. Her accent made it sound like *sked of heights*. "What? No."

"Last guy, Wes never tell got cliffs. The guy before never care."

He took another sip of water. "So, I'm the third caretaker?"

"Fourth, I think. First was me. Then had one guy, then another guy. But I always helped out in between—like the last few months, till he hired you."

"You were a caretaker?"

"Yup. I started, what, eight years ago? Maybe longer—I was the first person he hired. Carl Gunnerson was the last one—Carl from Colorado. You'd think he could deal with heights, but I think he lived in the flat part. He died, bad accident with his truck a couple years ago. I been helping out Wes off and on since then, staying a few nights a week, but since the lockdown I really need to be with my kids."

Grady stared out the open window. They'd left the city behind them. There was almost no traffic. Now and then a car would zip by in the other lane, or a 4Runner would barrel up behind them and pass, whether or not they were in a passing zone.

But everywhere, abandoned cars rose like mirages, parked on the roadside or marooned in fields of yellowing grass, hoods pulled up to reveal empty engine mounts and words spray-painted on broken windshields.

Aloha Express. Gone holoholo. Bye.

There were shopping carts, too, frames buckled, jammed with black trash bags, clothing, broken appliances. He didn't see any cops, which he guessed was a good thing, considering Dalita's disregard for stop signs and the truck's failing exhaust system.

Dalita's phone pinged again. She glanced at it and frowned. "Shit. I forgot to tell Wes I got you. Hey, boss," she said, setting the phone on speaker. "Sorry, got caught up talking."

"You get him?"

"Yeah, he's right here. I have you on speaker. Grady, say hi to Wes."

"Hey," said Grady. "I got here."

"Any problems with the flight? Dalita bring you something to eat?"

"Yeah. I mean, no, everything went fine," replied Grady. He and Dalita exchanged a look as she scrabbled in the space behind her seat. "No problems at all."

"Excellent. Dalita, what's your ETA?"

"Uh, maybe an hour. If we don't hit traffic."

"Ha ha. See you then," Wes said, and disconnected.

Dalita triumphantly held up a brown paper bag as the truck fishtailed. "Sorry! I forgot—I got you a burrito. You must be starving."

"Thanks." Grady unwrapped a squashed tortilla filled with beans and rice. He wolfed it down, licking salsa from his fingers.

"There's more water." Dalita cocked a thumb at several bottles jostling on the floor, glanced at him and made a sad face. "I feel bad I forgot your burrito. Got cookies, too."

"I'm all good," he said, willing it to be true.

CHAPTER 10

They continued to drive east. Behind them, the sun hung lower over a desert landscape: gray-green hills to the left, a broad plain to the right, all scrubby plants and rocks. On the opposite side of the highway, roads peeled off into the hills. The few houses Grady saw were modest. Cinder-block rectangles, modular homes, trailers, shacks with loose Tyvek flapping from the walls. Pickups were parked out front, older compacts and rusty RVs with orange extension cords running to carports. He'd flown halfway around the world to find himself surrounded by the same frigging shit he'd grown up with. Maybe Maine was the real world after all.

He turned his attention to the landscape on his right. Lots of cactus, dense thickets of saplings like overgrown weeds, a tree massed with neon-pink flowers that reminded him of Halloween as a kid, the girls all dressed as Disney princesses or fairies.

"Bougainvillea," said Dalita. "Not native. Those prickly pear not either, the koa haole too. Believe it or not, this used to be wetland. Some guys worked out a deal in the 1980s and they drained it. That was when the drug money came here, in the eighties. Before that was mostly hippies, and before that was surfers from the mainland. But the eighties, that's when everything really changed, when they built the resorts that stole all the water."

She gestured straight ahead: away from the dead-looking flatlands to the downslope of the dormant volcano, forests and dark cliffs giving way to the ocean. In the distance, a dark promontory seemed to hover between hazy sky and sea. "See that, way out there—that's all Wes's land. It ends at Hokuloa Point."

Hokuloa looked like something Grady couldn't put into words. He was used to the beauty of the Maine archipelago with its thousands of islands—cat spruce and granite ledges rising above denim-blue water, the drone of lobster boats, windjammers and smaller sailboats moving across the eastern horizon.

But he'd never sailed more than a few hours offshore, and even in the densest fog, there had always been the promise of a nearby island.

Hokuloa faded into . . . nothing, a mist that obscured sky and sea so only the faintest outline of the peninsula remained. The sight filled him with a slightly terrified exhilaration. What would it be like, to wake in a place like that? Would you worry the world around you might vanish?

"How far is it?" he asked Dalita.

"Farther than you think." She slowed the truck to a crawl, peering out the salt-grimed windshield. "From here to Wes's, maybe forty minutes. From his place to there . . ." She gestured to the end of the peninsula. "That's only about sixteen miles. His house is above where the wilderness begins, and it's a two-hour drive from there to Hokuloa Point. But you cannot go there. No one goes there but Wes."

Grady started to ask why, but she switched on the radio, cranking it up to sing along to an Adele song, her voice surprisingly sweet, almost childish. "I love this song!"

"My girlfriend used to like this," Grady shouted above the music and the roaring muffler. "Ex-girlfriend."

"Want me to turn it off?"

"No."

"How long were you together?"

The question ordinarily would put him on edge. Here, in another world, he found he didn't care. "Couple of years. We were at the same community college. Now she's at BU, getting her PhD. Archaeology."

"Like Lara Croft?"

Grady laughed. "Exactly like Lara Croft. She's married now."

"Huh. That bother you?"

Again, surprisingly, the question didn't faze him. "It did. Not so much now. It's been a while."

Dalita turned off the radio as a commercial came on. Lulu's Barbecue, takeout only. Cumulus clouds drifted across the sky, obscuring Hokuloa, so Grady looked out at the barren fields. He took a picture of a long-legged white bird standing in the high grass, regal-looking. Behind it, a squat concrete bunker rose from the otherwise empty plain.

Dalita eased up on the accelerator again, still humming, as Grady leaned out his window. The sunset had turned everything to gold—rocks, cactus, wiry gorse, everything except the bunker. Two stories high, it had a flat roof with vertical slits beneath, windows or ventilation shafts. No doors that Grady could see. Below the roofline, words were painted in big block letters:

NEVER FORGET THE MISSING
#ISLANDNALOWALE

Beneath were columns of names, dozens of them. *Ray Shoski, Kathyrn Cross, Cynni Brennan, Nanci Lee, Sam Arakawa . . .*

Grady turned, craning his neck to read more names on the building's side.

Brian Kapule
Kai Mirimoto
Nat Smith
Amanda Wellesley
Cory Desoto
Lance Nguyen

Grady looked at Dalita. "What the hell is that?"

"Communications building."

"What?"

She reached for her vape pen. She took a hit, glancing into the rearview mirror as the building dwindled behind them, and gunned the truck to seventy. "Damn, it's getting dark. Sorry, I wasn't paying attention."

"That building."

"Yeah, no—I mean I need to get home before dark. That building—there was a naval air station here during the Pacific War. World War II."

"I know what the Pacific War was."

"Well, there were landing strips here, hangars and shit, and that building was some kind of communications center. Like air traffic control."

"But what is it now? What's with all the names?"

"Those are people who've gone missing."

Grady stared back to where the building had dissolved into a glare of gold and red. "In one year?"

"Some, yeah. Some go way back. Couple times a year they paint over it."

"Who does?"

"The mayor. We're an island, but we're also a county. Our mayor's more like a state governor, and whoever's mayor, they have it painted over, because not good for tourists, yeah? But doesn't matter. The names always come back."

Grady frowned. "That's a lot of missing people for such a small island."

"People disappear here."

"Nalowale—what's that mean?"

"Lost, or vanished." Dalita tapped the gas pedal and the truck hit eighty, broken muffler rumbling like a thunderstorm. "Long ago, people on the other islands thought our island could disappear. Warriors would make the crossing in their canoes, but they couldn't find the island. There's this atmospheric thing—fog comes out of nowhere and settles on the coast. The people here would wait and attack the invaders at night, or leave them to the sharks. The reefs are filled with bones."

Grady couldn't tell if she was joking.

"It's true," she said. "Native Hawai'ians would bury iwi— bones—in the sand, or hide them in caves. Exposing them to sunlight was sacrilege. These are tourist bones. You can see them, snorkeling. They used to have tours that take people out to the reefs, but it's dangerous, also bad for the coral."

"Have you been there?"

"Sure, small kid time. Scared me shitless. All kinds coral growing up through the rib cages like freaking *Pirates of the Caribbean*. But the fish are beautiful. You just have to watch for tiger sharks. And whitetips."

"What's that?"

"Reef sharks. They're not really dangerous, but anything'll take a bite out of you if it's hungry." Dalita grinned. "No worries. They're not gonna come after you on dry land."

"I'm not worried. We have great whites in Maine."

"Sweet."

They drove on without seeing another vehicle, until at last they reached a Y-shaped intersection. The highway sheared off to the left. Straight ahead stretched a narrow road, chewed-up dirt and gravel. The spine of sharp green hills reared above the dirt road, and the desolate fields gave way to jungly undergrowth and tall green trees.

"We're on the downslope of the volcano," Dalita explained. "The road here is terrible—I've done the Road to Hana a couple times, and this is a hundred times worse. And the road from Wes's place across Hokuloa is even worse than that. A lava field cuts off most of the far end, but like I said, no one goes there except for Wes."

Grady peered out at the distant volcano, its slopes a dozen shades of green fissured with dull orange, as though the cliffs wept rust. The road ran roughly parallel to the coastline before he lost sight of it where a broken guardrail dangled fifty feet above black rocks and blue water.

"Jesus," he said. "The road's right there on the cliff."

"Cliff?" Dalita shook her head. "You'll see the cliffs. You'll *be* the cliffs. Just wait."

CHAPTER 11

They turned onto Hokuloa Road, where a mangled metal sign lay on the ground, overgrown with vines.

DANGEROUS ROAD

NO CELL SERVICE

DRIVE AT OWN RISK

Grady winced. "Is there really no cell service?"

"You can get it at Wes's house, and he has sketchy service at Hokuloa Point. Otherwise, no. A lot of the island's like that, except for the resorts. Big sign at the state park says you're better off with a first aid kit than a phone. That's one reason so many tourists get lost or disappear—they leave the marked trails and go off on their own. There're two helicopters on the island, one police and rescue, the other for medivac. But a helicopter can't find you in the rain forest. And the currents are some strong, so if you're not a good swimmer . . ." She drew a finger across her throat. "The resort beaches are pretty safe. But that's not where the best fishing or surfing is. This guidebook came out a few years ago, *Blue Island Secrets,* telling tourists how to find places where no one goes, not unless you know what you're doing. Some of those places are sacred. They were never meant to be public."

She downshifted as the truck began to climb. "Help yourself to that vape," she said, "if you need."

"I'm okay," Grady muttered, but already he felt carsick.

The truck rumbled along, chunks of broken rock flying up behind them. On Dalita's side, the land rose steeply from the roadbed, nearly vertical. An insane jungle sprang from the black rocks and reddish soil: palm trees, banana trees, vines as thick around as his calves with leaves the size of hubcaps. There were trees that looked like evergreens, but covered with green feathery growths instead of needles, with nests of red petals. Blades of orange flowers; dangling purple blossoms shaped like trumpets; small waxy white flowers clustered among gnarled roots and chunks of black stone. Trees he recognized as hibiscus, only here they grew as tall as poplars, their flowers red, yellow, white, orange. In spots, water-falls fell from the black rocks like silver chains, turning the road to soup.

After ten minutes the air grew noticeably more humid. The pickup felt like a moving sauna. He breathed in a lush, sweet scent. "What's that smell?"

"Not sure. Tuberose?"

They followed the switchbacks up and down, until they reached a fork in the road. The truck rolled to a halt—there was no stop sign.

Ahead of them the road continued, disappearing into the trees. Grady gazed out his window to where another road sheared off at a right angle.

"This is Hokuloa Road," Dalita said. "From here on it's wilder-ness. This is one of the only places on the island that's mostly been untouched. There..." She indicated the land sloping up behind them. "That's all a national forest preserve. No tourists allowed. No visitors, except for Native Hawai'ians and some scientists—they're replanting native trees along the border with the ranches. But this..." She turned to stare past Grady, out to Hokuloa Road. "It all belongs to Wes."

She gently tapped the gas pedal, and the truck made the ninety-degree turn, past a worn wooden sign nailed to a tree.

WARNING!

PRIVATE ROAD — HAZARDOUS CONDITIONS

NO TRESPASSING!

The one-lane road narrowed even more—a vehicle any bigger than the pickup wouldn't have been able to make it through. They might be a hundred feet above the ocean, the cliffs long black fingers of rock clutching at the surf. In places, vegetation and rocks had been swept away, by a rockslide or a vehicle that had plunged off the road. Grady saw two cars hung up on the cliffs below them, both vehicles mangled and overgrown with greenery. He could hear the waves smashing against the shore.

Grady's heart beat harder and faster, his mouth dry. He was tempted to roll up his window, to provide a barrier between himself and that gnawing blue mouth far below, but he remembered that people drowned because they were unable to smash free if their cars plunged into a lake or river.

"You okay?" asked Dalita.

"Yeah. Kind of."

He adjusted his seat belt. Ahead of them, a small sign was nailed into the rocks on the hillside.

5 MPH

He said, "Five miles an hour? First time I've seen that."

"This is where we no like run into traffic."

"Traffic?" Grady laughed.

"Yeah. Like Wes. Or me."

As the pickup crept around the turn, Grady fell silent. The road had deteriorated to crumbled lava and dirt, immense broken palm fronds and flowers strewn across it as though for some demented wedding ceremony. Leaves and branches scraped the side of the truck, reached through the window to tug at his hair. He thought of what the girl Jessica had said on the plane—*there are markers, if you know how to look for them, things to keep you safe*.

He saw no markers here. No guardrails, no walls, no warning

signs. Occasionally he spotted a pile of stones, a cairn, and wondered if these might be memorials for drivers who'd died here or, if they were older, built by the people who had lived here first. He forced himself to look out his window to see the road edge crumbling into the bright air.

"You all right?" Dalita glanced at him.

"Keep your eyes on the road."

"No worry, I do this all the time." She handed him the vape pen. "Seriously, it helps."

This time he shut his eyes and took a hit. The droning muffler and thumping waves faded into his breath, his heartbeat. The pickup rolled along like a miniature tank.

"What do you do," he said at last, "if a car comes the other way?"

"That never happens. But there's pullouts."

She gestured to a tiny crescent carved between the towering hillside and what passed for a roadbed. The space looked barely big enough to accommodate a person, let alone a vehicle. "And usually you can see them coming." She indicated where the road jackknifed in a series of hairpin turns, climbing higher and higher. "So you just pull over. And wait."

"Jesus."

Dalita sighed. "Take another hit. In two weeks, you going do this by yourself."

They continued to climb. The sky opened around them, colored like the watermelon tourmaline bracelet he'd given Rachel one Christmas—amethyst, tangerine, rose, pale green. He spotted a crude trail, deeply rutted and wide enough for a single vehicle.

"People *live* here?" he asked.

"There's a few surf breaks, so some hippies squatted here illegally in the seventies—the land belonged to Wes's father then. He hardly came to the island, though he built the original house where Wes is now. Wes renovated it long time back, and he built the 'ohana same time. But all the hippies are gone, dead or moved on. This guy

Leonardo—he works for Wes sometimes, and Wes lets him stay in an old shack when the swell comes."

"He climbs down that cliff with a surfboard?"

"There's a trail. I was there once for a party in high school." She fell silent, then said, "We shouldn't have been there. Leonardo shouldn't be there."

"Like in that guidebook? An Indian burial ground or something?"

He was trying to make a joke—the weed had eased his anxiety—but Dalita's expression hardened. "You need to be respectful here," she said. "We no need any more asshole haoles."

Grady flushed. "Sorry," he muttered. There'd been only one Black girl in his high school and she was adopted: between his flight and this trip to Hokuloa Road, he'd probably seen more not-white people than he had in his entire life. Dalita remained silent. He wondered if he'd blown it before he'd even gotten to Wes's place.

A few more minutes and the road leveled out, with bright blossoms scattered in the undergrowth like scraps of abandoned clothing. In front of them the road continued, but the pickup jolted to a stop. Dalita hopped out and walked to a metal security gate, a paved road winding up the hillside behind it. She punched in the passcode and returned to the truck.

"Where's that go?" Grady pointed to where Hokuloa Road continued on, past the gate.

"Hokuloa Point, eventually. Like I said, you can't go there. He built another gate so no one can get by. It's right where the lava field ends. I've seen pictures—it looks like Mordor. But this is just some billionaire's house."

She laughed as the security gate slowly swung open, and gunned the engine. They peeled up the driveway, Grady turning in time to see the gate close behind them.

CHAPTER 12

The rush of relief at getting off the cliff road overcame Grady's embarrassment. He remembered all the questions he should have asked Dalita before now. He glanced at her, measuring her mood, and said, "Anything I should know? About Wes?"

"No personal questions. He puts it on when he's talking to investors and the places he donates money to, all those environmental groups, Planned Parenthood. But he's not a people person."

She shifted gears and the truck came to a stop. "This is a hard place if you're not from here," she said, her tone warning, though not unkind. "You're not a tourist, so don't act like one. Respect the island. Carl Gunnerson died because he was fucking around, selling drugs to local kids."

"I don't sell drugs to teenagers," Grady retorted hotly. "Or anybody."

"No, I didn't think so."

"So was Carl killed? On purpose?"

"Not by anybody I know."

She began to drive again, the tires crushing a brittle palm frond that had fallen onto the driveway. "You not going see him much in person—he spends most of his time out at Hokuloa Point. There's a small house there. He inherited all this..." She gestured at the eastern horizon. "He has no right to it, but Hawai'ian land regulations are incredibly complicated. It's been in the courts for years, but Wes has deep pockets. Twenty years ago, he wanted to develop the point into another super-exclusive resort. Like Sensei on Lānaʻi. People would have to come by helicopter, or private boat. Native Hawaiʻian activist groups got involved, water rights activists, scientists talking about all the endangered species. Then bam: one day Wes withdraws all the permit applications."

"Maybe he just didn't need another hundred million dollars."

"No. He eats and sleeps and shits money. And he'd already shipped in construction materials, years ago. It's all still out there, waiting."

"For what?"

She shrugged. "I think he's building a secret compound. Like those billionaires who're gonna fly to New Zealand or wherever to escape COVID or the end of the world."

"What else should I know?"

"Everything's off-grid. Solar. Mostly you just keep an eye on things when he's away. A guy in Liʻulā named Uncle Honey, he picks up deliveries from UPS and Amazon and brings them up every couple weeks. Nobody else will deliver out here. After quarantine, you can take the truck to town for errands. Nothing's really open—a few bars in Makani and Liʻulā."

"Does he have any pets?"

"He keeps sea urchins. And a lot of birds."

The truck rounded another curve and the trees fell away, replaced by a sweep of tall grass. Stone steps led up to Minton's house, a sleek construction of cubes and reinforced steel that was nearly all windows, so the building appeared to melt into the darkening sky. Solar panels cladded the roof. A figure sat at a table on the second-floor deck, bent over a laptop.

The truck jerked to a stop and Dalita jumped out, reaching behind her seat for a handbag. She turned to wave up at the deck. "We're here!"

Grady made a face. With that busted muffler, Minton would have heard them from miles away. The figure on the deck stood and lifted a hand.

"Be right down," he shouted.

Grady got his stuff from the back of the truck. "Thanks for picking me up."

Dalita had already set the grocery bags and a thirty rack of PBR on the driveway. She motioned at his face—she'd put her mask on, and he quickly did the same.

"You should be all set," she said. "If you need anything, just text me. I can come back tomorrow afternoon. Any afternoon, unless I have to bring the kids somewhere."

"Yeah, sure," he said.

She clasped his arm, her grip strong and warm. "You going be all right."

"As long as I'm not a haole asshole."

She laughed. "Yups."

Up here, the air was cooler, heavy with unfamiliar scents—a spicy odor like crushed ferns, a fruity smell that made his mouth water, and also a pervasive, underlying smell of mildew and rotting leaves, a very faint but distinctive stink of carrion.

"Grady Kendall!"

He turned to see Wes striding toward them, unmasked, wearing an unbuttoned white shirt over a black sarong.

He stopped about ten feet from Grady and Dalita. "I'm Wes Minton."

Even in person, it was hard to tell how old Minton was. His hair was more gray than black, his eyes hooded and slightly downturned, with the icy sheen of an expensive hunting blade. Grady saw how his skin had been coarsened by sun damage. The lines beside his mouth weren't laugh lines. He reminded Grady of the judge who'd sentenced eighteen-year-old Donny to six months in prison, for possession of less than an ounce of marijuana.

"Very pleased to meet you," Grady said. "I—"

"You need anything, boss?" Dalita broke in. "I want to get back before dark."

Wes shook his head. "You go on. Thanks for picking him up."

"No worries. Grady, nice meeting you—just text me if you want me to pick something up for you. See you, Wes."

She climbed into her truck, whipping off her mask. Grady gazed after her wistfully as she waved and the truck barreled down the driveway.

CHAPTER 13

L et's get you settled," announced Minton. "You must be beat. We can talk tomorrow."

Grady walked with him, thick, rough grass crunching beneath his sneakers. Minton was barefoot, the sarong's hem taut against his calves. In a corner of the fabric was a bright yellow image, some kind of logo: a circle with crooked lines radiating from it, like a child's drawing of the sun.

"You'll be in the 'ohana unit." Minton gestured at a small wood-framed building about fifty feet from the main house. White-painted shiplap siding, a pocket-sized deck with two reclining outdoor chairs and a small table. The kind of faux-rustic accents Grady recognized from places in Maine owned by rich people from away. Behind the 'ohana loomed the forest, tall evergreens and unknown plants that cast long shadows across the grass.

Minton halted in front of the 'ohana's door. "I've got some calls to make, and Dalita should have everything set up for you. See you tomorrow."

Grady waited till Minton returned to the main house, then yanked off his mask. He pushed the door open and stepped inside.

The 'ohana was very small—400 square feet, tops. Nicely done up at first glance, but as he walked around he noted where the contractor had cut corners. LED lights in cheap lighting fixtures; plastic wall plates; double-glazed windows not top-of-the-line. The glossy wood floors were laminate, buckling in spots from moisture. Mildew freckled the walls in back, where the shadowy forest waited.

A soft yellow blanket was draped over the black leather couch—real leather, cracked with age. Probably a hand-me-down from the main house. There were two chairs, one an Eames knockoff, the other a more comfortable armchair. Overhead, a ceiling fan turned, so slowly he couldn't feel the air move.

The kitchen looked fancy, though here too everything had been done on a budget. Birch plywood cabinetry; countertops that looked like pink granite but, when tapped with a metal spoon, didn't give off the telltale ring of real stone. Open shelves held mismatched plates and cups, those wineglasses without stems.

There was a fancy German toaster and coffee machine, a fridge that probably cost what Grady owed on his truck back home. The label on the yellow blanket read 100% CASHMERE.

He went outside and brought in the groceries from the driveway. In addition to the PBR, Dalita'd gotten a few cans of a Maui lager, Bikini Blonde. He popped a can and finished his tour. The bathroom had a glass shower stall, fogged with soap scum. The bedroom held a queen bed with a tropical print, bamboo nightstands and bureau, a good-sized closet. For a caretaker's cottage, it was all pretty luxurious.

He wandered back into the living room, yawning. The bookcase held damp-swollen old paperbacks, guides to Hawai'ian wildlife and brochures with detailed instructions on what to do if you found an endangered seabird—'ua'u, a kind of petrel; 'ua'u kani, a shearwater—and cards with a phone number for sea turtle rescue. Also a year-old brochure advertising local attractions: zip lines, whale watching, snorkel rentals, helicopter tours, luaus. The pre-pandemic photos of smiling tourists and overeager kids made Grady feel sad as well as exhausted. He took another sip of his beer and walked to the window.

It wasn't yet 7:30, but the sky was black, as though it were a TV someone had turned off. Stars glittered overhead, more brilliant than he'd ever seen, even in the Allagash Wilderness. Birds fluttered and called from the trees, an unfamiliar chorus of croons and a single, persistent cry like scissors cutting heavy cloth.

He opened the french doors onto the side lawn, letting in a cool breeze that smelled of perfume. He stepped outside and inhaled. It wasn't perfume. The air really smelled like this, here. The sky really looked like this, so vast and beautiful it was like he'd fallen into a movie, something he'd always longed to happen when he was a kid. The tract houses and pickups he'd seen from the highway had made him fear that perhaps this place wasn't all that different from Maine. Now, despite his fatigue, he felt exultant, knowing he'd been wrong.

CHAPTER 14

H e had no trouble falling asleep but woke just after midnight, to the sound of heavy rain. The loud drumming soothed him back to sleep. When he woke again, the rain had stopped. It was 2 a.m., 8 a.m. back east. His mother would just be getting home from work. Donny and Zeke would just be starting. He lay in bed and scrolled through a string of messages from his brother, all joking variants on what a pussy Grady was for actually hightailing it to Hawai'i.

Fuck me didnt think youd ever really do it!!!

i love you too, Grady typed, and set down his phone.

He used the bathroom, went into the dark living room and sank onto the couch. He'd never been jet-lagged before: Was he now wide-awake or could he fall back asleep if he tried? He stared out the french doors to the overgrown lawn and the forest beyond. He'd turned off the ceiling fan before he went to bed, a good thing. He was surprised by how cool it was after the downpour—his bare arms had goose bumps.

He yawned. The air coming through the screens felt thick and sticky and seemed to coat the inside of his mouth, a sensation between a taste and smell that he could only describe as green. He stretched, paused when he heard an odd ticking noise from the ceiling. Peering into the darkness, he saw nothing. Seconds later, the same sound came from the opposite corner of the room.

Tkk, tkk, tkk, tkk.

Like someone tapping on the ceiling. There was no second floor to the 'ohana, and he couldn't imagine someone crawling on the roof. Some kind of insect, he decided. A cricket, or maybe a bird.

He opened one of the french doors, then its screen door, and stepped outside. Behind him, whatever it was *tkk*'ed again, more urgently. Palm fronds crackled in the night breeze, spattering the ground with moisture. He wondered if it might rain again, but the night sky was cloudless, save for a ragged arc of silver directly overhead: the Milky Way.

He'd seen it while camping, but that was nothing like this—a lunar brilliance edged with a black that seemed somehow more solid than the surrounding sky. He recalled what Jessica had told him on the plane, how the Milky Way looked different on the island. That had seemed unlikely but now struck him as, perhaps, true.

Gradually he grew aware of an odd odor, musky, though not like a skunk or fox—more rank, like roadkill. From the 'ohana came another insect alarm. *Tkk, tkk, tkk, tkk, tkk, tkk, tkk, tkk.* He turned to go back inside, and stopped.

An animal crouched at the edge of the forest, watching him, its head at about the height of Grady's waist. A dog, Grady thought, and remained motionless. It had erect pointed ears and a broad muzzle, slightly flattened. Stockier than a coyote, but he knew there were no coyotes here.

So a dog, a good-sized dog. Even in the darkness he could see that its fur was brindled brown or red; one of those dirt-colored mongrels bred to be mean. No collar or tag around its neck. Feral, probably. Not good.

He held his breath and took a step backward, very, very slowly, avoiding the dog's eyes. Donny had taught him that as a kid: they take eye contact as a challenge. But instead, as Grady moved, the dog swiftly reared up on its hind legs, as if to lunge. Somehow it stood without effort, as tall as he was, still staring at him: its eyes white with no pupils. The dog's eyes were now in the front of its head: a human's eyes, not a dog's.

With a muffled shout, Grady turned and stumbled back into the house.

CHAPTER 15

He slammed the door shut and turned the deadbolt before peering back outside. The dog remained standing at the edge of the forest and stared at the 'ohana. Grady felt along the wall for the light switch. Brightness flooded the lawn.

The dog was gone.

Grady scanned the forest, then made a quick search of the 'ohana, peering out windows, turning on another outside light. He saw nothing. He made sure both doors were locked, closed the windows he'd left open. He checked his phone: 3:17.

Shit. He hoped he hadn't woken Minton. He ran a hand across his forehead—he was soaked with sweat—and got himself a beer from the fridge. A proper pibbah, not one of Dalita's Bikini lagers. He sat on the couch and drank it slowly, waiting for his heart to stop pounding. When he finished the beer, he got another.

Gradually his heart slowed, his terror fading the way it did after the terrible dreams he still sometimes had about his father and Kayla. He felt embarrassed, even though there were no witnesses.

Maybe he'd been half asleep? He'd been traveling for almost twenty-four hours. And didn't some dogs have eyes like that? Like a bulldog, or those little pugs that always looked like they'd run into a four-wheeler.

But this dog hadn't remotely resembled a bulldog. It had been too big, for one thing, and the wrong color, that strange, dark, brindled red. He'd seen brindled mastiffs, but this dog wasn't that massive.

And it'd had pointed ears. It could have been an owl, he thought.

Were there owls in Hawai'i? Great horned owls were huge, and they had those ear tufts. Grady had seen one in broad daylight in the Allagash, sitting in a tree. It had scared the crap out of him, its head slowly rotating to watch him. But whoever'd heard of an owl as big as a person?

He finished his beer and stepped over to the french doors, opened one to peer through the screen door. Outside he saw only trees and the blazing tail of the Milky Way. He closed the screen door, again made sure the inside door was locked and returned to bed, this time carefully drawing the curtains closed.

CHAPTER 16

G rady woke to a faint sound. He thought it was the insect he'd heard the night before, then realized it was his phone vibrating. He rolled over to stare groggily at the screen: a text from Wes Minton.

Call me when you're up.

Groaning, he rubbed his eyes. It was after eight o'clock. He lay in bed, trying to source his unease: a dog, or a dream about a dog.

A dream, he told himself. Though he'd never had jet lag before, he knew it messed up your sleep, gave you insomnia and probably nightmares, too, maybe even those night terrors Zeke had told him about, when your eyes could be wide-open, seeing things that weren't there. Or it might have been a feral dog, twisted by shadows and starlight into something impossible.

Whatever: time to get up.

His room was stuffy and smelled of sweat and beer. He pulled apart the curtains to release an avalanche of sunlight. Birds called riotously, more birds than he'd ever heard in one place, like a frigging bird alarm.

Wincing, he walked to the bathroom and took a shower. He heard a loud, rhythmic *thunk, thunk* as the pump kicked in. Even after a full minute, the water barely got tepid. Off the fucking grid.

He washed quickly and got out. Drying off, he inspected his reflection in the bathroom mirror. He'd let his hair grow during the pandemic and hadn't cut it before coming here, figuring he'd botch the job. It brushed his shoulders, dark auburn and wavy, long enough to pull back in a ponytail, but he hated the way that looked. He didn't bother to shave his inch of stubble, just trimmed it a bit with his razor. With no real work, his muscle tone had gotten slack in the last few months, but he hoped that would change here.

He dressed in clean khakis and a rumpled white button-down, what passed for professional attire back home. In the kitchen, he couldn't begin to figure out the coffee machine, so he made coffee in one of those glass things with a plunger, then stepped outside with his steaming mug.

The sky burned as blue as a gas jet. The air had been cool when he woke, but already it had started to warm. Leaves stirred in the breeze, everything sparkling from the night's rain. The grass was still wet beneath his bare feet.

In daylight, the trees bordering the overgrown lawn seemed less wild, more like the cultivated ornamentals they almost certainly were. The dog he'd seen might well have wandered from some distant neighbor's place. For all Grady knew, it belonged to Minton. Dalita said he had no real pets, but maybe that had changed—lots of people were getting dogs during the pandemic.

The closer he looked at this property, the clearer it became that, for all the efforts to make it appear wild, Minton's compound was more like the resorts Grady had seen from the plane, meticulously designed if not well maintained. It was a rich person's fantasy of what Hawai'i should look like. He thought of the rich people in Maine, who managed their properties so that you never saw a blowdown or drifts of dead leaves. Their woodpiles tightly stacked like boxes of ammo, driveways plowed so you never saw a speck of snow.

It was fucking crazy. Nature was chaotic. Might as well accept that and not be so frigging tight-sphinctered. Grady took a final gulp of coffee and dumped the rest onto the grass, went inside and called Minton.

"Grady. How'd you sleep?"

"Fine."

"Good for you. Second night's always the worst for jet lag. How about you come here at ten? We can go over a few things, I'll show you the lay of the land. You like espresso?"

"Yeah, sure," Grady lied.

"Excellent. See you soon."

Grady squinted at his phone. 9:37 a.m., 3:37 p.m. back home. If she was lucky, his mother would sleep for another hour before waking for her shift. A wave of exhaustion hit him, two big thumbs pressing against his eyeballs. He ran water in the kitchen sink and splashed it on his face. *It was just a frigging dog,* he thought, even though the memory of its pupil-less eyes made his stomach churn. He stared at his reflection and realized he should've shaved—he looked like a bag of smashed assholes. He hoped he could get through the day without losing this job.

CHAPTER 17

A few minutes before ten he headed over to the main house, tugging on his mask. Minton sat at a long teak table on the first-
floor deck. He wore a plain red T-shirt, gray board shorts. No mask,
expensive sunglasses hiding his eyes.

The view from here was incredible.

It reminded him of Penobscot Bay, though the light felt different,
as though the sun was closer. In Maine, it could seem like the
landscape was in danger of running out of colors: you had blue and
green and gray and white and brown. Red barns, red-and-white
lighthouses. Lupines and invasive purple loosestrife livened things
up briefly in the summer, and October brought flaring orange and
scarlet. Grady always reminded his clients that, while a trendy
neutral palette was calming, by March they'd long for purple and red
and yellow.

Now the profusion of colors made him anxious. There was too
much of everything here: too many stars at night, too many strange
smells, too many sounds. The only thing there wasn't much of was
people. He sat in the single other chair, kitty-corner from Minton,
and forced a smile under his mask.

"Quite a view you got," Grady said.

Minton nodded without looking up from his laptop. A smart-
phone was propped alongside it, and a tablet, and Minton seemed
to be monitoring all of them at once, along with the smartwatch on
his wrist. There was also a set of binoculars, a German brand that
Grady recognized—two of his customers, a couple who owned a

fifty-four-foot Hinkley yacht, had a pair. The wife had told him they cost seven thousand dollars, which Grady hadn't believed. But he'd looked them up online and, yup, seven frigging grand.

"Just a sec." Minton's fingers moved across the keyboard, incredibly fast. He glanced at Grady, then the binoculars. "Check those out if you want."

Grady picked them up and peered through, whistling. He trained the sights on a tree at the foot of the driveway, watching as a small yellow-green bird hopped along a branch. "These are incredible."

Minton closed his laptop. "Done. You said you like espresso."

Before Grady could reply, Minton stood and slipped into the house. The wide glass doors were open, revealing an open-plan space, as sparely furnished as the 'ohana, though Grady suspected none of this furniture would be knockoffs. He set down the binoculars gingerly. He'd never spent that much money on anything, except maybe his student loans and repairs on his truck.

After a few minutes Minton reappeared, bearing two espresso cups. "Here you go. Hang on, I've got some bagels."

Grady picked up one of the thimble-sized cups, black with the same logo of a sun he'd seen on Wes's sarong the day before. A curl of lemon peel floated atop the espresso. He grimaced, and Minton returned with a plate of toasted bagels and a butter dish.

"They're from the freezer but still good. No cream cheese, sorry. I figured you might not have had breakfast yet."

"No, I didn't. Thanks—this is great."

Grady reached for a bagel. He realized he hadn't had dinner, either, unless you counted beer. He scraped on butter, raised his mask to take a bite, then, ravenous, wolfed down half.

"Sorry," he said, wiping away crumbs with a napkin. "I forgot to eat last night."

Minton smiled. He looked tired, a web of fine lines visible in the bright morning light. "That happens. How'd you sleep, really?"

"Okay for a while." Grady hesitated. "I got up once and saw a dog outside. Startled me."

"A dog?" Minton sipped his espresso. "What'd it look like?"

"It was hard to tell. Pointy ears. It looked like . . ." Grady recalled his queasy terror at those white, pupil-less eyes. "Like a coyote, maybe? But I don't think you have those."

"Coyotes? No. There are wild dogs—not a lot, and not around here. Wild boars are what you have to watch out for, but I hire a guy to take care of those. I haven't seen any for a while."

Minton picked up his phone and started scrolling. Grady ate his bagel, grateful for the interruption—the more he thought about it, the less convinced he was that he'd seen a dog. It could've been a boar, or more likely a deer. The wildlife guide had said there were deer here, some species from India, spotted all over, with large ears. He might have seen one of those.

Minton set his phone down, and Grady changed the topic. "You been here a long time?"

"Since 1993. I used to commute back and forth from L.A., but I got tired of it. Usually I go back a couple times a year, but not since the lockdown. It's been great, actually. No distractions from work. No tourists."

Grady wanted to ask what "work" consisted of, but Minton had again turned to his phone. He ate another bagel while Minton tapped out a long text message.

"Okay, yeah," Minton said. He picked up his bagel and took a bite. "Isn't it hard to eat with that mask?"

Grady nodded, his mouth full.

"So take it off. We're outside, you're on the other side of the table, the wind . . ." Minton shrugged. "I think we're safe."

Grady removed his mask and drew a grateful breath. "Thanks."

"When you're finished, I'll show you around. My father built this place—off the grid, though they didn't call it that back then. It's the only part of all our land that could be built on. Legally, anyway," Minton added, and laughed. "But he was never here so he sold the house and this piece of property to Niles Jarbash—ever hear of him?" Grady shook his head, and Minton continued. "Music producer, made a fortune in the eighties. He and his wife split up, and she kept the house—Maxine Kaiwi."

Grady recognized the name of the beautiful young woman from the photo online. "The model?"

Minton nodded. "She only lived here a few years, her and her daughter. Maxine didn't like how remote it was, but the little girl, she loved it. By then I'd decided I wanted to move to the island full-time, so I bought the house back from Maxine. Did a major renovation, built the ʻohana so I could have a caretaker when I go out to the point. There's not that much to be done here. Keep up with the lawn. Everything's solar. There's a backup propane generator in case of a hurricane or tsunami, but I've never had to use it."

"You get a lot of storms?"

"Haven't had a bad storm in years. But we get days of heavy clouds or fog, when there's not enough sun to run everything. In that case you want to keep the fridge fired up, and the water pump. And your phone."

Minton sipped what was left of his espresso, regarded the empty cup like it was a jewel between his fingers. "I grew these beans, out at the point. I spend as much time there as I can. Remote as hell, but I love it. That's why you're here. When I'm there, I need someone here to keep an eye on things. There've been a few times the roof sprang a leak. And there are some repairs I've been putting off—the last guy was supposed to get to them, but he never did. Dalita's good, but she's not much of a carpenter. You're a carpenter, right?"

"Also plumber, electrician, painter, roofer—I can do all that stuff. Pretty much anything you need."

"Like I said, I hope there won't be too much. Check on the main house at least once a day. I'll send you the code so you can let yourself in."

"You don't have a security system?"

"Maxine had a break-in when she first lived here with her daughter—there were still a couple people squatting on the land then. It was an hour and a half before the cops arrived. The police here can't handle anything. And I can barely get a cell signal out at the point—no Wi-Fi, so no way to watch a video monitor. I'd rather just have someone on-site."

"There's no security company on the island?"

Minton laughed. "You trying to do yourself out of a job?"

"Just curious. We have the same issues in Maine, especially on the islands."

"There's a security company in Li'ulā, but to be honest, I don't trust them any more than I trust the cops. There are a lot of conflicting interests. A lot of problems they don't want the tourists to know about. Homeless people everywhere, drugs. Trouble in paradise, right?" Minton shrugged. "You have enough food to get you through quarantine?"

"I think so. Dalita said she'll bring up more if I need it."

Minton slapped his palms on the table. "Okay, mask up. I'll give you the tour."

CHAPTER 18

Inside, the house looked expensive. Minton's taste ran to chrome and glass, buff-colored leather, white sheepskin rugs on the polished concrete floors. A custom-made bookcase had an entire shelf devoted to books about Hawai'ian birds. He followed Minton to the foot of the stairway and drew up short.

Against the wall stood the biggest fish tank Grady had ever seen outside the New England Aquarium, mounted on a massive oak-and-bluestone stand reinforced with steel. Only instead of fish it was filled with chunks of black lava, and smooth reddish rocks and lumpy white stones that, when he leaned in, turned out to be coral.

Also, sea urchins—lots and lots of sea urchins. They covered the tank's sandy bottom the way the urchins in the Gulf of Maine had in his childhood, before overfishing and warming waters had all but decimated them a decade ago. They didn't look like the sea urchins he'd grown up with on Penobscot Bay, gray-green and covered with small spikes. These resembled small, lavender jellyfish, only more opaque and covered with rows of tiny bumps.

"Don't stick your hand in there," Wes warned him. "I knew someone who stepped on one of those when he was snorkeling. Spine broke off and a year later worked itself out of his chin."

He started upstairs. Grady continued to stare into the tank, marveling. He'd worked for a rich young Belfast dot-commer who bred tarantulas and scorpions. At least this tank wasn't filled with spiders.

Wes's voice echoed from the landing above him. "You coming?"

Grady hurried upstairs, accompanying Minton through the master bedroom and two guest rooms. Framed photos lined each wall. A waterfall curtained by vines. A flame-orange bird, its long bill a yellow scimitar. Sea turtles clustered on a beach like abandoned plastic wading pools, a stunning photo of a surf break.

"Dalita's wife took that one — she's an amazing surf photographer. I took those." Minton indicated a picture of a beautiful bird, glossy black with yellow markings on its cheek and wings, with a long tail and a curved beak that held a large insect. "That's an 'ō'ō. They were proclaimed extinct over a hundred years ago. But I've seen them. At the point."

He mentioned this so offhandedly that it took Grady a few seconds to process it. "But how . . ." he started to ask, but Minton had already gone out onto the deck.

"I've had problems with rot here," Minton said, pointing at the rail. "That's something you can look into."

The wood on the deck was pressure-treated, but that was no match for decades of salt air and heavy rain. Grady dug a thumbnail into the railing, the wood spongy and fissured with insect borings.

Back inside, they continued Minton's inventory. The shower in the master bath dripped. The ceiling fans looked old, their wooden blades frosted with spiderwebs.

"One last thing up here and then I'll show you the solar setup," Minton said.

They walked down the hall to a back room. The door was closed, and when Minton opened it, light streamed into the hallway. A screen weighted with magnets separated them from what was inside; Minton held it aside so that Grady could walk in first.

He stepped into a high-ceilinged room, brilliant with skylights and floor-to-ceiling windows, and filled with plants in oversized terra cotta pots and wooden planters. An artificial waterfall cascaded four feet into a small concrete pool. Its burbling vied with a chorus of whistles and whirring sounds, a persistent cry like a squeaky door.

Grady looked around, delighted but also confused. If you lived in a tropical paradise, why would you need a garden on the second floor of your house?

He realized why as a brilliant scarlet bird zipped past him to land on a branch. It had an orange beak and black wings, a bright black eye that regarded him with intelligent curiosity. Within seconds an identical bird dive-bombed it and they both flew off. Grady saw that the room was filled with birds, thrusting their long beaks into tubular pink blossoms, swarming around clusters of yellow flowers and ferns, watching him from trees ten feet above his head.

"My aviary," Minton pronounced proudly. "I'm trying to establish a breeding colony. There's a drip irrigation system and a mister that comes on when it's needed. Everything's programmed, same as with the wana downstairs. When I'm here, you don't need to do anything. When I'm gone, just check to make sure everything looks the way it does now."

Minton gazed into the tangled web of leaves and branches, the darting bursts of yellow and red and orange. Grady again felt like the dreamworld had somehow swallowed the real one. He breathed in the odors of wet earth and water, the heavy green smell of the plants, and another, unfamiliar scent. Musky, though it also reminded him of stagnant water, or mildewed boat cushions, and a flowery scent like rotting lilacs. It wasn't unpleasant, just odd.

"It's the honeycreepers." Minton nodded at a bright orange bird hopping from branch to branch. "That smell. Can you imagine, coming to these islands twelve hundred years ago, and there were so many of those birds you were overwhelmed by their smell?"

Grady couldn't. It was as if Minton had told him that the sea urchins could talk.

"Birds were precious, and their feathers were worn by kings—made into capes and caps, even used for currency. There were special bird-catchers for the kings—po'e kia manu. A kia manu knew the birds by name and song—he knew where they lived, *how* they lived. He shared a sacred bond with them. The kia manu believed the birds had personalities—the 'i'iwi was cheerful, the 'ō'ō melancholy. But of course we humans used this knowledge to betray them."

This, Grady could believe. "How did they catch them?"

"They used kēpau, birdlime. It's sticky, so they'd smear it on branches or sticks, then carefully remove the birds so as not to damage the feathers. Sometimes they'd use one bird to lure another."

He stooped to pick up a dead leaf, crumbling it between his fingers. "You'll need to check and make sure the waterfall's going— sometimes the filter gets clogged. I've planted 'ōhi'a trees and other flowering species for the birds to feed on—they've had years to establish themselves, so it's a fairly self-sufficient little ecosystem. Uncle Honey brought in some of the native bees, and they've made themselves at home in the forest outside. There are a few small openings where they can get in, and other insects that pollinate the plants here. Keep an eye out for mildew around the windows."

He turned and walked out, leaving Grady to try imprinting the riotous display on his memory.

"You coming?" Minton called impatiently, and Grady hurried after him.

CHAPTER 19

He followed Minton downstairs and outside to the shed that held the solar battery bank and inverter. A standard setup—no bells or whistles here. Grady hadn't seen much that would drain the batteries, other than the hot water heaters and water pumps, possibly the irrigation system for the aviary.

He asked, "You don't have AC or any heating?"

"Don't need it. It cools off at night, but not much. When it gets hot, I just move with the sun, or pull the drapes."

"How do you get your water?"

"Catchment system, gravity fed. There's a pump that kicks in—I'm sure you've heard that. Tools and your truck are in the garage."

The detached garage had three bays, one occupied by a new, silvery-blue Tesla, another by an ancient pickup. The Tesla was a Y—an SUV model, brand-new but already with a few dings. The pickup was older than Grady, piss yellow, with a big dent in the hood and an even bigger one in the passenger door. Peeling bumper stickers, a bunch of empty Coors cans in the truck bed.

"Last guy liked his beer," Grady observed.

"That he did," said Minton.

The garage's remaining bay looked like an exploded yard sale. Sawhorses, a Craftsman lathe, a portable generator, a Sawzall and table saw were all nearly hidden beneath piles of other stuff: wet suits, a scuba tank and flippers, chain saws, hacksaws, a mountain bike, a motorcycle engine, an electric lawn mower. Six toolboxes, half of which looked like they'd never been opened.

"Looks like you're all set up for tools." Grady rescued a spirit level from a busted carton crammed with plastic goggles and a soiled drop cloth. "Okay if I spend a couple of hours organizing this?"

"Knock yourself out." Minton glanced down as his phone buzzed. "Look, I think that's everything. The truck is yours, once you're out of quarantine. Keys should be in there somewhere. Take it easy for the first couple of days. Jet lag can really slam you here—it takes about a week for your brain to adjust. There's nothing here that can't wait. I'll let you know if anything comes up."

He turned and walked back to the house. Grady linked his hands behind his neck, murmuring, "What the fuck?"

Who kept this much shit and never used it? Or maybe every caretaker before him had just bought more stuff, piling it onto the mountain that was already here. He spent the next few hours organizing. He moved aside plastic milk crates stuffed with flashlights. He uncovered Black & Decker power tools, some in boxes that had never been opened. When he'd cleared enough space, he moved the saws and worktables so they could actually be used. He found several plastic bins, all empty, that he could use for recyclables, and began to fill them with flattened cardboard boxes, empty water bottles. He'd transfer the recyclables to bags when the time came to take them to the dump. He also found a bunch of take-out containers that, when he made the mistake of opening them, released flying cockroaches as big as hummingbirds. He stuffed the containers into a bag, hoping the roaches wouldn't find their way into the house or 'ohana.

By late afternoon, he'd made a dent, but there was a ton of shit left to go through. Still, he could see part of the wall now, and navigate the space without tripping over an air compressor. His head pounded from exhaustion as he walked back to the 'ohana. He showered, then ate a granola bar for dinner, chasing it with a beer, undressed, and fell into bed.

Tired as he was, he couldn't sleep. He'd been so busy he hadn't thought about the weird dog he'd seen the night before. Minton didn't seem concerned, except for the possibility that it might have been a wild boar. But whatever Grady had seen, he sure as shit knew it hadn't been a boar. More likely he'd had some kind of bad dream he'd been unable to shake because he was so disoriented.

Still, the memory of its staring, pupil-less eyes clung to him like a hangover. What if it had been real, a feral dog sniffing around for food while Grady slept? What if it was out there now? Had he closed and locked the doors? Groggily, he started to sit up, but it was too much effort. The rain had already begun to fall, sluicing down the roof of the 'ohana and drowning out the monotonous *tkk, tkk, tkk* of whatever insect lived in the corners. Next thing Grady knew, it was morning.

CHAPTER 20

Grady's first week in quarantine passed, marked by brain-numbing heat during the day and drenching rain at night. Time was almost evenly divided between dark and light, with no real dusk or twilight. Night fell with the immediacy of a cranky neighbor yanking down a window curtain. When he woke every morning, it was to a brilliant day exactly like the one before.

He missed Maine, something he'd never experienced before. How could he, when he'd never been anywhere else? He'd always thought homesickness was some kind of made-up thing, like jet lag. Now he felt both, two persistent aches that didn't subside. Not even beer helped—every time he stumbled to the bathroom at 3 a.m., he'd glance at the window, overcome by dread that he might see something there.

The six-hour time difference made it hard to talk to anyone at home. Grady texted Zeke the photo he'd taken on the drive in, of the white, long-legged bird in the field.

shitpoke, replied Zeke, his name for a heron.

not a heron its an egret

shitpoke, Zeke texted back, along with a GIF of a cartoon bird exploding in midair. Grady laughed. But when he tried to describe how he felt to Donny, his brother was not sympathetic.

Your in fucking hawai shut TF up im at work

Minton was still around, but a day might pass before he'd reply to Grady's texts asking if he needed any work done. No thanks or Not today.

So Grady would stand in front of the 'ohana and stare out at the Pacific and remind himself that this was paradise. But the truth was, he'd have given anything to be back home.

CHAPTER 21

After several days, Grady's brain fog began to lift, along with the creeping dread that had dogged him since he arrived. Minton had said it could take a week to get over jet lag: now, for the first time, Grady felt like he could actually get some work done. Up till now, he'd spent much of his time poring over a book on Hawai'ian birds, and some field guides to local flora that he'd found in the 'ohana. He felt the same quiet joy and pride he'd experienced when he was training to be a Maine guide, memorizing animal tracks and spoor, differentiating between an osprey's cry and a bald eagle's, the silhouette of a red-tailed hawk or a gyrfalcon. Now he was absorbed by the variety and rarity of honeycreepers and other birds, the sad roll call of all the ones that were now extinct: 'ula-'ai-hawane, mamo, 'amakihi, the lesser and greater koa-finches.

Still, he was ready to do something other than read. He texted Minton. Gonna work on the garage again unless you need something else?

Minton replied within a few minutes. Thx no. Heading into town for groceries and errands, back late afternoon. U want anything?

No thx

Grady waited till Minton left, the blue Tesla sliding down the drive almost soundlessly. He felt ridiculously elated at being alone, with the warm sun streaming down on his face, surrounded by the smell of the sea and the faint scent of white hibiscus. It was like he'd been wearing dark glasses all this time, and only now saw everything clearly. He took a photo of a bright green lizard sunning itself on a rock and sent it to Zeke.

Nice togue bait, Zeke texted back.

Grady laughed and headed to the garage.

This time he focused on the built-in shelves jammed with gear. Hiking boots, running shoes, trekking poles, hats, and cartons of sunscreen. Also a box of random sneakers and flip-flops in different sizes.

Eventually he came across trash bags full of empty cans of Coors and Bikini Blonde lager. He felt like he was on an archaeological dig: he'd reached the Carl and Dalita levels. It was weird, going through a dead man's stuff, but he'd done it before, clearing out estates.

Grady piled these bags, along with the other trash bags, in the back of the pickup. There were enough redeemable cans to make some homeless person's payday. He wondered where all this crap ended up. Landfill? Shipped off-island? Obviously there was no trash removal service out here, other than Grady. He'd find out where the transfer station was in town, and get everything down there once he was out of quarantine.

After a few hours, he took a break. He returned to the 'ohana and got a beer, stood outside the garage and drank it, staring at Minton's house. Grady hadn't been inside since that first day. Minton wouldn't be back for a few hours, and he'd pretty much given Grady free rein with the place. He finished his beer and tossed the can into the back of the pickup, walked over to the main house, punched in the security code, and walked in.

Nothing looked any different from the last time he'd been here. Some empty coffee pods on the kitchen counter, a T-shirt slung over the couch. He felt a buzz of excitement, like when he and Zeke would enter an unoccupied camp during the winter, knock back a six-pack and a joint, then hike back out before they could be caught trespassing.

But Grady wasn't doing anything wrong here. This was his job, keeping an eye on things when the boss was away. Still, he crossed the room cautiously, glancing out the front windows for any sign of the Tesla's return, and halted when he reached the aquarium.

One night in the 'ohana, he'd spent a couple of hours on-line, reading about Hawai'ian sea urchins. The ones pictured with five-inch spikes weren't truly dangerous. But the lumpy, purplish ones—the kind that Wes kept in his aquarium—they really could kill you. Those were parasol urchins, found only in the waters off this island, though apparently related to a common species in West Pacific waters, called the flower urchin. The danger was posed not by their spines but by small protrusions that resembled tiny umbrellas. Brush against a parasol urchin, and you'd be injected with a quick-acting toxin. Grady had read gruesome accounts of paralyzed marine biologists, snorkelers, and pearl divers who died after having been stung. He wasn't surprised to learn that parasol urchins were near extinction due to loss of habitat, climate change, and sunscreen in the water. Go figure.

He stared at them for a few minutes, trying to detect any movement, finally went upstairs to the aviary. He let the screen fall shut behind him and stood in the middle of the room, entranced. Birds whistled everywhere and darted past him, completely unafraid—they seemed scarcely to notice him at all, hopping onto branches inches from his face, tilting their heads to gaze at him with keen black eyes. Once a brilliant crimson bird perched on his head, its tiny claws digging into his scalp. He inhaled its musty smell, closed his eyes, and tried to imagine a world where millions of these creatures had once filled the forests, a world without humans. He opened his eyes, and for a fraction of a second, he could almost believe it still existed.

A sound from downstairs made him jump—the front door closing. Minton had returned. Grady slipped back out into the hall, his heart racing even though he'd done nothing wrong.

"Hey, Wes, I'm up here!" he yelled from the top of the steps.

He hurried downstairs. Wes stood outside the kitchen, a canvas carry bag at his feet. He glanced up as Grady walked over.

"Sorry, I was checking on the birds," Grady said breathlessly. "You have anything else to bring in?"

Wes shook his head. "Nope. I'm going out to the point tomorrow—everything's already in the car. There's only one spot where I can get a signal out there, so if anything comes up, text me."

"How does that Tesla handle the roads?"

"The Y's great. Perfect for here. Good turning radius. And I never have to worry about oncoming traffic," Wes added with a grin. He set a few bags of coffee beans on the kitchen counter, and barely looked at Grady.

Grady stood awkwardly, waiting to be dismissed, or given some task to do. "I guess I'll head back," he said at last, and started for the door.

"Hang on."

Wes closed a cabinet and strode into the living room, making a beeline for the bookshelves. He ran his fingers over several books, pulled out a hefty volume, and handed it to Grady. "You can read about them online, but this'll give you better information. If you're really interested."

"Thanks." Grady glanced at the book: a guide to Hawai'ian forest birds, more like a textbook than an ordinary field guide. "I'll check it out."

"You do that," Wes said, returning to the kitchen. "I'll see you in a few days."

CHAPTER 22

Back in the ʻohana, Grady microwaved a food pouch—black bean chili and rice—from the carton of packaged meals he'd discovered in a cabinet, presumably left by his predecessor. He cut up an avocado from outside, dumped it into the bowl, opened a beer, and settled on the couch with the book Wes had given him.

He recognized some of the birds from the aviary: ʻelepaio, ʻamakihi, ʻakekeʻe, ʻiʻiwi, palila. ʻIʻiwi, a scarlet honeycreeper; ʻākohekohe, a feathered punk rocker with blaze-orange bands around its eyes and a white tufted mohawk. He wondered what their names meant, if they corresponded to their calls or held some deeper meaning when they had been named long ago. He went online to listen to birdcalls, entranced by their unfamiliar cries, playing them over and over again to memorize the sounds.

He worked his way through the thirty rack, poring over a chapter on extinct species—dozens of them, including the Hawaiʻian crow, which looked like a regular crow and had pretty much disappeared almost twenty years ago. A few pairs survived in breeding programs on the Big Island, but those released into the wild had been killed by predators or died from unknown causes.

Grady couldn't wrap his mind around it. He understood the logic of extinction, but how could a crow, a bird as common as dirt, just vanish? It was somehow easier to think of the prettier, more exotic birds dying out. He could hear Zeke's gleeful laugh in his head: *Hell, yeah, they're just asking for it when they look like that.*

Reading about the extinct honeycreepers left him depressed and also angry—though who could he be angry at? Grady was part of the fucking problem, just by being here on the island. At least Minton provided a haven for them.

He closed the book and went to bed. He set his laptop on the nightstand and listened to a local radio station he'd discovered. Between ads for used cars and Lulu's Barbecue, it played a mix of contemporary Hawai'ian songs—Jawaiian, which was like Hawai'ian reggae and local hip-hop, but also older music: steel guitars, men and women singing in Hawai'ian, their voices sometimes melancholic but mostly exuberant, like they were at a big party. He wished he could understand the words, especially to the songs that sounded like some sort of farewell, to a place or a lover, someone or something they would never see again. The music made him feel the way he had as a kid, listening to songs about heartbreak, years before his heart had been broken.

But mostly he wished he could find that big party he imagined, or even just a few people he could hang and share a couple of beers with. Given the pandemic, he wondered if that would ever happen here, or anywhere else.

CHAPTER 23

When he went to the garage early the next morning, Minton's car was already gone. He must've left before dawn. Grady turned to stare down the driveway, feeling a slight unease. For the first time, he was completely alone up here. A strong wind buffeted the palm trees overlooking the lawn: he heard the thrashing sound of a large frond as it broke off and fell to the ground.

He set down the toolbox he'd been carrying and walked across the grass, stooping to pick up a frond as long as his arm. It resembled a huge feather, brown and brittle, with spiky leaves as sharp as little knives. He walked to the edge of the woods and halted. Despite the brilliant blue sky and sun burning overhead, shadows moved within the forest, a shifting crosshatch of black and green and gold. As the wind gusted, he caught a whiff of the same rank scent he'd smelled that first night, like the honeycreepers' musk but more rancid. His neck prickling, he chucked the palm frond into the woods and hurried back to the garage.

He cleared off a workbench, setting it up like the one in his garage at home. He had better hand tools there, including some chisels that had belonged to his father and grandfather. By the time he'd finished with the workbench he felt calm, the morning's momentary unease forgotten. He stepped back, admiring the job, then made a circuit of the garage, picking up a pair of broken sunglasses and the crushed display panel from an old flip phone. He tossed them into a wastebasket and gave the built-in shelves a look-over. For the first time, he noticed a door hidden in the corner.

He walked over to examine it. He rapped and heard a dull *ting*—it was a commercial metal door, like a fire door. A metal hasp had been bolted to the frame, and from this hung a padlock. Not the kind you'd see on a garden shed but a military-grade Commando lock, with a shackle you'd need a laser to cut through.

He gave it a tug. It didn't budge. Grady tugged it again, then went outside, the afternoon heat hammering him instantly. He walked to the back and surveyed the exterior garage wall.

There was no outer door. Slowly he retraced his steps, his hand on the wall, palm flat as he tried to detect a seam. Unlike Minton's house, the garage had white vinyl siding, with a trim board under the eaves. When he reached the front again, he turned and back-tracked, the wall as warm as skin against his fingertips. Again he felt nothing.

He halted at the back corner, yawning. The locked metal door was odd, but rich people did weird things. He'd worked on homes that had safe rooms, storerooms for collections of porn or guns, plastic-wrapped paintings that had never seen daylight. One McMansion had a soundproof room for sex play, complete with harnesses and a trapeze and walls covered with red fake fur, so it felt like you were trapped inside a body cavity.

Minton could be sitting on a pile of cash or gold, maybe drugs. More likely he kept firearms there, or replacement parts for his brand-new Tesla. At home, people stole catalytic converters for the metals they contained—platinum, rhodium, palladium. A Tesla didn't have a catalytic converter, but in a closed ecosystem like this one, maybe there was a black market for Tesla parts. It seemed no matter where you went, rural Maine or some upscale compound in Hawai'i, you found the same old shit.

CHAPTER 24

Back in the ʻohana, Grady's phone buzzed: Unknown Caller. He answered, frowning.

"Grady Kendall?" a man asked cheerfully. "How are you feeling today?"

"Who's calling?"

"How are you feeling today?"

"Who is this?"

"Officer Padua, police department. Are you feeling okay?"

"Oh! I thought you were a spam call."

Officer Padua laughed like this was the funniest thing he'd heard all morning. "Yes! 'Your car warranty is up!' You feeling okay? Any fever, coughing, shortness of breath?"

"No. I feel fine."

"You still up there on Hokuloa Road? Have you left the premises?"

"Nope. I'm right here, haven't gone anywhere."

"Okay, good! Stay safe, I'll call you again tomorrow—mahalo!"

Grady was almost disappointed when he didn't call back the next day, or the next. He wondered if that girl Jessica from the plane had received a similar phone call. At least she was staying with a friend. He was bored out of his frigging mind. He'd finished up with the garage, done what he could with Minton's upstairs deck without having access to a hardware store, caulked the floor and drains in the ʻohana's bathroom and kitchen, hoping to stop the march of ants and the flying cockroaches that would erupt from the drain. The spotty Wi-Fi cut out when he played WOW. There was no TV, and no sports on in any case. The national news only made him anxious, so he read the online *Island Pilot*—police and COVID reports, travel updates.

A year ago, the island had seen a total of 279,000 visitors in July. This year, there had been 983. There were only three flights a week from the mainland. Yesterday, a total of thirty-four passengers had arrived—three returning residents, twelve airline crew, two military personnel. That left seventeen people like himself. All the resorts were shuttered—twenty-four thousand empty hotel rooms, more if you factored in family-owned motels or Airbnbs.

Tens of thousands of locals were surviving on unemployment and federal handouts. Over a thousand were houseless. He'd read about a village of several hundred houseless people on Oʻahu, which seemed in some ways more like a commune. But here, photos of encampments by the airport and on the beaches looked like scenes from a postapocalyptic movie.

When even local news made him too depressed, he'd return to the aviary.

He'd breathe in the ripe air as the birds flittered around him, unperturbed. Had they grown up inside this room, accustomed to Minton's presence? Or had he captured them, a species trusting of people and easily made into pets? Grady now recognized individual birds, noticing how one ʻiʻiwi—a male, from its brighter plumage—was more aggressive than the others. The tiny ʻelepaios were almost tame: all he had to do was stand with his hands open and they would perch there for as long as a minute before darting off.

As he watched them, his loneliness began to recede. Not just the loneliness of quarantine or the months of the pandemic but also the deeper, almost physical sense of isolation he'd experienced since he and Rachel had split, an ache like a pulled muscle. He definitely felt that he'd changed since arriving here, though he couldn't put a finger on what that change was. It was like some microscopic shift, like his molecules were being replaced or rearranged while he slept or watched the birds or stood outside at night staring at the stars.

Sometimes he thought the thing he'd seen outside the 'ohana had something to do with it, like it had been sending him a message or a warning, or even a threat.

He knew that was crazy. But it seemed a lot less crazy here than it would have been at home. Now, watching the birds thrust their beaks into flowers and soft bark in search of food, he realized how long it had been since he'd actually felt happy.

Yet they made him sad as well. They were wild birds. Surely they'd be happier back in the forest? Though there they might fall prey to feral cats and mongooses and wild dogs. And could birds even know what it was to feel happiness?

CHAPTER 25

Dalita called near the end of his final week of quarantine.

"Hey!" he exclaimed. "How're you doing?"

"Eh, how you doing? You stir-crazy yet?"

"Yeah." He laughed. "But only three more days."

"I'm going to Mak Supe this morning, you want anything? I can bring it up for you."

It was like she'd told him he just won a new truck. "That would be amazing! I haven't seen anyone since I got here."

"Wes at the point?"

"Yeah."

"Text me what you want. I'll let you know when I'm on my way."

He tried to tamp down his excitement. He didn't need groceries—he was mostly working through the carton of pre-pared meal pouches—but he made up a list, sent it to Dalita, and returned to the *Island Pilot*'s headlines.

LOCAL CELEBRITY ARRESTED FOR VIOLATING QUARANTINE

He'd learned from the *Pilot* just how many rich people lived here: a fucking boatload. If Minton ever wanted to party with other billionaires, he'd have plenty of company.

There were celebrities, too—not megastars, but reality TV stars and models, tech tycoons and franchise queens. Grady wondered who their caretakers were, where they hung out when they weren't mowing lawns or checking the nitrate levels in saltwater aquariums.

Maybe there was a twelve-step group for people like himself, losing their minds from boredom.

This local celebrity turned out to be a woman named Tinky Esposito, a hairdresser who specialized in resort weddings. She'd flown to Oʻahu for a weekend, then been photographed at a bar on this island the day after her return. Grady scribbled down the bar's name. It was in Makani, so maybe it was one of those bars the girl on the plane had referred to, a place they might meet up.

In other news, an experienced windsurfer had gone missing and was presumed drowned. The seas had been rough—the Coast Guard was calling off the search. A body had washed up on another beach, so damaged it was difficult to get an ID. The police suspected he was a homeless guy whose friends said they hadn't seen him for a few weeks.

Grady thought of the reef that Dalita had described to him, coral growing out of dead people's rib cages. He closed his laptop and went outside to wait for her.

He heard the truck five minutes before he saw it chugging up the drive. He quickly stepped back into the ʻohana—he didn't want her to know he'd been waiting like some overeager kid. When the engine fell silent, he ambled out to greet her.

"Howzit?" Dalita stepped from the cab, grinning. She wore a flowered bandanna over her cropped black hair, surf shorts, and a cropped red T-shirt emblazoned with another hula girl.

"I'm good." He touched his face. "Dang, I forgot my mask."

"You not sick."

"You don't know that."

"Yeah, I do. You'd be feeling something." She hauled out a couple of canvas totes. "My tūtū had it in February—they had her on a ventilator for a week. But she's okay now."

They carried the groceries into the ʻohana. Dalita set a thirty rack of PBR beside the fridge, watching him unpack the bags. "So, you lōlō yet?" she asked. "Going crazy?"

"I'm getting there."

"I used to go crazy here, and I wasn't under quarantine." She reached into the fridge for a lager. "It's beautiful, but how long can you just look at that shit? I don't wanna look at the water, I want to be *in* it. Right? Wes, he doesn't surf or anything. He just watches the birds. You like his fish tank?"

"It's pretty sweet."

"Yeah, just don't touch those wana—his sea urchins. Their sting can kill you." She swigged the beer, wiped her mouth. "He show you the aviary?"

Grady nodded. "That's crazy. Actually, it keeps me from going crazy. How long's he been keeping birds?"

"Long time. Long as I've known him, anyway."

"Where does he get them?"

"I never ask."

"What's it like at his other place? On Hokuloa Point?"

"I never been. Must be beautiful."

She smiled, her dark eyes glassy. He wondered if she was one of those people who were always stoned. As though she'd read his mind, she dug into her pocket and handed him a pill bottle. "Friend of mine makes these—maybe you like try. Help you through the rest of quarantine."

The bottle held brightly colored blobs: green, red, orange, yellow.

"THC gummies," explained Dalita. "They're not that strong."

"I don't really get high," Grady admitted. "I mean, I have, it just always makes me sleepy. Or paranoid."

"This is a nice buzz. Very calming. You could do only half of one." She shrugged. "Whatever, I just thought it might help pass the time."

"Well, thanks."

He lingered over putting all the groceries away. He didn't want her to leave. But she didn't leave. She wandered into the living room and stared at a corner of the ceiling. "He's still there."

"Who?"

"Moshi. That gecko—he always hangs out in the same place."

Grady gazed up at what looked like a grasshopper on the ceiling, saw it was actually a tiny lizard. "That's a gecko?"

"Sure. You don't hear him at night? *Tkkk, tkk, tkk.*" She grinned. "He kept me company. I wanted a dog, but Wes doesn't want dogs here."

"I saw a dog." Grady stared at the gecko's tiny splayed hands, its pinhead eyes. "The first night, I woke up. Actually, it was that guy who got my attention—" He gestured at the gecko, which skittered into a crack. "I heard that noise and came over to the door. There was a dog outside—I thought it was a coyote at first, but there are no coyotes here, right?"

Dalita nodded, her expression guarded, and he continued.

"Anyway, it just stood there watching me, and . . ." Grady hesitated. "And then it stood up—I must've fallen asleep on my feet, 'cause now I'm looking at this dog and it's standing there like a person, staring at me. The weirdest thing was, I'd swear it had a person's eyes . . ." He touched the inner corners of his eyes to illustrate. "Only they were all white, with no pupils. Weirdest frigging dream I've ever had. I swear, it was right there."

Dalita said nothing. At last she said, "That is one lōlō dream. I'll ask Lorelei—that sounds like one of her auntie's chickenskin stories."

"What stories?"

"You know, ghost stories. Like creepypastas—urban legends, like that. Only some are true, like the Nightmarchers."

"What's that?"

"Serious, you never heard? So many stories, they're famous. The ghosts of ancient warriors—you hear them drumming and see a line of torches coming down the mountain. You have to run inside and lie facedown on the floor and stay there till morning. If you look at them, they'll kill you. Lor's uncle Wei says they walked through his house when he was in high school. They came through the walls and walked right over him and went out the other side. He said he almost shit himself."

"That's fucked up."

"Yeah. Some stories, you know they're made up, but too many people see Nightmarchers. Not here so much, but on the Big Island. That dog…" She paused like she was about to tell him something. Instead she walked to the bookshelf, pulled out a faded attractions brochure and shook her head. "No sunset cruises this year. No fake lū'aus or snorkelers. So the fish are back. Lor was on the water a few days ago—she saw two manta rays and some seals. We haven't seen seals for years."

She put back the brochure and headed for the door. "I gotta go—I told Lor I'd be home before lunch."

Grady followed her, hiding his disappointment. "Thanks again for getting all this stuff. What do I owe you?"

She handed him the receipt. He looked at the total and whistled. Dalita laughed. "Sticker shock, yeah?"

"Seven dollars for a gallon of milk?"

"Eh, at least your beer was cheap. Did the police ever call to check on you?"

"Just once. He said they'd call every day, but I haven't heard anything since then."

"So lazy, the cops."

Outside, she surveyed the grounds appraisingly. "You're allowed to walk around here, you know. If you're going crazy. It says on the quarantine website, you can walk around where you're staying, as long as you don't leave the grounds. There're no paths, so it's easy to get lost. But you used to be a wilderness guide, yeah?"

Grady gave her a nod. He pointed at the garage. "I cleaned up in there."

"Whoa. Impressive."

"Yeah. I'll make a dump run when I'm done with quarantine."

Dalita swung into her truck's front seat. "Three more days," she yelled as she backed out. "You get 'em, Grady, almost pau quarantine!"

CHAPTER 26

He woke the next morning feeling alert, almost excited: like someone had pressed a reset button in his brain. Only two more days. He dressed, made coffee, and drank it as he wandered across the lawn, halting to peer at a messy web that looked like it had been spun by a minuscule drunk. A spider the size of a pencil eraser crouched near the center. Its body looked like a tiny anime face, a scowling warrior or demon. Elsewhere he found a bigger web, shining with last night's rain like silver spray paint. An enormous spider sat in the middle, with a fiery red body and neon-green head, its legs striped yellow and black.

His phone pinged.

Come to the house, I want to go over a few things.

Right there, Grady texted back, cursing to himself. When had Minton returned?

He met Grady on the front steps. He'd buzz-cut his hair, leaving a half inch of gray stubble that made him look like an aging Marine sergeant. Grady put on his crumpled mask and followed him into the house. "You get back last night?" he asked.

Minton nodded. "I needed to resupply. I'll head out again in a few hours. How've you been?"

"Good."

"Your quarantine is up, when? This weekend?"

"Yeah, Saturday."

"Excellent. I just wanted you to look at this." He gestured for Grady to accompany him into the master bathroom, and pointed at the tub. "That's not draining properly."

"I'll check it out." Grady bent to flip the drain switch up and down. "Probably just clogged."

They stepped out onto the upstairs deck. Wes leaned against the rail, glancing down to note where Grady had made his half-assed repairs. He looked back up at Grady and smiled. "How are my birds?"

"Great, I think. They're so beautiful."

"They really are. The wana, too, but those 'i'iwi . . ." He shook his head. "That's really why you're here, you know. To protect them." He smiled again, though this time it was more wistful. "Because I can't be in two places at once. If you ever find a dead bird, in the aviary or outside, put it in a ziplock bag in the freezer."

Grady winced. "I hope that never happens."

"Birds die, even here where they're safe. Same in some of the protected places on the island—people are living in tents next to sanctuaries, destroying the birds' habitat. There are not enough of them, and too many of us. I wish it was the other way around." He sighed. "Anyway, I've arranged for any dead birds to be used for research, but in the meantime I don't want them lying around. Rats," he added with a grimace. "I do everything I can, but they still find a way in."

Grady leaned on the railing beside Minton. From here you could see the coastline, seamed with black lava cliffs, the beach below laced with white breakers.

"Dalita told me about the fog here," he said. "How people used to get lost, and their boats wrecked on the coral reefs. She said she saw bones there. Is that true?"

"Could be. Ten years ago, me and some other folks petitioned to stop local businesses taking snorkelers to those reefs. All that sun-screen in the water kills the coral. And it's dangerous. Locals know to stay away. The reef you're talking about, off Hokuloa Point—they finally gave it protected status, so you can't go there anymore. There's a crosscurrent—you can be in two outriggers running parallel to each other and one will get pulled along twice as fast. Windsurfers are swept out to sea and never make it back. Those stories Dalita told you go back hundreds of years, a thousand, maybe. But bones wouldn't last long in that reef—they'd be smashed by the waves, or eaten by fish or algae. If anyone saw bones out there, police would be diving to recover them." Minton shrugged and started for the door. "But we have no tourists now, so it's a moot point. I'm off to finish packing. Uncle Honey's supposed to leave a couple boxes for me at the end of the driveway. You can help me load them into the car. I'll text you when I hear from him, should be in an hour or so."

A short while later, Grady received Minton's text. They met outside and climbed into the Tesla. The car purred along, driverless, as Minton leaned into the back seat to rummage through a heap of backpacks.

"It's the perfect car for here." Minton turned back, still not touching the wheel. "You've seen how much gas costs. In ten years, everyone on the island will be driving one."

The gate swung open as they approached the bottom of the drive. Two large plastic bins sat at the edge of the road. Minton remained in the car as Grady hopped out and placed the bins in the trunk, shoving aside outdoor gear, coils of rope, a first aid kit, and one of those hazard lights you stick on top of your car—this one was blue—along with a book on water management. He stepped away as the hatch swung back down.

"Thanks." Minton stuck his head out the window. "See you in a couple weeks. Text me if you need to."

The car drove off silently in a haze of red dust. Grady remained in the road. Behind him, the gate had already swung shut. He knew the code to open it. But he didn't want to.

He walked along the road in the direction Minton had gone, his heart beating hard. He was breaking the law. Even though he knew he'd hear a car long before he'd see it, he felt the surge of adrenaline he used to get riding shotgun with his brother when Donny was underage, or jacking deer with Zeke. When he'd gone about twenty feet, Grady stopped. All he heard was the wind in the trees.

But after a minute he picked out another sound. He thought it was the pulse of blood in his ears, but when he held his breath, he realized it was waves, crashing on the shore far below.

Only not so far, if he could hear it so clearly. A bird cried out, a bubbling song as though someone had pulled out a drain plug, and a lizard rustled in the vegetation near his feet. It must've been ninety degrees, yet Grady felt the hairs on his arms and neck stand up. He had no clue what was out here, beyond the confines of Minton's compound. *Chickenskin,* he thought. He turned to head back.

CHAPTER 27

The rest of that day—Thursday—passed with grueling slowness. Same with Friday, then Saturday, his final day. He checked on Minton's house multiple times. Fixed the bathroom tub drain, which was clogged with hair. Minton must have buzzed it when he was in the shower, though some of the hair was blond. Grady had seen no evidence of a girlfriend, or boyfriend, but the blond hair could belong to a previous caretaker, or a houseguest. He'd known people who waited years before they broke down and hired a plumber. God forbid they do the nasty job themselves.

As Saturday morning crept by, he couldn't stop thinking about Jessica, the girl from his flight. She too would be enduring her last day of quarantine, though she'd had her girlfriend for company. He wondered if she was gay, if this was a girlfriend girlfriend or a friend girlfriend. He'd already decided that Makani would be his first stop once he could get into town. He'd ask Dalita where people hung out. Offer to buy them drinks, her and her wife. Dinner, even. That way he wouldn't have to go alone.

He'd gotten up before sunrise, and by ten it already seemed like an entire day had passed. By noon, he felt like he was losing his mind. How had his brother survived months in prison?

He walked outside and thought of the three-day wilderness training he'd done at WMCC—seventy-two hours alone in the North Woods, with only a compass, three matches, and a plastic tarp. How had he gotten through that? The first two days it rained, and he spent most of the time huddled beneath the tarp in a shelter he'd constructed of pine boughs. His three attempts to make a fire failed. The only food he found was a handful of tiny sour wild strawberries and some wintergreen berries. On the last day, he managed to wrench his ankle, and had to be helped back to the pickup point.

He dropped out of the program after that. He couldn't see taking on any more student debt for something he obviously wasn't suited for.

He headed to the top of the driveway in front of Minton's house. From there he had a clear view of the entire peninsula. He gazed at the eastern horizon, where high white clouds slipped past the promontory by Hokuloa Point. What would it be like, to hike alone through this landscape? He'd always felt like he'd turned his back on something crucial when he failed his wilderness solo and never bothered to try again. Would he be someone else today if he'd continued with the program? If he'd successfully started a fire with one of the matches? If he hadn't quit his EMT job after Kayla's suicide? Why was he always so afraid of fucking up? His brother sure wasn't.

At least he'd gone for this job. He thought again of how no one on the island knew him. He didn't have to play it safe all the time. He could take chances, and maybe he wouldn't screw up. Even if he did, so what?

He continued to stare at the horizon, brooding. After a few minutes, he returned to the 'ohana and found the bottle of THC gummies Dalita had given him. He prized off the plastic cap and shook out a bright yellow blob, divided it in two, and popped half into his mouth.

The gummy tasted like it had been doused with condensed lemon juice and sugar, neither of which disguised the dank bite of cannabis. He swallowed it without chewing, rinsed his mouth out, drank some water, and brushed his teeth for good measure. The pungent residue remained on his tongue, now tinged with toothpaste.

He went to the living room. What he'd told Dalita was true—he didn't like to get high. He liked beer, the way you could measure it out, bottle by bottle, and calibrate the way it made you feel.

People talked about addiction like it was a disease, something you had no control over, but Grady didn't believe that. Drugs and hard liquor were like beautiful, dangerous animals. You made the choice to let them into your house, your body. If they tore you apart, that was on you.

Whereas beer was a lazy indoor cat. No surprises, no excitement. Just a comforting, dependable warmth while you watched a game or hung out with friends.

He briefly considered why he'd decided to take the gummy now. Part of it was curiosity. Part of it was so he could feel like he wasn't such a wuss. Was weed even illegal here?

He had only a few more hours left of quarantine. It would give him something to talk about the next time he saw Dalita. Mostly, though, he was just bored.

He yawned. He needed to get more oxygen into his lungs. He decided to take a walk.

He stepped outside and started down the driveway. The breeze lifted his T-shirt, rich with the scent of plumeria. He closed his eyes, still walking, and imagined he could taste the blossoms on his tongue.

When he opened his eyes, he stood just a few yards from the gate. How had he gotten here so fast?

Those gummies must be strong as fuck.

He turned to gaze up the driveway, where a windblown palm frond skittered across the pavement like a large brown rat. He continued. Punched in the code, waited as the gate swung open. Stepped out onto the road. Kept walking.

CHAPTER 28

From the corner of his eye, the ground seemed ablaze with ko'oloa 'ula, its red and yellow flowers like small, dangling hibiscus blossoms, and the air was sweet with the scent of nānū, which smelled like coconut suntan lotion—plants he'd learned the names of over the past two weeks. The sky seemed a richer blue here, as deep as twilight. He remembered something Rachel once told him, that ancient mariners had such acute vision that they could navigate by the stars even during daylight. Now he thought he saw sparks in the sky, shining, then disappearing.

When he lowered his head, he had the spins. He walked in the middle of the road, heading toward town, his arms held out to either side as though he were balancing on a tightrope. He saw tire tracks, presumably from Uncle Honey. Otherwise there were only the footprints of a big dog and those left by a good-sized bird or birds. The road was so narrow that, if there had been walls to either side, he could have touched them with his outstretched hands.

A hundred yards ahead, the vegetation sheared off and left a big blue hole in the greenery. It was difficult to spot the demarcation between sky and water. Wind-shredded clouds might have been the reflection of waves. The shadowy shapes of distant islands might have been clouds. He heard the wail of seabirds, and another noise, like the distant thrum of a generator. After a few more paces he halted. There was a steady vibration in his legs. When he stooped to press his palm against the ground, he felt it there, too, even more powerfully:

the weight of all the water in the world crashing against a sliver of rock in the middle of nowhere.

He straightened and stared at his hand, red with dust. When he wiped it on his jeans, it left streaks like blood.

"Jesus," he said aloud. He hadn't known it was possible to feel this stoned.

His face tingled, but that wasn't from the gummy. He'd forgotten to wear a hat or sunglasses. He had the beginnings of a bad sunburn, maybe sunstroke. He'd also forgotten his phone.

Still, he didn't want to go back. He found a palm tree and broke off a large, fan-shaped leaf, stuck the stem down the back of his T-shirt as a makeshift parasol. He resumed walking, and soon noticed another break on the seaward side of the road. He paused, trying to remember why this seemed familiar, at last recalled passing it in the truck with Dalita. Some guy who'd done work for Minton stayed in a shack here, Leonardo something. What had she said? *We shouldn't have been there.*

Grady walked to the head of the path, scarcely wider than a deer trail. Tire ruts had been washed away to reveal red rock, smooth and glistening like raw meat. Palm fronds hung over the trail, and vines bright with yellow flowers.

He hesitated. What if Leonardo was there now, right this minute? The faint buzz in his ears had become more of a low pulse, like waves or drumming, a sound that almost didn't register as a sound.

He shook his head. He was stoned, that was all. He tossed aside the palm frond parasol and started down the trail.

The path soon did a dogleg to the left. The undergrowth fell back, revealing an area that had been cleared, where spindly trees grew clumps of shiny red fruit like skinny bell peppers. A ladder leaned against one of the trunks. Grady picked a fruit and took a bite. His mouth flooded with a sweet flowery taste, like a girl's flavored lip gloss. He ate three in quick succession and, despite also remembering Dalita's warning—*We shouldn't have been there*—kept walking.

Another minute and he reached a small building with a concrete post at each corner, plywood walls reinforced with two-by-fours. Its corrugated metal roof was rusted out. Grady listened for any sound from inside but heard nothing.

A pickup truck was parked behind the shack—a Chevy, forty years old if it was a day, mottled black and gray where it had been repainted and repaired with Bondo. Red dust coated it, though the windshield was clear—it had been driven recently. No back plate, both taillights busted. A surfboard sat in the truck bed, partially covered by a ripped blue tarp. Alongside the shack, more surfboards lay on a metal rack.

"Hello?" he called softly, then more loudly. No one replied.

He jumped when a bird screamed. For a fraction of a second he thought it was a person, but then he caught the shadow of huge wings in the trees. He remained where he was, holding his breath.

The scream came again. A long, wavering cry—not a bird but a woman's voice—rising, then dropping to a low moan. It seemed to echo from the shore below the cliffs. Surely he'd misheard, but as he strained to hear, the cry grew more urgent and sounded nearer, like it was in the underbrush in front of him. He stood as still as he could, willing his heart to slow, his breathing to stop, listening. He stared at the green thicket as the moan rose to a shriek that might have had words in it, *Please!* or *Me!* or *See!*

Yet now it once more seemed farther off, echoing from the beach. Where the hell was it? *What* was it?

The scream faded into silence, then resumed. It clearly came from the beach. He scanned the trees, the sky. Seabirds screamed—they sometimes fooled you into thinking they were children's voices.

But there were no birds. Overhead the blue sky rippled as though a squall had moved in. The cries continued, only now they were an uncontrollable sobbing—a woman's voice. He took a deep breath, but it didn't seem to reach his lungs.

Go help her! he thought frantically, but how could he help her if he couldn't even breathe?

He clenched his hands and took a step, looking for something he could use as a weapon. He saw nothing within reach but dead palm fronds, dead grass. The woman's voice grew softer, as though she was losing strength, or was farther away. Had she been swept off by waves? Had that wild dog he'd seen attacked her?

Grady's chest heaved as he fought for air. He tried to yell, but it was like shouting in a dream, he heard the sound inside his head, but nothing came out. He should run to the beach—he was convinced now, a woman was being attacked or abducted—but terror had short-circuited all his instincts, everything he'd learned as an EMT: it was all he could do to remain upright, to not drop to his knees.

And what if it—he, whatever it was—came after him? He needed to get out of here, needed to run . . .

As abruptly as they had begun, the cries ceased. The air fell still, so silent he couldn't hear the wind or the waves. Grady gasped, his head throbbing like he'd been punched, but he jolted upright when a different strangled shout echoed from the beach: a man's voice, even more frantic than the woman's. His shouts rose to a howl, the words garbled, torn by something—wind? teeth?—into a series of hoarse grunts. Had the woman turned on her attacker? The grunting grew deeper, almost frantic, like a bear's warning *huff, huff.*

Grady knew that, whatever it was, it couldn't be a bear. And if it sensed or heard him, he'd be next. Above him the clouds parted like they'd been split with a knife, loosing a shaft of sunlight that made the leaves burn a thousand shades of green and gold behind him as he turned and fled.

CHAPTER 29

It took him three tries to punch in the security gate's passcode, his hand shook so badly. When the gate finally opened, he lurched into the driveway, doubled over and dry heaving.

When finally he looked back, Hokuloa Road was empty. He stumbled to the top of the drive, past Minton's house to the 'ohana, hurried inside to lock the front and side doors. He started to close all the windows but stopped when he realized that would make it difficult to hear if anyone was outside.

He went to the kitchen sink, ran the cold water and held his head under the tap. Then he filled a glass with water and drank it, filled it again, and again, till he felt like he might puke. His face was burning hot: whatever the fuck had happened down there, he definitely had sunstroke.

He checked all the rooms, but everything seemed just as he'd left it. He took a quick cold shower, wrapped a towel around his waist. He stared at his reflection in the mirror above the sink: his cheeks and forehead were bright red, his auburn hair silvered with sun. He walked, dripping, into the living room, where he turned the ceiling fan to high and sank onto the couch, closed his eyes, and let the air cool his face.

What the fuck was wrong with him? Why hadn't he helped them, whoever they were?

Why the fuck had he run?

His phone pinged. He picked it up and cursed. While he was

in the shower, a call had come in from an unknown number. He hit REDIAL.

"Police department, Officer Padua speaking."

"Yeah, this is Grady Kendall. I received a call from this number?"

"Grady who?" Padua sounded like he'd just woken up.

"Kendall." Grady could hear his own voice shaking and hoped that Padua could not. "I'm a visitor quarantining on Hokuloa Road, I was in the shower when——"

"How you feeling today, Mr. Kendall?"

"I'm fine."

"No fever, coughing, anything like that?"

"No, I'm good, I——"

"You still at Hokuloa Road?"

"Yeah."

"Well, your quarantine ends at"——he heard Padua tapping at a computer——"5:17 this afternoon. Let us know if you get a fever higher than 99.1 or develop coughing or other symptoms. Wear your mask, avoid crowded places. Okay, Mr. Kendall? Mahalo, enjoy your stay."

Grady set down his phone, shivering despite the heat. The memory of what he'd heard by the shack overwhelmed him. It had been an assault, right? Or an abduction, even a shark attack. Or a wild animal might have attacked a couple of sunbathers.

Yet what if he'd imagined it? The weed gummy, all the unfamiliar birds and animals and noises, the unrelenting heat and sun, his isolation . . . he could've had some sort of hallucination, like that white-eyed dog. He hadn't even seen anything, just heard it. His ears were ringing like they'd been boxed.

The cannabis might have caused all of this. He still felt so stoned he couldn't think straight.

He gazed around the living room: books piled on the floor, last night's empty beer cans on the coffee table. Everything looked exactly as it had when he'd left, which was pretty much the way it had looked since the day he arrived. What if he called Officer Padua to report what he'd heard—what he thought he'd heard—and the cops came all the way out here and found nothing?

Worse, what if they *did* find something, and held him for questioning? At the least, they'd wonder why he'd said nothing when Padua called. Technically, he'd violated quarantine—there were only a few hours left, but they could still charge him, maybe send him back to the mainland.

He pressed his hands to his face. Was he feverish? Delirious? Could he possibly have COVID? Didn't it cause hallucinations in some people?

When he was little and didn't want to go to school, insisting every cold was some exotic flu, his mother the nurse would say, "Don't hear zebras when it's horses, Grady."

He had sunstroke, that was all.

But what had he heard on the cliff? And what the fuck was wrong with him? Even his asshole brother would've run down there and pounded the shit out of whoever was attacking a woman.

"It's never too late to make something right." That was something else his mother used to say. He stood, still wearing the towel around his waist, walked into the bedroom, and opened the top drawer of his bureau, where he found his folding knife in its leather case.

CHAPTER 30

At home, he'd carried the knife everywhere, and while he used it when hunting and fishing, mostly it was a talisman. His mother hadn't told him how much it cost, but Donny had: "Almost two hundred and fifty bucks, dinkhead." Grady knew his brother coveted the knife, just as he knew all the reasons why their mother had never given one to Donny. Made in Norway, it had a four-inch stainless-steel blade that nestled in a birchwood handle, like a finger curling into a fist.

He opened the closet, yanked a white button-down shirt from a hanger and put it on. Even unbuttoned, it chafed his sunburned skin. He slathered his face and neck with sunscreen, went into the living room, and tapped out a message to Donny.

Going for a quick hike, not leaving property so ok w quarantine

He hesitated before hitting SEND. It was a lifelong habit to let someone know if he headed out alone into the woods, even for a short hike. Still, Donny might read too much into the message.

Not read too much—he'd read the truth, and know something was up. After a moment, Grady tapped SEND. If he didn't come back, after a few days Donny would get in touch with their mom, and she'd contact the police here on the island.

Grady thought again of the concrete bunker on the coastal plain. *NEVER FORGET THE MISSING.* He suddenly felt calm, like he was embarking on a round of WOW. It wasn't real, none of this was real.

He filled a water bottle, scrounged up a piece of paper, and wrote a note with the date, day of week, time, and the message "Checking out Leonardo's." If he didn't return, Dalita or Minton would find it. He propped the note on the kitchen counter, grabbed his Sea Dogs cap, and headed back to the shack.

CHAPTER 31

He walked fast, squinting nervously at trees and the crumbling edge of the cliffs. He'd brought his phone but forgotten his sunglasses. As he approached the trail to Leonardo's, he broke into a run. Otherwise he would lose his nerve. He couldn't rationalize why he was returning to the shack—it was too late to save whoever had been in danger. To find proof that he had witnessed something? Then he could go to the cops and absolve his cowardice. But could you witness something you hadn't seen?

He turned down the path. The only footprints were his own. He saw some broken branches, but that would have been him.

When the shack came into view, he halted. He removed the knife from his pocket, unfolded it, and grasped it lightly. That was how you handled a knife, his mom had taught him: like you handle a girl, gently. But while you always let a girl slip away if she wants to, you always hold on to a knife. You let it move your hand, not the other way around. Follow its weight and line and you'll find your mark.

He let his arm rest loosely beside his hip as he turned in a slow circle, taking in the trees, the way the leaves in the higher branches flashed from green to yellow as they moved in the wind. When he'd done a full rotation, he walked the last few steps to the pickup. He peered through the open driver's window at a litter of take-out coffee cups, empty water bottles, and a cell-phone charger. A beach towel covered the driver's seat. On the dashboard, a plastic hula girl on a spring. The inspection sticker had expired three years earlier.

Lax law enforcement, that or Leonardo got a pass. Maybe all the locals did.

Grady crouched to examine the tires—old, their treads worn. He caught a whiff of some fragrant plant, and saw a broken stalk of wild ginger, crushed beneath a front tire. When he touched it, it felt damp.

The truck hadn't been here long. A few hours, tops. So where was Leonardo?

Maybe there was a swell, and Leonardo had driven out to surf.

He walked to the shack and used his sleeve to clear away the residue of salt and cobwebs from a small window. Inside stood a Formica-topped table with two chairs, a drooping futon couch, and an armchair. Tightening his hold on the knife, Grady went to the front door—the only door. He covered his free hand with his shirtsleeve and turned the knob. It was unlocked.

He felt the gritty bite of sand beneath his shoes as he walked across the wooden floor. The room was surprisingly tidy, with the musty, resinous smell of a summer cabin that never dried out properly: damp pine boards and upholstery, weed smoke, salt. There were no appliances, just a cooler on a plywood counter beside a plastic basin that served as a sink. No electric outlets. An oil lantern hung from a beam. Add a woodstove and braided rugs, and you'd have a Maine hunting camp. Instead of a rack of antlers mounted on the wall, a wet suit dangled like a human cocoon, alongside a spearfishing gun and snorkeling gear. The only ornament was a seashell on the picture window's sill.

Grady circled the room again, spotting a bowl on the floor beside a chair, skimmed with milk and cereal. He went to the counter and opened the cooler. A milk carton sat in a few inches of water, along with two bottles of Bud Light. He continued to search for any sign of something unusual, but the few drawers yielded only kitchen utensils, some packets of soy sauce, a centipede that scuttled off before Grady could kill it. An oily scorch mark on the counter where someone had left a joint.

An old cotton blanket and lumpy pillow were tossed on the futon couch. On the floor beside it, a Stephen King paperback. Grady crouched to look underneath the couch, pulled out a small framed photo of a surfer, its glass surface smeared with white residue. A laminated driver's license was tucked into the edge of the frame, used for cutting up whatever drugs had been snorted from it.

Leonardo Sanchez, DOB 02/05/1989, EXP 02/05/2016

The photo showed a dark-haired, tanned guy wearing black square-framed glasses. Geeky-looking, not how Grady had imagined him. Sanchez would be thirty-one now.

Grady set aside the license and looked at the photo in the frame — a solidly built man bent forward on the lip of a wave, a wing of long dark hair lifted above his head as he leaned forward, as though about to leap into the water. This must be the older Sanchez. Grady knew nothing about surfing, but the photo was beautiful: the man, the glassy green wave and cobalt sky, all so perfectly composed, it might have been shot in a studio. Dalita obviously knew Sanchez. Had her wife, Lorelei, taken the picture? He stared at it another moment, then slid it beneath the couch.

He walked back outside and continued on the trail to the cliff. Overhead, a bird screeched as it followed him.

CHAPTER 32

He approached the top of the cliff cautiously, pushing past stands of bamboo and tall grass. The thick undergrowth had been cut back, leaving a space wide enough for two people to walk side by side. Or for one person to carry a surfboard. Grady felt a jolt of adrenaline. Had Leonardo Sanchez been the victim, or the killer?

He touched the handle of his knife, now folded again and returned to his pocket. He'd never attacked a person, never even dreamed of it. He forced himself not to think about whether he could do so now, if he had to. After another few minutes of walking, the vista before him opened to reveal the sea.

For a few seconds he forgot those horrible screams, forgot he was trespassing and violating his last hours of quarantine. He could only stare at the ocean: every shade of blue from indigo to aquamarine. The wind smelled fresh and saline, without the North Atlantic reek of decaying kelp.

Farther out, a line of swells broke against what must have been a reef. Closer to shore they became waves, the sound of their booming on the beach reverberating against the cliffs like an uneven drumbeat. They broke before reaching the area directly below him, a crescent of grayish sand fringed with immense, jagged black boulders that made it inaccessible except from this path. A keening cry startled him—the same bird that he'd heard before. He glanced around, but he was still alone.

At his feet, a switchback path had been hacked out of the earth.

He began to pick his way down, grabbing branches to keep his balance. More than once his feet skidded on the packed earth, but he caught himself before he could fall. How the hell could anyone do this toting a surfboard?

He found out when he reached the bottom. Right at the high-tide mark, a natural outcropping in the cliff formed a small cave, about six feet deep and twice as wide, high enough that a man could crouch inside. Two surfboards were stacked on the sand in front of it, secured with bungee cords to a tall black stone. The surf was deafening here, amplified by the cave. Steeling himself for what he might discover, Grady ducked behind the surfboards.

He saw nothing but sand and the stone walls of the chamber. No blood, no footprints. He wiped sweat from his face, eyes burning from the sunscreen, and made his way to the back of the chamber. The rock formation was shaped like a wave, and as the wind funneled through it, the sound of crashing surf deepened into a deep thrumming, almost a growl. When he pressed his palm against the ceiling, he could feel it vibrating.

A claustrophobic terror flooded him: the stone would collapse, the sand give way. He stumbled backward, tripping on the surfboards, and hit the ground. Catching his breath, he looked up.

The rock above him was covered with carved human figures. Some were straight lines with only a perpendicular line indicating a head. Others had triangular torsos with thick, jointed legs, smaller arms and heads, and, confusingly, spiral tails. Scattered among the figures were circles, some concentric, others with rays shooting from them: suns. One doglike creature's head tilted back to gaze at a crescent. Another doglike figure stood upright and held a spear.

Marveling, Grady touched the roof with a finger. He knew how long it took to carve something from a block of oak or maple. How many hours had someone spent here with a chisel, using stone tools that would also have taken unimaginable time and effort to create? And how long ago had they done it?

He crept along, the chamber growing narrower, until he reached a spot where he lay flat on his back, the roof an inch or two from his face. His shoulders ached, and he flinched as something cut his arm. A fragment of rock. He picked it up, hoping it might be an arrowhead or some other artifact. But it was just a broken bit of stone, and as he glanced around, he saw the floor in this spot was littered with more of the same.

He remembered the first summer he'd been with Rachel, when she was doing fieldwork for her undergrad degree. He'd accompanied her to a Red Paint People dig on an island near Vinalhaven, where she taught him to recognize rhyolite and flakes of chert left by knapping tools. He'd loved how she knew so much that he didn't. It was one of the things he missed most, how she made everything seem like an adventure, like they were always on the verge of discovering something.

"This is an ancient factory," she'd said, indicating the seemingly random bits of rock that had been buried beneath the soil.

The rocks in this chamber weren't evidence of ancient toolmaking. They'd been left by a jackhammer and modern chisels. Above him, someone had cut away a portion of the rock to a depth of several inches, removing a large piece, roughly two feet square.

"The fuck," Grady whispered.

Who the hell would do that? Grady felt like he did when he saw very old trees clear-cut to improve the view of some Masshole's second home, in violation of zoning rules. People were so fucked up. Even here.

He pushed himself back to look again at the petroglyphs that were unharmed.

The figures seemed to have been arranged in a pattern that related to that missing piece—the doglike forms all pointed that way, muzzles aimed at whatever had been there. To Grady, the petroglyphs weren't crude or sinister but beautiful. They meant something, though he had no idea what that might be.

Abruptly he grew aware that the thrumming he'd heard earlier had grown louder, almost a roar. Even flat on his back he felt dizzy.

Not enough air, he realized: he'd wedged himself against the back of the cave and was hyperventilating.

A weight seemed to crush his chest as the sunlight dissolved into black. When he tried to move, his limbs flopped helplessly against the sand. He was going to pass out.

A sharp sound cut through the sound of waves, a high yipping bark. With all his strength, Grady rolled onto his stomach, gasping. He could breathe again. The dog barked once more, louder, as Grady crawled across the floor of the chamber, out onto the beach.

Light engulfed him as he staggered to his feet. The stone chamber was once more a nondescript alcove. He turned to the water as the dog barked again.

It stood where the sand met the serrated line of boulders. A stocky dog, brindled black and red, with long legs, pointed ears, and a blunt muzzle. Its curling tail was distinctly not a coyote's. As Grady stared, the dog turned and jumped with ease onto the rocks. It picked its way carefully until it reached a stand of skeletal trees, where Grady lost sight of it.

CHAPTER 33

H e stood, catching his breath, then quickly walked to the water's edge. He bent to splash water on his face, and saw that the sand next to him had been disturbed. He clearly saw footprints where a person—a man, from their size—had dug his heels in.

He bent to get a better look. Dark spots dappled the sand beside the footprints. Blood? Before he could get a better look, a wave swept them away.

He straightened, hand on the knife in his pocket. He was alone now, but someone had just been here, and they'd been in bad shape. He scanned the shoreline, and saw a larger patch of something black spread across the sand. Before he could reach it, another wave washed onto the shore. He crouched and dug his fingers into the wet sand as the wave receded, but there was nothing there. Could it have been blood?

Grady scrambled to his feet, looking for the black dog. Was that what he'd heard earlier, someone being torn apart by a feral dog? But why hadn't the dog attacked him? Where was it now?

He squinted, nearly blinded by the dance of sunlight on water. The dark patch could have been anything—there were streaks of black sand on the beach, and clouds of tiny black flies. But a line had been dug into the sand, too, close by—a surfboard, Grady thought. Someone had just stepped onto the shore. And he must have dropped or dragged his board—he must have been attacked.

He, or she—it had been a woman's cries Grady had heard first.

He shaded his eyes and stared out to sea, but the sun on the water burned away whatever might have been there. When a wave lapped at his shoes, he stepped back, watching it erase the last traces of the attack. No one but Grady would ever know the footprints, and blood, had been there.

CHAPTER 34

Grady ran to the trailhead, hauled himself back up, and stood, breathless, at the top of the cliff, gazing down at the beach to see if someone or something was coming after him. It all looked as serenely beautiful as a postcard. Finally he walked back to the road.

He debated calling the police, but would they even believe him? He scarcely believed himself. He felt like he'd been in some kind of altered state ever since he stepped off the plane, and that fucking weed gummy had been a really bad idea.

The most likely scenario was that he'd heard some birds screaming—in the aviary, he'd occasionally been unnerved by the sudden cry of an ʻiʻiwi, like someone playing a harmonica. He'd just been so frigging high that he conflated an unfamiliar but normal sound with a person's screams. Weed always made him paranoid, and he'd spent enough hours listening to Zeke's stoned conspiracy theories and QAnon ravings to know how easy it was to fall down some crazy-ass rabbit hole and never climb out. Seriously, how likely was it that he'd landed here and witnessed a murder, or that anyone in this sunlit place had been murdered?

He slowed then, recalling the bunker he'd seen with Dalita. That hadn't been imaginary. *People disappear here,* she'd said. He recalled the carvings in the chamber. Generations of Native people had vanished, but those carvings had been there for a thousand years. He thought of the vandalized ceiling, the marks left by a jackhammer or modern chisel. Those, too, would remain.

CHAPTER 35

He returned to the compound, checked Minton's house to make sure nothing had been disturbed, then went to the 'ohana and did the same thing. All was as it had been, back before he'd eaten that weed gummy. An entire day seemed to have passed since then, but it was still only early afternoon. Despite the sun and warm breeze streaming through the windows, he felt a dread he'd only ever experienced in dreams, that he'd done something terrible and would be caught.

He texted Donny, telling him he'd returned safely from his hike. Donny texted back a GIF of a man falling from a cliff. Grady rolled his eyes, set aside his phone, and drank a beer, too fast, then a second. He settled on the couch with his laptop and killed the last hours of quarantine by obsessively checking the *Island Pilot* for any report of a murder. He stopped when he realized his search history might point to him as a suspect, and cleared the caches on his laptop and phone. He knew the police had ways of restoring that information. Still, there'd be no way to connect him. The waves would have washed away any footprints. The steady wind would have done the same around the shack, and on the road.

He had a momentary panic, that the dog he'd seen might have been a police dog, but that was ridiculous. He got another beer and refreshed the *Pilot*'s home page. A new headline took up most of the screen:

LOCAL SURFER MISSING

"Fuck," Grady muttered, and clicked on the link.

The Coast Guard has called off the search for a local man. Leonardo Sanchez, 31, was reported missing on Thursday after he failed to show up for work. Sanchez's primary residence is in the Kioha Apartments but he is known to stay on Hokuloa Road near Gunshot Point. Police did a welfare check at the apartment but found no sign that Sanchez had been there for several days, and also checked the Hokuloa Road property, where they found his truck but no sign of Sanchez. Friends say that Sanchez, an experienced surfer, often went out on the water alone at Gunshot Point. "I'm thinking he encountered a shark," a friend who asked to remain anonymous told the Island Pilot. *"Nothing else makes sense." Anyone with information is asked to contact police.*

Yet what he'd seen of Sanchez's truck, not to mention the footprints and surfboard tracks at the beach, suggested that Sanchez *had* been at his place. Dalita had said Sanchez would head out here to surf when the waves were running high. Maybe he'd skipped work Thursday night, laid low someplace, and gone down to the shack this morning, after the police checked on him. Maybe Sanchez was who Grady had heard being attacked.

Grady read the article again, his stomach turning. The police had searched Sanchez's place. When? Had he just missed them? Could they have had something to do with whatever he'd heard? What if they suddenly showed up here after all?

He slammed his laptop shut and shoved it away. He needed to stop thinking about this shit, needed to focus on something else, something normal, like finding a place to grab a beer and maybe meet up with Jessica Kiyoko.

His phone buzzed: Dalita. *Thank god.* He snatched it up.

"Hey!"

"Today's the day, yeah? You're done?"

"Not till 5:17. They time it to, like, the minute. Two weeks since I landed."

"Can you come by tomorrow lunchtime? Is Wes around?"

"No. He came back and left again, I think for a while."

"Perfect. So you come here around eleven, we can sit out back, you can meet Lorelei and everybody else."

"Like me!" a kid shouted in the background. "And fucking Peanut!"

"Watch it!" Dalita yelled at the kid. Then, to Grady, "Peanut's the fucking cat. You want a cat?"

"I'm guessing not this one."

"Smart. I'll text you the address," she said, and rang off.

Grady looked up Dalita's place online. The street view showed a small house behind a chain-link fence in a nondescript neighborhood miles from the nearest beach, backing onto acres of brown grass with stands of chinaberry, monkeypod trees, and gorse.

A pin identified the old pastureland as Lahiki Preserve. Googling it, Grady learned it had been part of a ranch, now under conservation easement. The land was to be restored as habitat for an endangered owl species. Grady stared at the withered landscape and shook his head. *Good luck with that,* he thought.

CHAPTER 36

The next morning he texted his mom, Donny, and Zeke to let them know he was out of quarantine. Then he walked over to the main house, ostensibly to make sure everything was safe, but mostly so he could visit the aviary. Just stepping inside it calmed him, at least for a short time: the birds' now-familiar scent; the way they seemed to trust him, even welcome him—landing on a nearby branch to regard him with a bright curious gaze, feeding from a kula blossom held gently between his fingers. He sighed with regret when he left, the sounds of birdsong and the artificial waterfall receding as he went back downstairs.

The *Island Pilot* had no further news about Leonardo Sanchez. Another homeless guy had gone missing, but otherwise there was nothing but recent COVID numbers and letters of complaint about the homeless encampments and beach closures. Grady only got his ass in gear when Dalita texted him midmorning.

Don't forget lunch! Don't bring anything just yourself.

He rinsed his coffee mug and went to the garage. He should have checked out the truck before now, but he wasn't a big car guy. The pickup was beat to shit—the passenger side looked like someone had taken a baseball bat to it, and the front bumper was attached with baling wire.

Still, when he turned the key, it seemed to run fine. He turned off the ignition, opened the glove compartment, and found an envelope crammed with an insurance card, registration, old records of oil and tire changes. There was also a rain poncho from a dollar store and a small LED flashlight, along with shreds of tobacco and cannabis seeds.

He closed the glove compartment and got out, swearing under his breath. He'd forgotten about the recyclables he'd loaded in the truck bed. He'd ask Dalita where to take them. He glanced at the faded bumper sticker, which sported a rainbow and the slogan DRIVE WITH ALOHA, only letters had been removed so it now read DRIVE WIT AL.

He patted the tailgate and wandered over to the padlocked door, gave the lock a tug. As ever, it didn't budge.

He returned to the 'ohana to grab his cap, a water bottle, sunscreen, and a towel. If he had time, he'd check out a beach, a real beach with people on it. As he passed through Minton's security gate, his heart started to pound, and didn't slow until he was well past Sanchez's place. He gripped the wheel so tightly he got trigger finger, approaching every hairpin turn as though an eighteen-wheeler might be careening toward him on the other side.

When he at last turned onto the highway, he felt a rush like he'd reached the top of a roller coaster. Vehicles! People! Not many of either, but still. He accelerated to eighty — he was afraid the truck might fly apart if he went any faster. He eased up when the drab coastal plain appeared in the distance. The concrete bunker looked like a black door cut into the barren landscape.

A car roared by him, passing in a NO PASSING zone and throwing up a smokescreen of dust. Grady glanced in his side mirror as the bunker receded behind him.

NEVER FORGET THE MISSING
#ISLANDNALOWALE

A mile farther, he spotted someone on the side of the road, an old Black man with curly white hair, dressed in layers of black clothing that flapped around him in the hot wind. He stared straight ahead as he pushed a shopping cart crammed with overflowing trash bags and other junk.

Poor old guy, dressed like that in this heat. Where was he headed? The bunker? The highway curved, and Grady lost sight of him.

When he finally reached town, he saw more chickens than people. A burly man wearing a Batman face mask guarded the door of Mak Supe, greeting people as they approached and pointing at their faces if they weren't wearing masks. Grady pulled into a parking spot and hopped out, tugging his on. The chickens pecking at the sidewalk barely moved as he walked by.

Batman gave him a thumbs-up and Grady went inside, welcomed by a blast of air-conditioning and a Spice Girls song ringing from a radio behind the register. He counted four other customers. Two young women who looked like they might be sisters stood behind the register, singing along with "Wannabe," faces hidden behind matching candy-striped masks as they rang up lottery tickets and cigarettes.

Grady wandered around the store, looking for something he might contribute to lunch. Dalita had told him not to bother, but his mom had always said to ignore that statement if a woman made it. Every-thing cost at least twice what it did at home. A lot of shelves were empty. There was no toilet paper or other paper products but a lot of beef jerky. Some flowers in a glass-fronted refrigerator turned out to be leis, each packaged in a plastic clamshell. He had no idea what the protocol was for giving leis to someone you didn't really know. It seemed like something a stupid white person might do, plus they were expensive.

He ended up buying a bag of tortilla chips and a jar of salsa, along with a six-pack of local beer. It was what he brought to parties at home.

"Mahalo," the girls at the register sang. He didn't get much change from his twenty.

Dalita's road was on the other side of town, one of many that led to similar-looking neighborhoods. He made the turn and eased the truck over several speed bumps, looking for her house number.

Chickens were everywhere. Some had long, brilliant orange and green tail feathers and crests, as spectacular as birds of paradise: strutting along the crumbling sidewalk, roosting in trees, ignored by the cats that lazed beneath the cars.

The houses were surrounded by chain-link fences and cement walks, all overflowing with flowering vines. Most houses had only one floor, though some sported DIY additions—a loft with a gable, a second story with a nice deck. Barking pit bulls charged as his truck crept past, then returned to loll under carport awnings.

The yards were crammed with stuff: Big Wheel trikes, wading pools, flowers and succulents in terra cotta pots, car parts, gas grills, fishing gear, surfboards. A propped-up vintage Mustang, new powerboats hitched to old trucks. The lawns were brown and patchy. Several houses, including Dalita's, had signs in front that showed a mountain and the words NO TMT.

He parked on the street and put on his mask, grabbed the beer, chips, and salsa, and walked up. Two small children raced tricycles across the lawn and yelled "Hi!" without looking at him.

Grady was checking to see if there was a scary-looking dog on-site when Dalita appeared in the doorway. In lieu of a mask, she wore a loosely tied blue bandanna. "You got here!" she yelled. "Come on in."

He opened the gate, sidestepping chunks of sidewalk chalk. He recognized Dalita's truck, parked beneath a carport alongside a Camry missing one back window, which had been replaced with cardboard. Dalita walked up, poking at his mask. "Come inside and meet Lorelei. You can take that off when we go out back."

The little house was cheerful, with woven mats on the floor, beachy-looking furniture, framed photos of surfers and epic waves. A fat tortoiseshell cat blinked at him from a chair.

Grady asked, "Is that fucking Peanut?"

Dalita laughed. "The one and only."

Someone moved in the kitchen, where a radio blasted hip-hop. He smelled pork simmering, and barbecue sauce.

"Lor's a photographer," Dalita said as Grady admired a picture of a massive wave, a tiny surfer trapped in its curl like an insect in a green bottle. "That's me, at Jaws on Maui."

"Are you frigging kidding me? That's a great shot."

"I know. Weddings pay the bills, but she's a genius with the water. Lor! Come meet Grady."

A tall, broad-shouldered older woman filled the kitchen doorway, dark-skinned, her buzz-cut hair dyed a green that played up eyes the color of sea glass. She wore bone earrings shaped like fish, a loose white shift patterned with big orange flowers. A tattoo of a wave circled one upper arm.

She tugged a neck gaiter over her face and said, "Aloha, Grady." He couldn't see her smile, but her eyes crinkled. "You survived quarantine."

"I guess so." He laughed uneasily, thinking of what had happened yesterday. "Barely."

"That bad?"

"Not really. I'm glad it's over."

"Us too." Lorelei had a deep voice, calm and confident, and smelled of lavender. Grady could imagine her presiding over weddings as easily as photographing them. "You and Lita go outside. I'll be there in a few."

Grady turned to Dalita, holding up the six-pack, chips, and salsa. "I wasn't sure what to bring."

"Beer is appropriate for every occasion."

He followed her to the backyard. It was larger than he'd expected, with papaya and banana trees planted around a wooden fence blocking a view of the depressing nature preserve, and a garden bed with tomatoes and peppers in wire cages. Stacked lumber lay beside the garden.

"Home improvement project," Dalita said as he stepped over to investigate. "We're pulling down an extra twelve hundred dollars a week with that unemployment bonus, so we're gonna build the kids a play set."

Grady crouched to inspect the wood. "You're going to want pressure-treated wood. At least for the base."

"I know. They were sold out—everybody's sold out. I got some Thompson's WaterSeal. They were almost out of that, too. Every-body's doing the same thing, building a shed or lānai or whatever." She looked at the pile of wood and shrugged. "It's okay, the kids'll outgrow it in a year. Just trying to get them out of the house so we don't go insane. Have a seat."

A blue-striped beach umbrella shaded a picnic table set with plastic bowls, paper plates, napkins weighted with painted rocks. Dalita set down the beer, tore open the bag of chips and dumped them into a bowl.

"You brought all the major food groups." She opened the jar of salsa and dumped it into another bowl. "Help yourself. And you can lose the mask. You haven't seen anybody, yeah?"

"Just you and Minton."

Grady cracked a beer, and Dalita did the same, digging into the chips.

"Nice sunburn," she said, taking in his exposed face. "Sorry I didn't call more. Lor was at Kaniai this week, taking photos for this millionaire tech bro who lives out there. A parasailor. It's dangerous, even in his big boat, but she loves it. So I had the kids."

"Those two out front?"

"Three. Stella and Paolo, they're the little ones. Tim's with his dad this weekend. He's mine—he's fifteen, dad lives out past Kaniai." She broke into a grin as the back door opened. "Stella by starlight! This is Grady."

Grady got along with kids, one of the things clients liked about him. He didn't mind if they hung around watching him pound nails—it was better than when the clients lingered, running their mouths and giving him advice, thinking they knew what they were talking about because they watched *Property Brothers*. Kids were a lot easier to deal with, and sometimes he'd ask the older ones to give him a hand.

This girl looked around seven. Skinny and long-legged, with fly-away black hair and pale green eyes. She wore a *Frozen* T-shirt and had a fake—he hoped it was fake—butterfly tattoo on one arm.

"Hi." He nodded, smiling.

The girl smiled back, not shy at all, threw her skinny arms around Dalita's neck and tried to climb into her lap. "Can I eat?"

"Soon," said Dalita. "Ow! Go ask Mama if you can help bring out stuff."

"But I'm starving."

"The faster the food gets out here, the faster you eat."

The girl made a face, hopped from Dalita's lap, and scooted back into the house. "They're going lōlō." Dalita reached for another chip. "Usually we get to the beach, but they had a shark flag up, so we decided to wait."

"Shark flag." Grady gulped a mouthful of beer. He thought of Sanchez's shack, footprints on the beach and blood like engine oil soaking into the sand. "Last night," he said, "that Leonardo guy you mentioned, the surfer? I read he went missing."

"Yeah. This morning they found his board out past Gunshot Point, nearby where you are. Couple of guys spearfishing, one of them recognized it."

"They think a shark got him?"

"I don't think so—no marks on the board. But another fisher-man did see a shark up north shore. He was pretty sure it was one great white, so he called it in, and the Coast Guard sent out a spotter plane."

"Was it?"

"Not likely. Attacks are rare, and most here are tiger sharks. They'll take a chunk out of a surfboard or your leg, but they never killed anybody that I know of."

"So what do they think happened to him?" he asked, trying to sound casual. "Leonardo?"

"Don't know. Maybe was one shark. I laugh if was."

"Who?" Grady turned as a boy a little older than Stella emerged from the house, carrying a tray heaped with sandwiches. "Leonardo Sanchez?"

"No. Mind your business." Dalita took the tray from him. "Grady, this is Paolo Big Ears. Paolo, this is Grady. Go tell Mama we need more napkins."

Lunch was pulled pork on hamburger buns. Lorelei joined them, tugging down her neck gaiter as she yelled at the kids snatching food. "Hey! Where's your manners?"

"I'm a shark!" Paolo laughed.

"Oh my god, they need to be in school," moaned Lorelei.

"It's summer—they wouldn't be in school," retorted Dalita. "They need to be at soccer camp. Nature camp. Anything. Grady, please eat."

Grady did. Lorelei helped herself to the beer he'd brought. "I like this better than that shit Bikini beer you get, Lita."

"Got it," said Dalita. "No more shit beer."

Lorelei laughed. She wiped her mouth with the back of her hand and took another pulled pork sandwich. "Grady, what do you think of our island?"

"This is the first I've seen it," he said. "But, yeah, it's beautiful. Different from Maine."

"How's your boss?"

"I don't see him much. Or anyone." Grady swallowed a bite of his sandwich. "This is great pulled pork. Do you make your own barbecue sauce?"

Lorelei nodded. "Of course."

"Liar." Stella nabbed another sandwich. "She gets that orange sauce from Lulu's."

"I augment my sauce with Lulu's Barbecue," Lorelei said airily. She grasped Stella by the wrist, pulling her close to kiss her. "Go get us a couple more beers, please. And ask Paolo to bring out that fruit salad."

Dalita leaned over to wipe barbecue sauce from Lorelei's mouth. "Grady read about Leonardo," she said when the kids were out of earshot. She glanced at Grady. "Was that on the *Pilot*?"

He nodded, and Lorelei shrugged. "Well, I won't miss him. You saw a girl went missing, right?"

"What?"

"Late Thursday night, I think. It was just reported an hour ago," Lorelei went on. "From California, I think. She got here right around when you did, about two weeks ago. She was breaking quarantine, she went to a bar in the Quad—"

"That's in Makani," said Dalita. "Big tourist hangout, and even though there're no tourists, they opened most of the bars after the Fourth of July. For the locals."

Lorelei nodded. "She and a friend were at Fitzhugh's. I guess her girlfriend left early. A security camera caught the girl leaving, but she never made it home."

Grady stared at Dalita. He tried to swallow, but his throat felt scorched. "What was—did it say her name?"

"Jessica, I think."

"'Jessica Kiyoko,'" said Lorelei, reading off her phone. "Twenty-seven years old, Century City, California."

"Century City," he repeated. "Fuck."

Lorelei cocked her head. "Do you know her?"

"Yeah. I mean, no. There was a girl named Jessica on my flight—we talked for a few minutes. Said we'd meet up when quarantine was over. She told me places had started to open, out where she was staying."

"Maybe it's not the same girl," Dalita said.

"Here." Lorelei handed her phone to Grady.

TOURIST BREAKS QUARANTINE, REPORTED MISSING

27-year-old Jessica Kiyoko was reported missing after she failed to return to the residence of the friend she was staying with early Friday morning. The visitor from California had broken quarantine to go to Fitzhugh's Irish Pub in the Quadrangle district of Makani, accompanied by her friend, Raina Mayhew, of Makani. Mayhew left around 11 p.m. She told police that she had last seen Kiyoko with several people she knew from an earlier trip to the island. Travis Olehu, one of that group, said that Kiyoko left the bar shortly after midnight. "I asked if she wanted me to walk her home, but she said no because it was so close to Corner Street." When Kiyoko didn't return or reply to repeated phone calls and text messages, Mayhew notified police. Security footage showed Kiyoko walking across the Quadrangle by Corner Street with an unidentified man behind her. Anyone with information as to her whereabouts or the identity of the man in the security photo is asked to contact the island police.

Grady enlarged the security photo, grainy black-and-white. A blurry white circle indicated the only streetlight. The girl's face was unmasked and she was smiling. He recognized her crooked front teeth and curly black hair, pulled back in a loose ponytail. About thirty feet behind her walked a man in a black hooded sweatshirt, head slightly lowered. A dark bandanna covered his mouth and nose, shadowed by the hood. His hands were in his pockets, and he leaned forward, hunched as though he walked into the wind, or as though he was getting ready to lunge.

Grady handed the phone back to Lorelei, hoping she didn't see his hand shake. "That's her," he said as he struggled to keep his voice steady. "That's Jessica."

CHAPTER 37

O h my god," Dalita murmured. "So you do know her."

"No." He took a deep breath to remain calm. "Like I said, I just talked to her for a few minutes on the plane. She told me her name was Jessica. And Raina—the girl who picked her up, that was her name. I saw her outside the terminal."

Dalita glanced at Lorelei. "You think he should go to the cops?"

"Why?" Lorelei looked at Grady. "Unless you know something else? Like this guy in the photo?"

"Jeez, no. How could I even recognize him in the dark?"

"He did it." Dalita smacked the table. "Look at him, the way he's dressed—he knew no one could ID him."

"Maybe she met somebody else she knew," Grady said, feeling slightly desperate. "This guy, he could just be a guy in a hoodie and a bandanna face mask."

"*Nobody* in the Quad wears a mask," said Dalita. "Every time I drive by there, everybody drinking and hanging out, no mask."

"Who are they?"

"Locals who don't give a fuck. Maybe a few tourists, but there cannot be more than a hundred on the whole island right now. Locals are the ones spreading the virus. They fly to O'ahu for the weekend to party, then come back. Nobody is quarantining."

"Grady did," said Lorelei.

"How do we know that?" Dalita winked at him. "He's up there alone—he could've got up to all kinds of shit."

"Not really." Grady forced a smile. "Just cleaning out Wes's garage."

"That's a major accomplishment." Dalita opened another beer. "Seen any more wild dogs?"

The question caught him off guard. This was his chance to mention the screams, the feral dog on the beach. But what the hell would he say?

I was lying. I broke quarantine and I think I heard someone—two people—being attacked. But I never found any bodies and probably I imagined it because I was so fucking stoned.

He could feel the women watching him. "No," he replied.

"I told Lor," Dalita said. "About your dream. Dog spirits are a big thing in Hawai'i, Lor used to tell Tim stories about them, scared the shit out of him. He started wetting the bed. That was the end of that."

Lorelei stood and gathered the empty plates. "Can I help?" Grady asked, hoping to change the subject.

"No, you stay here with Dalita. I'll enlist the kids."

She walked inside, where Grady heard her yelling for Paolo and Stella.

"That's so weird you know that girl," Dalita said.

Grady ran a hand through his hair. Why the hell did she keep bringing it up? "You were right." He sighed. "People do disappear here."

"It's on the national news," Dalita said. "You don't want to read the comments. Everybody blaming her, especially here. 'Stupid haole bitch, she broke quarantine, she deserved it.' That shit. Too many girls, they're killed, or sometimes trafficked off-island. Used to be, no one did a fucking thing, especially if the girls were Black or brown. At least now we have HNP."

"HNP?"

"Ho'ōla Nā Pua—New Life for Our Children. Still harder to get attention if it's not a white girl gone missing."

"Jessica's not white."

"If it was a guy . . ."

"Some of the names on that bunker are guys," Grady argued.

"Some."

"But not enough? Leonardo Sanchez, maybe he'll balance it out. If he's dead."

"Brah, that's harsh," Dalita said. "That building, it's the tip of the iceberg. Have you seen the homeless camp out by the sewage treatment plant? They say twenty residents have disappeared in the last five years. Probably more—they're not reported as missing, because they're already missing."

"The camp by the city airport?"

"Yeah, just past the airport, by the state park. The beach over there is awesome—I used to surf there, but it got really sketchy. Six years ago some homeless people jumped this photographer Lor knew, local guy—he was taking pictures of the sunrise. No one knows what happened, but he was killed. One of the attackers got seven years. Since then, they keep breaking up the camp and moving people out—they're using the pandemic as an excuse. Big problem, people can't afford to live here anymore. But finally the health department and police gave up—everybody's too scared of COVID. So they just leave them alone now. Seriously, it looks like *Mad Max* out there."

Grady rubbed his arms, chilled. "That's awful."

"I'll tell you what's awful." Behind them the screen door opened. Lorelei stepped out and sat beside Dalita. "Thirty thousand empty hotel rooms and people are sleeping in their cars. Working people can't afford to live here. I inherited this place from my tūtū, otherwise we couldn't afford to live here."

No one spoke. From inside came the kids' voices, arguing over the iPad. Grady stared at his beer. At last he asked, "Why did Wes hire me?"

"I'll let Dalita take that one," Lorelei said.

Dalita shrugged. "You're a carpenter, right? You can fix stuff and keep an eye on things."

"All I've done is unclog a drain and straighten up his garage, put a couple screws in the deck railing. And keep an eye on the birds."

"Well, that's what caretakers do, right?"

"But it hardly seems like he's there at all."

"So? Isn't that part of the job, too? It means you have the place to yourself. People would kill to live there, Grady."

"I'm just wondering why he didn't hire someone local, someone who knows the island. That's how people usually handle it."

"I'm local," retorted Dalita, and Grady saw that Lorelei was watching her.

"Yeah, but it sounded like you were just filling in for that last guy, Carl," Grady countered. "Carl from Colorado. Who was before him?"

"Long time was, when Wes still thought he could build his resort," said Dalita. "I left when I got pregnant with Tim."

"You forgot Al," said Lorelei. "Al from Utah. He only lasted a few months."

"Why'd he leave?"

"No one knows. One day he was gone. No note or phone call. Wes said he thought he missed his family."

"Jesus." Grady laughed, but he felt disturbed. "It's like the frigging *Shining*."

"Leonardo Sanchez filled in after Al," said Lorelei, her deep voice calm, as though soothing a nervous child. "He's local."

Grady drank the rest of his beer as Lorelei went back inside. Dalita stared at him, eyebrows raised. "You okay?"

He gazed at the empty bottle. *I should tell them,* he thought, feeling trapped. *I should tell them—why the fuck don't I just tell them?*

He couldn't do it. Running over the events in his own mind was bad enough. If Zeke or Donny had recounted them to him, Grady would've told him to sober up.

And these two women hardly knew him. Dalita might go to Minton and tell him the new caretaker was batshit crazy. Or she'd laugh at Grady for diving into the deep end after doing one of her weed gummies. That might almost be a relief, since part of his brain needed to believe he might have hallucinated it all. He blinked and saw that Lorelei had returned and was staring at him, too, her brow furrowed.

"I'm fine," he said, and opened another beer. "Just, it's been a while since I've seen anyone. Even before I got here, the only people I ever saw were my mom and my friend Zeke."

Lorelei nodded, sunlight turning her carved fish earring to gold. "It can be hard, coming here. Tourists, people who move here because they like to surf or they're rich or whatever—they all have an idea in their head of what this place is like. Some people never adjust to the reality. Rich people, they can just avoid it. Everyone else . . ."

"Jesus, Lor." Dalita smacked her wife's arm. "It's his first day out of quarantine!"

"It's true." Lorelei shrugged, but she smiled at him. "Probably you'll be all right. It's a bizarre time to be here. To be anywhere. And it's interesting, what Lita said about the dog spirit you saw. Why would it appear to you?"

"I have no frigging clue," Grady snapped.

"I know." Lorelei held his gaze until he looked down, flustered. "That's what's so interesting."

CHAPTER 38

T hose TMT signs out front," he said, hoping again to change the
subject. "What's that about?"

"Thirty Meter Telescope," said Dalita. "They want to put one
on top Mauna Kea, on the Big Island, the most sacred place for
Hawai'ians. We've been protesting it for years."

Lorelei nodded. "There's a word, 'āina. It means 'the land.' Aloha
'āina is 'love for the land.' Hawai'ians believe we're here to protect
it—everyone should protect it, even visitors. If you're going to stay
here, you need to learn these things."

Again she stared at Grady, her green eyes and emerald hair
incandescent in the sun. He didn't look away but felt himself flush.
She knows I'm lying, he thought. *Not about what, but she knows.* He was
relieved when Dalita broke in.

"Everything here has been totally fucked up by developers," she
said. "The forest, the waterfalls—there are signs everywhere telling
people to stay on the paths. The tourists ignore them. Then everybody is shocked when some haole jumps into a pool and breaks his
neck. Things here are sacred *and* dangerous. If you live here, you
know that."

"What about Wes?" asked Grady. "All that property he owns."

Lorelei shook her head. "By haole law, he owns that peninsula, but
it's not his land. We could make a court case, but that's expensive
and the Native resources are limited. At least he gave up on the
resort. After that got shot down, he had some kind of Come to Jesus
moment."

"What changed his mind?"

"He told me once he'd found an injured ʻiʻiwi near his house," said Dalita. "A mongoose must have gotten it. He tried to save it, but he couldn't and . . ." She opened her hands, shrugging. "He said he couldn't understand it himself but he felt different after. I mean, he has choke money, it's not like he needs more."

"So now he donates to all those land trusts?"

"Sure. It makes his conscience feel better. It makes him feel he belongs here. Wes is like one of those white guys who give themselves a Hawaiʻian name without knowing you only get that from a kumu."

Lorelei shot Grady a look that made him realize he, too, might be that kind of white guy. He'd never truly registered that the land where he was living had been stolen from the people who'd been here for more than a thousand years. He'd wondered where the real Hawaiʻians were: they were here at this picnic table, at Mak Supe, everywhere. He was the one who wasn't real.

He turned, so Lorelei couldn't read his expression.

"He treats our peninsula like his own private resort," Lorelei continued. "He says he's going to leave it to the island, but . . ." She touched her biceps, and her fingers seemed to become part of the wave tattoo. "We shall see."

From inside came an aggrieved shout, followed by a thump and screaming. "'Scuse me." Dalita hurried into the house.

Lorelei turned to Grady. "Minton hired you because you're not from here," she said. "He wants someone who won't ask questions."

"So I won't ask any questions."

"That's not what I'm telling you." Lorelei's eyes glittered. "Maybe you should."

CHAPTER 39

Grady looked up as Dalita stepped back outside.

"Was Paolo acting up?" asked Lorelei.

"Stella. No blood or broken bones."

Grady expected Dalita to sit, but she remained behind Lorelei's chair, hands on her wife's shoulders. It was time for him to go.

"Well, I better head out," he said, and stood. "Thanks for lunch."

Dalita walked him to the front of the house, the two stopping beside the truck. Grady glanced at the bags of recycling in back. "Shit, I forgot—where do I take those?"

"Transfer station's out on the highway south, but they close at two. They'll be open on Monday. No worry, your truck looks local, all that crap in the bed."

"I guess I'll just drive around. I haven't been anywhere since I got here."

"You should do the cliff walk at Keawa. That's where the resorts are. Not real cliffs like Hokuloa Road—there's a walkway between the beaches and hotels. You can't keep people off the beaches, even at the private resorts, but they're all closed anyway. Park by the Royal Keawa—you'll see signs for the path. It's about forty-five minutes each way, but if you get tired, you can walk back on Shearwater Road, behind the hotels. That way's only twenty minutes."

Grady nodded. He felt increasingly queasy and off-balance—the news of Jessica Kiyoko's disappearance, the dead or missing caretakers, Lorelei's anger. "Is Lorelei Hawai'ian?" he asked.

"Her great-grandfather. She also get same as me, Filipino, white, Black. But her family has been here longer than mine."

She glanced into the truck cab. "No more valuables inside, yeah? Don't lock it, and leave the windows down. There're a lot of smash-and-grabs, especially where people go hike. Usually they target rentals, but a couple weeks ago someone broke Lor's side window and stole a bag of groceries while she was swimming." She flicked her gaze toward the street. "How's driving Hokuloa Road?"

"Fine. I went slow. It would be beautiful if I could actually look at it."

He opened the truck door and got inside. Dalita rapped the hood. "A hui hou. See you."

Heading out of town, he obsessively ran over the time of Jessica Kiyoko's disappearance. Could she have been the woman he'd heard on the beach yesterday? Someone could have held her captive before bringing her there.

The obvious suspect would be Sanchez himself—he'd been reported missing on Thursday, too.

He banged the steering wheel in frustration, then saw on his phone map that he'd missed the turn to the resorts. He made the next left and backtracked, passing a street sign that sounded familiar. Corner Street. As he turned onto the access road for the Royal Keawa Resort, he remembered—Corner Street was near where Jessica Kiyoko had been staying. He thought of driving down there but decided that would be too creepy, like he was a stalker, or one of the rubberneckers who'd gawk at a crash scene when he was out on an emergency call.

The access road behind the resort was in rough shape, crumbled blacktop and sand. It wound between high hedges of an unearthly green. Birds rustled in the leaves, and he felt a welcome excitement at recognizing them from his field guides—saffron finches, a red-vented bulbul. All introduced species but still beautiful.

The occasional gap in the hedges revealed glimpses of another world. A huge circular drive lined with scores of dumpsters.

Warehouse-sized maintenance buildings. Trailers surrounded by stacks of PVC pipes and huge wooden spindles coiled with steel cables. Parking lots filled with empty tiki bars, wooden outrigger canoes, bins holding Polynesian masks and Chinese lanterns. A raised platform with a pagoda and a thatched hut. Smiling plastic tropical fish, smiling plastic sea turtles. It looked like Disneyland had puked up the contents of its storage sheds.

Another road split off from the access road, smooth white asphalt lined with neat black curbstones—the road for resort guests. It snaked up a gentle slope between wide green lawns, sparkling beneath the spinning rainbow arcs of sprinklers. Palm trees and papayas grew among clumps of bird-of-paradise, yellow and orange hibiscus, wine-colored plumeria.

Grady slowed to a halt, letting the truck idle as the hot wind filled the cab with the fragrance of plumeria. After a minute he drove on, until he saw a sign that read NATURE TRAIL PARKING. He pulled into the lot—his was the only vehicle—parked and got out.

The asphalt glittered with beads of glass, mounded up like sand. Dalita wasn't kidding about those smash-and-grabs. He reached inside the truck for his hat.

The parking lot was also walled in by tall hedges, though these hadn't been pruned in a while. Unruly sprigs and branches erupted like a bad green haircut. A large sign reminded visitors that smoking, skateboards, dogs, and bicycles were forbidden, and only hotel guests were welcome on the resort grounds.

He stepped onto the path, and there it was: the Hawai'i from the tourist brochures. Behind an ornate metal fence topped with foot-long spikes, a fairy-tale castle rose above lawns and tropical gardens. The castle was ten stories tall and as long as a football field, cladded in white and turquoise stucco. Its minarets and balconies looked more *Aladdin* than Hawai'i. There was a huge pool—pools—with waterfalls and jade-green water, shaded by palms and hibiscus and surrounded by orderly rows of teak lounge chairs, each with a beach umbrella emblazoned with the resort's logo. The only things missing were guests.

Small brown-and-gray birds hopped across the grass—nutmeg mannikins—and cardinals chittered from an outdoor bar shaped like an oversized canoe. Two scraggly calico cats watched Grady from behind the fence, one with a dead rat between its paws. As he walked by, the cat scampered off, leaving the rat for the ants and cockroaches.

He passed resort after resort, each with its own logo and theme: tropical paradise, faux-rustic haven, a concrete-and-steel monstrosity that looked like Cruise Ship in Outer Space. All those folded beach towels and umbrellas, all those immaculate lawns and pristine pools—who tended it all? He felt like he'd wandered onto the set of *Left Behind*. He wished Rachel could see it, Rachel with her love of dead cultures and ancient monuments, burial mounds and ruined pyramids.

Mesmerized, he walked for a good half hour before he stopped, feeling like an idiot. He still hadn't seen the ocean.

He turned, stunned by what was there—a beach just as meticulously curated as the resorts. Sand the color of underdone toast, an unbroken line of turquoise rollers.

And, at last, people. A woman and two children sat on towels beneath a small umbrella. In the distance, a solitary surfer. On the horizon, a freighter. The blinding sun made everything look radioactive.

He left the path, walking across the beach to the water. Beneath his sneakers, the sand felt as soft as talcum powder. He looked for seashells or coral but saw only yellowing fragments of broken shell, like toenail clippings, and tiny granules of bright turquoise plastic.

When he reached the waves, he crouched and let the water cover his outstretched fingers. Something scuttled across the sand by his foot, a small ghostly shape that disappeared when he looked at it. He straightened, and again saw a flicker at the corner of his vision. If he remained still, ripples appeared beneath the sand.

Dozens, no hundreds, of spidery crabs, no bigger than a finger joint. They swarmed from under the sand, their carapaces nearly transparent.

He bent to get a better look at what they'd found to feed on. And blinked. It couldn't be—an eye? Iris a curdled yellow-brown, the eyelid nibbled to pink lace.

Grady recoiled, tasting bile. Surely it wasn't a human eye. He forced himself to stoop closer. The ghost crabs continued to dine, as though Grady was nothing but a passing shadow.

The eye was nearly all pupil, the brownish color deepening to black with a rim of gray like a lunar eclipse. Weren't shark eyes black? Yet something about it did seem disturbingly human. The eyelid, for one—sharks didn't have eyelids, did they?

He knew it was irrational—he was miles away—but he couldn't shake it: Could this possibly have come from whoever had been killed on Hokuloa Road? Or were the beaches here possibly littered with body parts? That couldn't be right. He thought of the list of the missing. Dalita's reef of bones. Minton had scoffed, but the bodies had to end up somewhere.

Not just human bodies, he reasoned, but animals, too—sharks and sea turtles, sick birds. Fish that couldn't survive the change in water temperature.

It's from a shark, he thought, *a fucking dead shark,* and furiously kicked sand over the eye. The ghost crabs scattered but almost immediately returned, digging so they could continue to feed.

CHAPTER 40

He hurried from the beach, his stomach knotted, and walked past yet another resort, this one called Serenity. More empty sea-facing balconies, more empty deck chairs. An Olympic-sized pool with a mosaic of sea turtles. MAHALO FROM SERENITY, read the sign above the locked gate. PLEASE BE SAFE, A HUI HOU. Behind the fence, two security guards chatted inside a bamboo-sided café that now served as storage for boogie boards and swim noodles.

At least someone's still punching the clock, Grady thought wearily. He checked the time. He'd been gone for almost forty-five minutes, so he must be near the end of the trail. He was utterly beat, ready to go home and hit an early bedtime. He'd take Dalita's suggestion, walk back along Shearwater Road.

After a few minutes, the resort path petered out. When he got to the street-facing side of the resort wall, the carefully curated flowering vines gave way to dead vegetation, peeling off in a forlorn brown curtain.

Grady kicked aside discarded face masks and plastic bottles as he trudged through to a big public parking lot, a third of its spaces occupied by pickups, cars, hippie vans, and a shiny Airstream trailer, many clearly serving as homes. Beyond the lot stretched a beach, at last dotted with small family groups—parents and kids, couples. Grady counted five surfers in the water, and others unloading surf-boards and paddleboards from their trucks. Signs reminded people to wear masks and practice social distancing, though nobody was.

He bet that resort staff warned visitors to stay away from here, even though it looked safe and far more welcoming than the creepy stage sets he'd just seen.

He found Shearwater Road. It ran alongside a neglected park— benches on dry grass, metal fixtures that had held trash bins, removed to discourage congregating. A man with a straw hat pulled over his face dozed, a beer can at his feet. On another bench, two large women fanned themselves as they talked. A circular concrete walkway served as an informal skate park where three boys on skateboards swooped, wheels clattering.

Grady watched as a guy in dripping board shorts walked to an outdoor shower and rinsed off. When he left, Grady stepped over and drank greedily from the accompanying water fountain. A pickup cruised along Shearwater, blasting metal, its bed loaded with PVC pipe and an old toilet.

Wiping his mouth, Grady walked to the corner, where a street-light had been turned into a community bulletin board. Flyers covered it, from ground level to as high as he could reach. At home in Maine, the flyers would have been for missing cats. These were all for missing people.

Kristian Salvadoro, b. 2007, last seen in Lula on October 11, 2019. Wearing red hoodie/black shorts, carrying skateboard.

The photo, crackled beneath its lamination, showed a boy making devil horns with his hands.

Pls call with information. Thank you and god bless.

The flyers were taped one on top of another, the faces erased by weather and time, the names in faded boldface type or scrawled Magic Marker. Grady pried up months-old postings to reveal the older flyers beneath, some going back a decade or more.

Medardo Gill, last seen sometime in March 2020. Camps longtime on south shore beach with his dog, Grappa. Family in Maui has had no contact with him since March.

Harold O'hu 87 wandered from his home on Mackinaw Road the night of 7 July 2015. Harold has diabetes and dementia...

18 year old Cynthia "Cynni" Brennan last seen wearing Red and Blue two piece bathing suit at Marena Beach where she has been camping for six mos. She is a strong swimmer and may be in the Hokuloa area.

Grady circled the pole, his arms breaking out in goose bumps as he forced himself to read every flyer. He'd seen the names on the bunker, but until now, he never really believed there could be so many missing. He could never remember each name, but at least he could register them. Maybe he could find the pattern that might connect them all.

Only there was no pattern. They were strong swimmers, old people with dementia, homeless people. Children and teenagers, mothers and fathers. Runaways and tourists who had been on the island only for a day or week. They were all ages, all colors, all genders. Surely they couldn't all have drowned, or been abducted, or murdered.

Dazed, he thought of the maybe-woman screaming on the beach and felt sick: Was her picture here? Would it be here next time he looked?

Had that been Jessica?

Behind him the skateboarders' din grew louder. Grady looked over to see one kid catch some air, pumping his fist as he landed, shouting, "Shoots uuright!" Grady turned back to a photo of a smiling young man, his eyes very dark brown, almost black, against dark skin, his black hair shoulder-length. A stylized dolphin was tattooed on his chest.

Cory Desoto, 26 years old, Missing 7/8/20. From O'ahu, no fixed address. Last known to be sleeping on North Beach. If you have seen Cory please call . . .

Grady began to move more urgently, standing on tiptoe and kneeling on the ground, searching for a new flyer with Jessica Kiyoko's name. Finally he got shakily to his feet, exhausted and depressed. Maybe it was a good thing her friend Raina hadn't needed to post one of these yet. He had to get out of here. He turned to leave but stopped when he saw it.

MISSING SINCE LAST THURSDAY JULY 23: JESSICA KIYOKO. FROM L.A. BUT STAYING IN MAKANI. SHE WAS AT FITZHUGH'S IRISH PUB AND LEFT ALONE AROUND MIDNIGHT. PHOTO SHOWS A MAN BEHIND HER. IF YOU HAVE SEEN JESSICA OR RECOGNIZE THIS MAN PLEASE CALL RAINA . . .

There was a phone number, along with the same black-and-white security photo and also a color one of Jessica. Her curly hair fell around her face, she wore a white T-shirt with a flowered scarf tied loosely around her neck, and she was smiling at whoever was taking the picture.

Grady took a photo of Raina's name and number, and nearly ran to his truck. Behind him, he heard a shout followed by laughter and curses as one of the skateboarders wiped out.

CHAPTER 41

He drove back to Corner Street. This was his chance to do the right thing, maybe his only chance. Connect the dots, talk to Jessica's friend and learn if Jessica had known Leonardo Sanchez, if there was some possibility that Jessica might have been the person he'd heard—or he thought he'd heard—on the beach.

But if he didn't act fast he'd lose his nerve. When he spotted an open grocery, he pulled over and ran in for a six-pack. Back in the pickup, he popped a beer to calm his nerves, drank it, and called Raina Mayhew. Her phone rang over into voicemail, so he left a message.

"Hey. My name is Grady. I was on the flight with Jessica from Los Angeles and we talked for a while. I just heard about what happened, so, uh, call me if you can. Thanks."

He set the phone down and stared at it, wishing he could just show up and pound on Raina Mayhew's door. But she might refuse to see him, or think he'd had something to do with Jessica's disappearance. A flock of chickens surrounded his truck, pecking at the street.

After ten minutes he gave up. He began to drive to Minton's, clutching the wheel in his anger and disappointment. He'd only gone a block when his phone vibrated. He recognized the number.

"Raina?" he asked, pulling over in front of a shuttered T-shirt emporium. "Thanks for calling back."

"Who are you?"

"Uh, my name's Grady Kendall. I was on the flight with Jessica, we talked for a while. I was there when she got her stuff in the baggage claim—I saw you when you picked her up. I don't know if you remember."

"I don't."

She was silent for so long he thought she might have hung up. "Hello?"

"I do remember." She sounded reluctant to admit it. "That guy by baggage claim—Jess said she'd talked to him. She said he seemed nice, kind of shy."

"Yeah, I guess." Grady laughed nervously. "She was really nice, we talked about maybe meeting up later, when we were out of quarantine . . ."

"Are you going to give me more shit about her breaking quarantine?"

"No! No, of course not—I just, I was just upset about it! I feel terrible—I wanted to say how bad I felt. Feel. She was really nice," he repeated, knowing he sounded like a jerk. "I'm sorry."

Again he expected Raina to hang up, but after another long pause, she said, "Well, thanks. Have you talked to the police?"

"What?"

"The police," she demanded. "Have you spoken to the police?"

Was this a trick question? "No," he said, hoping that was the right answer.

"Where are you?"

"Tiki's? A T-shirt shop on Corner Street."

"Look, I have to be somewhere later, but I could meet you in fifteen, for a little while, if you want. You know where Fitzhugh's is? Next block, I'll meet you there."

The Quad was a bunch of bars and casual restaurants, all facing a big parking lot that functioned as a courtyard. A dozen vehicles sat in an area meant to hold a hundred. Bar doors hung open, releasing the smells of scorched grease, fried fish, spilled beer, weed. Every place had variations on the same cheesy decor—fishing nets and seashells, plastic pineapples and plastic leis. Reggae music and oldies. Two men in chef's aprons shared a smoke and gave Grady the stink eye as he pulled in, their masks dangling below their chins.

Fitzhugh's occupied the far end, with a line of motorcycles parked in front—crotch rockets, a Triumph in mint condition. The pub was by far the largest—two stories tall, with upper and lower decks and a weathered sign. FITZHUGH'S IRISH PUB EST. 1983. HAPPY HOUR EVERY DAY 4–6.

A few drinkers leaned out of open windows to talk to those on the downstairs deck. There were more people than he'd expected. No one wore a mask. It looked more like a shipboard bar than an Irish pub. Grady stood awkwardly, pulled out his phone to hide his unease.

"You Grady?"

He looked up with relief that she hadn't stood him up. "Yeah. Raina?"

Without a word she walked inside, leaving Grady to catch up.

CHAPTER 42

Raina Mayhew was a slight, wiry—make that scrawny—girl his own age. Tanned light-brown skin, long bleached-blond hair that had probably been sleek and straight before the lockdown but now looked ragged. She wore tight sky-blue pants that ended halfway up her calves, the fabric spotted with burn holes, and a low-cut paisley blouse. Wood-soled sandals with two-inch heels that clomped loudly on the floor. He thought she had on heavy eye makeup, but as they drew up to the bar, he saw that her eyes were dark-circled and raw-looking.

The room was dim and wood-paneled, a relief after the glaring sun outside. Drinkers sat at a handful of tables scattered around the big space. The only concession to tropical decor was a small shark mounted on the wall, a string of blue Christmas lights draped around it.

"What's your pleasure?" yelled the bartender, the only person wearing a mask. Her eyes widened as she recognized Raina. "Oh my god—how are you?"

She leaned over the counter to hug Raina. Two men at a high top turned to watch, giving Grady a once-over.

"I'm okay," said Raina. She seemed uncomfortable. "Haiku ale."

"Same," said Grady.

He took out a couple of bills and set them on the counter. When the bartender returned with their beers, Raina grabbed hers and made a beeline for a side door. Again Grady hurried after her, upstairs to the empty second-floor deck. Raina headed for a table in a back corner, where she slumped in a chair. Grady sat across from her, scooting his chair away from the table.

"I don't have fucking COVID," snapped Raina. She had a hard gaze and very dark eyes—the irises almost purplish, so her eyes looked all pupil. She would have been pretty if she hadn't looked like she was on the verge of throwing a punch.

Grady nodded. "I know. I mean, I don't know, but I assume you don't. I hope you don't," he added, and ventured a small smile.

Raina looked at him like he was an idiot. "So you met Jess on the plane. Do you live in L.A.?" She stared at his face, shaking her head as she answered her own question. "Ever hear of sunscreen?"

"I forgot it yesterday."

"I can tell. What'd you talk about?"

"Nothing, really." He pressed the cold beer bottle against his forehead. "You know, where are you from. I'm from Maine."

"Why didn't you call the cops?"

He took a swallow of beer. "I only found out a few hours ago. I just got out of quarantine. I've hardly seen anyone."

"And you called me instead of the cops?"

"I saw your flyer down by the public beach."

"All the beaches here are public."

Christ, this one was a ballbuster. "Look," he said, "I didn't mean to bother you. I was just heading home, so—"

"Because the cops here are fucking useless," she broke in. "They just cover up whatever shit is going on."

"What *is* going on? The woman who picked me up at the airport, we drove past that deserted building with the names on it and she told me about all the people who've gone missing here. Then I read the news about Jessica, and at the beach I saw that pole with the flyers and I recognized her." He pulled out his phone, brought up the photo he'd taken. "That's where I saw your number."

"Hale o Nalowale." Raina sipped her beer. "That's what it's called. The building. House of the Vanished. They kill us, but we still have our names. Someone will put Jess's up there. Not me. If she's gone, she's gone. She might be dead already. Probably she is."

"Don't say that."

"Why?" she sneered. "Because I'll jinx it? Because it's kapu? If she's dead, she's dead. If not, she's been trafficked off-island."

"How?" Grady retorted as anger got the better of him. "There're no flights, no cruise ships."

"Boats. You have a boat, you can go anywhere. You think the police watch every cove in Hawai'i? You can move drugs, people, animals, plants, just like they did a thousand years ago." She shrugged. "But maybe she's alive and still here and no one knows. They busted up a prostitution ring here ten years ago, they were grooming high school girls. Fourteen-year-olds!" She raised her voice. *"Right here."*

"On this deck?"

Raina gaped at him in disgust. "Oh my fucking god."

She stood and stomped off down the steps.

"Whoo hoo." Grady let his breath out in a long whistle. He finished his beer and had just started to his feet when Raina clomped back with two more. She set them down and slid into her chair.

"No, not right here and, yes, right here," she said. She rubbed her lower lip, which was bitten up and seamed with dried blood. "They did bring the girls here sometimes. Some of them looked older," she allowed. "But they were kids. It was a swim coach at the high school. He got older boys he knew to do it. Buy 'em drinks, get high with them. Lonnie, the bartender then, he just looked the other way."

She picked up her beer and drained half the bottle. Grady didn't touch his. This girl was a loose cannon, and he didn't want to be the one who lit her fuse. He ran through different questions, trying to determine which might be safest.

"How'd you meet?" he asked at last. "You and Jessica?"

"I had to leave here." Raina stared at her beer bottle, her expression sad. "They sent me to live with my cousin's family outside L.A. A real shithole, the place stank, like it literally stank. One day a sinkhole opened and the trailer next to ours fell in. It was during the day so nobody was killed. That night we wake up and there are all these black helicopters, bullhorns shouting at us to stay inside and take cover. A whole fucking SWAT team. Turns out people in the trailer next to ours had an underground meth lab. They were hiding in the tunnels. Cops killed one of them when he came out with a semiautomatic. Blew out our bathroom window."

She twirled a lock of her bleached-out hair. "Soon as I turned eighteen I got the fuck out of there and came back here. The only person I missed from California was Jessie—she was in my year at high school. We were best friends from day one. She went to USC, but we always stayed in touch. She came here a few times—from L.A. it's only five hours. I was constantly on her to move here. Once the lockdown started, she decided that would be a good time. So that's why she came."

Raina ground her palms against her swollen eyes, then looked up at Grady. "I can't cry," she said. "Too much of that, years of it. My body just sucks it all back in. People always say I should talk to someone, like a therapist, but I think I should talk to a scientist. Have you ever heard of that? Someone who can't cry?"

"No," said Grady.

He tried to square this sad but possibly crazy person with her confident friend on the plane, Jessica with her silver toenail polish and pink flowered flip-flops. He glanced down at the Quad. More cars and motorcycles had arrived. People stood alongside their vehicles, laughing like normal. Hip-hop wafted up from the bar, heavy bass and a woman's suggestive voice. He turned back to Raina.

"Why'd they send you to California?"

"You don't get it." Her bloodshot gaze grew almost pitying. "That was me, here." She patted the table. "The girls from the high school. That's how I know."

CHAPTER 43

'm so sorry," Grady stammered. "That's horrible."

"I'm fine. It was a long time ago. Just, people treat you different after something like that. Some of them, they thought I got what was coming, right? But most people aren't like that." She sighed. "But I can always tell—they're all thinking about it. A place this small—no one forgets anything. Half the locals are related. That was another reason why I wanted Jessie here, someone who didn't care. Who knew me differently."

Grady wanted to touch her hand, but he couldn't do that, not to a woman he'd just met. At last he said, "It's—I'm glad you're okay. Obviously."

"I wish Jessie was." Raina didn't sound worried but terse. Resigned, almost. "She's getting her PhD, if she liked it here she was going to transfer to UH Mānoa. I went there for undergrad—marine biology. I dropped out before I finished—I couldn't take on any more debt, and my mo needed my help because of her COPD. And I was depressed," she admitted. "I tried meds, but they didn't help. For a long time, I just felt like shit for being that girl who gave blow jobs to tourists at the Drifter's Inn."

"But you were a kid! You shouldn't blame yourself."

"I don't blame myself." Raina eyed him coldly. "And some of it wasn't so bad. They don't want you to say that. Not the sex part—that was fucking gross. But this one developer from Tahoe really liked me, he took me to O'ahu a couple times. He told people I was his daughter."

Grady fought to hide his shock. "Didn't—didn't you try to get away? Or call the police?"

"I was scared to—I didn't trust them. And my parents are super-strict Christians, I didn't feel like I could tell them. I'd left when I was fourteen and moved in with some friends who had a group house in Kahawai. That's how I met Leonardo—I thought he liked me, but he was grooming me. He was four years older. I stayed in school—that was one good thing. Anyone asked, I said I was going to O'ahu with my uncle. Uncle Tahoe. Mostly he was at meetings during the day, so I stayed in the room and watched TV. It sounds bad, but it was kind of a vacation." She laughed at Grady's horrified expression. "I know, right? He took me to the mall and bought me nice clothes and makeup and books. We saw *Eclipse*. I loved those books. *Twilight*."

"Did they even arrest him?"

"Nope. None of them. They just flew back to Tahoe or Cincinnati or wherever. I never knew their real names. Honestly? I just blocked it all out, except the good parts, like the mall. The rest was like it happened to someone else." She rubbed her eyes again. "They did bust the swim coach. He's out now and moved to the mainland. The local boys got their wrists slapped because they were still teenagers. They're the ones I think should be in jail. Because they *knew* us."

"Are they still on the island?"

She didn't reply. Downstairs, an old Rolling Stones song came on.

"My mom likes this song," said Grady finally.

"Everyone's mom likes this song. Except mine."

"All those people who disappear—someone has to be killing them, right? Some of them, anyway. I get that people can fall off a boat or get lost in the rain forest or whatever, but all those flyers, and the names on that building—this place must have a really, really high number of unsolved cases."

Grady waited, but still she said nothing. "Well, what is it?" he insisted. "What do you think is going on? You grew up here!"

"Where do you get this shit?"

But her expression had softened. The alcohol, Grady thought. Skinny as she was, it wouldn't take much to put her away. She peeled off a long strip of the bottle's label.

"What I think is, there's more than one killer," she said at last.

"Like a gang?"

"No. But you could still have more than one killer."

"Not a chance." Grady shook his head. "They'd get caught. This place is too small."

"This island is seven hundred square miles. It's the best place in the world to kill someone. Tourists save up their whole lives to come here. They're throwing money around like crazy, but people here are *poor*. The tourist industry doesn't want the tourists to think there're any risks, even though there are literally a million ways you could die. That's why they all stay in the resorts—it's like they're in a zoo. You here before the pandemic?"

"No."

"They shuttled tourists around in buses, from beach to beach or whale watch to parasailing or whatever. Lava stone massages. You can't drive anywhere because mostly there's just one road, and if there's an accident or heavy rain, everything gets backed up for hours."

"Yeah, but that's better than everyone renting a car."

"They *all* rent cars. The shuttles are so the resorts can try to keep an eye on them, make sure no one disappears. Because if a visitor disappears, it's a shit show for the mayor. Like, Jessie disappears and makes the national news. Locals disappear, it's never publicized. Like when girls are trafficked. No one believes it, no one wants to believe it, and so they pretend it never happens." She laughed bitterly. "Only time it gets serious is when it's a haole. And then, it's always their fault. They were walking alone at night, they were surfing where it wasn't safe, they went out on a boat with someone who's not licensed. Since they're never seen again, there's no murder, right? It's presumed death by misadventure or whatever you call it."

She shot him a hard smile. "That's my *perspective* on that."

"But I saw the flyers—people are still disappearing, even since lockdown. That can't be by misadventure. There's a serial killer here."

"Maybe. But sometimes people want to disappear. Suicide tourism—that's a thing. Or they want to escape and they go into the wilderness and live there. That's a thing, too. Or they disappear with no reason, but that's been happening forever. That's what the old people say in their chickenskin stories." She leaned across the table and ran her fingernails along his bare arm, watching the goose bumps rise.

"Nightmarchers," said Grady. "Dalita told me about them."

"Dalita? Who lives with Lorelei the māhū? How do you know her?"

"I'm the caretaker at Wes Minton's house on Hokuloa Road. Dalita's been helping me out with stuff."

Footsteps and voices echoed from the stairs, and a group of boisterous sunburned white women holding margarita glasses hauled themselves onto the deck. One waved and yelled down to the parking lot. "Nathan! Up here."

Cursing, Raina finished her beer. Grady pushed his nearly full bottle across the table. She grabbed it and stood.

"I can't deal with this shit," she said in a loud voice.

He walked out with her. A few people recognized Raina and called out a greeting. She stared straight ahead, her only response an occasional nod. Neither she nor Grady spoke, and he felt more and more anxious. Raina's red-rimmed eyes warned him not to push her, but he still knew next to nothing about Jessie. Like, why did they become friends so quickly? Why microbiology?

And, though he didn't want to admit it, the most burning question of all: Were Raina and Jessie lovers? If not, did Jessie have a boyfriend?

He blurted, "Was she seeing anyone here?"

"Seeing someone?" Raina snorted. "You a stalker?"

"No. Just, we talked about meeting up after quarantine and I was hoping I'd run into her. I liked her. She seemed nice."

"'Nice'? You mean, you want to fuck her."

"No! I just wanted to see her again."

"So you don't want to fuck her?' Raina scrutinized him. "You a Christian?"

"No, goddammit! Forget it, okay? I just hope she's not dead. Is that good enough for you?"

He stormed to the pickup. Raina followed him. She finished his beer and tossed the empty into the truck bed. Her mouth opened to make another retort, but then she looked down and her eyes widened.

"Dump run," Grady said. "Only I missed the dump."

Raina ran her hand along the rear bumper. "Where'd you get this truck?"

"It's Minton's. He keeps it for the caretaker."

She touched the buckled metal. "Sheesh. He's a goddamn billionaire and he can't buy you a new truck?"

She walked around the pickup, examining the bashed-up passenger door, ended up alongside Grady. She stared at the bumper sticker — DRIVE WIT AL. "He was okay," she said, kicking the bumper. "A Mormon or something, he went back home to Utah. But the other one, not Leonardo, the next guy — "

"Carl Gunnerson," broke in Grady. "Carl from Colorado."

"Right. He sold weed to kids living on the beach, but then he got into X and ice. He was driving home one night and his truck went off Hokuloa Road. It hitched up on a boulder, so it didn't go down the cliff, but he got thrown through the windshield. The truck was old, no airbags. Minton wasn't around so no one even knew for, like, a week. Leonardo went out there to surf—he was the one who called it in. They even brought in rescue dogs but never found him."

"When was this?"

"Maybe two years ago? There's a memorial for him on the road."

"Do they know what happened?"

That cold light returned to her eyes. "Carl Gunnerson died

because he was fucking with the island. Hokuloa Road's supposed to be haunted. Nobody who knows the island will stay on Hokuloa Road."

"Leonardo Sanchez did."

"Yeah, but you heard what happened to him, right?"

"Only that he's missing, and maybe a shark got him."

"A shark didn't get him. Something bad's up there."

Grady wished he could argue with her, but something bad *was* up there. "You're right. It's a strange place."

Raina turned to leave, glancing at his goose-pimpled arm. "I wouldn't drive that truck," she said, and walked away.

CHAPTER 44

He headed back to Minton's. When he passed the bunker, Hale o Nalowale, he made a point of keeping his eyes on the road. Like holding your breath past a graveyard; like never driving past the cemetery outside Rockland where his father was buried.

When he turned onto Hokuloa Road, the sun was behind him, low in the sky. The reflection on the ocean was blinding, even through his sunglasses. It was like the road had been designed to kill you, day or night.

Eventually trees and shady upland forest made it easier to see. He clocked another set of tire tracks—they seemed headed in the same direction he was. A motorcycle. He downshifted into first, frowning.

He spotted a cairn ten minutes later, on the ocean side of the road. He stopped, switched off the ignition, and got out, brooding on what Raina had said, that Carl Gunnerson had died *because he was fucking with the island*. Raina was superstitious—she'd said herself that this place was haunted. Grady had never believed in that kind of crap, but Raina's explanation was starting to seem as good as any.

Wind raked his cheeks as he walked. He heard the boom of waves against the foot of the cliffs. Beside the road, remnants of a stone wall showed where the truck had plowed through. The ground had been churned up to expose crumbled black lava, now overgrown with sourbush and thorny vines.

A lizard skittered away as he followed the truck's path. Even a few years later, he could see where it had taken out some small trees and left a deep rut, before it got hung up on a cone-shaped boulder that reminded him of the one on Sanchez's beach. This rock was smooth and black, almost glassy, pitted with tiny holes. Bits of broken glass still winked from the ground.

Grady tried to re-create the scene in his mind's eye. It was hard to fathom how, or why, anyone familiar with these switchbacks would drive at enough speed to veer off the road. You'd have had to be going fast to plow through that low stone wall and go through the windshield. Carl could have been drunk or on drugs. With no body, there'd have been no toxicology test. He might have swerved to avoid oncoming headlights, though supposedly no one ever drove this road but Minton, Minton's caretaker, Sanchez, and maybe that guy Uncle Honey. But Raina had said Minton was gone when the accident occurred, and she hadn't mentioned another name.

Or Carl could have been avoiding something in the road.

Grady thought of the thing he'd seen his first night here: that doglike figure, standing upright like a man. He pushed away that image, replacing it with the dog by the beach, a deer, or a wild boar. Raina hadn't mentioned any sign of an animal—why should she if Carl had swerved to avoid it?

He walked a short way down the hill, to the boulder. He rested a hand on it, then snatched it back, fingers tingling as though he'd touched a live wire.

He scanned the ground for a line. Nothing. Warily he touched the rock again with a fingertip.

And, yes, he felt a vibration, like someone was running heavy equipment nearby. He pressed his palm to the stone. It felt sun-warmed, the pitted surface at once smooth and coarse, sandpaper with honey poured over it. The vibration didn't stop. He bent to press his hand on the ground. No vibration.

A geological anomaly—the rock must be acting like a tuning fork, amplifying the ocean pounding at the shore below. He walked around to gaze down at the sea.

The ground here wasn't steep at all. It flattened out, covered by a thicket of Christmasberry and a stand of ʻōhiʻa lehua that gave way to gorse, sourbush, and finally, a good fifty feet away, the top of the cliff.

There was no way someone could have been thrown that far, even if he'd been hurtling along at eighty miles an hour. He might have bounced off the hood, then rolled a few yards. The odds of surviving that kind of impact were nil to none, yet even if Carl had somehow survived, would he have had the strength to crawl? If he had, why would he have crawled away from the road, and not toward it?

And as in any and all of these cases, why hadn't they ever found his body?

CHAPTER 45

On his way to the pickup, he stopped at the cairn, which he now knew was Carl's memorial. The white rocks were pieces of coral, the rest black lava. He picked up a chunk of coral that had fallen and set it back on the pile before returning to the truck and climbing inside. He turned the ignition and drove on. Outside Minton's gate were more motorcycle tracks, from the same bike. It looked like it had come from Hokuloa Point, driven down to the highway, then returned here. Inside the gate, the tracks headed up the drive.

Grady swore. He opened the gate and gunned it, the truck's wheels spewing gravel until he reached Minton's house. A late-model KTM motorcycle was parked in front. An off-road bike, not top of the line, but it would still set you back twelve grand. This one was covered with dried mud and leaves. Two aluminum panniers had been mounted in back. Minton sat at the table on the downstairs deck, staring at his phone.

"How're you doing?" he called, like he hadn't been gone for three days.

"I'm fine," Grady replied, relieved. He walked over slowly, trying to compose his thoughts. Had he missed a text saying Minton was returning? Or was this a test, Minton checking up on him?

Minton didn't look up until Grady stopped by the porch rail. "I needed a few supplies in town. I got all the way there before I realized I left the keys to the panniers back at Hokuloa Point.

I'm always losing keys." He shook his head, grinning ruefully. "But I have an extra set here, so I grabbed them and went back to shop."

Grady relaxed. "You should have called, I could've done it for you."

"No worries. I've done it before, forgotten the keys. I'll just stay here tonight and head back in the morning. How's the first day out of quarantine?"

"Good. I went into town."

"Want to join me? I just opened a bottle." He picked up a glass of white wine and gestured at the front door. "Or there's beer if you want."

"Sure, thanks. I'll grab a beer."

He went inside and got a bottle of some local microbrew from the fridge. The cap didn't screw off, so he looked through drawers until he found a church key, went back outside, taking a sip of his beer and trying not to grimace. A guava IPA.

Minton gestured for Grady to sit. "What'd you do in town?"

"Not much. I went by Dalita's, she invited me over for lunch. I was gonna go to the dump but it got late."

"No worries," Minton said again. "That stuff has been sitting in the garage for months. You check out the beaches?"

"I did that cliff walk by the resorts. It's strange with everything in lockdown."

"Those places are losing millions of dollars a month. Tens of millions. They furloughed all the waitstaff and housekeeping, but they still have to maintain the grounds. It's costing them a fortune."

"All that water in a drought. People's wells must run dry."

"They do. You can buy a piece of property and wait decades before you're allowed to put in a well."

"What about the resorts?"

"It's Chinatown, Jake."

Grady looked at him blankly.

Minton shook his head and drank more of his wine. "Nothing. Want another beer?"

"No thanks."

"I saw you checking out Carl Gunnerson's memorial." Grady blinked but said nothing as Wes continued. "I can see that part of the road from the upstairs deck. That was a terrible thing."

"What happened?"

"No idea. I was out at the point for a few weeks. He worked for me for a long while. From Colorado Springs. I would've thought that he'd be accustomed to mountain driving, but he wasn't—he was spooked by the road. Good worker, though. He put in that new catchment tank for rainwater. Dalita thought he had some issues with drinking. She heard stories about him not getting along with the locals."

"Did she know him?"

"Not really. She said he used to hang out at the resort bars. That night he may have had one too many. They never found his body, so who knows? It's easy to lose your way here."

He stared at his wineglass, then at Grady, like Grady was another glass and Minton was trying to determine if he was half empty or half full.

"I get that," Grady agreed, because it seemed like one of them should say something. "About losing your way. You see that in Maine. I was in a program to be a Maine guide—people were always getting lost or injured, sometimes killed."

"Here, they say that some newcomers, the island doesn't want them. The island doesn't welcome them. They never fit in. Their marriage breaks up, they lose their job. Their house burns down. Eventually they leave. Or die."

Minton gazed out to where the ocean glimmered in the fading light. "Other people, the island welcomes them in. They find a job, they fall in love, they make a home here and have children and stay."

Gazing at him, Grady felt his heart twinge. Had Minton ever

done any of those things? Would he? "Is that what happened to you?" Grady asked at last.

Minton shook his head, still staring at the water. "I'll tell you the truth, Grady—I've been here all these years, and I'm still not sure."

CHAPTER 46

Minton sighed and turned to Grady. "How do *you* feel? About being here?"

"I don't know." Grady looked up to see the first star winking in the night sky. "It's not what I expected. I thought it would be like Florida."

Minton laughed. "Well, maybe the hotels."

"Yeah. But it's hard to get a handle, with everything locked down. Not that I've ever seen it any different, but it feels . . ." Grady's voice drifted off. "I don't know how it feels. You'd think it'd be sleepy or quiet, but it doesn't feel like that. It feels unsettled. Like something's about to happen."

"Something good? Like the pandemic ending?"

Grady wanted to respond, *No, definitely not something good*. He shrugged. "I don't know."

For a few minutes neither of them spoke, listening as birds made their soft calls from the trees, roosting for the night. From upstairs came low whistles and twitters from the honeycreepers as they did the same thing in the aviary. As he listened to them, Grady almost let go of the thought that something bad could happen. This felt like one of those after-work conversations he occasionally had with contractors or homeowners, when you'd crack a couple of beers and maybe pass around a jibbah. He'd learned to take these moments as they came, and also to get as much out of them as he could—a line on another job, the name of a guy who had a truck for sale, maybe an invitation to go sailing.

He sipped his beer, then asked, "What happened to his body? Carl?"

"No idea. Police thought maybe he'd crawled away only to fall off the cliff."

"I guess that could happen. But he'd have to go a long way before it got steep enough to fall off. And he would've been beat up, getting thrown through the windshield, right?"

After a moment, Minton yawned. He picked up his glass and stood. "I'm going to try for an early start tomorrow, though I might wait till Tuesday—I've got a Zoom meeting with the Audubon people. Good chatting with you, Grady. Maybe I'll see you before I take off."

Grady hopped to his feet. "Anything you want me to do while you're gone?"

Minton glanced at the KTM in the driveway. "I think I'm all set. I won't be back for a few weeks. But I'll text you if I think of anything. Have a good night."

"You too."

Grady remained on the deck, watching darkness overtake the ocean as he fought an unexpected wave of unease. He recalled a night the previous summer, when he'd worked on Vinalhaven, building an addition for a couple, Bree and Jon Farris, whose home overlooked the Fox Island Thoroughfare. They had three young kids, one a daughter, Sophia, who'd recently undergone treatment for a rare form of brain cancer. Seasoned boat people, they gave a lot of parties, especially after the island's weekly J/24 races. When the Farrises' boat was shorthanded, Grady signed on as crew.

One weekend after a race, the weather turned bad and the ferry was canceled. The Farrises invited Grady to stay over. He ended up on the deck, drinking with Bree late into the night. The talk turned to bad weather, near misses, and disasters at sea, including a hurricane the year before that had pummeled the Caribbean, where a two-masted yacht out of Newport sent out a Mayday signal. The couple who owned it were well-known in the global sailing community—they'd logged hundreds of hours at sea, including several round-the-world trips with their two kids, both of whom had been with them on this cruise.

The Coast Guard located the yacht weeks later, floating sideways in calm waters a hundred miles from shore. Everyone aboard was missing, along with the boat's life rafts and PFDs. The latter included so-called gumby suits—cold-water survival suits, bright orange, with inflatable pillows to hold the wearer's head above water. News stories fixated on the life rafts, with people speculating as to whether anyone might still be alive, perhaps on some remote island.

"Jon and I were sailing back from St. Thomas in September," Bree said. "Sophia's doctor had told us she could come along—it was the first cruise we'd taken all together since she got sick. I had the night watch. Beautiful night—there was a full moon."

She leaned over the deck rail, gazing at the rain lashing Penobscot Bay. "I saw this orange thing floating, very far away. It looked like a big pumpkin bobbing up and down. Just drifting."

"A pumpkin?" Grady asked, not understanding.

"It was one of those gumby suits, just drifting along."

"Was it where they found the boat?"

"No. Miles away, hundreds of miles. The current took it."

"Did you call the Coast Guard?"

"No. We'd've had to wait, and file a report. Talk to everyone . . . No. I didn't want to distress the children. Sophie—she's still so fragile. I told Jon when I woke him. It was gone by then."

"They would have been dead for a long time," she added as she turned to Grady, her gray eyes anguished. "It's better that no one ever found them."

Grady shivered at the memory, and returned to the 'ohana. He poured the rest of the guava IPA onto the grass, tossed the empty into the back of the pickup, grabbed the six-pack of PBR he'd bought, and went inside. He got out his laptop and checked to see if Jessica Kiyoko had been found. She had not.

He spent the next few hours drinking steadily while he Googled her, telling himself he wasn't a stalker but a concerned friend. In his head he could hear Raina sneering, but he bet she was doing pretty much the same thing. The beer dropped a blurry curtain between his search and everything else that had happened in the past twenty-four hours—the beach, the screams, Leonardo's disappearance, crabs swarming around an eyeball on the sand. He knew if he pulled the curtain aside it would all still be there, waiting. For now, he continued to drink and trawl the internet.

He found a couple of references to research papers Jessie had assisted on, dealing with the decline of phytoplankton in the Northern Hemisphere; also an Instagram feed where she seemed to post only intermittently. Photos of the lab where she worked before COVID, pictures of phytoplankton enlarged under a microscope, which looked like stills from a movie about aliens. No photos of her with Raina, though there were a few with a tall white guy, tanned and grinning. He looked too geeky to be her boyfriend. A coworker, Grady thought, though if pressed he had to admit Jessica had seemed kind of geeky, too, with her big glasses and silly flip-flops.

He wondered if Jessie had felt the way he did, the first time she came here, amazed by how beautiful it was but also unnerved. She would have known about Raina's history: Had there been other strange, even sinister, things that she'd learned? He thought again about their conversation on the plane; what were the odds that, of everyone on this island, he'd first met her? He desperately hoped that she was safe. He felt linked to her somehow, as though they'd both been exposed to and survived the same rare virus. He felt cheated of their chance to talk about it.

Fuck, he thought, realizing he'd finished the six-pack. He was right lawn-chaired. He closed his laptop and passed out on the couch. When he woke late the next morning with a hangover, Minton's KTM was already gone.

CHAPTER 47

H e showered and dressed and swallowed some ibuprofen, made coffee and drank it standing in the kitchen. He couldn't muster the energy for food. It was lunchtime, and while he'd been up for only an hour, the midday heat and a hangover had already sapped him. What he really felt like was a nap.

Instead he walked over to the main house and went up to the aviary. As he slipped past the screen, an 'i'iwi, its plumage flickering orange and crimson as a flame, fluttered past his head. He stopped, holding out one hand, and the bird flew down to settle in his palm. Grady stared at it in delight, his headache forgotten. This 'i'iwi was smaller than the others—a baby? He hadn't seen a nest, wasn't sure what he would do if he did see one.

Let it be, he thought. Wes seemed to know what he was doing. Grady hoped so, anyway. He watched the little 'i'iwi until it darted off once more, then he sat for another half hour, listening to the slurred whistles and creaking cries of the other birds as they fluttered around him. At last he stood and walked around the sunlit space, looking for any sign of disturbance—injured birds, cockroaches, leaks in the ceiling. He picked up a bit of broken eggshell, the size of his pinkie nail and as thin as a piece of paper, dropped it, and bent to retrieve an orange feather. It was too small to keep safely in his pocket, where it would be crushed.

And it also seemed wrong to take it from here. Didn't some birds feather their nests? He set it gently beneath a fern, and went back to the 'ohana.

He drank some orange juice from the container and flopped onto the couch. As his hangover receded, along with the bright memory of the little 'i'iwi, he thought of Jessie, and Raina, and Leonardo Sanchez. But he refused to open his laptop, or check his phone for local news. He considered driving into town to get more beer, but he didn't have the energy. He could raid Minton's liquor cabinet, but that seemed like a slippery slope.

So he finished off the orange juice and pounded back more water, trying to flush bad thoughts from his head along with the alcohol.

He felt like he should do something constructive, but why? Minton obviously didn't give a fuck. Why should he? The hot breeze made him yawn. He didn't have the brainpower for a game, even if he could get enough bandwidth to log in. He had a couple of movies downloaded on his laptop but didn't feel like that, either.

At last he went outside, dragged a lawn chair into the shade of the avocado tree. Behind him, he heard the wind blow the screen door open. He didn't bother to get up and close it now.

Eventually he drifted off. When a sound woke him, a dog or owl or other night bird, he sat up, wincing as he rubbed his neck.

It was dark. *Fuck,* he thought. He'd slept all day, though at least it was still early enough that the almost-nightly rains hadn't started. Overhead, thin cirrus clouds obscured most of the moon. What time was it?

He checked his phone: no messages. He shivered as the breeze found its way under his T-shirt. He stood and walked inside to pull on his hoodie. Returning to the dark living room, he froze.

A silhouetted figure faced him from just beyond the french doors. Both the inside and screen doors were wide open.

He blinked, slowly walked forward. The figure stood, motionless, on the edge of the grass. It was as tall as he was—no, taller, its shape all wrong, its arms twisted, slender legs bent at the knees. It was bizarrely elongated, as though crouched and stretched at the same time. Grady heard a soft repetitive *huh, huh* sound, but that was him, struggling to breathe.

The figure didn't move. Its face too was all wrong, ears tugged upward to a point, its eyes a smeary white. No pupils, no irises. Its mouth yawned open, and Grady realized the face had no mouth, just a black, shapeless mass that spread like mold, enveloping its misshapen limbs and torso and head, the sky and trees and grass: everything but those blank white eyes.

A terrible smell seeped through, the scent of carrion, roadkill, fox musk carried on a sudden gust. The screen door swung toward him, and Grady tried to grab it before it could slam shut. His fingers ripped through the wire mesh and he lost his balance, his forehead slamming into the doorframe as his legs buckled and he dropped to his knees, head flaring with pain. He lurched to his feet, but the grass was now empty. Palm fronds rattled in the breeze. In the 'ohana, a gecko ticked, and a second gecko answered.

Grady touched the lump on his forehead—it was like he'd been hit by a two-by-four. He took care to shut the door, put ice in a towel and lay on the couch. The pain didn't go away. After a while, he trudged to the bathroom and took more ibuprofen.

He couldn't go to bed. If he had a concussion, he didn't want to fall asleep and not wake up.

And he couldn't bear the thought of dreaming about what he'd just seen. What *had* he seen? Why did it keep showing up?

He had no idea. Recalling its blank eyes and mouthless face, he wasn't sure he wanted to find out. So he lay on the couch and listened to the hunting geckos until the room grew pink with sunlight.

CHAPTER 48

He spent most of the next day resting. He rallied enough to check Minton's house and the garage, and found nothing out of order. The urchins were safe in their tank. The 'i'iwi and other birds whistled and gurgled, darting through their elaborate enclosure. For once Grady couldn't bear to watch them — their flashing feathers and constant cries pierced his head like needles.

Back in the 'ohana, he tried to check for news about Jessica, but just looking at the screen nauseated him. He felt like this was some kind of payback for doing nothing about the scene on the beach, but he knew that was crazy. He'd gotten drunk, had a monster hangover, passed out in a lawn chair. His brain had replayed the same nightmare image that he'd seen — imagined he'd seen — his first night here.

Now he felt lethargic and had a horrible headache. He continued to swallow ibuprofen and ice his forehead. By late afternoon, the swelling had gone down slightly. The bathroom mirror showed him a goose egg and the green tracery of a bruise, painful to the touch. When he checked the screen door, he found that he'd not only torn the mesh but also split part of the side panel. He'd have to replace the broken panel, that or buy or build a new door.

He tried not to think about the night before. Again he wondered whether this might be an off-brand COVID symptom, a hallucination. But he wasn't feverish and his breathing was fine. The fragrance of night-blooming jasmine was already stealing back through the open windows, so his sense of smell wasn't impaired. He wasn't suffering from heat stroke.

Grady considered the possibility that what he'd seen was real, whatever "real" meant in this strange place. He still didn't believe in ghosts, but as afternoon receded into early nightfall, he grew uneasy.

It didn't have to be a ghost. There could be a flesh-and-blood person out there. The same person who'd killed Sanchez and perhaps Jessie? It wasn't impossible. Maybe Grady's failure to contact the police meant that he'd set himself up to be the next victim.

The idea chilled him. Jessie and Sanchez had disappeared without a trace: Why not Grady? If something happened and he had to call 911, it would be an hour before anyone could get here.

He tried to think rationally. No one was stalking him. He'd lost his balance and cracked his head. Still, he got a tire iron from the garage and placed it at his bedside, and closed and locked all the doors and windows before he went to bed.

CHAPTER 49

I n the morning, he called his mom, which made him so homesick he felt like crying after. To distract himself, he took a video with his phone—palm trees, the rim of gold where the sun met the sea—and texted it to Donny.

oh dude u suck, Donny shot back.

Grady grinned. Miss you too, bro.

The grass steamed as the sun burned off last night's rain. He mustered the nerve to inspect the spot where he'd seen the eerie figure but saw nothing except an avocado that had rolled there.

He ate it defiantly while he scrolled for news about Jessica. She still hadn't been found. He'd pissed away an entire two days when he might have done something to help look for her.

And his refusal to notify the police about what he'd heard on the beach continued to gnaw at his gut. Like that story about the murderer driven crazy by the sound of a beating heart. Maybe Grady's guilt was making him see things, driving him nuts until he collapsed or confessed.

But he'd seen the white-eyed dog creature before he'd gone to the beach, not after. This place was bizarre enough without him adding supernatural blame to the mix. He finished the avocado and logged into one of the Reddit forums devoted to missing persons on the island.

Malihini girl disappears and it's big news like when any haole disappears. My brah 'Anuhe went missing a week ago but no one cares cuz he lives on the beach.

Our police department is fucked! Corrupt! Someday bodies will show up and they will admit the truth—a serial killer lives here!

Grady scanned more posts. Many berated the police for not pursuing the disappearance of so many houseless people. Some posts were recent; others went back years. Grady shared his brother's hatred of cops, but he had to wonder what they could do in cases like these. Some of the names were obviously nicknames—Yaya, Hellgirl, Giant Andre, Myrlynne—and so many people seemed estranged from their families, many for good reason.

But then they just fell through human-sized holes and were never heard from again. Donny had lived on the streets in Portland for a while, and he always talked about friends who were drug addicts, alcoholics, or just old-fashioned crazy. Whenever their mother brought up affordable housing and lack of medical care, Donny would just yell, "I should fucking know!"

So there'd be a war of attrition right there, thought Grady, people dying from exposure, ODs, or, these days, COVID. And didn't homeless people sometimes go home?

Still, the number of missing people here was disturbing. Nationwide, Hawai'i ranked alongside Maine, both per capita and in the actual number of people who'd disappeared. But this island had far more unsolved cases than the rest of the state.

Island-related forums, websites, and articles repeated all the reasons he already knew. Police corruption, drug cartels, human trafficking, weather, or wilderness-related misadventures. Deaths incurred while boating, swimming, surfing, windsurfing, parasailing, hiking, flying. Private planes disappeared. Friends watched from the beach as people swam out to go snorkeling, never to be seen again. Wind filled rainbow-colored parasails and bore their occupants away.

Most of those deaths had witnesses, or at least reasonable explanations. But there remained an inexplicable number of people who simply vanished. Some, like Jessica Kiyoko, left ghostly images on CCTV or security cameras. Others went out to take a walk or stormed away from the dinner table after an argument and were never seen again. The sole common denominator was that they all vanished without a trace.

Yet something had to be linking them. He backtracked through websites and forums, reading and rereading all those accounts of heartbreak, loss, grief, even hope.

I know you're out there, baby—if you're reading this, call me! Love you always!

He wiped his eyes, bleary with fatigue and tears. How could people endure so much loss? How had his mother, after his dad's death? As a kid, he'd always found his father's suicide incomprehensible. That was before he knew about the booze and depression, the money missing from the office where he worked.

Yet these disappearances were different. There was no rational explanation.

But there might be an irrational one. What if something else linked them? Something no one talked about, because they either didn't know about it or were too afraid? Something that was now hunting Grady?

CHAPTER 50

He quickly made himself coffee and returned to his laptop. He'd learned to avoid sites where people posted photos of blurry lights above Haleakalā as evidence of UFOs and alien abductions, or recordings of humpback whales that purportedly held information.

Still, he gave in and typed the words "dog man Hawai'i."

Most results had to do with dogs and their owners. A few recounted the same news story from five years earlier, of a man killing and eating a dog. A site devoted to Hawai'ian myth and legend had a section about cannibal dog-men on O'ahu and Maui, including one named Kaupe. The stories had been collected early in the twentieth century, though he assumed they were much older, gruesome folktales or a Hawai'ian version of the werewolf legend. A link to an academic website brought up an article that speculated these might be ancient folk memories of a ritual dating back thousands of years.

He skimmed the article, dense with footnotes about the Lapita culture. They'd settled in what was now known as Polynesia. The Polynesians were brilliant navigators who'd made their way to the Hawai'ian archipelago, utilizing their incredible abilities to read waves and clouds, and to follow the stars. Grady fell down a rabbit hole and perused constellation maps, transfixed by the Hawai'ian names. Aldebaran was Kapu-ahi, Sacred Fire; Betelgeuse, Kaulua-koko, Blood Star. Sirius was sometimes called 'A'ā, which meant

Bright Burning One and sometimes also identified with ʻā—a booby, a bird that navigators followed because it returned each evening to its island nest after hunting all day at sea. A constellation representing a great shark swam through the Milky Way.

And there was Hokuloa, the Great Star of the Morning: a chiefess star, a woman leader. It dizzied Grady to think of it: a world where people could gaze at the same stars he did yet see and experience an utterly different cosmos. He felt like he'd eaten another one of Dalita's gummies.

He clicked back to the main article and scrolled down to the comments section—people arguing about distortion of ritual practices, a discussion of DNA and the evolution of dogs in Southeast Asia. Nothing to link the thing he'd seen with missing people. He was ready to give up for the day, maybe forever, when he saw the name of the island.

> *Usually you hear about Kaupe on Oʻahu, but when I was growing up, there were a lot of stories about a monster like Kaupe on this island. Everybody back then knew about him, you weren't supposed to go to Hokuloa because that's where he lived and hunted. Supposedly people driving Hokuloa Road at night saw him and their cars would go off the cliffs. I never saw him but I also wasn't stupid enough to drive there at night lol.*

He came across a single other reference in Google Books, from an obscure late-nineteenth-century text on Pacific Islands folklore, compiled by a white missionary.

> *Here some believe the spirit Kaupe is the island's guardian spirit. He haunts the isolated southeastern region and is said to take the shape of either a dog or a man.*

Grady stared at the screen. On the plane, Jessie had mentioned ghosts, and something about a spirit dog. But it was insane to think any of that could be real, though a murderer might use the old stories as a way to cover his tracks, or even disguise himself, like Jason Voorhees with his hockey mask.

Of course Jason Voorhees wasn't real either. Still, before he went to sleep, Grady made sure the tire iron was still beside his bed.

CHAPTER 51

Next morning, the swelling on his forehead had nearly disappeared. The ugly bruise remained, purple and yellow, and a distinct dark line where the rail had smacked him. At least he felt much better.

After he'd eaten breakfast, he steeled himself to go outside and stare into the woods. Nothing there but a lizard on a rock. Smaller than his hand, the lizard had jade-green skin brightening to turquoise and dusted with gold, its back spotted with what looked like chromium-yellow and red paint drips. It had sky-blue patches above its eyes, blue feet with sucker pads on each toe. Grady reached for his phone to take a picture, but the lizard skittered off into the grass.

He checked the local news for any updates on Jessica Kiyoko or Leonardo Sanchez. Still nothing. To keep himself from all this doomscrolling, he did a Google search for the lizard and learned it was a gold dust day gecko, native to Madagascar. In 1974, college students had released eight of them in Honolulu.

And here was one, nearly fifty years later. Too late, Grady realized he should have killed it—an introduced species, it probably had caused all kinds of damage to endemic island plants and animals. Yet he didn't have the heart to kill something so beautiful. And humans were an invasive species that had done far more damage.

He started to type in Jessica's name again, slammed the laptop closed, and shoved it away. He had to get out of here, before he started asking weird-ass questions about Jessica on Reddit forums.

Beer was a bad distraction: he'd finally go to the dump and unload those recyclables. Afterward, he'd run by a hardware store and pick up what he needed to repair the screen door. He took its measurements and made a list, went to the garage to make sure the right tools were there. Before he left, he gave the padlocked door a tug. It didn't budge.

The island had a big-box store, the one all the contractors he knew called Home Despot, an Ace Hardware, and two independents. The chain stores had online ordering and curbside pickup only. Grady wasn't an established contractor here, so he wouldn't get any discounts, besides which he preferred the smaller, family-owned stores. He located one a half hour away, in Nai'a on the southwest side. Nai'a meant "dolphin"—he'd read that in one of his field guides. Maybe he would see some from the beach. He filled his water bottle and hit the road. The hardware store didn't open till ten, so he had an hour to kill.

He found the drive easier this time. He bumped along Hokuloa Road, the morning's warmth not yet tipping into unbearable heat. After he passed Sanchez's place, Grady felt a lightening in his chest. A mirage shimmered ahead, a peacock with its tail fanned out. Its long trembling feathers collapsed like a folding umbrella as he approached, and it high-stepped into the underbrush.

The highway seemed eerily quiet after the jaw-cracking miles of Hokuloa Road. Grady drove fast, happy to feel the wind on his face. His mood receded when he saw a dark shape on the side of the road, a large animal that had been hit by a vehicle. He slowed and saw it was a dog, a black dog with pointed ears, like the one he'd seen at Sanchez's place.

It couldn't be the same dog this far away, though maybe wild dogs wandered over a wider area than he thought. It was more likely there was an interbred pack of them. It didn't have a collar, and while muscular and big-boned, its prominent ribs suggested it had gone awhile without a good meal. He continued on, peeling past a few cars for the mindless thrill of speed. When the old airfield appeared, desolate in the morning sun, it took a few seconds for his brain to process what was different.

The names were gone. The bunker had been painted a dead white that sucked into it what little color was in the surrounding wasteland, like somewhere a nuclear bomb had been detonated. Before, the building had been a memorial: Hale o Nalowale, a plea to keep searching. Now it looked like a warning, a reminder that the island could make anyone disappear, including Jessie.

And, if he wasn't careful, maybe him, too.

CHAPTER 52

He found the transfer station with no trouble, sorted out the recyclables into their appropriate dumpsters, dropped off the bags of trash, and left the bags of cans and bottles in a donations bin to benefit the island's Forest Bird Recovery Project. An elderly woman picked through a dumpster for scrap metal to sell elsewhere—a rusted car exhaust pipe, a large pail without a bottom. Another old woman helped her carry everything back to a 4Runner, and they rattled off.

Grady followed a different route to the south side of the island, one that took him inland for several miles. The countryside was different here, desert-like, with thickets of low-growing trees with long feathery leaves, and taller trees with lethal-looking thorns that shaded stands of cactus. Small brown goats grazed everywhere, and a large bird soared overhead. He watched it dive, skimming above an open patch of ground before it flapped back into the air, one taloned foot clutching something that writhed.

Eventually he reached the turnoff for the southwest coast. Behind him rose the volcano, distant enough that, for the first time since landing, he saw that it *was* a volcano and not merely a mountain overshadowing the peninsula. The sight of its green flanks, giving way almost to black near the summit, gave him goose bumps. He could never have imagined that someday he would live on the downslope of a sleeping volcano. He watched it recede in the rearview mirror, until it was indistinguishable from the clouds.

The road widened into a two-lane highway that ran along the

beach. Cars and pickups were parked in the shade, surfboards propped alongside. People sat in beach chairs, holding coffee mugs or cans of beer. Weathered old hippie couples; a group of muscular guys, arms crossed as they stared out at the swells, watching a dozen or so surfers bob up and down.

Grady searched in vain for a place to park. People were living here, too. Not everyone—most cars seemed to belong to surfers or parasailors. But plenty appeared to have been here for weeks or months, their tires half buried in sand, windows covered by sheets, cardboard, or reflective fabric. Coolers sat alongside folding tables and chairs. There were children's toys and bicycles. One truck had a generator. Music blasted from boom boxes or car radios. The air was ripe with the smell of meat frying on portable grills, the skunky scent of weed, coconut suntan lotion. The vibe was less *Mad Max* than a low-key music festival.

He saw a spot between a 4Runner and a Taurus, but as he put on his turn signal, a naked older man emerged from the 4Runner. He stretched and hobbled over to a stand of trees to take a leak. Grady kept driving.

Just beyond the trees sat a Westfalia camper van, once white but now liberally splotched with Bondo and loose strips of silver duct tape. Its roof was popped up and its back door was open, so Grady could see blankets and sleeping bags inside, stacked plastic bins that held clothing or utensils.

A lone flip-flop lay on the sand beside the door, where three people his own age stood talking. A white girl and two guys, all lean and fit. The girl wore a string bikini, her hair in multicolored dreadlocks. One of the guys was white, with matted blond hair and a sarong worn low around his hips. The other guy had buzz-cut dark hair and brown skin. His blue Hawai'ian shirt flapped in the wind, giving Grady a glimpse of the spiral tattoos that covered his entire chest and arms. Nearby, a folding table held a camp stove.

Without realizing it, Grady had let the truck slow to a crawl. The guy with the matted blond hair turned to stare. Embarrassed, Grady lifted a hand in a half-hearted wave. The guy continued to stare, his pale gray eyes wide and angry.

No, not angry—scary, the way Donny's eyes used to get when he was tweaking. Grady knew he should look away, but he couldn't. The guy's eyes widened even more, and Grady saw the deep lines scored around them, white against his tanned skin. Slowly, holding Grady's gaze, his mouth began to open, wider and wider, to reveal white teeth and the black space behind them. He looked like he was screaming, but no sound came from his mouth. His eyes never left Grady.

"Scotty!"

Grady jerked as someone shouted—the girl. She grabbed the flip-flop from the ground and swatted the blond guy with it. He started to laugh, eyes crinkling and his mouth still open. The buzz-cut guy with the tattoos turned to look at Grady, too. Unsettled, Grady drove on, careful not to accelerate—he didn't want them to think they'd spooked him.

But they had. The blond guy, Scotty, watched Grady's truck recede. He raised his arms like a referee signaling a touchdown, tilting his head back to stare at the sky, into the sun, his mouth split into an ecstatic grin.

With a shudder, Grady tapped the accelerator. Scotty's wild gaze and yawning mouth reminded him of the figure he'd seen, or imagined, outside the 'ohana. It was impossible that Scotty could have been there, but the thought still disturbed him. He pushed it away as he continued to drive alongside the beach, which broadened, then narrowed to a sandy spit only a few yards wide.

On the other side of the two-lane road rose a wall of reddish stone. Road signs warned of falling rocks, and for a long stretch, the hillside was covered with a heavy-duty net of metal chains and orange plastic, to keep boulders from crashing onto the highway. Homes perched atop the bluffs, contemporary glass-faced mansions like Wes's. The kind of houses that always looked empty and cold, even with the sun beating down on their meticulously planted stands of papaya and guava and palm. Grady noted the pickups parked in driveways, almost certainly belonging to landscapers or a caretaker like himself. Who were they? Did they hang out at Fitzhugh's? The hardware store?

The bluffs ended and he drove through a handful of tiny towns, places that might have been cheerful a year ago. Food trucks and roadside stands advertised fresh fruit, banana bread, flowers, all now closed and desolate. When Grady spotted an open food truck selling fish tacos, he pulled over.

"Howzit?" the man in the truck called as Grady approached.

Grady ordered, and the man slapped a couple of tortillas onto a paper plate and started filling them. "You pau surf already? Some good the conditions today."

"Not today."

The man handed him the plate. "Mahalo."

"Mahalo," said Grady, momentarily flattered to be taken for a local.

He ate as he drove on, wishing he had a beer to calm his nerves as he replayed the scene on the beach. All those people living in their trucks and vans . . . could Jessica be there, too, or somewhere like it? It would be a good place to hide in plain sight. Or to be hidden, he thought grimly, as the town of Nai'a appeared before him.

CHAPTER 53

Nai'a resembled the kind of weather-beaten beachfront town that had almost disappeared from New England. Three surf shops, only one open. A couple of shut-down restaurants, an open-air bar still in business. Smoothie shacks and a dusty souvenir shop, its windows covered with white paper scrawled in Magic Marker.

Mahalo for 27 Good Years

He parked behind the hardware store, which had a gallon of hand sanitizer by the door and a handwritten sign that read *Mahalo for Wearing Mask*. Inside was cool, the hum of air-conditioning and the comfortingly familiar smells of fertilizer and paint thinner, chalky drywall and citronella. A stocky old man walked over.

"Can I help you with anything?"

"Yeah. I'm looking for some mesh to repair a screen door. And some paint."

"Sure thing."

He motioned for Grady to follow him outside, where lumber was stored in a separate building. Grady felt soothed by orderly stacks of cut pine, and even the chemical odor of particleboard. A sign above an empty pallet read SORRY NO PRESSURE-TREATED WOOD TILL FURTHER NOTICE.

Grady remembered the pile of wood in Dalita and Lorelei's backyard. He took out his phone and texted Dalita.

Hey, you got a post-hole digger?

The man returned with the mesh for the screen door. "Any-thing else?"

"Yeah, probably, but I'll find it. Thanks."

"Okay, I'll put this on the front counter."

The man walked away and Grady's phone pinged.

whats that

Grady laughed. You around? I'm at hardware store, need anything?

No. ima here, come have lunch

Grady found primer and white paint, a couple of brushes. He brought them to the front counter, did another sweep of the store to grab a post-hole digger. He'd seen one in Minton's garage but hadn't thought to bring it. But this way he could give it to Dalita and Lorelei as a gift.

He nabbed the last gallon of Thompson's WaterSeal. Dalita had said she'd bought some, but it would be good to have extra. He could always make use of it at Minton's place. They'd also need something for any part of the play set that touched the ground. He settled on roofing tar, and some heavy-duty brushes to apply it. After he paid for everything, the man helped him carry it to the pickup.

"I know this truck," he said as he studied the DRIVE WIT AL bumper sticker.

"Yeah, friend of mine used to own it," Grady said, immediately more anxious, and swung into the front seat. "Thanks, man. Mahalo."

CHAPTER 54

When he reached Dalita's house, the two kids were playing with a big plastic fire truck in the driveway, Paolo steering while his younger sister pushed him.

"Good deal." Grady hopped out of the pickup and gave the boy a high five. "Your moms home?"

Stella ran off into the house, yelling, "Momalita! That man is here."

Grady grabbed the post-hole digger, his toolbox, and the cans of sealant and roofing tar from the back of the truck and set them down. Dalita stepped onto the sidewalk, shading her eyes.

"What man? Oh, *that* man." She shook her head. "You barely even a man. My son Tim's here, he can help you if you need to carry anything else in."

"No prob, I've got it."

Frowning, Dalita peered at Grady's face. "What happened to you? Get in a fight at Fitzie's?"

"I bashed my head against the screen door. I had to go to the hardware store so I can repair the screen. I got you some stuff." Grady pointed. "Some more WaterSeal in case you need it, and—hey, watch it!"

He nabbed the post-hole digger from Paolo, who was trying to swing it at his sister, and handed it to Dalita. "You really need one of these if you're going to be putting anything in the ground. And this, and this . . ." He hefted the can of roofing tar in one hand, and in the other a six-pack of PBR he'd picked up on the way here. "That WaterSeal's okay for rain and stuff, but it's not going to do anything if the posts are buried." He looked at Stella. "Otherwise the whole thing's gonna tip over first time you climb on it."

Stella grinned. "Yeah!"

"They'd love that." Dalita took the six-pack and walked inside, Grady trailing behind her. She shoved the beer into the fridge and they headed into the backyard. "I should just leave those boards where they are and let them bash each other with them. That's the most fun, right, kids?"

Paolo and Stella ran for the stacked lumber and tried to drag a piece across the lawn. Lorelei strode outside, followed by a heavyset teenager in a cropped The Hu T-shirt and cargo shorts.

"Hey, that's enough, you two," she yelled. "Stella, go feed your lizards—one of them is eating the gecko. Paolo, your turn to clean the cat box."

Stella shrieked, either in delight or dismay. She ran inside, followed by her brother. The teenage boy, Tim, stood in the shade and avoided eye contact with Grady. He looked like he worked out, with well-defined muscles in his chest and arms, but his face had a softness that made Grady think he'd probably been a pudgy kid not that long ago. He had large dark eyes and curly black hair, like his mother's, that hung past his shoulders. A sweet kid, maybe someone who got knocked around a bit by other boys, though Grady bet Lorelei and Dalita would kick ass if they ever caught that going on.

"I'm Grady." Grady held out his hand, then dropped it. "Sorry, I keep forgetting."

"He's okay." Dalita turned to Tim. "He's been in quarantine this whole time. This is Tim."

Tim raised his head to give Grady a studied look, taking in the goose egg on Grady's forehead. "Nice to meet you." His voice was high and boyish.

"You too." Grady turned to Dalita. "So, where're the instructions for this thing?"

They went inside, where Stella stared raptly at a small terrarium. "I watched Kuku eat him," she said without looking up. "His tail was hanging out of Kuku's mouth."

"Sweet." Tim peered over.

"That's disgusting." Dalita rifled a stack of papers until she found a ziplock bag. "Here we go."

Back outside, Grady perused the instructions and accompanying hardware—screws, bolts, hinges, brackets, and safety handles, swing hangers. Dalita watched him with interest.

"What do you do if you don't have the right tools?"

"You make do."

"It's all supposed to be precut and premeasured." Dalita began sorting the lumber. "And numbered."

"Yeah, well, let's make sure. Measure twice, cut once. I always measure three times. Tim, you down for this?" Tim nodded with disinterest. "Okay, your first job is to go through this list and make sure everything's here, all the screws and stuff, and also all the lumber."

They spent the next hours doing the preliminary work. Tim and Grady took turns manning the post-hole digger. After a while, Lorelei came out and peered at Grady's forehead.

"I hope Lita didn't give you that."

"He walked into a 'door,'" Dalita explained, making quotes with her fingers. "You finish your Zoom call?"

"Yeah. Wedding at that farm in 'Io. Two grooms, four witnesses. Everybody's from Seattle. They say they've quarantined. First wedding I've shot since April," she said to Grady. "At least it's something. What can I do to help?"

She joined Dalita in applying WaterSeal to the wood, leaning each piece against the house to dry in the sun. Stella and Paolo ran over periodically to plead to help.

"Go make sure there's no spiders in those post holes," Dalita ordered. "And watch out for fire ants!"

The sealant needed two hours to dry, so they took a break. The adults each had a beer while Tim nursed a Capri Sun. The younger kids took turns holding the resigned-looking cat, Peanut. Tim's phone rang, its tone a hoarse male voice bellowing in a language Grady couldn't recognize. Tim hurried inside.

"Mongolian heavy metal," explained Lorelei. "He and his friends, they have a band."

"Had a band," said Dalita. "Before COVID fucked up everything." She sighed. "This probably means I'll have to drive him back to his dad's."

"Take the kids. Grady and I can finish here." Lorelei gazed at the tools and lumber scattered across the lawn. She laughed. "Or something."

"Can someone drive me and Iko to Kahawai?"

Grady looked up to see Tim in the doorway, phone still pressed to his ear.

"Yeah, I'll take you." Dalita got to her feet. "Stella and Paolo, let's move!"

"Noooo," Tim started to complain, but Dalita cut him off.

"That's the deal. Unless your dad wants to come get you. Lor, I'll take them for shave ice after I drop off Tim, so you and Grady can keep working. Grady, you had shave ice yet?"

"What is it?"

"Basically a sno-cone, but a hundred times better. Too bad, the play set not pau. Next time."

CHAPTER 55

D alita and the kids left. Grady finished his beer. He was surprised at how strong Lorelei was. He'd expected that with Dalita, because she'd worked as Minton's caretaker. Lorelei seemed more of a city girl, with her emerald buzz cut and bone jewelry, that elegant tattoo. But she could heft the posts with no trouble, and handled tools with ease.

As they worked, the late-afternoon sun moved past the papaya trees, beating down on their heads. They were both drenched in sweat. "I could use some of that shaved ice," Grady said. He removed his T-shirt and used it to mop his face.

"Here it's shave ice," Lorelei corrected him. "She must've taken the kids to the beach. Tim's dad lets him and his friends practice at his place—he lives up-country, so the neighbors won't complain."

"It's good that everyone seems to get along."

Lorelei nodded. "Yeah, we do. You have to here—everyone knows everyone else's business. And it's just better for the kids. You want another beer? Or something else? I'm gonna have a gin and tonic."

They went inside, Grady grateful to be out of the sun. He got a PBR while Lorelei made herself a gin and tonic, heavy on the ice and lemon. She pressed the glass to her cheek as they walked back out, standing under the eaves to survey the play set.

"It looks good." Lorelei raised her glass to Grady, and he clinked his beer can against it. "That would have sat there for another month before we even started on it. Thanks for helping out."

"No prob. I was happy to have something to do. I've been going kind of stir-crazy up there."

He took a long swallow, and Lorelei wrinkled her nose. "I honestly do not see how you can drink that."

"Nothin' bettah than a pibbah," Grady replied, putting on a thick Maine accent. "'Cep a pibbah and a jibbah. PBR and a joint," he translated.

"I can fix that." Lorelei stepped inside, returning with a tightly rolled joint and another beer for Grady.

He eyed the joint warily. Considering how toasted he'd gotten on Dalita's weed gummy, maybe he should stick with beer.

Still, there was something to be said for cold ones and rolled ones on a sunny afternoon in Hawai'i with friends. "Thanks," he said, and accepted the joint.

CHAPTER 56

They shared a few hits, settling at the picnic table beneath the umbrella. Grady stared at the trees. He recognized a small flock of birds, warbling as they hopped from branch to branch, searching for insects.

"Java sparrows," he said, pointing. "Right? And that's a house finch by the tricycle."

Lorelei shrugged. "If you say so. Tell me, what do you do up there all day at Wes's?"

"Learn about birds." He laughed. "Not much. I feel like I'm baby-sitting a house. And the aviary."

"Isn't that what caretakers do?"

"I guess." Grady gazed at the play set. "But when I've done stuff like that before, the owners have a list of projects. Wes doesn't. He's never around, and I feel weird starting on stuff without talking to him first."

"He's out at the point?"

"Yeah. Have you been there?"

"The only person I know who's ever been there is Uncle Honey."

"The delivery guy?"

She nodded. "He does that for Wes, but he was a research scientist from Harvard. He came here years ago for vacation and never left. Now he's working with a biotech firm to kill off the mosquitoes. We had no mosquitoes in Hawai'i till 1827—an English ship dumped barrels of stagnant water on Maui. Boom: avian malaria and mass bird die-offs on all the islands. They carry dengue fever too—there was an outbreak in Maui ten, fifteen years ago. Yet another reason they should make the day we killed Captain Cook a state holiday.

"But the mosquitoes didn't reach here till the early 1900s. Same thing happened: native species went extinct. The biotech company says they can eliminate the mosquitoes through gene editing." Lorelei made a face. "What could possibly go wrong? But Wes wants to have a research station out there. You can do a lot with a billion dollars."

Seeming agitated, she stood and nipped inside, returning with a freshly brimming drink for herself and a plate of cut-up pineapple and papaya, which she set in front of Grady.

"Hokuloa was protected by the same family for centuries," she said as he picked up a chunk of papaya. "They didn't own the land, not like haoles do, but they kept an eye on it. People were respectful, so there wasn't much trouble.

"But after a while, the family's children moved to the mainland, or died, and almost no one was left. By the early 1900s, the responsibility fell to a girl named Irma Ohelo, who left and went to Hollywood. She became a silent movie star called Vera Ashanti."

"I never heard of her."

"No one has, now. But for a couple of years she was the shit—she did all these quote, unquote exotic movies where she played the jungle princess or high priestess. Eventually she cashed out, married an old rich guy, and moved to Florida. When he died, she moved back here. She still had a claim to the land, but she knew not to build at Hokuloa Point, except for a little cottage where she could sleep. She put in a narrow road—no room to pass, just big enough she could get out there in whatever kind of car she had. No one ever went out there because they knew it was precious land. Sacred. Wes didn't do much to the road, but he did build out there. Nobody knows what he's done, really, but I heard he put in some big house. Illegal, but you get enough money . . ." She shrugged. "I know he built a big gate to keep everybody out."

"How did Wes end up owning the peninsula?"

"He inherited it. Irma Ohelo had no kids. Complicated story—I heard she had no will, so Hokuloa went to a great-nephew named Otto, whose family had moved to L.A. from the Big Island. Not a blood relation—related by marriage. He planned to develop it, but in the meantime he built the original big house on the property where Wes lives now. Otto hardly ever stayed there, so he sold it to Niles Jarbash.

"Then Otto died, and his son, Wes, inherited it all. By then, Niles and his wife had divorced, and she'd gotten the house, which she sold to Wes. He moved here from Los Angeles. First thing he does, he goes out that little road to Hokuloa Point, sees the tiny house Irma built there, and immediately decides he's going to build an exclusive resort—totally off the grid. A dozen luxury houses, staff who'd be housed in a separate building. No vehicles. Everyone would have to arrive by boat or helicopter. He even had a name picked out—Kanaka Sun."

"What's 'kanaka' mean?"

"A man or a person. It doesn't make sense, but that's what Wes is like. He hired a graphic designer to come up with a logo, ordered uniforms for the staff, met with investors. Then, boom." Lorelei laughed in triumph. "Turns out he can't do a damn thing. Irma had put the entire peninsula under protective covenants. She should have just donated it to the island, but she never wanted anybody to go there. She wanted it to remain as it was."

"Is it?"

"Like I said, I heard he got some big house out there. Probably he paid off someone. Many people."

"Could Wes ever sell the land?"

"No. It has to remain in the family. And there is no family, other than Wes. I'll give him that—he turned on a dime once it became clear he couldn't develop it," Lorelei said with grudging admiration. "Like I told you, he got obsessed with the birds."

Grady nodded. "I get that. They're what keep me sane out there. Maybe him, too," he added, and laughed. "He told me he's seen honeycreepers out on Hokuloa Point that are extinct everywhere else. Where does he find them, the ones he keeps?"

"I don't know. It's illegal to catch them, but rich people make their own laws. He might've found the eggs and hand-raised them. Hard to do, though by now he may have established a breeding colony. But those birds shouldn't be caged. They're not pets."

Grady shifted uneasily. He'd thought the birds might be neutral for conversation, but obviously not. For a few moments neither of them spoke. Finally Grady took a long swallow of his beer, and then asked, "Why does Dalita hate Leonardo Sanchez?"

"I don't think anyone actually likes Leonardo, not after what he did."

"You mean the high school girls?"

Lorelei nodded. "And other things. But that was the worst. How'd you hear about it?"

"Somewhere online," he lied. "An old news story. What do you think's happened to him?"

She shook her head. "No idea. I know some people won't shed a tear if he's dead."

"Why do you think he's dead?"

"I don't. But he went missing while he was out surfing, and they found his board but not him. That sounds like he might have drowned or run into a shark."

"Don't you think it's weird that he and Jessica Kiyoko both went missing around the same time?"

Lorelei cocked her head, staring at him. "Weird how?"

"Just that they both disappeared. He has this history with women, right? Grooming girls, all that shit. It seems strange to me that he went missing around the same time she did."

"So what do you think happened?"

"I don't know," Grady said, increasingly uncomfortable under her intense gaze. "But what if he had something to do with her disappearance?"

"They didn't know each other."

"They knew people in common." He hesitated, thinking this through for the first time. "The person Jessie was staying with—Raina Mayhew. She was one of the girls Sanchez groomed, back when she was in high school."

"How do you know this, Grady?"

He wanted to lie again. Instead he stared at the table and said, "I talked to her. Raina. I saw a missing-person flyer with her number and called her."

"Have you talked to the police? Has she?"

"No. And I don't know. I doubt it."

Behind them, the door banged open for Dalita, holding a canvas bag of groceries. Lorelei frowned at her. "Where're the kids?"

"I ran into Suze and her kids at Mak Supe. They were headed to Kahawai, so I said Paolo and Stella could go with them. She's gonna bring them home in a bit. And guess what?" She turned to Grady. "Your girlfriend from the airplane—they found that guy with the hoodie, the guy in the security photo. Hang on and I'll tell you."

CHAPTER 57

D alita rejoined them, carrying a glass of white wine.

"I told Suze you knew that girl," she said to Grady. "Her brother's a PD dispatcher—he hears stuff. The guy in the security footage went to the police—you know him, Lor. Django Russo."

"Django?"

"Yeah, but he didn't do anything. Someone told him he was in that photo and he looked at it and said, 'Yeah, that's me.' Django walked out of Fitzie's right after that girl did. He said he kept an eye on her—she seemed drunk, and he didn't recognize her, so he assumed she might get lost. But she seemed to know where she was going, so he just went on home."

"But no one's heard from her since then," broke in Grady.

Dalita shook her head. "She's only been gone a few days—"

"Seven days! A week."

"Look who's counting!" Dalita snapped her fingers. "You getting little bit obsessed with this, yeah? You said yourself you only talked to her for a couple minutes on the plane."

"And by baggage claim."

Dalita leaned across the table. "I feel for that girl's family—they must be going out of their minds. But you're not her family, Grady. And she can turn up still."

"And if she doesn't, her name'll be up there on that fucking bunker with all the rest," he said. "So he had an alibi? Your pal Django?"

"He did," replied Dalita. "His roommate vouched for him—the two played *Fortnite* till three a.m. The police looked at the website and it all checked out." Her voice grew gentler. "They searching for her, Grady. But there's nothing you or either of us can do about it, not unless you know something?"

A sick feeling overcame Grady. For an instant the brilliant afternoon darkened.

"Grady. You okay?"

Dalita was staring at him. He waited for the nausea to fade, but it didn't. He squeezed his eyes shut, opened them again. "I need to tell you something," he said.

CHAPTER 58

I t all came out then, like he really was sick and spewing words. He told them how he'd gotten stoned, broken quarantine, and wandered down to Leonardo Sanchez's shack. He told them what he'd heard there, and what he'd later found on the beach, and also about the wild dog, the vandalized chamber, the ghost crabs and the eyeball. The thing that upset them most was the vandalized chamber.

"They stole the ki'i pōhaku?" Dalita demanded, and Lorelei cursed so loudly that Grady flinched. "With a fucking *jackhammer?*"

"You need to call the Conservation Department," Lorelei broke in.

"Really?"

Lorelei gave him a look as disdainful as it was condescending, and Grady turned away, ashamed. He'd been so fixated on his own fear, his guilt over not calling the police about a possible murder, his compulsion to find Jessica—it hadn't even crossed his mind to notify someone about the vandalized chamber.

"I'll call them," he said, without meeting Lorelei's gaze. "The conservation people, about the vandals."

"I'll give you their number. What else?"

He finished by telling them about seeing the doglike figure again the night he smashed his head against the door. He fell silent, then looked from Dalita to Lorelei. "So am I out of my mind?"

Neither of them spoke. But neither of them looked like they thought he was crazy.

Lorelei said, "So you heard someone screaming, a woman, and then you heard someone else being attacked. A man."

Grady nodded.

"Well." Lorelei took a sip of her drink. "My uncle Wei might say you saw a dog spirit. Heard it. There are a lot of dog spirits in Hawai'i. There are a lot of stories even now—urban legends—about one very dangerous dog spirit, a cannibal."

"Kaupe," said Grady. "I read about it online. Is that like kapu?"

"No," said Lorelei. "Totally different words. Kapu means 'forbidden,' something you don't do, or a place you don't go. But it also means 'sacred.' You still see signs everywhere, like 'No Parking' signs, that say 'Kapu.' A joke but serious. It's a way of showing respect. Kaupe is a kupua—a supernatural being. He lures people using a voice like somebody in danger. Then when you go to help them, he eats you."

She took another swallow of gin. "I studied folk literature and oral traditions at UH. Talk story. Ghost stories we heard as kids, urban legends. A lot of those came from Japanese immigrants, but there are also very ancient stories that people have been sharing for over a thousand years. Like the dog spirits. The details get changed around, so now people see dog-men by the Target access road, or they see dog-men with the Nightmarchers, not just in their ancestral home in Waikiki. They look like men, only they have tails."

Grady's eyes widened.

"You've heard of them?" asked Lorelei.

"I—I saw them. Pictures, online," he stammered, reluctant to bring up the chamber again. "But whatever I saw outside the 'ohana . . . it looked different. I guess because it seemed so real," he added with a shaky laugh.

Lorelei shrugged. "Maybe it was real."

"I gotta check in with Suze, see how the kids're doing," Dalita announced, and stood. "Lor knows more mo'olelo than all my uncles and aunties combined."

Grady wished he could follow her inside. He stared at his beer, conscious of Lorelei watching him. "That thing," he said at last. "Kaupe. Does it want to kill me?"

He regretted the question the second he asked it. Not because it felt ridiculous but because he was starting to fear it might be true.

"I don't know," Lorelei said slowly. "My father's parents and great-grandparents, they understand a lot more about these things than I ever will. My father's from here—he's mostly Hawai'ian and Filipino—but my mom's from Chicago, Roseland. I never knew her parents, or anyone from that side of the family. I've only been there once. But I always wanted to know about my ancestors—that's why I studied folklore. Things like what you saw—kupua, supernatural beings—if they exist, they're not going to think or act the way we do. They're not going to care about the same things."

Grady stared at her. Were they really having this conversation? Zeke would have produced more weed and excitedly jumped right in, but Grady felt like he'd wandered into a church where he didn't know anyone and didn't understand any of the rules.

Lorelei, though, seemed to be gaining steam. "It *is* strange that someone like you would see it, Grady. But maybe it can't tell us apart—where we're from, if we're Hawai'ian or not. I've always wanted to see something like that—like the Nightmarchers, even though when my uncle did, it terrified him." She glanced at Grady and shrugged. "I don't think it wants to kill you. I think it would have done that already if it wanted to."

"Thanks," he said weakly.

"And maybe the peninsula has remained unspoiled so long because its kupua protected it. Maybe the kupua was dormant, like Haleakalā, but something disturbed it. Someone."

"Me?"

She gave him a thin smile. "I doubt you're that important. More likely it's Wes, or whoever stole the ki'i pōhaku. But it might want to use you."

He started to argue but stopped. Could any of this be true? He'd been trying to convince himself that it couldn't possibly be, but that would mean he was delusional, or having some sort of breakdown.

Was this what had happened to his father? Had he cracked up, then killed himself?

He stared at Lorelei. She didn't seem to be regarding him as though she thought he was crazy. Arrogant and complacent and clueless, definitely, but not crazy.

"How would it use me?" he asked slowly.

Before she could reply, Dalita stepped back outside and held up her phone, her face tight.

"It's Tim," she said. "They found a body on the beach."

CHAPTER 59

The next few minutes were a flurry of pings, as Dalita frantically texted and read Tim's replies aloud.

"His dad drove him and his friends to Kahawai," she said. "I don't like him going there—last year they busted someone from Honolulu selling heroin and fentanyl. But his dad doesn't worry like I do."

"Is Tim okay?"

"He says they're all fine. He's with Bobby Lee and Sando. They're good kids," she added for Grady's benefit. "A surfer saw a body in the water—Akira, the bartender from Low Tide—and he called 911. Someone on a Jet Ski got there before the ambulance and brought the body to shore. The police are there now questioning everyone."

Grady's mind spun, praying, *Not Jessie, not Jessie, please don't let it be Jessie,* even though he knew how futile that was. He didn't believe in God. Until he came here, he didn't believe in creatures that lured you by screaming like a woman in danger. Now he was starting to realize he'd been wrong about at least one of those things.

"Do they know if it's a man or a woman?" he asked. "The body?"

"Tim didn't say. Or, no—he said Akira thought at first it might be Leonardo. So I guess it's a man."

Dalita raised her screen so they could see the photo sent by Tim. Uniformed figures surrounded something on the sand, observed by scattered onlookers. Grady squinted at the screen. "Do you think it's Leonardo?"

Dalita shook her head. "Police not going say nothing till they notify his family. Whoever he is."

Grady ran his hands through his hair. He had to get out of here. Drive to that beach, see the body for himself. Maybe something on it would absolve his constant guilt over not running to help when he first heard those screams.

"I gotta go." He stood. "Thanks for lunch."

"Thank *you*." Dalita lowered her phone, and he saw the effort it took for her to smile. "You put together that entire play set. It would have taken me and Lor a month."

"It would have taken us a year." Lorelei touched Grady's arm. "Come for dinner in a few days? We can sit outside."

"That would be great," he said, and left.

He drove through town, pulling over in front of a strip mall. Everything was closed except for a tiny coffee shop, its front door propped open with a sidewalk sign.

WE ARE OPEN!
BEST COFFEE ON ISLAND
ASK ANYONE THEY'LL TELL YOU

Grady pulled on his mask and hurried inside. He needed to clear his head. The middle-aged Japanese woman behind the counter greeted him cheerfully.

"Beautiful day!"

"Sure is." He hadn't seen a day yet that wasn't.

He waited while she heated milk for his latte. A pair of tablets sat on the counter, one for the register, the other open to the *Island Pilot* home page.

BREAKING NEWS: BODY FOUND AT KAHAWAI

"Here you are." The woman set down his latte, glancing at the tablet. "They found a man there."

"They know it's a man?" Grady paid with his debit card, leaving a five-dollar tip.

"My sister told me it's a young man who went missing a while ago. He got in trouble with those people by the old high school, living in a school bus." She wiped her eyes on a paper napkin. "That's a bad place."

"Kahawai?"

"The old high school, but Kahawai, too. That beach used to be so beautiful—we went there all the time when we were kids. Drum circles, surfing. Then runoff from the pineapple plantation got into the gulch. The pollution caused a big die-off, fishes and coral—whatever was in that runoff, it ate right through everything. They had to shut the beach for a while. That was a long time ago. Then the plantation closed and they cleaned it up. You used to be able to drink out of that stream. But maybe you know all this."

"No." He stepped away from the counter, lowering his mask to sip his latte. "This is good."

"Mahalo. It's the best coffee on the island. Don't believe me, they'll tell you." She flapped a hand at the empty sidewalk. "I still got customers. But afternoons are slow. Everything slow, because of COVID. You're visiting?"

"Yeah. From Maine."

"I went there once, Acadia. It was beautiful." She laughed at his surprised expression. "I took a cruise up to Newfoundland. You come here, we go there. It all comes around. This will end."

She looked again at the tablet. "Someone died there last spring, but that was a flash flood. That girl they found in the forest, she was lucky."

"What girl?"

"That girl from Li'ulā who went for a hike and they didn't find her for almost two weeks. Last fall. Local woman, she went up to the waterfall and she ends up in Pohihihi Gulch. Two weeks. If it had rained she would've drowned. Those gulches, you have to watch out for them. Nice talking to you," she said, turning away. "You have a good day, now."

"You too." In the doorway he stopped. "That beach, Kahawai—how far away is that?"

"Half an hour. Everything is half an hour, except Hokuloa. But you can't go there," she said.

CHAPTER 60

At Kahawai Beach, the pavement ended but the road continued onto the sand, ending at a low wall of rough black stone. Beyond it, a parking area held a dozen trucks and beat-up cars, a Westfalia van, and an old Airstream with a pop-up tent beside it. Also, two police cars, one with its blue lights still flashing, and an ambulance. A couple of cops chatted with the EMTs — strong, intimidating guys wearing sunglasses and sturdy black boots. He felt a flicker of envy. He wouldn't have been able to cut it on this crew. They looked more like bouncers or bodyguards.

He parked, got out, and scanned the beach, not sure what he was looking for. The body was hidden under a white tarp. The police had staked out a staging area around it with yellow tape, but apart from a small knot of rubberneckers, most people seemed to have lost interest. Surfers chased the barrel waves while several old men ambled along the shore, talking. A golden retriever loped across the parking lot until a cop yelled at its owner.

Grady walked down to the ocean, one of the cops glancing up as he passed. When he reached the water, he stood and watched the surfers for a few minutes. His bruised forehead stung as sweat trickled down it, and he adjusted his cap. Turning, he headed to the big black rocks at the far end of the beach. His arms ached from the work he'd done that afternoon, lifting heavy lumber.

"Hey!" someone yelled at him.

Grady hadn't seen that three people stood in front of the rocks. He halted, lowering his sunglasses to get a better look. Two guys and a girl, a small beer cooler at her feet: the same three people he'd seen alongside the Westfalia van that morning on the beach highway. The girl now wore a sunhat and a loose white shift, and Grady recognized crazy-eyed Scotty in his sarong. The other guy, the one with the buzz cut, wore sunglasses, but Grady had the distinct impression he wasn't giving him a friendly look.

The girl had her hands on her hips and her head cocked. Grady uneasily looked from her to the others. He lifted his chin to acknowledge them, and started walking to the parking lot.

"Hey!" the buzz-cut guy yelled again. "That your truck over there?"

Grady paused. Had someone broken into the pickup? He glanced in the direction of the parking lot.

" 'Drive wit Al.' " The man strode toward Grady. "That you?"

Grady said nothing. Coming to a stop, the man smelled of rum and weed, but he didn't move like someone who was drunk or stoned. He moved like the guys on Grady's high school wrestling team, sizing him up, intent.

"Chris," the girl called.

The guy, Chris, ignored her. He stared at Grady.

"You work for him. Minton, out on Hokuloa Road." He pushed up his sunglasses to get a better look at Grady, took in his bruised forehead and shook his head. "Someone got there first," he said.

He swung at Grady, so fast Grady couldn't even blink. His fist slammed him in the gut, right below his ribs. Grady gagged as his sunglasses went flying. He doubled over, tried to duck as Chris took another swing, this time clipping his shoulder. Grady fell to the sand, clutching his abdomen.

"Chris." Dimly he saw the girl above him, grabbing Chris by the arm and staring in the direction of the cops. "Come on. You know it's not him."

"I don't give a fuck. He's at Minton's . . ."

The girl pulled him away. Grady spat out blood where he'd bitten his lip. He lay there until he could breathe again, then gingerly pushed himself up. The sun beat down as he touched his chest, ran his fingers across his ribs. Nothing seemed broken.

"What the fuck," he murmured.

He saw his cap and sunglasses, both undamaged, put them on and slowly got to his feet. Chris, the girl, and Scotty stood by the rocks, staring past Grady. He glanced over his shoulder. One of the cops was looking their way. Grady lifted his hand, indicating everything was fine, just another haole getting decked on the beach. He didn't know what the fuck had just happened, or why, but he knew the police wouldn't make it better.

Grady took a deep breath and started back to the lot, glancing behind him to see Chris with his arms crossed, watching him. The girl sat in the driver's seat of the van.

"Chris!" she yelled. "Come on."

Yeah, you do that, Chris, Grady thought, and angrily kicked at a rock. He got only a few more feet before someone grabbed his arm.

"I know what you saw." It was Scotty.

The wind stirred his long, matted blond hair. He was so thin his ribs looked like they might poke through his skin, like a pencil through paper. He was younger than Grady, his skin thickened and turned the color of old brick by sun and salt. The bruised flesh around his eyes appeared charred.

"On Hokuloa Road. I've seen it, too."

Scotty had a young voice. Maybe he wasn't even twenty, maybe he was still a teenager, everything young about him burned away like he'd been set on fire. His eyes were the palest gray Grady had ever seen.

"I know what you saw," he repeated. "It told me, too."

He stared at Grady without blinking and opened his mouth, wider and wider, head tilting back until Grady couldn't see his lips anymore, only his teeth, a few of them missing. Grady tried to take a step back, but somehow he couldn't. He could only stare at Scotty's swollen tongue, his throat, and then something else, something with long sticklike legs that emerged from Scotty's throat, its legs twitching against his blackened lips.

No. This couldn't be happening. Grady struck wildly at the air and started to run, his feet sliding on the sand. He nearly tripped, but he caught himself, looked back to see Scotty still there, his hands limp at his sides and his black mouth yawning in a soundless scream as he stared straight into the sun.

CHAPTER 61

G rady reached the parking lot and stopped in the shade of a tall metal sign, retching as he fought to catch his breath. *What the fuck, what the fuck was that?*

Chest heaving, Grady could barely bring himself to look back, but when he did, Scotty was still on the beach, kicking at the waves, laughing to himself.

No one in the parking lot took any notice of Grady. He removed his sunglasses and rubbed his eyes, wiped his mouth on his sleeve. Not much more blood.

He started toward the pickup, whirled when he heard some-one running up behind him. He relaxed, unclenching his fists. "Raina. Hi."

She frowned, taking in his face. "You okay?"

"Yeah." He rubbed his shoulder. "Just some asshole took a swing at me."

Raina glanced at Scotty, now standing in knee-deep water, his back to them. "Not Scotty?"

"No, his friend. Big guy, Chris. So ugly even the tide wouldn't take him out. He doesn't seem to like my truck. Minton's truck," he corrected himself. He looked at the water, shuddering at the memory of those sticklike legs protruding from a person's mouth. "Is his name really Scotty?"

"That's what everyone calls him. Like, 'Beam me up, Scotty.' His real name's Lucas. He used to be fine, this sweet kid. But something bad happened to him. A couple years ago he started talking about how he'd been kidnapped and seen aliens and monsters. Now he's a lost soul."

"Well, his friend's an asshole."

"Chris isn't a bad guy. He and his girlfriend keep an eye on Scotty. Keep him safe, get him to eat when they can. Did you say something to him? Chris?"

"No, I didn't fucking say something! He said something about the truck, asked if it was mine. Then he decked me. He doesn't seem to like Minton."

"Nobody likes Minton." She reached to touch his forehead. "He do that to you?"

Grady flinched. He got why Dalita and Lorelei didn't like Minton, but what was with this asshole Chris, and now Raina? "No. I'm fine. Forget it."

"All right," she said. She looked better than the last time he'd seen her, dressed in a flowy blue dress with no sleeves, her hair pulled back in a loose braid. No mask. She had on a little makeup, pink on her lips and something shimmery on her cheeks. Blue fingernail polish. When she lifted her sunglasses, her dark eyes appeared golden in the sun. "How's it otherwise?"

"Same. I was in town, helping out Dalita with something, and her son texted they found a body on the beach. I guess it's a man?"

"That's what I heard."

She nudged the sand with one foot. Grady nodded in the direction of the police. "So that's good, maybe. It's not Jessie."

"Not so good for him. I heard it might be Leonardo."

Grady stared at her. "Leonardo, the guy who . . ."

She nodded, her eyes bright with relief, or malice, or both. "Someone was bringing heroin and ice here, fentanyl, coming from other islands by boat. I heard this beach was where they'd drop it. He stopped grooming girls for sex and started selling them that shit. He's not a good dude."

Grady watched a man step over the yellow tape, the cops moving aside so he could examine the body.

"That's Fairchild," said Raina. "The police detective. He's the one told me I needed to make better choices. I'm fourteen and being pimped out and I need to make better choices. Better choices in police, for sure." She looked up at Grady. "So, what do you think? Need a drink?"

"Yeah," he said, still dazed from getting sucker-punched. And anything was better than staying near Scotty. Plus, after his desperate Google searches, he could use her perspective. "Fitzhugh's?"

"Let's go to my house. I don't feel like seeing anyone. You remember the address? Yeah? Okay, I'll meet you there."

She turned and walked to her old Outback. Grady headed to his truck. He removed a metal scraper from his toolbox and stooped to scrub the faded sticker from his bumper, letting the bits of shriveled plastic blow away in the wind.

CHAPTER 62

He stopped to buy a six-pack for himself and a chilled bottle of white wine for Raina. She'd been drinking beer last time at Fitzie's, but maybe she'd appreciate the effort, make it easier for him to find out more about Jessie. Driving to her place, he almost popped a beer in the car, to wash away the thought of Scotty's ravaged face and something crawling from his mouth. Instead he turned up the radio as loud as it would go, not even registering what blasted out of the speakers.

Raina's apartment was small, the living room opening onto the kitchen. It was very, very neat, and very, very yellow. Yellow futon couch with bright yellow pillows, a galley kitchen with yellow and orange cookware stacked on metal shelves. Small flat-screen TV above a yellow circular table with two chairs. The walls were decorated with a hat woven of palm leaves and dried leis, and a framed poster from the island aquarium — an underwater shot of a coral reef teeming with fish, a huge sea turtle floating lazily in the foreground. On the floor beside the couch sat a suitcase he recognized as Jessie's, draped with an oversized pink T-shirt.

Raina handed him a beer and poured herself some wine. "Sit wherever you want."

He settled on the futon, beneath a paper light fixture hanging from the ceiling. "IKEA?"

"How'd you know?"

"I'm a carpenter. I installed a lamp just like that one. Fluffy Cloud, right? The name of the lamp?"

She nodded. "You have a good memory."

"You never forget your first Fluffy Cloud," he said, and she laughed.

He popped his beer, took a drink, and leaned back against the couch. It was a relief to be sitting somewhere different, especially after busting his nut for most of the afternoon, putting up the play set. Getting clocked by someone he didn't even know.

And he had to admit, it felt good to be here with Raina. She seemed more relaxed than he'd ever seen her, not that he'd seen her much. Probably because she was in her own place. Though maybe she'd decided he was an okay guy, and not just another asshole haole. He hoped that was the case.

She noticed him looking at her and smiled. "So you install a lot of lamps?"

"Enough. Before everything shut down. I do woodworking and electrical, some plumbing. Mostly carpentry. What about you?"

"I worked at the aquarium." She cocked a thumb at the poster of the sea turtle. "It's on the west side of the island—you probably haven't been there. And it's closed because of the pandemic."

"An aquarium. Sweet," he said. "Because of your marine biology, right?"

"Not that sweet—I worked in the gift shop. So mostly just dealing with a million tourists every day, and two million schoolkids." She laughed again. "Minimum wage, but I did get some health insurance. Best thing was I could go to the aquarium whenever I wanted for free. And lectures, stuff like that. They have these scientists come in and talk about sea turtles, humpbacks, coral reefs. Birds, too. I took some marine biology classes there. Not for credit—adult ed—but one day I'll go back and finish my degree. Jessie said she'd help me with the applications for financial aid. And Laura, the woman in charge of education, she told me I could apply to become a docent. COVID shut all that down. I really miss working there," she said wistfully.

"But not the two million schoolkids."

"I don't even miss one of them. Well, maybe one or two. It's definitely lonelier now." She kicked off her sandals and flexed her bare feet, tanned except for a white V from the straps. "I can't hardly see anyone because of my mom's COPD. I can't take a chance of making her sick. I used to see her every day. And Jessie . . ." Her eyes welled. "I really wanted her to be here."

Grady swallowed, unsure how to react. Before he could reply, she said, "At least I get unemployment. When everything opens up again, it'll be easier."

"You think everything will reopen?"

"You joking? Fast as they can. The island wants those tourist dollars. People from Houston need their hot stone massages and mai tai dolphin cruises."

"At least you're not cooped up in a city apartment." Grady took a long pull at his beer. "Like in Maine, at least we can go outside."

He realized he was staring at her and looked away. Again he marveled at how neat her apartment was. Most of the guys he knew were slobs. So were most of the women. Like Rachel. Especially Rachel. That was one of the things they used to argue about when he'd stay over at her place. It was like being in his brother's bedroom.

He said, "Your place is really nice."

"Thanks. My dad was a real neat freak when I was growing up."

"Are you close to him?"

"He took off when I was in high school. I don't even know if he's alive. This one therapist, that's all she ever wanted to talk about—my dad and how I felt. Like that was what messed me up, not getting fucked by a bunch of old men when I was fourteen."

"I'm sorry."

"For what? You didn't rape me."

"I've never raped anyone." He finished his beer and stared at the floor, pushing down his anger. When he felt more calm he asked, "Okay if I get another?"

"Sure."

He got his beer and sat back on the couch. Neither of them spoke.

"Maybe this might help them figure out what's been going on," Grady said at last. "The police."

"What do you mean? What might help them?"

"That body on the beach." He paused. Just a few hours ago, he wouldn't have spoken so openly. But that reluctance was gone. "What if it's all connected somehow," he said, "all the disappearances here. Not just Jessie but her and everyone else. What if there's someone, one person, who's attacking them?"

"Like who?"

"Like Leonardo, for one."

"Leonardo?" She seemed taken aback.

"Yeah, Leonardo! He's pimping out high school girls, selling heroin. He might've abducted Jessie."

"Jessie? Why would he abduct Jessie?"

"Why not? He knows you. Did he know her, too?"

"No. I mean, she knows who he is, she knows what happened to me—"

"So who's to say he didn't follow her coming out of Fitzie's?"

Raina shook her head. "I don't think he'd do that."

"Why not?"

"It would be too stupid, even for him. Dealing drugs—I'm sure the cops are in on that. But if Leonardo abducted someone now, after what happened with me—he'd never get away with it."

"Even if the cops looked the other way?"

"Cops here do what they can to cover their ass, and keep the tourists coming. No tourists now, so I think they'd be more focused on covering their ass."

"Okay." Grady nodded. "But still, this body, it might—"

"It might *crack the case*? Brah, you are smoking some Hawai'i Five-O."

"Yeah, okay," he snapped. "I get it—I'm a haole and I don't understand anything that happens here."

"You're right," she said. "You don't."

"But *something* is happening. If there's a serial killer, this is when you find him, while the island's on lockdown. The cops could go through a list of everyone who's landed in the last few months and track wherever they've been."

"You realize that would include you."

"Well, yeah," he said, though he hadn't. "But you get my point. A serial killer could visit here repeatedly over the years, commit a murder, leave, and never get found out. There're no tourists on the island now, and people are still disappearing! That suggests that—"

"Stop." Raina raised a hand. "You think there's a single solution— one person, one killer, all these dead people? Over, like, decades or a hundred years? And you—special Grady—for some reason, you're the one who's figured it out?"

She leaned forward, and for a second he thought she'd take his hand. "What if it's one murderer for every victim—not one killer, dozens of them. Hundreds."

"That's crazy," Grady said.

"Crazy?" Raina countered triumphantly, like he'd walked into a trap. "When a woman is killed here, or anywhere, it's nearly always by the guy she's with, or someone she knows."

"Yeah, okay," he said. It *had* been a trap. "That's true. But a lot of the missing people here, they're not women—"

"But nothing. They could still all be killed by someone they know."

"But that means there could be—I dunno—a hundred murderers on this island."

"Just like everywhere."

"Right." He recalled when he met Raina at Fitzhugh's, how she'd seemed kind of crazy but mostly vulnerable. Now she seemed kind of crazy again.

Then again, he was the one who'd been seeing things. He thought again of Scotty, his burned-out face and pinhole eyes, his mouth opening like a black hole had been torn in his face.

"Point taken," he said at last. "But all those people, they've . . . vanished. How could so many guys kill their wives or girlfriends or kids or whoever, and somehow make their bodies completely disappear?" He hesitated, took a deep breath. "It could be something else."

Raina stared at him.

"What if it's something nobody has seriously considered yet?" Grady went on, slowly. "What if it's . . . something . . . that no one ever talks about?"

CHAPTER 63

Raina stared at him. "What do you mean?"

"The other night—"

A knock at the door made them both jump.

"Rainy Day!" a stout, bearded man yelled as he stepped inside, a plastic bag in each hand. "Dinner delivery—oh, you got company."

"Angelo!" Raina ran over to him and hugged him as though Grady wasn't there. "Aw, thank you!"

"Mochiko chicken and mac salad. I went to Spunky's. There're some fries, too."

"You're the best!" She took the bags and peered inside one, releasing the smell of fried chicken. Angelo looked at Grady.

"This is Grady, he's someone I met a few days ago," Raina explained. "A friend of Jess's."

Angelo nodded. He was beefy, not as tall as Grady, dark-skinned, his brown hair shaved close at the sides and sticking up in a modified brush cut at the top, which made him look like a cop. He wore a rumpled white shirt, the sleeves rolled up, and black pants. A lanyard was tucked into his shirt pocket, its cord dangling across his chest.

"Do I need to put my mask on?" he called after Raina, who'd walked into the kitchen area.

"Only if you want. I think he's safe. You safe, Grady?"

Grady looked at Angelo and shrugged. "I guess."

"I only got two plates." Angelo sank into a chair. He watched as Raina opened cardboard containers and exclaimed over the contents. "I woulda got more if I knew." He gave Grady a pained look.

"That's okay." Grady put his hands on his knees, his mouth watering. The food smelled fantastic. "I guess I should go . . ."

"Don't be stupid—there's plenty," said Raina. "We can share."

"Well, thanks." Grady smiled at her, then at Angelo. "Thanks, man."

Angelo sighed. "Yeah, sure. Just I didn't know." He hooked a finger through the lanyard cord, pulled the card from his shirt pocket and slid it into his wallet. "I'm Angelo Viela. Raina's cousin."

"Grady Kendall. I got a job here a few weeks ago."

It felt awkward not to shake hands. Grady glanced to where Raina was scooping food onto plates. Angelo took out his cell phone, only to hop up when Raina appeared with a plate in each hand.

"Let's eat on the deck." She handed one plate to Grady, the other to her cousin. "Angelo, you want a beer? You're off duty, right?"

"Sure. I'm done till Monday."

"Won't Lois be mad you didn't bring any to her?"

"She and the kids went to Ma's for dinner. I'm too tired. You're all I can stand right now."

The deck turned out to be a tiny back balcony, concrete floor and metal railing, with a few chairs, a TV tray, and a lush yellow hibiscus in a terra cotta pot. Raina sat, motioning for Grady to take the chair beside hers. Angelo scooted his chair away in a futile effort at social distancing.

"Brah, relax," Raina scolded him, and pointed her fork at Grady. "He's been in quarantine."

"Yeah, okay." Angelo started eating. "You at the hotel by the airport?"

"No. I'm a caretaker." Grady took a bite of chicken. "Man, this is delicious," he said, hoping to avoid the topic of Minton's.

"Spunky's makes the best mochiko chicken." Raina ate a piece in two bites.

"Caretaker, huh? Yeah, a lot of those big stars aren't here," said Angelo between mouthfuls. "They're stuck in California or Wyoming or some shit."

"I didn't know so many celebrities lived here," said Grady.

Angelo nodded. "Shit ton famous people live here."

"Angelo works at Serenity," said Raina.

"The resort? I thought they were all closed."

"I'm security," said Angelo.

"The *only* security," Raina said. "There're, like, three thousand rooms, and he's the only guy."

"Not that many," Angelo allowed. "One thousand seven hundred and forty-two. But, yeah, it's nuts. Tomas over at Royal Keawa, at least there's him and two other guys, they can talk and shit. I just talk to myself and listen to the squawker. I do get more exercise, walking." He patted his belly. "Lost seven pounds."

Raina and Angelo made small talk as they ate. Grady couldn't see much physical resemblance between the two of them, but they could be second cousins. Or maybe "cousin" meant something different, and they were just close family friends. He was content to half listen, staring out across the parking lot. Two boys skateboarded past, pushing off from cars and yelling at each other, their voices as high as birds'. Cigarette smoke drifted from another apartment, the echo of an argument that dissolved into laughter. He tuned back in to the conversation.

"Yeah, I was there," Raina was saying. "I wanted to know if it was Jessie. That's how I ran into this one. He and Jess met on the plane over."

Angelo shook his head. "She's a good girl, Jessie. Thank the Lord it wasn't her at Kahawai. I still think she'll turn up, Rainy." He reached over to squeeze her shoulder. "Like that girl in the forest. She was saved."

"But Jessie wasn't in the forest. She was right outside the Quad. Someone abducted her."

"I still think she'll be okay. That wasn't her on the beach, anyway."

Grady turned to Angelo. "Do you know who it was?"

"Just that it was a male. They won't have ID'd him yet."

Angelo paused to eat a mouthful of macaroni salad and went on. "But you know, a call came through dispatch yesterday, I listened in. Guy fishing in his boat way out past Hokuloa Cove saw someone swimming. Trying to swim—the current is real bad there. He radioed it in and took his boat over, but by then the person was gone."

"Huh. I didn't see that online." Grady set his empty plate on the table.

"Everyone is so worked up over all the COVID since Fourth of July, police don't want to give them something else to scream about. Could have been a turtle. Or, you know, a shark might have gotten him."

Raina shuddered. "Don't say that."

"They didn't find anything. No distress calls. Police contacted that rich guy at Hokuloa. He said he hadn't seen anyone."

"It could be the same person," said Grady. "The body on the beach."

"Yeah, maybe. Current doesn't run that way usually. But tourists go out alone, they get in trouble easy. The area around Hokuloa Point is a dangerous place to be snorkeling." Angelo took another bite of mac salad. "And Kahawai's sketchy. Plainclothes policeman took one of those kids away a few weeks ago. Jimmy Tobin told me, my daughter's boyfriend? One of those homeless kids camping there—Jimmy said he was selling ice." He sighed loudly. "It's not like when we were kids, Rainy Day."

"We used to do mushrooms! You wanted to swim out to see the whales and I had to drag you back!"

"Yeah, sure." Angelo shrugged. "But we weren't selling them."

"I was!"

Grady finished his beer. "So, you think it might be Leonardo?"

Raina laughed. "I should be so lucky."

CHAPTER 64

Grady got to his feet. He felt like he'd overstayed his welcome, even though he'd been there first. "Nice to meet you," he said to Angelo. "Thanks for dinner."

Angelo nodded. "See you."

Raina followed Grady out the apartment door. She leaned over the rail, staring down at the street before turning back to him. "Sorry about my cousin."

"Why? He seems nice. The food was great."

"Yeah, no, Angelo's the best. Just..." She cocked her head, a strand of hair falling across one cheek. "I wasn't expecting him. Let me know if you want to hang out sometime."

"Oh." Grady tried not to look too surprised. "Sure. I'll text you."

Impulsively, he leaned over to put his arm around her. Not tightly, but in the awkward pandemic hug that felt like the way he'd slow-danced with girls in sixth grade. Afraid to get too close, but for different reasons. Her hair felt soft, not bleached out and stiff. Her skin smelled of sweat, of lemons and plumeria.

"I'd like that," he said.

She drew away from him. "Angelo, he's like my brother. He's a really good guy."

"I'm sorry about Sanchez—I shouldn't have brought it up."

"It's not a secret. Everyone knows he groomed girls back then, only no one has ever done anything."

He longed to tell her about the screams he'd heard by Sanchez's place. Instead he said, "That's creepy, what Angelo said about that swimmer."

"Yeah. But he's right, it might have been something else. A sea turtle. That fisherman—your eyes get burned out, staring at the sun and water all day. And probably he was wasted."

Grady smiled. "Wouldn't be a fisherman if he wasn't. I'm glad I ran into you. Thank Angelo again for dinner," he said, and Raina slipped back inside.

Shadows fell swiftly behind him on the drive to Hokuloa Road, though the fields still held a glimmer of alpenglow. He passed the same old man pushing his shopping cart along the highway, his hair a pale flag in the wind. As the truck drew nearer, Hale o Nalowale rose from the dark plain. A passing truck's headlights momentarily illuminated its walls, no longer an unbroken expanse of white. Names had been painted on them in red letters.

Maximillian Shindo
Leonardo Sanchez
Ray Shoski
Amanda Wellesley
Cory Desoto
Lance Nguyen
Jessica Kiyoko . . .

At the base of the building stood a figure. It didn't turn to look at Grady's truck, just continued to paint in slow, careful motions.

NEVER FORGET THE MISSING
#ISLANDNALOWALE

CHAPTER 65

In the morning, the 'ohana's windows were opaque with moisture. A fine mist hung over everything, palms and glossy-leaved
kōpikos visible only as ghostly columns fading into nothing. He was
fogged in.

At home, this would have been an irritation—no ferry to get to
a job site, no sailing—or just plain depressing. Here, after weeks
of mostly perfect weather, the fog seemed like a gift. He pulled on
jeans, a T-shirt, and a flannel shirt against the clammy air, his socks
and work boots, and made breakfast. He cut into an avocado and he
checked the local news. Jessica Kiyoko's parents were now offering a
$35,000 reward for any news or information as to her whereabouts.
Grady had to stop reading when he saw the photo of her parents,
their faces skinned by grief. He recalled her name in big red letters
on Hale o Nalowale and felt a stab of fear.

He reminded himself that Raina's cousin Angelo was right: Jessica
could still show up alive. Sometimes people didn't want to be found.
Grady knew a guy who'd disappeared on a solo canoe trip in the
Allagash. His girlfriend was convinced he'd died, but it turned out
he'd joined a Buddhist monastery in Vermont without telling anyone.
What would be worse, knowing someone you loved had died or
learning they were essentially a stranger?

He returned to reading. An article about the body at Kahawai
Beach took up most of the *Pilot*'s home page. They'd announced he
was a young man in his late teens. They were still trying to identify
him. The police had posted a reminder that riptides and currents

posed a constant danger even to those familiar with local conditions. In the comments, people speculated about a shark attack.

No bad tide yesterday, Great Whites seen around here, why aren't we told the truth? Because they want the tourists back!

my uncle spotted one off Lanai last week. Sharks don't care about COVID!

Mayor don't care about our people disappearing! Other things to worry about beside chinese virus

Don't be racist, great whites don't care about that either lol

neither do whites lol

that kid was def from oahu, no one reported missing here

he's a homeless kid, my brother knows him. no one cares until they die then they still dont care

One post had a caption beneath a photo of teeth marks on a leg, crimson V's growing smaller as they marched down the calf.

Why you don't want to get shark bit

Grady rubbed his eyes. So the body on the beach hadn't been Leonardo's. That meant that he could be—probably was—still alive.

And Jessie was still missing, which meant that possibly she, too, could still be alive, perhaps with Leonardo. But where?

He decided to visit the aviary. He felt a sharp pang of guilt as he realized he hadn't done that in a few days, hadn't even checked on the main house. The birds always soothed him, but in a way that made him feel alert, not sleepy. It would clear his head, plus he'd be doing what he was being paid to do.

Outside, thick mist hung everywhere, but a strange metallic brightness tinged the air—the sun, making its presence felt. The dew on the spiderwebs looked like mercury splashed from a broken barometer. The air smelled like lettuce gone slimy in a plastic bag. When something rustled, he tensed, expecting to see a rat. Instead, a brown creature ran out, like a furry snake. A mongoose, the first he'd seen.

When it was out of sight, Grady followed the tree line down the hillside. The thick fog altered noises, something he'd noticed before when sailing. Noises were at once muffled and loud: a bell buoy might sound distant, but within minutes its low clang would echo near the bow.

Now it was the birdcalls that were muted—the 'elepaio's reverse wolf whistle more melancholy, the crooning of the spotted doves lower and less insistent. Even the wind seemed reined in.

As he approached the gate, another sound disturbed the quiet morning. A vehicle. It didn't sound like Dalita's truck. Grady listened for a few seconds, then hurried to the security gate.

CHAPTER 66

H e reached the gate before the vehicle did, stood where he'd be hidden by the oleander hedge. Not that he needed to hide—the fog was even thicker down here, coiling in the updraft from the cliffs. The rank green smell had dissipated to a fainter, boggy odor. When he licked his lips, he tasted salt.

He waited. He wasn't afraid but expectant. Would the vehicle stop? Head on toward Hokuloa Point? Could it be Minton? The Tesla might have gone past the compound in the middle of the night or early morning, and Grady wouldn't have heard.

It wasn't the Tesla but Raina's old Subaru, emerging from the fog like a maroon ghost. It jerked to a stop—she'd braked too quickly, taken by surprise when the gate appeared, or by the fact that he waited behind it. Grady waved, but his stomach turned. Something had happened and Raina had driven here to tell him, rather than calling. Raina rolled down the driver's window and peered out.

"Hi." She smiled, looking embarrassed. "How you doing?"

"I'm fine. Everything okay?"

"Yeah, sure."

"I mean Jessica—is she all right? Did you hear something?"

"Oh! No, I haven't heard anything." Now she seemed even more embarrassed. "Actually, I was just going for a drive. Then the fog rolled in, and . . ."

"And you just happened to end up here?"

"Kinda."

"You want to come up to the house?"

"Is your boss around?"

"He's at the point, I don't think he'll be back for weeks. Come on, I'll let you in." He opened the gate and, once she was inside, got into the car. "You want coffee? Have you been up here before?"

"Never. But I knew where it was. Angelo has a drone—he goes out on his boat and shoots footage all around the island. You wouldn't believe some of the houses here. People have way too much money."

"Has he ever gotten pictures of Hokuloa Point?"

"Angelo hasn't, but one of his security buddies has—he sent it to Angelo. He showed it to me. Crazy." She drove slowly, peering at the fog. The wiper blades squeaked as they smeared mist across the windshield.

"Is it foggy down in Makani?"

"Nope. Bright and sunny. Hot. No fog when I turned onto Hokuloa Road. The higher you go the worse it gets."

"It'll burn off."

"You don't mind I came up here, right?" She gave him a quick look. She'd put on eyeliner and mascara and lip gloss, her hair pulled back in a loose ponytail. "I was just driving and thought, *What the hell, I'll see what you're up to*. I go crazy. Most of my friends, they're still partying, but I got to worry about my mom, if I ever get the chance to go see her. At least I know you're safe."

Grady wasn't sure if he should take that as a compliment.

She parked alongside his truck, got out, and stared up at Minton's house. She wore a faded blue T-shirt and worn jeans, a pair of old hiking shoes. "That's so ugly. If I had that much money, I'd build a plantation house on the beach."

"What, like a Southern plantation? That would be even uglier."

"No—you know, an old-style wooden house, with a nice porch and a lānai. This . . ." She squinted at the soaring windows and steel trusses, glinting in the fog. "It looks like a glass elevator. Like in that old Willy Wonka movie. That scared me when I was a kid."

He laughed, glanced at her car. For the first time he noticed a bumper sticker—old, a wave and the words EDDIE WOULD GO. "What's that mean?"

"It's a saying in Hawai'i. This Hawai'ian surfer, Eddie Aikau—he was an incredible big-wave surfer, and also a lifeguard. He saved more than five hundred people over the years—monster waves, all kinds of weather. I can't believe you never heard of him." She sounded slightly annoyed. "He died trying to rescue the crew of the *Hokulea* when it capsized."

"Hokuloa?"

"No—*Hokulea*. A voyaging canoe. They built it to sail to Tahiti, navigating by the stars. It capsized off Moloka'i. Eddie drowned, trying to save the people onboard. He was only thirty-one."

"Was this recent?"

"No. In the seventies. Biggest surf contest in the world is named after him. You see those bumper stickers everywhere here. He's a legend in Hawai'i."

Raina's tone and expression made Grady acutely aware he wasn't a legend, here or anywhere else. He shrugged. "So, you want to see inside? The aviary is pretty amazing."

"Sure."

They went into the house. Raina seemed unimpressed by the sleek furniture and cathedral ceiling, but she stopped at the aquarium. "He raises wana?" She stared at the spiky lumps, the spectral drift of plankton and algae that fed them. "Oh my god. That's freaking weird."

"Not so weird. I was reading about it—they eat algae, keeping the tank clean for fish. If he had any fish," he added sheepishly.

"That's not what I mean. These are parasol urchins." She drew closer to the glass, maneuvering to stare at a small lavender mound clinging to the coral. "They're poisonous—like, fatally poisonous. If you touch one, you could die." She glanced at Grady. "You *would* die, probably—you'd never be able to get to a hospital in time."

"Yeah, Wes told me. It's not like I'm gonna stick my hand in there—they don't need to be fed, I just have to check on the filtration system, stuff like that."

"They're also endangered. Coral bleaching's changed their habitat." Raina straightened, pushing a strand of blond hair from her face. "There's a small breeding colony at the aquarium, but he's got more in there than we do."

She gave Grady a strange look. "It's against the law to have them. Do you know why he keeps them here?"

"He didn't say. It's not like it's a secret—he showed them to me right off. And he didn't say anything about me not telling anybody. Dalita knows, for one. That tank's been here for a while."

He hoped he didn't sound defensive. The last thing he needed was someone riding him, filing some kind of official complaint. "Maybe it's a breeding colony, too," he added. "He's involved with all those environmental groups. 'Save the sea urchins.'"

"Yeah, I guess." Raina appeared unconvinced. "It's just weird," she said. "He sounds weird."

"He's rich as fuck. People like that, they're always weird."

He wondered if he should abort this mission. If the parasol urchins triggered Raina, she'd probably flip a tit over the aviary. But before he could suggest going back outside, she'd already started up the stairway.

"It's up here, right?"

"Yeah, but hold on . . ."

He caught up with her on the landing. From down the hallway they could hear the waterfall's murmur, the plaintive cries and whistles. As they approached the screened entry, Raina slowed her steps, her expression now childlike, almost frightened.

"They really are in here," she breathed. "I thought you might be kidding."

He shook his head, holding the screen open so she could go inside. "No," he said. "It's for real."

Moist, cool air enveloped them, heavy with the birds' fruity musk and the scent of the yellow, fuzzy flowers the 'i'iwi fed on. Raina turned in a circle, staring at the trees that reached to the ceiling high above them.

"Those are 'ōhi'a," she marveled.

Grady squinted up at the canopy, blade-shaped leaves stirring like thousands of green feathers. "Is that what they are?"

"Yeah. Forest birds love them, they feed on the flowers—lehua, that's what the flowers are called." She turned to him, brow furrowed. "Doesn't it seem really strange to you? This private forest inside a house?"

"Sure," Grady replied, bristling slightly. "But I don't ask a lot of questions. Every week my paycheck shows up in my bank account, and I hardly see him. Mostly he's out at Hokuloa Point, which is why I'm here, keeping an eye on things."

Raina rubbed her bare arms, watching a larger brilliant red-orange bird with black wings dive-bomb another. "These male birds are super-territorial. They must fight a lot here, in such an enclosed space."

"Do they? I didn't know," admitted Grady, feeling stupid. "I never noticed. Are you cold? I can get you a hoodie."

"It's the fog, it gets into your bones. That's what my auntie always says." She stared entranced as the smaller bird darted into a patch of tall ferns. "This is all just . . . bizarre. I feel like I'm trapped here with them. Like I'm a gigantic bird."

Grady shrugged, unsure how to respond. To him, the aviary had always seemed magical, a place that transported him into the forest without him ever having to leave Wes's house. "They're not really trapped," he said defensively. "They don't even know they're not in the forest."

"If they can't leave, they're trapped. You can live in a nice house and still be trapped." She pointed at a small bird. "Wow! That looks like an 'ākepa."

Grady squinted at it. "A what?"

"An 'ākepa. See?"

He tracked the little bird as it hopped along a branch, the same bird, he thought, that had landed on his palm. "Isn't that just a smaller 'i'iwi? A baby?"

"I don't think so." She stood on tiptoe to get a better look. "Its beak is totally different, for one. Look, there's another." She turned to Grady. "They're endangered, I think. I know. It can't be legal for him to have them here."

"He must have a permit." Grady tried to hide his impatience. "Like I said, he's probably working with some nature group. Otherwise why keep them?"

"Bird trafficking?"

Grady laughed. "The guy's a billionaire. He doesn't need to traffic frigging birds. Those other ones, the 'i'iwi . . ." He pointed at one of the bigger birds with a curved beak. "What about them?"

"I don't think they're endangered. But I don't know if you can keep them as pets."

"They're not pets." Grady again felt an obscure urge to defend Minton. "He's breeding them. Like with those Hawai'ian crows—they keep trying to reintroduce them into the wild."

"Maybe." She hugged herself, and he saw her arms were goose-pimpled. "I will borrow that hoodie, if that's okay."

"Yeah, of course."

They walked back into the hall. Grady started downstairs but stopped when he looked back to see Raina had entered Minton's bedroom.

"What is this?" she asked in a low voice as Grady stepped alongside her.

She stood in front of the photograph of the bird with an insect in its beak, its feathers so glossy they seemed to have been doused in black ink, then daubed with sulfur-yellow paint.

Grady said, "Wes took that photo. A bird, I forget its name."

"It's a Moloka'i 'ō'ō. I've seen a taxidermied one. He can't have taken that picture—they're extinct."

"Oh, yeah—he told me that. He said he saw one at Hokuloa Point."

"That's impossible. No one's seen one in a hundred years."

"Well, maybe they're wrong. Or maybe he is—it might be a different bird."

"Maybe," Raina said doubtfully. "Have you ever seen one in the aviary?"

"No. I'd remember if I did. And he didn't mention having one here."

She rubbed her arms again, as though the photo chilled her. "Let's go," she said.

They went back outside, Grady disappointed that she'd been unimpressed by the things he most loved about this place—the seemingly tame birds, the fact that Wes had created a miniature of the island inside his own house.

But now the enchanted space seemed tainted. He didn't remotely believe Wes was smuggling birds, or even keeping them illegally: it was more the idea that the birds might actually know or sense they were trapped.

"Now, this is nice." She touched his arm as the 'ohana appeared from the mist. "This is where you live?"

"If you call this living." It was something Zeke used to say, and she laughed.

Inside, Grady retrieved his hoodie, then made coffee. They sat on the couch, Raina wrapping the yellow cashmere blanket around her, too.

"You still cold?" he asked.

"No." She stroked the blanket like it was a cat. "This is just so soft."

"It came with the place." Grady settled at the other end of the couch. "I don't travel with my own cashmere blanket."

She laughed again. He liked that she was here, that she was wearing his hoodie. "Do you drive up Hokuloa Road a lot?" he asked.

"No. When I was in high school, like I told you. That party. A couple of times with Jessie when she was staying with me. We always turned around when we reached the gate."

"The road doesn't bother you?"

"Nope. I grew up here. And there're other places almost as bad as Hokuloa Road. Just go slow. I was a little nervous about driving back in the fog," she admitted.

She cupped her coffee mug, cocked her head to regard him with those pale golden eyes. He'd never seen a girl—anyone—whose eyes changed color according to the light. "You don't get scared up here by yourself?"

He took a sip of coffee before answering. "Do you remember yesterday, when we were talking about everyone who disappears here? I said that maybe it wasn't a person doing it—maybe it was something else."

"I remember. Then Angelo came."

"I think I might've seen it. Heard it . . . " He hesitated. "Kaupe."

Raina sucked her breath in, glancing at the door as though some-one might be there. He walked over and locked it, and returned to the couch.

"You heard it here?" Raina asked in a low voice.

"No. On the beach."

He told her what had happened, from his first night when he'd seen the dog figure outside the 'ohana to hearing the attack. She didn't interrupt or ask questions, though when he talked about going into Sanchez's shack, she bunched up the blanket like she wanted to rip it.

"I saw it again a few nights ago." He touched the lump on his head. "That's how I got this . . ."

"It attacked you?"

"No. I saw it, standing out there . . ." He stared at the door, chagrined. "It startled me, and I bashed my head against the door."

Raina sank deeper into the couch. "You actually heard it."

He nodded without taking his eyes off her, like she'd disappear if he did. Raina believed him. Lorelei had seemed to believe him, too—but that conversation had felt more like he was being grilled, like he'd been not just the witness to something terrible but also, perhaps, a perpetrator. He felt light-headed with gratitude, and relief.

"So you know what it is," he murmured.

"Yeah. Kaupe."

"I'd never even heard of it before—it just showed up when I got here. What the hell does it want?"

"Maybe it doesn't like your boss keeping all those birds in a cage."

"Then why doesn't it go after him?" He felt off-balance again, talking about whatever it was like it actually existed. "Why does it keep coming after me?"

"It hasn't actually hurt you, right? I mean, you hit your head, but it didn't attack you. Maybe it's just trying to get your attention. Like a ghost."

"I've never seen a ghost."

"Me neither." She stood. "I want to go there — to Leonardo's place."

"Why? It's dangerous."

"I still want to go. There're two of us. You think he might have something to do with Jessie? I want to see for myself. I've been there before." Her gaze fixed on Grady, her eyes no longer golden but again that dark, almost purplish brown. "Nothing could be worse than what happened that time. Let's go."

CHAPTER 67

Raina carefully folded the cashmere blanket, held it against her cheek, and draped it over the couch. "'Scuse me."

She headed to the bathroom. Grady went into the bedroom, got his knife, and stuck it in his jeans pocket. Back in the living room, he texted Donny.

Going for a hike on Hokuloa Road

His brother replied:

what is this a code? are you getting laid?

No i'm really going for a hike and if I fall off a cliff i want someone to know

well that's good because falling off a cliff your odds are better

i love you too bro

pussy

Grady heard the bathroom door open. "I'm ready," Raina said.

They walked down the driveway. The fog was even thicker. Raina tugged her hood up against the damp. Their feet slapped loudly against the ground, the sound echoing eerily.

A bird called out from the mist-shrouded treetops, and Raina stopped and tipped her head, listening. When Grady started to speak, she pressed her hand against his mouth. The bird called again—a piercing string of notes, more like music than birdsong. Raina's fingers remained on his lips. She seemed transfixed.

The bird cried a third time. After a few seconds another bird answered, from higher up the hillside. This second call was fainter and higher pitched, not as musical as the first. But its tone, to Grady's ear, sounded similar. He held his breath, thought he heard the flutter of wings in the forest canopy. Raina remained motionless beside him. At last she let her hand drop.

"What?" he whispered.

She didn't reply, just started walking again, but more slowly, pausing now and then to listen. When they reached the bottom of the drive, the gate emerged from the fog like a ship's rail, an illusion heightened by the sound of waves from the unseen cliffs. Grady opened it and they stepped out. His skin felt chill and clammy, and he shivered, wishing he'd grabbed his sweater.

"Oh, brah, you're cold!" Raina exclaimed. "And I got your hoodie—you want it? I'm okay now."

She started to unzip the hoodie he'd given her, but he gently grasped her hand. "Hell no. I'm from Maine. We go out snowshoeing in shorts and a T-shirt."

"Really?"

He laughed. Out of nowhere, he felt a kind of loose happiness he hadn't experienced in years, the way he used to feel with Rachel. "It's not cold, really. Fog's so clammy, it gets under your skin. Just keep moving."

They walked as though in a dream down the broken road, kicking up rust-colored dirt and chunks of lava. Giant ferns appeared through the milky haze, and trees strung with flowers like Christmas stars.

"What was that bird?" Grady asked after a few minutes. "It really sounded like music. I've never heard anything like that."

"It sounded like an 'ō'ū." Raina tugged her hair from its ponytail, tucking it beneath her shirt collar as though it were a scarf. "Which is impossible. I saw an episode about them online—somebody recorded one in 1987, a male 'ō'ū calling for a mate. But a female never replied. They used to be on all the islands. Now they're gone."

She looked so sad that Grady wanted to put his arm around her, but he didn't. "It sounded like another bird answered it," he said. "Did you hear that?"

"Yeah. But probably that was another kind of bird. The 'ō'ū was a type of honeycreeper, and there are still a lot of different species of honeycreepers around."

"It would be amazing if there actually was one here. Like that other bird—it would be like finding Bigfoot. Were they like that other bird?"

"The one in the photo? No. Different bird. But they're both extinct." Raina stared into the trees.

The fog had begun to fade, as though someone had adjusted their camera filter. Trees and rocks took shape and Grady began to differentiate between the green and dull bronze leaves of 'āla'a and the glossier pāpala, with their tiny threadlike red flowers. 'Ōhi'a trees grew here as well, with their bright red flowers beloved of the birds in Wes's aviary. Through a gap in the vegetation he glimpsed the fruit trees that grew by Leonardo's shack. Raina halted.

"This is it. I remember those mountain apples—I was here when he planted them. That was, what? Almost thirteen years ago," she said. "I thought Leo was my boyfriend. I was fourteen the first time, his friends were already out of high school."

She fell silent as they walked, side by side, to the trees. Grady knew better than to say *I'm sorry.* He picked two apples, cleaned the larger one on his T-shirt, and handed it to her. He bit into the other. It was waxy, with an odd, light taste, and made his mouth feel dry. He finished it in two bites.

"It's good," he said, and smiled tentatively.

Raina didn't smile back. "Thanks." She ate the apple, dropped the core, and picked a second fruit. Didn't bite into it, just stared at it, like it was a Magic 8-Ball.

"We don't have to go in there," said Grady. "I shouldn't have told you all that. I didn't know what happened to you here —I just thought everything might tie together. The missing people, that thing I heard. But this is a bad place for you, Raina. We should go back."

"I can make up my own mind about if I want to go back." Raina took a bite of her second mountain apple. "This therapist, she used to tell me I held trauma in my body. I told her that was bullshit. I think places hold trauma."

"You mean the shack?"

"This island. All the islands. Maybe everywhere, now."

She walked on, stopping to glance inside Sanchez's truck. Grady stayed beside her. When they reached the shack, he moved to open the door, but Raina pushed past him and went inside.

The windows dripped with moisture, leaving dirty streaks as though someone had tried to claw through the glass. Grady propped the door open to let in some air as Raina paced the small room. She opened the cooler and sniffed, picked up a paperback and dropped it onto the floor, lifted one leg of a wet suit hanging from the wall and let go of it in disgust.

"Nothing's changed," she murmured. "It looks exactly the same, like he was just here."

She continued her search—peering under the futon couch, criss-crossing the small room in frustration. She grabbed the lumpy pillow and held it to her nose, tossed it away.

"She was never here," she said. Her face crumpled, disappointment but also relief. "He was, but Jessie wasn't with him."

She walked to the picture window, its view of the ocean obscured by fog. She ran a hand along the sill, the wood warped, and picked up the seashell.

"He used to have so many of these," she said. "Cone shells—he'd find them on sandbars when he was surfing, or when he went snorkeling in the reefs. We have them at the aquarium, too." She held it up to the window. The filtered light made the shell appear translucent, almost filmy, like it was made of cloth. "He liked them because they're poisonous. A lot of cone shells are, but this kind can kill you."

"How?"

"It hides under the sand, and when a fish comes along it shoots this retractable needle and poisons it, then eats it. It's like the parasol urchins—if you step on one, or pick it up, it can kill you. Even through divers' gloves. There's no antidote."

She set the cone shell back on the windowsill. "He must've taken all the rest of them somewhere else."

She started to walk away from the window, then turned, took the cone shell and pocketed it. "There was a big swell last week—he would have been on the water. Let's go down to the beach."

CHAPTER 68

They returned outside. The last remnants of fog hung above the tallest trees, quickly fading into blue sky. The sun's heat pressed suddenly against Grady's face: once again he'd forgotten his cap, sunglasses, sunscreen. Raina continued ahead of him, stopping where the trail grew steep. He drew up alongside her. Below them, the path disappeared. The small difference in altitude meant that the sun hadn't yet burned through this fog to the shore below.

Raina seemed familiar with the trail. She started down, grabbing branches without looking at them, nudging her feet between rocks as though sensing the firm ground beneath.

Grady moved more cautiously. Within a few minutes, he'd lost sight of her. "You still there?" he called.

"I'm here!"

Her voice seemed to come from far away. She must have reached the beach. He tried to clamber down more quickly, but his leg shot out from under him. Lava crumbled into a rain of loose scree. For a fraction of a second he hung in the empty air, before landing hard on his back. Grabbing a branch, he heaved himself to his feet. He stood there, panting, and called out again.

"Raina! You okay?"

No reply.

The waves sounded louder than they had only minutes ago: he was near the bottom. Wind and spray mingled with the haze, so thick that he couldn't see his feet. He thought of the legend Dalita had told him, about the uncanny fog that kept invaders from finding the island. He gritted his teeth, navigating the last few steps until he felt solid ground beneath him.

He could see nothing on the beach. The waves sounded close. He stooped to touch the sand, cool but dry. He looked around for Raina but saw only formless gray. A bright pearl glowed above where he guessed the horizon was—the sun. He smelled salt and an underlying funk, a dead animal or fish rotting.

"Raina!" He heard a sound behind him and touched the knife he'd kept folded in his pocket. "Raina?"

His skin crawled as he listened to waves hissing on the sand. When he took a step, a low moan came from the rocks to his left, hidden by the fog.

"Raina?"

The moaning grew louder: a woman's voice that rose into a scream, then abrupt silence, as though someone had covered her mouth.

"Raina!" he shouted.

The scream came again. She sounded not just terrified but in pain. Grady pulled out his knife, flipped it open, and took a step toward the rocks.

A dark form stood there, barely discernible in the fog. Gradually its outlines grew clearer. A figure as tall as Grady, taller, with no arms or legs, its head a black smear above a body shaped like an upright casket. No eyes or nose or mouth.

Then it moved. And it did have a mouth—a whitish cloud that slowly expanded then contracted against the smear, as though breathing, growing larger until all Grady could see was an awful yawning void.

Raina screamed again and Grady recognized his name in the garbled consonants. Heart pounding, he rose onto the balls of his feet, his fingers tightening on the knife's handle as he steeled himself to launch.

Before he could, someone grabbed him by the throat with one hand, pressing the other over his mouth. The screams rose to an anguished shriek. Grady lashed out, but the knife fell from his hand,

and he was dragged across the sand. The screams continued, a sustained howl of agony and terror that drowned out the sound of the waves, the wind, everything except for a voice hissing in his ear.

"Shut up, shut up! It's me——"

He struggled to shake free but couldn't. The hand dropped from his mouth to grab his chin, turning his head till he saw her face inches from his own.

Raina.

CHAPTER 69

She pulled him to the chamber, both of them bent double as they dropped to their knees and scrambled beneath the outcropping. Grady clutched at the sand, but his knife was gone, left on the beach. He looked up to see Raina in the shadows, a finger pressed against her lips as she furiously shook her head. She scooted back as far as she could go, farther than he could because she was smaller.

He remained where he was, within the curl of the stone wave so that he, too, remained in shadow. He groped for anything he might use as a weapon, but there was nothing. Still kneeling, he edged backward until he reached the wall, where he crouched like an animal, his back wedged against the rock above him.

The fog was dispersing, not blown by the wind but sucked into the sea, drawn into each retreating wave like a video played backward. On the rocks, the dark figure had diminished to a shadow cast by something that wasn't there. It continued to scream, a high, sobbing wail.

His mother's voice the night his father had shot himself.

He began to cry, his fingers kneading the sand as Raina put her arms around him. "Don't," she whispered into his ear. "Don't go to it."

He nodded, wiped his eyes and focused on the rock above him, so close his breath warmed the stone. Natural indentations in the rock resembled a face—eyes, a slit for a mouth. Someone had carved zigzag lines around it: when Grady moved his head, the image shifted from face to spider to sun. If he remained still, he could see all three at once, a silent dance of shadow and stone and light.

"Grady. Grady, are you all right?"

Raina touched his arm. He recoiled, then gasped as he realized the sobbing cries had stopped. He shut his eyes, trying to regain control.

"Yeah, I'm okay." It hurt to speak, as though he'd been the one screaming. Raina put her arms around him, and he felt her shaking. He slipped his arms from hers to hold her tight, too. "It's okay," he whispered. "It's gone, I think it's gone . . ."

They remained there for a long time, not talking. After a while Raina drew away.

"It's gone," she said. The light fell on her face: he saw she'd been crying, too.

"What did you hear?"

"Myself." Her voice was hoarse. "I heard myself screaming. But it wasn't me."

She lowered her head, pushing herself back to stare at the chamber's ceiling.

"I've been here before," she said, sounding very far away. Her fingers traced something on the rock. "Leo showed me, he showed all of us—" She cried out, snatching her hand back so violently he thought she'd been bitten.

He bellied up alongside her. "What is it?"

"It's gone—the ki'i pōhaku of the sun. It's not here." She pointed to where the chamber had been vandalized. "There was a carving of the sun. It's—someone's hacked it out of here . . ."

"I know—I saw when I was here before. But we need to get back outside."

He took her hand. She yanked it away. She pressed her fingers against the stone, then struck it with her palm, hard. "Goddamn it!"

"Raina," Grady urged her. "Come on. Please."

She continued to curse, but when he crawled back out onto the beach, she followed.

Grady felt like he'd been pummeled: his entire body ached and his ears rang. He looked around and saw his knife, retrieved it and stuck it back into his pocket. Raina stood unsteadily, staring back at the chamber, the cone-shaped rock where the two surfboards were still tied.

"That motherfucker," she said, and spat onto the sand.

Grady stayed where he was, blinking in the sunlight. The air smelled sharp and clean, that high salt smell he associated with wind snapping at full sails, with cold spray and the sound of seabirds. Here the spray felt blood-warm and the heat like a fist.

A whistling cry echoed from high above him. He looked up to see a huge bird, its wingspan easily three feet, tail streaming like the contrails of a jet. He watched until it flew out of sight, then he walked silently with Raina, back to the path.

CHAPTER 70

They didn't speak until they reached Hokuloa Road. Whenever he glanced over at Raina, she refused to meet his gaze.

"Are you okay?" he finally asked. The air was heavy with the lemon-drop scent of lantana, the smell of dust. "Raina?"

"Yes." She let her breath out, like she'd been holding it a long time. Her face was freckled with sand, her hair matted. "I heard someone screaming. Someone—" She stopped. "Someone else. But then it was like I was hearing myself. Is that what you heard?"

"Kind of. I thought it was you—I thought someone was attacking you. But then . . ." He squeezed his eyes shut, hearing that terrible sound again. His mother's screams, a shadow swinging across the garage floor. "It sounded like someone else I know."

"Me too."

He waited for her to say whose voice she'd heard, but she remained silent. "What is it doing?"

"I don't know." She shivered. "The stories, they say it sometimes imitates someone you love—to lure you." She seemed to shrink into the folds of his hoodie. "Chickenskin."

When they got to the 'ohana, Raina went inside to clean up. Grady waited by her Subaru, staring dully down the hillside.

He wondered if this was how people who'd survived a plane crash felt. No one else could possibly understand what you'd been through, but what you'd been through was not the kind of thing you'd want to sit around and reminisce about together. It struck him that this was what had happened with his mother, him, and Donny, after their father killed himself.

And now it had happened with Raina. The only reason she was here at this moment was because he'd exchanged thirty words with her friend on a plane, a friend who had since disappeared. Whatever they'd just experienced—were they somehow fated to share that? Did Kaupe lure them there on purpose, for a reason they couldn't grasp?

Or was this all totally random?

Whatever had occurred, it seemed to have rewired his brain. He felt overwhelmed by an emotion he couldn't understand or describe—fear but also yearning. Maybe it was just shock. He wished he could talk about it with Raina, but he didn't know where to begin.

She returned a few minutes later, her face clean and her hair once more pulled into a ponytail. They stood awkwardly in the driveway, the day around them serene. Deep blue sky, high white clouds, the forest trees such a bright, hopeful green he couldn't bear to look at them.

At last he said, "You okay driving back?"

"Yeah, sure." For a few seconds she was silent, like she was thinking hard. "Listen," she said finally, crossing her arms on her chest. "I know you're not from here, so you can't really understand. But whoever stole that carving did a terrible thing. Ki'i pōhaku are sacred—that whole place down there is supposed to be kapu. Leo should never, ever have been living there. I should never have been there."

She looked up at Grady. "He's the one who did it. Vandalized it."

"You can't prove that."

"I don't need to. It's exactly what he'd do. I bet it's in his place in town. In his game room with his fucking flat-screen TV."

"Wouldn't the police have seen it when they searched there?"

"Maybe. I bet he sold it."

"Do you think...whatever it was we heard...do you think it killed him?"

"Brah, I told you before. I hope so." She turned to open her car door. "Damn, I'm tired. I'll be fine," she said, cutting him off as he began to protest. "Seriously."

She unzipped his hoodie, pulled it off, and handed it to him. "Thanks for letting me borrow this."

She started to get into the car, but Grady stopped her. "Wait." She sighed but remained where she was, waiting for him to go on. "What do you think happened to us?"

"Grady, you were there!"

"I know that. But—*why* do you think it happened? It started by imitating your voice, so I'd go to you. Why does it keep coming to me?"

"I don't know," she snapped. "Maybe it needs you. Maybe it wants you to do something for it."

"But what?"

"I have no clue, Grady. Look, I'm exhausted. You think you're the fucking chosen one, figure it out."

She got into her car, leaving the door open as she turned the ignition and waited for the AC to kick in. The radio came on, one of the Hawai'ian songs from the station Grady loved, steel guitar and a man who sounded like he was singing goodbye.

"You want to meet up for a beer?" Grady asked tentatively. "Not today—tomorrow, maybe?"

"Maybe. I need to think. But, yeah, probably. I'll text you, okay?"

"You'll need the security code to get out," he said, and gave it to her.

"See you." She reached out the open window to grab his hand. Her eyes were red, and he wondered if she was lying, if this would be the last time he ever saw her. But he couldn't ask her that, so he just watched as she drove off.

CHAPTER 71

Grady found it impossible to concentrate after Raina left. He felt wired, his body on fire. Every time he tried to make sense of what had happened, his brain resisted: he had to knuckle his eyes or run cold water on his face, anything to eradicate the memory of that screaming shape. When he glanced at the time, he was shocked to see it was only late morning.

Despite that, he went to the fridge for a beer, then did an about-face. "Screw it," he said.

He walked over to Minton's, let himself in, and headed straight for Minton's liquor cabinet. Grady scanned the bottles, all kinds of top-shelf booze—rum, gin, tequila, mescal, bottles of different single malts. He went for a bottle of Glenfiddich—not so rare if Minton noticed some had been drunk—and carried it up to the aviary.

He sat on the floor and took a swallow of whiskey, wishing the fire in his throat would burn away the memory of the beach. For once, the birds didn't soothe him. They seemed agitated by his presence, their cries more urgent as they fluttered into the upper branches of the trees. He took another drink of whiskey and stood, walking around the room to see if something else might have disturbed them, a rat or mongoose that had somehow managed to make its way inside. The thought sickened him, but he found no sign of any predator, only the usual detritus of fallen leaves and twigs, bird droppings, stray feathers. He removed a palm frond from one of the big terra cotta pots holding a good-sized tree, for a few minutes stood and stared up at the green canopy not far above him.

The birds had all but disappeared into the foliage. He heard a low rustle of wings, and a low warning chirp. Otherwise, he might have been alone. The near-silence disturbed him. Was this what it was like everywhere else in Hawai'i—all the birds in retreat, or nonexistent? An awful melancholy seized him, and a loneliness that felt like fear: the same quiet anguish he'd felt the past spring, when he'd heard no spring peepers in the wetland near his house. He waited another minute, to see if the birds might emerge from hiding, then returned to the 'ohana.

Immediately, everything that had happened since he and Raina sat here this morning crashed over him. That thing on the beach— whatever it was, it must be hunting him. At the very least, it knew he was here and wasn't happy about it. And now Grady had dragged Raina into this whole fucking mess. He wished he'd asked her to stick around, or insisted that he follow her back in the truck, to make sure she was safe.

But that would have just seemed creepy, and the truth was, he was the one who no longer felt safe. He gulped down the whiskey, dug out his phone, and called Dalita.

"Hey," he said. "What're you doing?"

"Finishing lunch. Lor took the kids to the beach."

"You feel like company?"

"Sure. I was just gonna take a hike in the forest. You have hiking shoes?"

"I'm made of hiking shoes."

She laughed. "Are you drunk?"

"Kind of."

"Maybe not the best idea to drive—"

"I'll be fine. You were the one told me to do it when I'm stoned."

"That's different."

"I'll be fine."

"I'll text you a pin. But——"

He hung up. He changed into jeans and his boots, filled a water bottle for the trip. He didn't want to talk to Dalita about what had happened with Raina. He just wanted to be with someone, someplace other than here.

CHAPTER 72

As he drew near Hale o Nalowale, he saw the same homeless man pushing his shopping cart. Grady slowed the truck to a crawl alongside him. "Hey," he said.

The man looked at him without surprise, dark brown eyes in a face shriveled like a walnut by the sun.

"Here." Grady stopped the truck. He took a twenty from his wallet and handed it to the man, along with his water bottle. "You take care."

"Mahalo."

The man nodded and Grady drove on, past Hale o Nalowale. His phone pinged, the text from Dalita with a pin for the Ounawai Forest Preserve.

> I'll meet you in the lower parking lot. if it's full go to the next one

The forest was in a mountainous area a short distance from town. He followed a series of hairpin turns, through thick woods and past numerous houses, more prosperous-looking than the ones in town. After three miles he saw the sign for the preserve. He pulled onto a gravel road, drove until he reached a large parking area.

Pickups and Subarus with bike racks were scattered around the lot. A large family sat in lawn chairs around Weber grills and coolers—kids, grandparents, parents, teenagers. Food was spread across a big folding table, mounds of grilled chicken and pork, plastic bowls of salads, bags of chips. The smell of charred meat made Grady ravenous.

"Grady!"

"Hey," he said as he joined Dalita. "Hope you haven't been waiting."

She wore sturdy shoes, long shorts, and a long-sleeved shirt, a small backpack slung over one shoulder. Her dark curls were reined in by a pink baseball cap, eyes hidden by big pink sunglasses. "I just got here. Look, Stella found a dead shark." She held up her phone to show a photo. "Very exciting."

"Very disgusting."

"Right? She had a fit when Lor said she couldn't bring it home."

Dalita turned and started walking, past an array of signs—plant and tree identifications, maps of mountain bike trails and where it was okay or not okay to walk your dog. "You up for a long walk or a short walk?"

"Either one."

"We'll take a medium walk." She gestured to a path, well-trodden, yet another sign beside it.

STAY ON TRAIL!

AVOID GULCHES ESPECIALLY DURING RAIN. FLASH FLOODS OCCUR VERY SUDDENLY LEAVING YOU NO TIME TO REACH HIGHER GROUND.

STAY ON TRAIL!

"I guess we should stay on the trail," said Grady.

Walking with Dalita calmed him, and also sobered him up. He didn't exactly forget the morning's events, but they gradually receded, like a hangover. Through the trees he glimpsed other walkers, some with leashed dogs. Children's voices echoed from not far away, and the buzz of fat bike tires zipping down nearby trails. After a few minutes, he and Dalita were surrounded by towering trees—conifers, a tropical variety of ash, gum trees—stands of huge ferns, and thickets of underbrush.

"This was a forest plantation—building lumber," Dalita said. "Most of these trees are introduced species. Then the company went bust. They donated the land to the island to avoid taxes, something like that."

Grady looked up at the green spires blotting out the sky. "It looks wild."

"Well, it is wild now. This is where that girl got lost last year. She was lucky they found her." She glanced at Grady. "Any news about the girl on the plane?"

"I haven't really looked at the news today." He looked down so she couldn't read his expression and see he was lying. "Raina, her friend, I talked to her, and she hadn't heard anything. I guess that's good news."

Dalita was an excellent hiking companion. She knew the names of trees—swamp mahogany, paperbark, toon—and sounded interested when he told her about the woods in Maine and his time at WMCC.

"Maybe you could become a guide here," she said as they picked their way down a steep part of the trail. "Train to be a docent or something. Wes might not care if you did that part-time."

"Maybe."

Grady paused to survey a gorge that cut sharply through the forest, an almost perfect V that sloped steeply to the bottom fifty feet below them, damp and boggy. A narrow path zigzagged along both sides. The fall might not kill you, but there were dead trees everywhere, and rocks. It would definitely be a challenge to pull yourself back up to the trail.

"This is what they warn you about." He stepped aside to let Dalita go first along the path. "The gorge."

"Gulch," she corrected him. "Flash flood, you'd never get out in time."

A loud crack echoed above them, followed by the sound of thrashing leaves and a muffled crash. Grady jumped, nearly losing his balance. "What the hell was that?"

"Gum trees. They get shallow roots—they fall all the time. You gotta keep your ears open."

After that he noticed the sound often, a random explosion followed by a crash. As they descended into the gulch it grew dark, like an early sunset, but when he looked up at the sky, far above the trees, it was bright blue. He was relieved when they reached the opposite side of the ravine and began to climb out.

Golden light slanted through the canopy, falling onto tall stands of pale yellow ferns and drifts of brown leaves. They might have been in the Maine woods in autumn. But it smelled different—the sharp medicinal scent of eucalyptus, a honeyed fragrance he couldn't identify. A pang cut through Grady's momentary sunlit mood. He looked at Dalita.

"That body on the beach—have they found out anything?"

She withdrew her phone, brought up a photo that could have come from any number of missing-person flyers. A sweet-looking young man, dark-skinned, with deep-set eyes and a big smile.

"The kids called him 'Anuhe," said Dalita. "I don't know if it was to his face or not—it means 'caterpillar.' The police are still trying to find out his real name so they can contact his family. Tim said they hung out a few times at Kahawai." She handed the phone to Grady. "I cannot handle this kine anymore," she said, her voice breaking. "That could be my son. He's someone's son."

The photo was on the *Island Pilot* home page. Grady scrolled down to a second photo, a detail of the green T-shirt the boy had been wearing. The T-shirt had an insignia in the middle, a circle with lines radiating from it. It reminded him of the petroglyphs.

He gave the phone back to Dalita. "Not a lot to go on," he said, and she sighed in agreement.

CHAPTER 73

They started walking again, waving at a masked woman who jogged past in lizard-green leggings and a tank top.

"We're almost back where we started," said Dalita. "Next time we can take the trail that goes all the way to the top. Gorgeous, the views up there."

"What did Tim say about him? 'Anuhe? You said they hung out together."

"Nothing much. He said he was a good guy, little bit older, maybe few years. Quiet. Tim thought he was from Honolulu—before the pandemic, we got a lot of runaways from O'ahu. Tim said he mostly slept on the beach, but a few times he stayed with some other kids who have an up-country group house. He said 'Anuhe was selling mushrooms at some point."

"Did Tim tell the cops that?"

"Of course not. That's somebody's child. It's not like he was a serious dealer. Probably 'Anuhe stole them from other kids he knew and tried to sell them to make money. Tim said he's been around since Halloween."

"Before the pandemic."

"Yeah. Back then there was tourists, he'd have panhandled. Or have a job, dishwashing or something. Raking lawns. A lot of homeless kids, people try to help them out. I've tried. Give them a hot meal, offer to buy them a plane ticket home. It's tough. Especially when you realize that for them, sleeping on the beach and dumpster diving is better than going home. Tim's friend

Meegan said 'Anuhe got picked up by the cops one night a few weeks ago."

"That's the last time anyone saw him?"

She nodded. "They were partying, Meegan said he wandered off to pee. Next thing, she saw blue lights by where he'd gone, and the car drove off. And that was it. The police say they don't have a record of anybody fitting his description being brought in. Probably whoever picked him up just gave him a warning and let him go."

They'd reached Dalita's truck. Grady leaned against the tailgate, musing. "So he gets into a cop car, they drive off, and boom: game over. No one hears from him again, until he washes up on that same beach a few weeks later. It doesn't make sense. Wouldn't he have texted or called his friends?"

"He never have his phone," said Dalita. "They haven't been able to find it."

"Did Meegan get a good look at the car?"

"She said it cop car—you know, blue car, flashing lights."

Grady stared across the parking lot. The picnicking family had left. A black dog nosed around where they'd been, scrounging for scraps.

"It wasn't a cop," Grady said at last.

"What?"

"That car. It wasn't a cop. It was someone pretending to be a cop. My mom knew a guy who did that in Maine. Bought a decommissioned Crown Vic and drove it around. He had one of those portable hazard lights and he'd stick it on top of the car and follow people he knew, flash the lights and scare them."

"What an asshole."

"But people do that. Pretend to be cops, then kill people."

"You don't need to pretend." Dalita gave him a hard look. "You can actually be a cop and kill people."

"I know! But I swear, there was some guy who did that. I heard a podcast—he'd pretend to be a cop and pull over cars with women in them."

Dalita shook her head. "Grady, this conversation is freaking me out. I gotta go, Lor and the kids will be back by now."

"Yeah, okay. Thanks for letting me walk with you."

"Of course." She made that shaka sign with her hand that people did here. "We still want to do dinner, I just need to check with Lor. Maybe Sunday?"

"That would be great."

He waited as she got into the truck, then said, "One last question — the police here, I haven't seen them except for yesterday at the beach. What kind of cars do they drive?"

"Some cops just drive their own cars, maybe with a light on top. Otherwise it's Teslas," she replied. "Like Wes says — ten years, everybody here going be driving one."

CHAPTER 74

After she left, Grady sat in the truck, hands tight on the wheel, ignition off. He stared into the trees, trying to piece together what he'd seen at Kahawai the day before. Two police cars, an ambulance. The ambulance had been an older Ford, standard issue, maybe some bells and whistles inside because it had to serve an island. He'd clocked it because of his training as an EMT. The police cars, he couldn't remember anything about them.

The same thing could've happened to Jessica. A guy who scoped out bars for a young woman walking home alone, someone who looked like a tourist, intoxicated. He'd pull over, flash his lights. She might have gotten in without question—she knew she was guilty of breaking quarantine.

"Shit."

He started the truck and left the parking lot. He drove slowly, hoping his mind would relax so he'd find the pattern he knew was there: Jessie, 'Anuhe. Missing homeless people, screaming ghosts, spider suns. When he reached the main road, he decided to take the long way back, past the resorts. He felt more jangled than when he'd left the preserve.

He drove by strip malls so generic they might have been anywhere. The few people shopping wore masks and speed-walked, like they were afraid to be outside. Fewer than a dozen cars were parked at the supermarket. A long line straggled in front of the post office, masked customers laden with arms full of packages.

He almost ran the light at the intersection where he turned onto the resort road. Not that it would have mattered. The only other vehicle was a convertible whose middle-aged driver sat texting. The light changed and her car didn't budge. When Grady checked the rearview mirror a minute later, her car was still there.

The speed limit dropped to 25, and the resorts rose before him. From the cliff walk along the beach, they'd seemed absurdly stately but grand, with their mosaic pools and tiki bars and swooping balconies. Like a scene from an old movie, waiting for the stars to race across the lawn and dive into the pool.

Now, from the main road, they just looked huge and ugly. Everything was silent, except for the sound of lawn mowers and the cries of birds. He drove on, past the Royal This, the Grand That, slowing when he saw a car pulled alongside a hotel lawn, blue lights flashing.

The car was definitely a Tesla, a real police car, with a real cop—dark-skinned, his cap pushed back on his forehead, hands on his hips as he stared at another man, who was white, dreadlocked, and naked. The cop looked aggravated, like someone's dad trying to convince his kid to get in the car so he could drive them to school.

Grady put the truck into neutral, so that it barely crept forward, and adjusted the sun visor. As the pickup inched closer, he got a better view of the guy arguing with the cop.

Not arguing: he just stood there staring, his sarong at his feet, as though his skinny body no longer had enough mass to hold it up. Scotty. His friends with the Westfalia must have finally bailed on him. He looked like he was out of his mind on something, with the same wild expression and charred eyes.

Grady shifted into gear. Unless he did an illegal U-turn, he'd have to pass them. He kept close to the centerline, creeping along at the speed limit. The cop didn't give him a glance.

But Scotty's head whipped around. For a second, his gaze met Grady's.

"He won't help you!" he shouted. "Don't believe him!"

Grady flinched and stared back at the road. Still, he clocked how Scotty's mouth gaped open, until it seemed like his lips might split and his sun-blackened face peel away.

CHAPTER 75

When Grady got back to the 'ohana, he tried to normalize things as fast as he could. He made avocado toast, washing it down with a PBR. Raina had called Scotty a lost soul, raving about alien abductions. Grady couldn't blame him for resisting the cop.

He won't help you! Don't believe him!

Grady wouldn't believe a cop, either. He didn't know who he believed anymore.

He texted Donny — another day in paradise! snowing there yet? — a deliberately lame attempt at humor that got an immediate reaction, a photo of Donny's fellow road crew members, all giving him the finger. In retaliation, Grady sent a picture of the cloudless blue sky and distant Pacific.

Seconds later his phone pinged. He read Donny's scatological response and grinned, momentarily fortified. He sent the same photo of the ocean to his mom with a heart emoji. Miss you, hope you're doing well, let's talk soon.

She texted back a photo of herself in full hospital PPE, her face unrecognizable behind its shield and mask. Love you too, so glad you're there not here. tomorrow i have two days off in a row!

Grady texted a row of hearts and texted Zeke last of all, a photo of distant blue water and a seabird soaring calmly overhead. Zeke responded with a photo of a huge, dead eight-point buck in the bed of his pickup. Grady laughed, replied with a thumbs-up emoji, and put the phone back in his pocket. He still felt shaky, but he was safe, his mother and brother and Zeke were safe. So was Raina, so were Dalita and Lorelei and their family. He refused to think about Jessica.

When he finished his beer, he grabbed the half-empty Glenfiddich bottle he'd taken from Minton's earlier, walked over to the main house to return it. When he opened the liquor cupboard, the door wobbled—one of the screws had come loose. He tightened it with his finger, made a mental note to come back with a Phillips-head screwdriver, started to close the cupboard. Stopped.

A large metal water bottle with a logo sat on the top shelf, creamsicle orange. He'd seen similar water bottles at L.L. Bean, where they cost fifty bucks. Grady picked it up, feeling a tightness in his throat as he stared at the logo: a black circle surrounded by irregular lines—the same logo that had been on 'Anuhe's green T-shirt.

CHAPTER 76

He remembered now where he'd seen it before: on Minton's sarong, the evening Grady had arrived; and the next morning, on his espresso cup.

He even had a name picked out, Lorelei had told him. *Kanaka Sun. He hired a graphic designer to come up with a logo . . .*

He set the water bottle on the counter, took a photo, and put it back where he'd found it. He returned to the 'ohana, making an effort to walk slowly, as though nothing unusual had happened, as though someone might be watching him. Once inside, he hurried into the kitchen, where he grabbed hold of the counter and waited for the wave of dizziness to pass, murmuring, *"Fuck, fuck, fuck,"* beneath his breath. After a minute he got out his phone and texted Minton, hoping it wouldn't be days before he replied.

Going to town tomorrow. Need anything?

He took a fast shower, washing away the salt and sweat and sand from a day that already felt forty-eight hours long. When he got out, he found a message waiting.

thx don't need anything attm. well supplied here

Grady sank onto the bed in relief, jumping up when the phone pinged again.

you might check solar panels if you had same high wind as here. If not no worries

Will do, Grady texted back. take care

He dressed quickly and raced outside, entered the garage and searched everywhere for something that might help him make sense of what he'd seen. He found nothing with the same logo. He racked his brain, trying to recall if there'd been anything he'd come across while cleaning out the garage. Could he have thrown away some clue or shred of evidence?

He looked up and stared across the garage, at the door with the Commando lock.

"Fuck me," he said.

He ran over and yanked at it, kicked the door fruitlessly. He could attack the outside wall with a Sawzall, but that would take time. And if he was somehow wrong about this, it would be impossible to explain why he'd hacked through his employer's garage.

There had to be a key. Minton had told him when he drove the KTM back to the house, *I'm always losing keys . . . I have an extra set here.*

He raced into the house, ran upstairs, and searched the bedroom, bathroom, bureaus, closets. Even the aviary, where the honeycreepers flew everywhere, crying in alarm as he dug his fingers into terra cotta pots and searched the pool beneath the fake waterfall. Discouraged and angry, he stormed downstairs, halting to gaze into the wana aquarium.

That would be a great place to hide a key, only every time you needed it, you'd have to don heavy-duty gloves and take the chance of poisoning yourself. Minton wouldn't bother. He felt smug here, in his cozy fortress. He'd hide the key, but someplace where he'd be able to access it easily.

Grady looked around the living room, thinking of his brother, Donny. How when he was a teenager, he'd hide his weed and X and crack in his bedroom. A Bible that was actually a safe. A Band-Aid container. A box of Oreos with a plastic baggie hidden in the bottom.

Grady ran into the kitchen, looked through drawers and beneath the sink, the freezer. He inspected the liquor cabinet, then yanked open a cupboard, examining bags of granola, organic muesli, Irish steel-cut oatmeal, and organic flaxseed. He replaced them, then grabbed a box of shredded wheat from the shelf's back corner. The box was heavy, and jingled when he picked it up.

He dumped its contents onto the counter. Dozens of keys, mostly ordinary household keys, including one to a post office box and some old skeleton keys, the kind he used to believe would unlock a treasure chest, if only he could find one. He spread them across the counter, examining each until he saw the one he wanted: a gold-colored metal key stamped with the word "Commando."

He swept the other keys back into the shredded wheat box, shoved it back where he'd found it, and ran outside to the garage. Past the neatly organized boxes and shelves of tools, past the cabinets full of outdoor gear, the mountain bike and scuba gear and lawn mower. When he reached the padlocked door, he slipped the key into the lock and turned it, praying that it was right, that the pins inside the lock would engage. They did.

He tugged the shackle, and it slid away from the body of the lock. He removed it from the door hasp, freed the latch. The door opened inward. He pocketed the lock, felt around till he located a light switch, and stepped inside.

The room was dim, lit by a 40-watt LED bulb, and smaller than he'd expected—four by six, the size of a deep closet. The same concrete floor as the garage, reinforced walls. A dropped ceiling eight feet above the floor. No access panel here, no openings or panels anywhere. Metal shelving took up most of the space, bolted to the walls.

Three shelves, the top one empty. The second shelf held two large Sterilite storage bins, their sides translucent so Grady could see they were empty. He took each one down and checked to make sure, put them back.

The lowest shelf held four identical opaque bins. He opened the first. It contained stacks of men's pants, dark khaki green, all neatly folded and brand-new with tags attached. Grady held up a pair and looked at the tag. His size. He went through the rest, sixteen pairs in total. Different sizes but otherwise identical, all carefully folded, all retaining a whiff of that new-clothes smell he associated with back-to-school shopping.

Grady tried to recall if he'd seen Minton wear pants like these. Possibly. He'd heard of people buying things in bulk during the pandemic, but this seemed odd. He went through the pants again, checking all the pockets. Empty. He examined the manufacturer's label: a well-known American company, the pants made in the US. Minton wasn't spending his money on cheap clothes from China that would end up in a landfill.

But where were these supposed to end up? Grady stared at the mountain of khaki, then carefully refolded and restacked everything, hoping to replicate how orderly they'd appeared when he opened the bin. When he was finished, he closed the bin and opened the one beside it.

This one held cotton plaid boxer shorts. Again, there were sixteen, brand-new, neatly folded and stacked. A different US manufacturer. This time he didn't bother to remove them all. Just slid his hands between each pair, looking for—what? Currency, packets of drugs? He found neither. It was a bin full of frigging boxers.

He closed the bin, set it on the floor, pulled out the one behind it. He yanked off the lid and stared at stacks of folded T-shirts, all the same shade of jade-green, each with the logo of a spidery black sun.

CHAPTER 77

"What the hell," Grady whispered, and picked up a shirt. The tag read MEN'S MEDIUM. As with everything else, it was made in the US, 100% COTTON. If Grady hadn't just seen a photo of the same shirt worn by a dead guy, he would've thought Minton was a hoarder. Or one of those frugal rich people, hanging on to the staff uniforms he'd bought for his failed resort.

But Grady had never seen Minton wear a T-shirt like this. He set it aside and went through the same drill as before, checking to be sure nothing else was hidden. As with the khakis and boxers, there were sixteen. He took a photo of the restacked T-shirts, a second photo that zeroed in on the logo. He closed the bin and pulled out the final container. Cargo shorts, the same brand and color as the khaki pants, and stacks of white athletic socks.

He swore again, put the bins back where he'd found them. He leaned against the wall, bewildered. Why keep all these clothes? Why not donate them to a homeless shelter or Goodwill?

Maybe he didn't want reminders of his aborted venture floating around the island. But why keep them locked up in a secret storage space in the garage?

After a minute, Grady got to his knees and peered beneath the shelving unit. He saw nothing, and turned on his cell phone's flashlight to look more closely. He barely made out two small square shapes against the back wall. There wasn't enough room for him to squeeze under the bottom shelf, so he stood, dashed back into the garage, returning with a broom. He used the handle to push the objects toward him, one at a time.

Two metal boxes: one the size of a shoebox, the other smaller. The larger box was heavier. He shook it cautiously and heard things moving around inside. When he shook the other box, its contents didn't move. Both boxes were locked.

Grady stared at them, at last picked them up and got to his feet. He inspected the room to make sure it looked as it had when he'd entered, grabbed the broom, turned off the light, stepped back out. He replaced the Commando padlock and returned to Minton's kitchen. He got out the shredded wheat box and once more sorted through the keys, trying every one on the locked metal boxes.

He found the key for the smaller box first. He opened it to find a taped-up wad of Bubble Wrap. He unpeeled the tape, unwrapped it to reveal three small white pharmaceutical boxes, each labeled flunitrazepam. He took a picture of the labels and boxes, rewrapped them, and locked them back inside. He started looking for the other key.

He was sweating now, hyperaware that what he was doing could in no way be considered part of his duties. Minton had said he'd be gone another week, but what if he'd lied, what if even now he was driving back to the house in his silent car? Grady's chest hurt. He'd lost track of which keys were which and had to start again, his hands damp. Outside, the sun had dipped below the treetops. Bars of golden light slanted through the windows to fall across the counter.

If Minton returned now, Grady was fucked. Probably he was fucked no matter what.

He found the key and slipped it into the keyhole of the larger box. It turned like a charm. The lid opened easily.

The golden light fell onto a box of cell phones, more than a dozen of them, none new. Flip phones and TracFones, iPhones and Galaxies, old Motorolas and Nokias, and the same model iPhone that Grady owned, only blue, not red. He hesitated, then turned it on.

The screenshot showed a boogie board on the sand, a pair of

flip-flop-clad feet—a guy's feet—and a can of Bikini Blonde beer. A photo taken by some local guy, probably around Grady's own age, give or take a few years. The same guy who owned the phone, someone who was almost certainly dead.

He immediately turned off the phone and closed his eyes, feeling faint. When he knew he wouldn't be sick, he took a photo of each cell phone, put them back into the strongbox, and locked it again. He kept the keys for the two boxes, and the one for the Commando padlock. He swept the other keys into the shredded wheat carton and replaced it in the cupboard. Picking up the metal boxes and the three keys, he returned to the 'ohana.

CHAPTER 78

He went online and searched for flights to Boston. There were no direct flights to the mainland—they'd been cut back due to the pandemic. The next available flight to Oʻahu was the next day, but there were no flights from Honolulu to the mainland for two days after that. He'd have to stay in a hotel until then, and he wasn't even certain that would be possible, because of the interisland quarantine.

In any event, he couldn't afford it. Working for Minton had boosted his bank account, but not that much. He only had a debit card, not a credit card.

He ran his hands through his hair. Call the cops, he should call the cops. But would they believe him? Minton would have a perfectly legitimate reason for keeping all that stuff. The clothing with the logos, for sure. And people lost their phones all the time. Minton gave millions of dollars to preserve the environment. Maybe he walked around the beaches, picking up discarded cell phones.

If Grady could come up with those excuses off the top of his head, Minton the gazillionaire could do better. He'd have lawyers on retainer, he could sue Grady for slander. Boot him off the island, keep him from ever getting hired again. Grady had watched enough true-crime shows to know that, without a smoking gun, murderers got off all the time. Especially rich white ones. If Grady went to the cops, it was more possible that he'd be under suspicion. At the very least, he'd be questioned, maybe held at the station. He'd read about people who got the virus after getting tossed into the drunk tank.

Worst-case scenario, he could be the fall guy for Minton. Grady was five thousand miles from home. He knew virtually no one here. He couldn't afford an attorney.

He was fucked.

He stared at the photo he'd taken of the pharmaceutical boxes and copied out the name of the drug, typed it into his laptop's search bar, and went to the DEA website. A photo showed an identical box, along with pictures of the pills inside, white or green.

Generic: flunitrazepam. Also known as Rohypnol. A powerful benzo-diazepine derivative, a Schedule IV substance under the Controlled Substances Act, not approved for manufacture, sale, use, or importation to the United States. High doses, particularly when combined with CNS depressant drugs such as alcohol and heroin, can cause severe sedation, unconsciousness, slow heart rate, and suppression of respiration that may be sufficient to result in death. Rohypnol is also referred to as a "date rape" drug . . .

The drug could be used to treat insomnia—but not in this country. Which meant Minton was either dealing it or using it himself. He'd never mentioned insomnia: every time Grady had seen him, Minton seemed wide-awake, even hyper. There was no legal reason for him to have these pills.

Grady grabbed the box containing the drugs as well as the cell-phone box and ran to Minton's garage. He opened the Commando lock and entered the secret room, using the broom to shove the boxes back where he'd discovered them. He was shaking so hard it took him two tries to get the Commando hasp into its slot.

It would be early afternoon at home in Maine. He texted his brother as he returned to the 'ohana.

what happens if you get roofied?

wtf you desperate???

no asshole what does it feel like? could you go to work next day

hell no never tried it i never had to use it on anyone else!!! srsly
not worth it lil brother even for those hawaiian girls ☠

just curious watching a movie

ok well dont!!!! Listen to the voice of Unreason!

kk thx

what movie??

Grady texted Donny an emoji of an alien and set aside his phone.

Minton didn't use flunitrazepam to help him sleep. He was using
it to drug people—judging from the clothes locked up in the
storage room, men. Grady took a deep breath. He'd seen plenty of
unisex uniforms, khakis and T-shirts. So maybe women, too. Maybe
Jessica Kiyoko.

CHAPTER 79

He hadn't gone through the cell phones to see if any still worked, except for that one with the screenshot of a beach scene, or heard who might pick up if he returned a call. The thought had made him sick to his stomach.

It's a collection, he thought. That was one of the things serial killers did, right? Collect trophies of the people they murdered. He thought of all those missing-person flyers, the names painted on the walls of Hale o Nalowale. He thought of 'Anuhe, the young man who had been found on the beach. He was no longer among the disappeared: even if he was dead, he'd been found. Would they do an autopsy? Probably not. A homeless man, presumed drowned. Was one of those phones his?

Grady shut his eyes. 'Anuhe had been living on the beach, maybe selling psilocybin to his friends. He'd last been seen getting into a cop car a couple of weeks ago, though the police had no record of him being brought in.

Angelo—Raina's cousin—had mentioned something when they were hanging out at her place.

A call came through dispatch yesterday . . . Guy fishing in a boat out past Hokuloa Cove saw someone swimming . . . He radioed it in and took his boat over, but by then the person was gone.

Grady typed "Hokuloa Cove" into his laptop, clicked on the map, waited for the image to pop up. The cove was near the easternmost tip of Hokuloa Peninsula.

Not many miles from where Wes Minton was now.

CHAPTER 80

It could work like this: Minton would scope out some vulnerable homeless person, someone sleeping on a remote beach. He'd approach them, pretend to be a cop. In the dark, his Tesla might look like a police car, especially with a flashing blue light blinding them. Especially if they were young and scared, maybe high, or drunk. Once in the car, he'd drug them and drive them down Hokuloa Road, out to Hokuloa Point.

Or maybe he didn't need to do all that. Maybe he could just offer them a ride, a beer, some drugs. Pay them for sex. Once they reached the point, he could keep them for days, weeks, months even. Lorelei had implied the point was accessible by boat. When he needed to, he could just dump them in the Pacific. If that swimmer had been 'Anuhe? Somehow, he'd survived long enough to escape, to be spotted by that fisherman. He'd almost made it back.

The reefs are filled with bones. Wes Minton had said that wasn't true, but he was lying.

Or I could be losing my mind, thought Grady. Dog-men, vanishing people, those horrible screams . . .

But Raina had been with him yesterday—whatever had happened, she'd heard it. She'd been part of it.

And Jessica might be part of it, too. He couldn't shake the sense, as irrational as it was, that their paths had crossed for a reason. It wasn't just that she'd reminded him, in an uncanny fashion, of Kayla MacIntosh; or that Kayla's suicide, and his father's, and Jessie's disappearance all seemed like points on a star chart he couldn't read. Because there were other points there, too — Scotty, with his mad stare and gaping mouth; Raina and Kaupe; the sea urchins and the birds in Minton's aviary. All those people whose cell phones filled a metal strongbox. All those people whose names were written on an abandoned building in the middle of a burned-out field. Minton himself.

And Scotty again. *He won't help you! Don't believe him!* Minton must have taken him, too, only Scotty had somehow managed to escape. But what about what Grady himself had seen, or imagined he had — something crawling from Scotty's mouth, or into it? Could that have something to do with Kaupe? Had Scotty encountered it, too?

Grady clutched his head, feeling like he, too, was on the verge of losing his shit completely. What the fuck had he fallen into? A world where people disappeared and ghosts screamed with the voices of people he cared about, a world where Scotty might actually be the only one who knew the truth about what was going on?

Without wanting to, without even knowing it, Grady had become part of a mystery, not just of those who'd vanished here but of something deeper, something he couldn't understand. His whole life, he'd fucked up or lost so many things. His dad. His brother. His own chance to finish college. His failed, four-year relationship with Rachel. The EMT job. Kayla. Every epithet Donny had ever thrown at him echoed through Grady's head: *fucking coward, loser, pussy, piece of shit*. No wonder some terrible creature wanted to kill him.

Except it didn't kill me, he thought. It had scared the shit out of him, but it hadn't hurt him. What if it was trying to communicate? Send him a warning. Tell him something . . .

But if this thing did exist, wouldn't it communicate with someone from the island? Or Minton, who was trying to save Hokuloa, protect what still survived of the wilderness here?

Only Minton wasn't the good guy.

The cell phones. The roofie drugs. All those missing people.

Minton couldn't have killed all of them, but he could have killed some—many—and no one would have noticed a pattern. The island would cover for him, with its riptides and lethal currents, cliffs and impenetrable forests.

And Grady, without realizing it, had covered for him, too. Watching his house so Minton could go out to Hokuloa Point, making sure everything would be fine when he returned. Grady couldn't imagine Dalita had known anything about this, but the other caretakers might have figured it out. That was why they'd disappeared—Minton had killed them. Or perhaps Kaupe had, trying to protect the peninsula from interlopers.

But Leonardo Sanchez—he might have helped Minton. Maybe Sanchez hadn't been the surfer killed by Kaupe on the beach with the petroglyphs. He could be with him right now, out at the point. Maybe Minton didn't abduct just homeless men but women, too. Like Jessie. Meanwhile, here was Grady, living in Minton's 'ohana and making this possible.

And, he had to admit, he was probably as expendable as all those others had been.

He thought of Dalita's question and his own response: *What do you do if you don't have the right tools? You make do.* What if Grady just happened to be the tool at hand—not the best one but the one within reach? The haole was the problem: let a haole clean it up.

And what was it Lorelei had said about the kupua? *If they exist, they're not going to think or act the way we do. They're not going to care about the same things.*

Kaupe was a dog spirit, so maybe Grady was being harried, the way border collies harried sheep at the dog trials at the Common Ground Fair. The sheep didn't understand why. They just ran where directed.

He pulled over his laptop, hesitated. Whatever else he might find at Minton's isolated compound, there was a chance Jessie was out there. As long as that was even a remote possibility, he had to go. He opened the map app and typed in "Hokuloa Road."

CHAPTER 81

U sing the satellite view, he traced Hokuloa Road toward the eastern end of the peninsula. From above, the journey appeared intimidating. The road hugged the cliffs in a series of zigzags that seemed impossible to navigate in a vehicle, but Minton, and Irma Ohelo before him, had managed. Grady thought of Maine roads he'd driven in blizzards. As much a matter of body memory as quick reaction time. He could drive the truck out there, at least part of the way, then walk. But the thought of driving that stretch of unfamiliar road made him feel sick and dizzy. He remembered the mangled vehicles he'd seen on the cliffs, caught by a spur of rock before they could plunge into the waves crashing below. And he might run into Wes, and then what? He couldn't do it.

Even walking would be a challenge, especially if it rained. When it rained. There would be constant danger of falling rocks and mudslides.

After about sixteen miles, a gate blocked the road, more Area 51 than standard neighborhood design. Hard to gauge how tall it was, based on the satellite shot. Grady's best guess was twenty feet, too high to scale, wedged between the rocks. He couldn't imagine anyone getting past it. For several miles before the gate, an ancient lava flow had taken out the vegetation, all the way to the sea—a motionless river of black stone. Hokuloa Road cut through the lava, near where it reached the cliffs, work that Irma Ohelo must have commissioned almost a century ago.

Past that point, the entire tip of the peninsula had been redacted from the satellite map. All Grady could see were interlocking red squares and smudges, green, black, and blue, that represented forest, black cliffs, and blue ocean.

He searched in vain for aerial views, drone photos, pictures of the rain forest. There was one thirty-seven-second video taken years ago by an enterprising hiker as he approached the lava field. Minton's efforts at keeping his name from appearing online extended to his private wilderness as well. Grady could only imagine this shaky footage remained as a deterrent. The lava field seemed like a good place to disappear.

He closed his laptop, hurried into the bedroom to empty his backpack, then went into the kitchen to take stock. He had five packaged seitan meals his predecessor had left plus one chicken tikka. A few cans of beans were too heavy to carry, so he added a container of sesame rice crackers, packets of seasoned nori seaweed—better than nothing, though it would make him thirsty. In the morning he'd nab granola from Minton's place, along with whatever else he could use. He retrieved four empty plastic water bottles from the recycling bin, filled them and shoved them in the pack.

At home, Zeke had a bug-out bag, which included firearms and ammo. Grady had his knife and the Leatherman tool he'd checked in his suitcase but never removed. Now he stowed it in his backpack, along with rolled-up socks and two T-shirts, his flannel shirt, a hoodie, underwear, and sunscreen. He charged his phone and plugged in his backup battery, too.

He made a mental checklist of what else he'd need, what he'd have to do without. He cursed himself for not bringing his old-fashioned compass. He had a compass on his phone but would have to conserve the battery as much as possible. Minton's garage would provide some stuff—fishing line, a tarp—and Grady could come up with a makeshift first aid kit. Fill a vial with bleach for purifying water. He'd seen that rain poncho and flashlight in the pickup, he'd grab those; also a blanket, and his sunglasses.

He wouldn't bother with a sleeping bag—it wouldn't get that

cold at night. He found some matches in the kitchen, along with a cigarette lighter. He put the matches in a ziplock bag and the lighter in his pocket. Finally, he went back to the kitchen for a beer. He turned off all the lights and sat outside.

Overhead the sky had darkened to a velvety blue-black, the Milky Way a trembling cloud above the treetops. An owl called from the forest, a pueo. It sounded like a small dog barking. He drank his beer, reciting in his head the Hawai'ian names of stars and constellations he'd memorized: Kapu-ahi, Kaulua-koko, 'A'ā.

He walked over to Minton's house. He'd never seen any indication that Minton owned a gun, but now he searched for one. He found nothing. No guns, no weapons of any sort hidden in the bedroom closet, not even a can of pepper spray. If Minton did have a gun, he'd probably keep it with him at his compound.

Grady left Minton's bedroom and went to the aviary. Pushed aside the screen and stood there for a moment in the dark. The breeze wafted through the screened windows, stirring branches and leaves and bearing the scent of jasmine, a faint hint of the sea. He listened for any sounds from the 'i'iwi or 'apapane or 'ākepa but heard only the rustle of leaves and palm fronds. He breathed in the now-familiar musk of the sleeping honeycreepers, lilacs and rot and something he would never know the name of. After a few minutes he left, letting the screen fall closed behind him, and returned to the 'ohana. He longed to have another beer but needed a clear head. He found his phone and called Raina.

CHAPTER 82

R aina answered right away.

"Hey," she said.

"Hey. How's it going?" He heard background noise, hoped she wasn't at Fitzie's but home, where she could talk without being overheard. After a moment the noise stopped. She'd been watching something on TV. "You got a minute?"

"Sure. You okay?"

He took a deep breath. "Okay, listen . . ." He told her about what he'd found in the garage. She was so quiet he had to ask, "You still there?"

"I'm listening," she said. "Go on."

She didn't interrupt him until he told her about his plan.

"That's just plain crazy, Grady. You can't do that. No one goes out there."

"How do you know?"

"How about this: nobody goes out to Hokuloa Point and comes back. The island doesn't want us there. It doesn't want you there."

"Then how come Irma Ohelo? How come Wes Minton?"

"Irma's family protected it. Wes——"

"I think it wants me to go there. The thing on the beach. I think it's been trying to tell me about Minton. You were with me. You heard it, you saw it."

"God, Grady. Maybe you should just call the cops."

"Money talks, Raina. Everybody here tells me how useless the cops are. *You* told me! I need to go. And you can't tell anyone. Not yet, anyway."

There was a long moment before she replied. "Yeah, okay. But you still can't go there alone. You'll die."

"You can't come with me or you'll die, too."

"The fuck, I'm not going out there."

Grady felt the tiniest disappointment. "I wasn't going to ask you."

"Why are you doing this?" she demanded. "You don't know Jessie, you don't have a clue who she is or what she's like. Like you don't know me, like you don't know anything about this place. You're another haole guy who lands here and thinks he's going to be the hero. You think you're going to find all those disappeared people, just waiting for you to save them?"

"No. But Jessie might be there—"

"Jessie is not out there!" She sounded like she was crying. "You're being an asshole, Grady."

She disconnected. Grady stared at his phone. She was right, he knew she was right. But what else could he do? He couldn't stay here, knowing what he did, suspecting what he did. He couldn't afford to return to Maine, not unless he broke down and asked his mother to send him the money. Even then, Minton might guess why he'd fled. Minton could kill him, too. Arrange for an accident back in Maine. Kill his mother, anyone connected with Grady Kendall.

He was overcome with revulsion and dread as he thought about the strongbox full of cell phones back in the padlocked storage room. His phone rang and he snatched it up.

"I'm sorry," Raina said. "It's just, first Jessie, now you—"

"I know. I'm sorry. I shouldn't have sprung it on you like that." He took a breath. "Look, I wanted to ask you a question. That was why I called."

"What?"

"You said your cousin Angelo had some drone footage of Hokuloa Point. Do you think he'd share it with me?"

"No." He heard her take a drink. "It was his friend, not him, but he doesn't have it anymore. Something happened—it got wiped from his computer."

"Like, hacked?"

"I don't know. He said that one day it was just gone. He didn't think he was hacked, just . . . it disappeared."

"Okay. But do you remember anything about it? Anything that might be good for me to know?"

"Not really." He heard her take another drink. "There's a big dock, and he has a powerboat. I assumed it was his. Not a super yacht, like a bowrider."

"Good, this is all good. What about the grounds?"

"I don't know. There's a house—the old house that was originally there. It looked like he put on a big addition or something. But you couldn't really tell. Mostly it's just forest, and the cliffs."

"What about getting there?"

"You can't get there, Grady." She no longer sounded angry, just resigned and sad. "It's all forest except for the lava field. The only way is if you take Hokuloa Road, and he has that huge gate to keep anyone from getting there. Supposedly there's an old road across the lava field that the Hawai'ians used. My great-grandfather had some friends who found it and hiked across it, but that was a hundred years ago. Every year tourists try to find it—they get lost in the forest and have to be rescued. Some of them just never come back."

"I've spent time in the wilderness."

"But not here." He heard ice rattle in her glass. "Jesus, I don't know, Grady," she said at last. She still sounded resigned, but also maybe the tiniest bit excited. "Maybe you're right. Maybe it wants you to do this."

"I think it does. I'm the right tool for the job. Like you need a hammer but you only have a pipe wrench." He laughed, and was relieved when she did, too. "I'll be okay, Raina. I have wilderness training. I was an EMT. I can do this." As he spoke, he felt something ease in his chest, as though a poison he'd swallowed years ago had finally dissolved. "It's the right thing to do."

"It's the insane thing to do, Grady."

"Yeah, maybe. Probably. But I'm still doing it."

CHAPTER 83

After she rang off, he forwarded her all the photos he'd taken in the locked room.

Don't show anyone, he texted. Not unless you have to.

omg don't say that

I'll be ok

He sat and thought of the thing he and Raina had seen on the beach: both dog-like and coffin-like. It had been terrifying, yet what if he was right and it hadn't been threatening him? What if it had been warning him, or sending a signal?

That was when he thought of Scotty. After Chris took a swing at him at Kahawai Beach, Scotty had said something to Grady.

I know what you saw. It told me, too.

It had appeared to Scotty, who had recognized that the thing wasn't just screaming but communicating.

It told me, too.

That on its own would be enough to send you into the deep end, Grady thought shakily. Poor frigging Scotty.

He picked up his phone and called Raina again.

"Listen," he said. "I wanted to say I'm really sorry I got you into this. I'll text you if I get into trouble, and I'll let you know when I get there if we should call the police. If you don't hear from me in three days, call Dalita—I'll give you her number."

"Have you told her about what you found at Minton's?"

"No. I haven't told anyone except for you."

"Why not?"

"Will you do that? Call Dalita in three days? And I'll text you contact info for my mom."

"Jesus." Her voice rose—anxiety, not anger. "Okay, yes, I'll call her. I can't believe you're laying this on me."

"I can't either. I really am an asshole. But how can I not go?"

For a long moment she said nothing. "Okay," she said. "I hope you do find something there. I hope you come back."

"Thank you." He took a deep breath. "I think you're really brave, Raina. Braver than anyone I've ever known. I'll see you in a few days."

"I hope so," she said in a soft voice.

CHAPTER 84

H e closed his laptop, collapsed into bed, and somehow managed to fall asleep. In the night he woke, to snarls and a high-pitched shrilling outside. He lay in bed, holding his breath, as he listened to palm fronds snapping, the crack of a broken branch, growls, and a horrible gurgling squeal interrupted by the distinct sound of teeth crunching on bone.

The squeals grew fainter as the victor fed, until Grady heard only low grunts and panting, followed by footsteps as the animal retreated into the forest. Grady remained motionless, afraid even to grab his phone.

Whatever it was, it sounded big. A wild boar? Feral dog? The night breeze flowed through a window, jasmine cut with a stink of body odor that made him gag. The bad smell dispersed as the nightly rains came, as though someone had switched on a celestial faucet.

He woke again just before sunrise, to the expectant cries of a bulbul and the croons of mourning doves. He thought of what he'd heard in the night. It was a full minute before he remembered that this morning he would leave for Hokuloa Point.

He padded barefoot into the kitchen, looking through the screen door at the cloudless sky, the steaming grass, and the forest canopy, traced in gold. Carefully, he pushed the door open.

He nearly stepped on it: a head. Football-sized, lying on the grass just outside, a mass so mangled he couldn't tell what kind of creature it had been. Its flesh was torn and its gray and black fur matted.

Shuddering, Grady grabbed a stick and poked the thing, turning it over to get a better look.

Pink tendons and shreds of flesh hung between its upper and lower jaws, which had been wrenched apart to expose the rows of sharp teeth in its long, narrow snout. Its eyes had been gouged out, but its ears remained, delicately cupped and as translucent as petals. Part of its spine protruded from the skull, surrounded by strands of white muscle like the tendrils of a jellyfish. Grady ran through every mammal he could think of—dog, cat, mongoose?

No, he realized, it was a rat, or what was left of one. The biggest rat he'd ever seen. With a head that large, it must have been the size of a small pit bull.

It seemed to have fought like one, too. He scanned the lawn, looking for animal tracks. He saw nothing. He found a shovel and chucked the rat's head into the woods.

What the hell was big enough and fierce enough to have killed that thing? Grady couldn't shake the question, even as he resumed packing. And why had it been left for him? As a warning?

Or—and this was an even more unnerving thought—had it been left as a gift? The way a cat would leave a mouse on the doorstep for its owner?

CHAPTER 85

H e quickly made coffee and texted Raina Dalita's contact info, and his mom's. He told her he'd bury the key to the Commando lock beneath a rock at the edge of the forest, where he'd first seen Kaupe, and send her a picture of the rock so she could find it. He hit SEND, then wrote a text to Dalita.

> Minton just dumped a project on me, need to fix some stuff w solar system, will probably take a few days so can't meet for dinner. Maybe next week?

Dalita replied soon after. Lor has that wedding so I'll be w kids all weekend. Next week better. See you soon!

He texted his brother—Taking a hike to explore the mysteries of Hokuloa Point. Well-provisioned—and another to his mom that read, Hope it's a good weekend, love you!

He texted Raina again. Thanks for everything. Stay safe.

He turned off his phone before any of them could reply and make him lose his nerve, and walked over to Wes's place to scavenge a few last supplies. Small tarp, fishing line, bungee cords. A sun hat with a flap to protect his neck. He filled the water bottle with the Kanaka Sun logo and took that, too, along with the smallest bottle in the liquor cabinet, some kind of artisanal tequila. The expensive German binoculars, which were magically lightweight and foldable. He made a bedroll of the tarp and the yellow cashmere blanket. The blanket made him think of Raina. He should have just given it to her.

Last of all, he went upstairs to the aviary. He opened all the windows, removed the screens, and stepped back to see if the birds would fly out. For a long time, none did.

But finally one bird zipped out—an ʻākepa, a female—and a few minutes later another ʻākepa followed, and then an ʻiʻiwi. He waited until, with a great fluttering and chorus of their creaking songs, a sudden exodus of scarlet honeycreepers streamed from the aviary's trees, out the largest window into the blue air, a bright ribbon that tore into innumerable threads as the birds separated, disappearing into the forest.

CHAPTER 86

He returned to the ʻohana, slung on his pack, and headed outside. The day was warm and clear. A golden archipelago floated above the eastern horizon, clouds that gradually faded into the blue. A skein of large white birds circled the cliffs in the direction he would take, their cries carried by the wind. Grady watched them as he ate an avocado with the last of his salsa. He shouldn't care if he didn't return and left a mess for Minton, or, more likely, Dalita, but he cleaned up anyway.

"Okay," he said aloud. "Now or never."

He checked the outside doors of the ʻohana. He'd already closed up the main house. As he walked down the driveway, his heart lifted. In spite of whatever terrors awaited him, this was a beautiful place, the most beautiful place he'd ever been. He punched in the gate's security code, waited for it to open, and headed out onto Hokuloa Road.

CHAPTER 87

For the first few miles, he walked on the uphill side of Hokuloa Road, to avoid leaving tracks. Below him, the road was the same combination of red dust, crushed black lava, sand and gravel. Stands of clumping bamboo and tree ferns alternated with thickets of kolomona, blocking his view of the sea, although he still heard its monotonous boom and crash.

After an hour or so, the vegetation changed. On his left, the land climbed ever more steeply, and the trees thinned out. He caught far-off glimpses of black, like patches of night sky showing through the daylight—the lava field, still many miles off.

He spotted a stand of trees with a high canopy providing shade, settled there to have lunch. He recognized few of the plants here, with less encroachment by introduced species and more of whatever had flourished here hundreds of years ago. He sat where the trees hid him from the road, habit more than necessity, and ate the contents of one of the seitan pouches. It tasted pretty gross cold, but it was better than nothing. It felt good to sit. Even better was to feel his leg muscles ache, the way they used to when he'd take a long hike in the Allagash.

The air felt different here, almost cool. He'd been steadily climbing the entire time he'd been walking. The sea smell was stronger. He heard a seabird, perhaps one he'd seen from Minton's house, its cries louder now. He adjusted his hat and sunglasses and clambered to his feet, shading his eyes to scan the sky, but didn't see the bird.

He walked back down to the road. A carpet of matted greenery grew between the trees, dotted with small white flowers and a grayish herb that released a sharp, pleasant scent when he stepped on it. He halted when he reached a natural berm, a long mound of earth overgrown with the creeping herb and tiny purple flowers. He climbed the berm, clutching his hat as a sudden updraft shook him.

Below, the hill sloped down to the shore, a stretch of white sand. Aquamarine waves rolled onto the beach, dissolving into white and gold spray. He watched for a few minutes, then continued walking.

He camped that night on the forested hillside. He wanted to be able to watch the road below. He checked for centipedes, also fire ants, an invasive species but one that didn't seem to have made its way here. He strung the tarp beneath branches, to provide some shelter when it rained, and ate, watching the last light leak from the sky. He had the beginnings of a blister on one ankle. He'd brought his work boots but not good socks—these were lightweight and worn cotton, not wool. He'd double up the next day.

Night fell swiftly. He caught flickers of starlight between the moving leaves. The moon rose, nearly full. There were no clouds. The forest was full of noises—creaking branches, the cries of unfamiliar birds, a soft snuffling that receded when he sat up, knife in hand. Despite all this, he slept, wearing his hoodie over a flannel shirt, and wrapped in the yellow cashmere blanket he'd packed as part of his bedroll.

He woke as the sky started to pale, from blue-violet to dove-gray. For the first time he could remember, it hadn't rained at night. His phone had clocked that he'd gone over ten miles yesterday, which meant he was about six miles from the point's gate. He was unsure how far Minton's compound was from there. He recalled when his plane had made its final approach, that fleeting glimpse he'd had, windows catching a flash of sun, a white beach. By tonight he might be within sight of it.

He'd have to cross the lava field first, to avoid the road and the possibility of running into Wes, and the impossibility of getting past the security gate. He would have given anything for a map—a real map, a paper map. He'd put his phone into low battery mode, checked if he had reception here. He didn't, so he turned it off.

As the sun rose, he drank some water and ate another one of the packets of seitan chili. Daylight revealed the ground swarming with insects—small wasps with T-shaped wings, long, straggling legs, and sweeping antennae. They appeared oddly toylike. A closer look showed they were moths, not wasps, with transparent white-and-brown wings like a dragonfly's. He repacked everything and walked back down to the road.

The morning passed quickly. The beauty of his surroundings lulled Grady into a strange half-sleep. Unbounded turquoise ocean and black cliffs to one side and the sprawling slope above him, ferns the size of cars and the fleshy tongues of koli'i blossoms, everything alive with unfamiliar insects and birds. Once he saw a powerboat out on the water, a leisure fishing craft with two small figures aboard. He moved behind a tree. A helicopter droned in the distance, barely a dot in the cloudless sky, heading to Kaua'i, perhaps, or going to O'ahu.

Otherwise it was only him and the sun. He kept to the sides of the road, following the shade. When his shadow disappeared he knew it was noon, and paused to eat beneath an overspreading tree. Water trickled steadily down the hillside, seeping into the dust of the road. A good sign. He might find other rivulets ahead, even a stream or waterfall. Once he stopped to rest and dozed for a few minutes without meaning to, waking to a sharp sound—a dog's bark, echoing from far above him.

He scrambled to his feet and gazed up the mountainside. The dog barked again, farther off now. Grady had seen no sign of human presence. *It must be a wild dog,* he thought. He got out his knife and hacked off a low branch, leaned on it to make sure it was sturdy enough to serve as both walking stick and weapon, and resumed his trek.

The lava field appeared without warning as he rounded a long curve. In front of him and to the left of the road, the forest ended.

In its place stretched a wilderness of black rock. He clambered up the hillside, got out the binoculars, and surveyed the landscape.

He'd stupidly imagined it as a real field, like a pasture, only crumbly with black gravel. Instead it looked as though millions of tons of immense, jagged black boulders had dropped from the sky—like a glacial moraine, only far more threatening. He saw no path, no place to stop and rest, no shade.

He turned to look down at the road. From here he could see where, miles away, the gate blocked its access, a high wall of black stone extending to one side, and a sheer drop to the ocean on the other.

He'd have to cross here, on the slope above the gate.

He cut another branch, so he had a pair of rudimentary walking poles. His work boots were sturdy and thick-soled but only came just above his ankles. To traverse this safely, he'd need serious search-and-rescue, tactical-grade boots, steel-plated and made of heavy leather. Not to mention knee and elbow pads in case he fell.

If he did, he might not get up again. He'd die here, and like so many others on the island, his body might never be found.

He couldn't fall.

He drank what remained of the first water bottle, leaving four full ones. He turned on his phone and again checked for a signal. None. He decided to leave it on—he could make use of the compass, if nothing else. He adjusted his sunglasses and sun hat, kept a steady hold on his makeshift poles, and began to cross.

CHAPTER 88

I t was less like walking than climbing a mountain where you never gained elevation. With each step, he had to raise his leg as high as he could, lean forward as he balanced on the sticks, then place his foot down, hoping that the stones beneath wouldn't give way. The lava was like nothing he'd ever known: black shading to deep maroon, the color of marrow in a fresh-cut bone. It was pitted like a sponge and sharp enough to draw blood. Heat rose from the ground as though from a grill.

He moved with excruciating slowness, every step straining his thighs and his arms. At first he tried to find a path among the stones, some route that would avoid the biggest, or most dangerous, rocks. That was hopeless. The rocks seemed random. Maybe a vulcanologist could have made sense of it, but Grady couldn't. He forged on.

If he'd planned this out, he might have made the crossing at night—he would have avoided the deadly heat. Sweat rolled down his face, burning his eyes as his sunscreen melted. His cheeks felt charred from sunburn. His lips were hot: when he licked them they felt brittle and tasted of blood. Without the shelter of the trees, the wind battered him. He was within a mile of the sea—the trade winds howled up from the cliffs and across the lava field, nearly knocking him down.

He was afraid to take out his phone—he might drop it—so he had no idea how long he'd been walking. An hour? Three? A seemingly endless landscape reflected the sun, shimmering like black glass. How far had he walked?

Halfway, maybe. He could see nothing but lava now. He'd tried to follow a straight course but the lack of landmarks, and his inability to accurately locate where the sun was in the sky, made that impossible. He could be wandering in circles.

Once he lost his footing, and barely caught himself. Later, he saw something gleam against the ground, the first thing he'd seen that wasn't lava. He halted to look at it, panting. The lower jawbone of an animal, bleached an unearthly white, its pointed teeth as delicate as needles. He picked it up, so light it might have been made of paper.

Grady looked around but saw no other bones. How had it gotten here? What had killed it? A bird? He'd neither seen nor heard any since stepping foot on the lava, not even a faraway tern or petrel. He set the jawbone back down and continued on.

A moment later, he knew he'd moved too fast. His left foot lodged between two large stones. Before he could stop himself, he fell forward, his foot locked in place. Pain seared his ankle—the same ankle he'd injured during his wilderness training years ago—then flared everywhere as he slammed down.

He lay still, eyes squeezed shut as he fought for breath. For a minute or so he didn't move, trying to determine if he'd broken something. If he'd shattered his ankle, he was done. He summoned the strength to push himself up, the lava biting his palms, gasped when he finally managed to reach a sitting position. He checked that his knife and phone were undamaged. His sunglasses dangled from the lanyard around his neck, though one of the lenses had been badly scraped. He still had his hat.

Wincing, he pulled off his backpack. His lower leg and ankle throbbed, but nothing felt broken. He remained where he was for some time. He drank some water. He'd need his strength, but he was afraid if he ate anything, he'd puke.

He looked around for the walking sticks. One of them had snapped. The other lay a few yards away, though it might have been on the moon. He knew he'd have to get it if he had any hope of continuing.

At last he began the process of attempting to stand. He used the backpack and sturdier-looking part of the broken stick for leverage, and, inch by inch, pushed himself until he was upright. His left foot throbbed, but he didn't get the shooting pain he associated with a serious sprain.

He slid the pack back over his aching shoulders. He used the shortened stick as a cane and hobbled, bent over like an old man, to retrieve the other. It was intact. He jammed the broken stick between some rocks, wishing he had something to use as a flag or marker. He didn't want to part with any clothing yet—if he survived, he'd need it. His knuckles and palms were ripped up, but it would have been worse if he didn't have hands calloused by years of carpentry.

He turned in a circle, trying to figure out where he was. He could no longer see the gate. He'd completely lost his bearings. The endless expanse of lava shimmered in the heat. He closed his eyes for a few seconds, and struck out once more.

Every step was agonizing. His ankle ached. Pain radiated from where he'd scraped his arms. His face and hands felt like they'd been set on fire. He tried to distract himself, but he couldn't bear to think of people he knew. His mother, Donny, Zeke; Raina, Dalita and Lorelei and their kids...if his mind dwelled on any of them, he'd start to cry and never stop. Same thing when he thought of home, of Penobscot Bay, winter nights when the stars seemed to crackle in the night sky. He tried to muster rage against Minton, imagine holding a knife to his throat while demanding that he release Jessie. But exhaustion and a near-total inability to picture himself killing anyone made this impossible.

So he kept his eyes on the ground directly in front of him, measuring his progress in inches. Once he thought he might black out from the heat: he stopped, swaying as he clutched the stick, and after a few moments moved on.

Seconds later he halted. A sound echoed over the wind, ringing off the stones. Another dog's bark. Grady turned to scan the field but saw nothing. He took another step, and the bark came again.

Twenty feet ahead of him, a chunk of lava moved, only it wasn't a rock but a large dog, brindled red and black. He couldn't see its legs, but they must have been long for it to pick its way among the jagged stones. It had pointed ears, a curling tail. Lips curling back from its mouth in a snarl, it raced toward him.

CHAPTER 89

The dog moved impossibly fast before halting a few yards away. Its ears flattened against its skull and it lowered into a crouch, as though to spring. Instead, it then straightened, turned, and picked its way back among the rocks, until it abruptly disappeared.

Grady stared, afraid to go forward or back. A minute later, he heard it bark again. Now it stood atop a flattened ridge, the ground beneath it unexpectedly dun-colored, not black.

"The fuck," Grady whispered.

He hobbled in the direction the dog had taken. After a few dozen steps, he reached where the lava had been crushed to form a path about six feet wide, winding up toward the volcano's summit.

In the other direction, the path ran toward the ocean. He caught the blue glitter of water, a sense of the world unfurling. A few feet in front of him, the dog had turned onto a narrow side path. He'd have to take his chances.

He limped to the trail. Here, the crumbled lava was more like gravel—still treacherously loose, and sharp, but a fall wouldn't kill him. Far above him reared the volcano, a heavy gray veil of cloud hanging over its summit. He saw no further sign of the dog.

After fifteen minutes, the lava field ended as abruptly as it had started. Grady stepped off the path onto a brown strip of tussocky earth, facing a forest so green it hurt to look at it. Leaning on his stick, he walked slowly beneath branches covered with pink flowers. He touched a tree trunk: moisture welled from its bark. There would be water here, even if he had to purify it.

He removed his pack, and eased himself onto the ground. He leaned against the tree, longing to close his eyes, but he was afraid to fall asleep. He got out one of the water bottles, drank, then poured a small amount onto one of his clean T-shirts. He dabbed his face with it, then his arm. He'd been wearing a long-sleeved shirt to protect himself from the sun, but his fall had torn the fabric and left a two-inch gash above his elbow. The cut wasn't deep, but here he was worried about infection. On one of the Reddit forums he'd read about rat lungworm, a disease just as awful as it sounded, and leptospirosis, which sounded like Maine's beaver fever. He opened the plastic container that held his first aid supplies.

He hadn't brought enough antiseptic wipes, that was for sure. He used several to clean the cut, then his abraded cheek, and covered his exposed skin as best he could with Band-Aids. If he had to, he could use the tequila as a disinfectant. Right now he'd rather drink it.

He had remembered to pack an ACE bandage. After his humiliating experience in the Allagash, he never went hunting or hiking without one. He removed his boot and sock, whistling in pain. His ankle had swollen; a nasty bruise would come up in the next few days. He wrapped it with the bandage, put on a clean sock, then pulled the sock he'd been wearing over it. He'd wait till tomorrow to put his boot back on. By morning the swelling might have gone down enough.

It was still daylight, but the sun had dropped closer to the horizon. It would get dark quickly. Exhaustion had taken hold of him like a fever. He spread out the tarp and cashmere blanket, pulled on his hoodie, and opened the package of chicken tikka. He could only choke down half of it, so he set aside what remained for breakfast. He drank more water and took three ibuprofen, opened the small black bottle of tequila and took a long swallow. He knew you weren't supposed to drink when injured, but he needed something to take the edge off.

Who had made that path? he wondered. It must have been built by the people who lived here hundreds of years ago. Had they been here already when the volcano had last erupted? He didn't even know when that had been—six hundred years ago? Seven hundred? Before European contact. He longed to know more about them, whoever they were—where they'd come from, how they'd lived. Where they'd lived.

Of course their descendants were still here, trying to survive the pandemic like everyone else. They must know about the trail. It must be a sacred place, like the rock chamber on the beach. He probably shouldn't even be here.

Grady took another mouthful of tequila, then poured a bit onto the ground. He wished he knew a prayer to volcanos. Instead he said, "Thanks." Zeke did that whenever they drank outdoors—poured a little beer or home-brewed mead onto the grass as an offering to Odin. Grady didn't believe in Odin any more than he believed in Jesus. Still, better safe than sorry.

He put away the bottle and eased himself onto the tarp, propped his injured foot on his pack to help with the swelling, and wrapped the blanket around him. Above, the sun still shone through the shifting patchwork of leaves. His body ached as though he'd fallen down a set of concrete stairs. Despite that, within minutes he was asleep.

CHAPTER 90

He woke before dawn to a persistent drone, like that of a small aircraft. He blinked but didn't see an airplane, though the droning continued. He checked the gash on his arm, cleaned it again and put on new Band-Aids, rewrapped his ankle. He'd forgotten yesterday to check on the binoculars—had they broken when he fell?

They were intact. That was one good thing, anyway.

He ate quickly, then cleaned up, testing out his ankle as he walked a few yards from his camp. Still sore, but better than when he'd wrenched it in the Allagash. If he could spend a day with his leg up, resting, it would probably be better by tomorrow. That wasn't going to happen, so he took more ibuprofen, smeared on sunscreen, broke camp, and started out again.

Woods surrounded him, the lower rain forest that had sprung up millions of years ago, composed of plants he'd never seen before. Trees whose pale, gnarled branches looked like exposed muscle, covered with small leaves and red brush-like flowers. He soon realized what the droning was.

Both air and flowers were alive with bees. He paused; his mom was allergic—she always carried an EpiPen—but she wasn't afraid of them. "You have to move slowly," she'd said. "Don't be aggressive. They respond to our pheromones, men especially—they can smell anger or aggression and they'll sting you."

Grady felt anything but aggressive right now. And he had no choice but to move slowly, putting his stick down and barely letting his bad foot touch the ground. The bees unnerved him. There were so many, not hundreds but thousands, tens of thousands—in places the branches bowed beneath their weight, as though covered with a rippling brown rug.

More zipped past him. Now and then one would momentarily alight on his hand, tiny legs tickling his scraped-up knuckles. He had to resist the urge to swat it.

He walked among plants escaped from a Dr. Seuss book. Leaves like black-spotted tongues; hanging vines with drooping, pale green flowers like clusters of luna moths. 'Ākohekohes perched in the trees like punked-out starlings, curved black beaks dipping into 'ōhi'a flowers. Like the bees, they paid no attention to him.

After half an hour of walking, the trees thinned and a clearing opened up. It took a moment for Grady's eyes to adjust, and even then he couldn't focus properly. He removed his sunglasses, thinking the scratched lens was causing some refraction, and stared in wonder.

Everywhere around him, the air flickered green and pale blue, almost white. Fluttering shapes fell like rain, then rose again, drifts of petals in a storm.

Except they weren't flowers but butterflies. They flew into his face, landed in his hair, smeared his sunglasses with greenish powder from their wings. They fed upon the low-growing flowers, so it was impossible to avoid stepping on them. He quickly retreated to the edge of the clearing. He brushed them off his shirt, sad for those he'd inadvertently killed but also grossed out.

Instead, he made his way within the trees again, realizing that every-where around him, birds sang or flew or perched, so many that he couldn't tell apart their songs, moving through the woods like a vast school of fish might move through the sea. He glimpsed flashes of yellow and fiery orange, like feathered sparklers burning in the greenery. Their scent filled his nostrils: overripe guavas, moldering wood, musk.

Was this what it had been like when the first people came here?

As swiftly as the eerie symphony had started, it began to fade, as the birds fluttered off to places where he couldn't follow them.

He stopped to lean against a tree. His ankle ached, and he still needed the walking stick, but he obviously hadn't been as badly hurt as he'd feared. He drank some water—he had three full bottles left, which might be enough to get him to Minton's compound.

And then what? His messed-up ankle meant he wouldn't be able to move quickly in a fight, not that he ever had. And it wasn't like he was truly capable of killing anyone. He needed Donny here to egg him on, goad him into doing something Grady knew he would never be able to do. Or Zeke, who could offer a prayer to Odin, then, without hesitation, slit a buck's throat and watch the blood spill onto the ground.

There was also the possibility that Grady was wrong. Jessie might have taken off on her own without telling Raina—a horrible thing to imagine, but better surely than thinking she was dead. Grady hadn't believed it when Minton told him he'd photographed an extinct bird—but what if that was true? Wesley Minton might be exactly who people thought he was—a wealthy recluse who'd helped save this tiny, astonishing piece of the world. If Grady wrongly accused Minton, he'd be doomed as the asshole who tried to take down one of the good guys. The media would love it. Donny would say, *I told you so, dickweed*.

But he couldn't go back, not if there was the tiniest chance he might find Jessica. He wondered now if hers was the voice Raina had first heard on the beach. *It sometimes imitates someone you love—to lure you.*

He cleaned his sunglasses on his shirt, checked his phone again for a nonexistent signal, then used its compass to get a bearing, registering due east. The unseen peninsula ended there, a spur of rock and sand surrounded by thousands of miles of open ocean. He swallowed another mouthful of water and headed on.

The gulch appeared so unexpectedly that he took a step into empty air. Grabbing a woody vine, he pulled himself back to more stable ground, and peered down.

He'd disturbed the earth already, exposing grub-like roots and a mulch of brown leaves. Something white glistened a few yards down, a fast-food container dislodged by his fall, the first human-made thing he'd seen since leaving the 'ohana. He bellied down at the edge of the ravine, ignoring the tiny spiders that crawled across his face, and moved forward inch by inch until he grasped the broken container and scooted back up.

He turned it in his hands. Not a Styrofoam container but a broken bowl, greenish white and flecked with dirt, its surface rough beneath his fingertips. As he held it to the light, he saw where it had shattered, and a deep impression above the broken curve: what remained of an eye socket.

It wasn't a bowl or cup but a fragment of a human skull.

CHAPTER 91

He almost dropped it, barely clutching it in one hand as he inched back from the top of the ravine. A sheen of moisture covered the skull's interior. He flicked a beetle from the eye socket.

He was shocked by how heavy it was—he knew from his anatomy classes that an intact skull could weigh more than a pound. This fragment was roughly a quarter. He had no idea if it belonged to a man or a woman, only that it looked like an adult's. He set it on the ground in front of him, stared at it for a long time, then at last put it into his backpack.

He jammed his walking stick into the ground. He tied a sock around it as a marker, so he could find his way back. He tightened his pack on his shoulders and scooted again to the top of the gulch. Inch by inch, he made his way down. He dug into the slope as he went but found nothing save soft chunks of rotting bark and handfuls of leaf mold. Finally he reached the floor.

It took a few moments for his eyes to adjust. He'd entered a world of green twilight, the forest trees above him impossibly far away. A few grew on the steep slopes, their skeletal branches struggling toward the light. But ferns were everywhere: some like gargantuan versions of Maine's cinnamon ferns, others with fronds like yard-long fingers, covered with rows of brown spores. The floor of the gulch was about ten feet wide. If a flash flood came through, he'd drown in minutes.

He craned his neck to check for any sign of rain, but all he saw were slivers of blue. Behind him, the gulch receded into shadow.

Ahead of him it brightened. That was east. He decided to explore down here for a short while, then find his way back to the sock.

He started by heading west, behind him, though "behind" and "in front" were almost meaningless here: there was only up and down, shadow and near-shadow. He walked in the middle of the gulch, using his good foot to move away layers of decomposing leaves. His clothes and skin grew sticky with sweat and dirt, leaf mold, insects. He tasted the air in the back of his mouth, as though he'd swallowed a chunk of moss.

He halted to peer under fountains of ferns, moved decaying logs that exploded into musty-smelling clouds. Once he saw a star-shaped object he took to be a pink flower, sprouting from the ground. He stooped to get a better look and saw it was a fleshy fungus swarming with flies, its six arms like those of a starfish, only forked. It smelled putrid, alien roadkill that had sat in the sun on a hot day. Did anything live on the island that hadn't come from outer space?

The western end of the gulch finally ended in a rock face. Long vines dangled from a few last twisted trees. He tugged one, and a brown bird darted past him with a reverse wolf whistle—an 'elepaio.

He turned and reversed his steps. It was easy to tell where he'd walked—the ground chewed up by his footsteps, small plants uprooted, rotting debris scattered everywhere. It might have been years, decades or perhaps centuries, since someone had walked here.

Except for whoever that skull belonged to. He'd been so mesmerized by the steady rhythm of his journey that he'd nearly forgotten his purpose. When he saw the sock flag at the top of the gulch, he paused to sit on a rock. He drank some water and retrieved the skull from his pack. He gazed at it, no longer repelled, but sad.

Who were you? he thought. *Who are you?* He replaced it in his pack and forged on.

Within minutes, his foot had uncovered something long and brown beneath the loose soil. Despite its discoloration, he recognized it: a human femur. He swept aside the dirt until he uncovered another bone, this one a rib. He continued to dig but found nothing else.

He reburied the remains and continued until he spotted a patch of whitish green, a confusion of bones banked against a truck-sized boulder. They must have washed up there in a flood. Or possibly someone had fallen and been unable to climb back up?

Or the body could have been dumped here.

A skull's greenish crown poked from the soil. Grady dug around it, exposing a leathery patch with coarse blond hairs still attached. He turned it over and saw its teeth were intact. Two lower molars had fillings in them.

He prodded the other bones with his foot, disturbing centipedes and beetles. There was no smell of carrion, just rotting vegetation. He exposed part of a rib cage. Something was twisted around the ribs, a fern that, when he touched it, shed particles of black soil. It wasn't a fern but the remnants of a T-shirt, jade-green and stitched with black mold.

CHAPTER 92

*F*uck, fuck, fuck, Grady thought. He examined the scrap of fabric, searching for an identifying logo, a label, a name. No dice. It tore as he handled it, the threads brittle with decay.

It could belong to anyone, he told himself. A random hiker, some freaking hippie tripping his or her ass off, oblivious until they took a misstep and tumbled to their death. Or got caught unawares in a sudden rainstorm.

Grady recalled the clot of blond hair he'd removed from the drain in Wes's house. What were the odds that these remains were *not* those of a murder victim?

Not so good, he thought.

He dropped the tattered fabric, stood, and gazed at the jumble of bones at his feet. Someone with a name; a son or daughter, a parent, a lover. He removed the broken skull from his pack and gently set it down, feeling like he should say something, like a prayer. But he didn't believe in God, especially now.

It was much more difficult climbing up the gulch than it had been coming down. He was exhausted; his foot ached. But he finally heaved himself onto level ground.

He must have dozed off: he opened his eyes, confused as to where he was. Camden Hills State Park? The Allagash? He tried to make sense of the oppressive heat and unfamiliar trees, the fiery pulse in his ankle. With a crushing dread, he remembered: he was on the Hokuloa Peninsula. He had no choice but to keep going.

He sipped some water. He had enough to last till tomorrow, if he was frugal. He took another bearing with his phone compass. He left the sock flag as a marker for where he'd found the remains, cut another walking stick, and headed east. After about an hour, he reached a clearing and stopped.

In the shade of some tall ferns was an area of soil as dark as coffee grounds. An uneven circle a few feet in diameter, stitched with small vines and seedlings. Grady crouched, wincing in pain, and dug until his fingers touched something—a piece of fabric, filthy but recognizable as plaid flannel. He dug more quickly, uncovering part of a sleeve, green-and-yellow plaid patched with mold.

He paused to wipe sweat from his face. At this rate, it would take him hours to uncover whatever was buried here. He rooted through his pack for the makeshift first aid kit, packed in a plastic container. He stashed its contents in the backpack and used the empty container to dig until he'd unearthed a heap of clothing, or what remained of it.

The smell rocked him back on his heels. Not the stench of a rotting body but the stink of urine and sweat and human shit. A flannel shirt disintegrated into ribbons when he tried to lift it. There was more to a pair of denim jeans, though they, too, fell apart when he lifted them. He grabbed a stick and poked at a smaller wad of decayed fabric, lifting a sock like a shed snakeskin. He used the stick to push aside the rotting clothes, and kept digging with the plastic container, light-headed in anticipation of unearthing a body.

But there was no body, just a pile of rotting fabric barely recognizable as clothing. He separated everything with the stick: jeans, a shirt, socks. The jeans were large, the shirt, too, suggesting they belonged to a man. So did a frayed elastic band, all that was left of a pair of jockey shorts. No shoes. No watch or jewelry or anything else that wouldn't decay quickly in this hothouse microclimate, where it might take only weeks or months to decompose. He stopped when he'd dug a hole about two feet in diameter and the same depth, and found nothing else.

Where was the body?

CHAPTER 93

He filled in the hole, stood, and scraped leaves and vines across the area he'd uncovered. If you knew what you were looking for, you'd be able to tell that the soil had been disturbed. To anyone else, it would be part of the patchwork of ground cover.

Someone had buried those clothes, and it had to have been Minton. Why? This spot was so remote—the police would never come here to search for anyone who might have gone missing. In any case, the bodies would decay quickly, more quickly than fabric.

And even out here, the corpses might draw predators, Grady thought. Wild dogs, rats, mongooses—all the creatures Minton wanted to keep from his sanctuary. He'd find another way to dispose of whoever he killed.

The reefs are filled with bones.

But the clothes, those would be proof. He started walking again, halting to investigate every patch of ground that appeared darker or lighter than the soil around it. Now and then he heard the twittering of a bird that perched somewhere just out of sight, an 'ākohekohe's odd gurgles and grunts, almost like a dog's.

He soon discovered another site, this one deeper than the first. Digging, he pulled out the remnants of an oversized T-shirt and a pair of board shorts, the latter filthy but nearly intact.

He checked the zippered pockets—empty—and the label. Manufactured in China, nylon and polyester. That was why they hadn't rotted away, and no doubt why they were buried deeper. Again, there were no shoes and, other than the board shorts, nothing that wouldn't surrender to the relentless march of decay. The person who'd buried them knew what he was doing.

He filled in the hole and tried to cover his tracks. Over the next hour he found three other burial sites. All but one contained clothing that had belonged to a man, or at least someone man-sized.

The other held the remains of a pair of pink short shorts, a web of cotton and spandex, as well as a small T-shirt, its color no longer discernible.

CHAPTER 94

G rady drew a shaking breath and tried to think reasonably. Jessica had disappeared almost two weeks ago. Not enough time for her clothes to have rotted like this, for a colony of mushrooms to have sprung up where they were buried. As with the other sites, there was no sign of a body, or shoes.

Whether or not they'd been Jessie's, the clothes had belonged to someone's daughter or girlfriend, sister or wife or mother. Grady thought of the clothing he'd found in Minton's padlocked room. T-shirts. Khaki pants. Cargo shorts, socks, plaid boxer shorts . . .

He stared at the T-shirt, puckered and dotted with mildew. Something at its hem moved in the breeze, a loose thread. He looked closer and saw it was a single human hair, dark and coiled like a guitar string.

His knees buckled and he almost fell. The skull fragments, the buried clothes . . . once they'd been part of someone alive, someone who lived on the island or had come here as a visitor, someone who'd gazed in wonder at the ocean, hiked with a loved one through the rain forest. He'd come out here with a half-cocked plan of uncovering some mystery, but he hadn't imagined what the reality would be. Pieces of bone, a girl's hair. How could Minton have done this? he thought, head reeling. How could anyone?

Don't think about it, he told himself, and gritted his teeth. *Just keep going.*

He covered up the remnants of clothing, checked his phone's compass against the sun's dying arc in the sky. The afternoon was beginning to fade. He started once more to walk. The ground grew rough, seeded with good-sized rocks. If there were more clothes buried here, he saw no sign of them.

The trees thinned. He was nearing the ocean. The vegetation had changed yet again, though now it was obviously because of human intervention.

Many large trees had been cut down, their stumps now covered with moss and vines, swarming insects, fungi. He wondered if these had been koa trees, prized for their wood. One of the stumps was still raw-looking—a recent cut. It looked like it had been made by a two-man saw. One operator could have been Minton, but Grady had seen no evidence that he'd ever used a tool more powerful than a corkscrew.

The area hadn't been clear-cut—that would have been visible from the air—and while he could easily see where the large trees had been harvested, it looked as though the cutting had been done with care. An attempt at sustainability, maybe.

Or, Grady thought, warily scanning the surrounding forest, maybe the work had been done so as not to draw any attention to it.

He was more cautious after that, listening for voices, footsteps. But except where the trees had been harvested, the forest seemed untouched, alive with birds and insects. Wind stirred the upper canopy, cool on his sunburned cheeks.

He came upon a waterfall, flowing down a rocky outcropping into a small pool, the water so clear he could see the stones on the bottom. He filled his two empty water bottles, cupped his hands and drank, splashing water on his face. After that he felt better, and he began to move more quickly.

Not long after, he heard the first cries of seabirds. Soon he was no longer hiking through a forest but stepping out of one. Filmy grass covered the ground, wispy like a baby's hair, and thick moss that made it feel as though he was walking on a mattress. The cooler air smelled fresh, the heavy greenhouse odor dispersed. He couldn't yet see the ocean, but he wiped away tears of relief, knowing it was there.

CHAPTER 95

He walked more warily now: he was no longer in the wilderness. A trail appeared among the trees, overgrown but still passable. Not a trail: the remains of an actual road. He passed two sites that had been clear-cut for good-sized houses, now overgrown, though he could make out the footprint for each structure. There was also an outbuilding, now ramshackle.

Grady stopped and turned slowly in a circle, looking at the sky and forest around him. Here again, the building and construction sites would not be visible from the air. And even from a very short distance, they would be difficult if not impossible to see from the ground. He walked to the outbuilding, cracked the door to peer inside, and entered.

Bands of light filtered through cracks in the walls, igniting dust motes and a skein of flies that swirled high above him. The structure smelled of cut wood and WD-40, though there was no wood stacked here, no power tools or hand tools, and also of something long dead.

Grady pinched his nose, pulled out the mask still in his pocket and put it on.

Other than a single plastic bin like those back in Minton's garage, the storage building was empty. He walked to the bin, dreading what he'd find inside, knelt and opened it.

He reeled back on his heels. Even through the mask, the smell made him gag.

But he saw nothing in the bin but stacks of books and brochures.

He blinked, then gingerly picked up one of the books. It had a red cover, curled from damp, and he recognized the title—one of those twelve-step books Donny used to bring home, when attending AA or NA meetings was part of his probation. Grady flipped through it but found nothing tucked between its pages.

The other books were similar—different titles, but all related to helping people with various addictions. Same with the brochures, most of which were moldering.

Grady shook his head. Did Minton hold twelve-step meetings here? The idea was laughable. But as he examined the rest of the books, he found nothing unusual, except for that powerful odor of decay. He moved aside a stack of damp brochures, the paper stuck together and ink bleeding so he could no longer decipher the titles, and ran his fingers across the bottom of the plastic bin.

Something was stuck there, like a piece of cardboard. He dug his fingers beneath it and pulled it up, grimacing. It wasn't cardboard but a desiccated fruit rind, a papaya—no, part of a coconut shell. He used his knife to pick it up.

What he'd thought was a coconut shell was a section of scalp, the flesh shriveled and darkened by decay. A patch of light-brown hair still clung to one side. Grady examined it, holding it at arm's length and turning it to catch the light. He could just make out four V-shaped marks, black, almost like stitches. He'd seen these before, too, in the comments section of that *Pilot* piece about Kahawai Beach and shark attacks.

But what the fuck was this? All that remained of someone Minton had tossed off a boat? It seemed too grisly for a trophy, plus why would it have been in a box of books? Maybe it had washed ashore, and Minton had just tossed it into a box and forgotten about it?

Grady scooted forward and dropped the gruesome relic where he'd found it. Quickly he covered it again with the books and brochures, replaced the lid, and stumbled back outside.

CHAPTER 96

I t took him a few minutes to get a handle on his revulsion. He gulped some water, trying to keep from puking. His mouth was as dry as sand, his heart beating way too fast. Shakily, he stepped beneath a huge koa tree, its gray trunk large enough to hide him. He laid his hands on its smooth bark and peered down.

He stood atop a rise that overlooked Minton's compound. Below him, the ground sloped down to a wooded area that surrounded two or three acres, the land meticulously cleared so that groupings of native trees and shrubs concealed vegetable gardens, papaya and avocado and banana trees, coconut palms, coffee plants. Tucked into the forest trees were a few small outbuildings and an elaborate system of water catchment tanks. In the lee of the rise where he stood, a line of solar panels mounted on posts surrounded a small pool, fed by a waterfall.

Grady shaded his eyes and moved aside, staring at the solar panels. As with the other construction he'd seen here, they'd been designed and placed to blend in with their surroundings: if you weren't looking directly at the panels, or looking for them, you'd mistake them for the reflection of sunlight on water.

Four of the compact outbuildings appeared to be bungalows. The others looked like storage sheds. At the far end, a house was perched atop a cliff, tucked within towering trees so that, even from here, Grady couldn't see it clearly. This must be Irma Ohelo's house—renovated, legally or not, by Minton at some point.

At the edge of the forest, shorts and green T-shirts flapped from a clothesline. In the driveway sat Wes's Tesla, even more dinged up than last time Grady had seen it, and the KTM bike. A string of prayer flags hung across the house's long porch, their bright colors faded by the sun.

Grady squinted at the house. Surrounded by trees as it was, it still would command an impressive view of the ocean.

And, weirdly, it still appeared to be under construction, with new-looking koa wood siding, milled from trees that must have taken decades to mature. The windows were dark-tinted, like those in a limousine.

Yet why would you want black windows on a house in Hawai'i? They would make it difficult to see out—and impossible to see in, Grady realized. Difficult to spot, too, if you were trying to determine if someone was building something where they shouldn't.

There also seemed to be some kind of underground structure being constructed near the house, a bunker or addition. Grady had read about wealthy people in cities who built vast rooms beneath their existing homes—they couldn't build up, so they went down. Zeke had spoken about doing the same thing, to ride out a nuclear war or the liberal zombie uprising or whatever crazy shit he was obsessed with at the time.

Could Minton—the guy who claimed to love endangered birds and the environment, the guy who donated to land trusts—could he actually be building some kind of stripped-down Fortress of Solitude here in the Hokuloa wilderness?

And how could he have built it? Who the hell was doing the work? Grady couldn't imagine excavators or other large equipment out here, but you could still build a house with manual labor. People did that all the time in rural Maine. Native trees would have been used for construction for hundreds of years. With a reliable work-force, you could get a substantial amount of construction done. It would take a long time, but now, during the pandemic, people had lots of time.

There'd clearly been a ton of work done here in the last ten or twenty years. The four bungalows nestled in the forest had board-and-batten siding painted green and white, metal roofs. Perfect for Airbnbs or glamping cabins, or as tiny permanent living spaces. Rich COVID refugees would pay out the nose to live under such rustic conditions, only a short walk down the cliffs to a private beach. Had Wes somehow secured building permits for these after all?

No fucking way. He'd constructed them illegally. No code enforcement officer would ever come out here. And if one ever raised a red flag, it would be easy to bribe them, by promising to donate millions of dollars to island environmental causes.

Grady trained the binoculars on the land sloping down to the cliffs. A nearly invisible set of metal steps, painted mottled gray and black to blend in with the cliff, led to a dock. Dalita had said that the original development plans included private boat access, so there must be a deepwater mooring. That or they launched Zodiacs to carry people to shore. Anything could be done if you had enough money.

He started at a sound from below and quickly edged behind the tree. A figure emerged from behind the trees near the main house. Grady froze, terror flooding him as he flashed back to the thing on the beach.

But then he saw it was a man, carrying a rake and dressed in one of Minton's jade-green T-shirts and khaki pants. He looked like a member of a landscaping crew—young, dark-skinned, tall and well-built, with shoulder-length dark hair.

As he focused the binoculars on the man's face, Grady clearly saw his eyes: deep chocolate-brown, almost black. Grady had seen this guy before. Where the hell had he seen him?

The young man walked to a storage shed beneath the trees, paused, then continued to one of the bungalows. He leaned the rake against the wall and went inside. A few minutes later he reemerged. He'd changed into a flowered Hawai'ian shirt, bright yellow, unbuttoned so Grady could see the dolphin tattoo on his chest. He retraced his steps, weaving in and out of the trees until he reached the main house.

CHAPTER 97

Grady lowered the binoculars, his thoughts frantic.

Dolphin tattoo, dolphin tattoo...

It came back to him like a remembered dream—one of the flyers by the skate park. A photo of a handsome young man who'd been missing nearly a month. He'd been homeless, living on the same stretch of beach where Grady had first seen Scotty. Grady couldn't remember his name, but this was him, it was definitely him. He watched the young man take the house steps, two at a time. Wes opened the door to greet him. Grady strained to hear what they were saying, but he was too far away. Wes clapped a hand on the young man's shoulder and they walked inside, the door closing behind them.

Grady scanned the grounds, then focused on the young man's bungalow. A chain saw and more tools sat beneath the eaves—a shovel and pickaxe, crowbars, a rolling toolbox. There were more tools by the other bungalows. Wheelbarrows. Pruning shears. Pole saws and weed whackers, hedge shears, a table saw, spirit levels...

Even without seeing what was inside the storage shed, Grady suspected there was enough equipment to keep a small army of landscapers and workers busy for years. Though you wouldn't need an army, just one or two people. Homeless guys, guys tired of chasing their demons and sleeping rough. Donny used to mock the well-meaning people who ministered to the homeless in Portland, offering them meals, clothing, a cot in a shelter. Sometimes they'd encourage him to attend meetings in a church basement, give him a card with the Serenity Prayer on it. "I got my Higher Power right here, bub," he'd laugh, shaking a bottle or a little baggie of white power in Grady's face. "All the serenity I need."

But not everyone was a hard case like Donny. Some guys—young guys, kids almost—they might be homesick or desperate, trusting or naive enough to go along with someone who promised them a place to live in exchange for a job. Or . . .

Grady recalled the blue hazard light he'd seen in the Tesla's trunk; recalled how Wes had buzzed his hair, so he looked like a cop. A plainclothes cop, someone who could intimidate a homeless kid into getting into his car. It could work like that, too. Perhaps he drugged them, though maybe he'd save that for when he needed to kill them. Probably he'd bring in only one or two at a time, so it wouldn't seem overly suspicious when they were never seen again. But the police didn't know or care about the disappearances of homeless people. When rumors popped up on Reddit forums, they'd be dismissed as crackpot ravings. Same if someone managed to survive, like Scotty seemingly had.

It was such a simple, foolproof plan. Basically, the same plan that the entire country ran on. Use the poor, whoever they were, then dispose of them.

And they wouldn't have to be men, either. He could bring women here, too, for work, or sex. Runaways living on the beach, tourists just arrived. Ask if they wanted to spend a weekend at a luxurious, hidden compound. An attractive older man, well-spoken and obviously well-off, driving an expensive car. He wouldn't have to kidnap them. All he'd have to do is get rid of the corpses. Take them out on his boat to go snorkeling, give them a roofie, and slip them overboard. The sharks would do the rest.

"Fuck," whispered Grady. He felt as though he'd stepped off the edge of a cliff he hadn't known was there, plunging into a chasm that had no bottom. He wasn't looking at a secret vacation compound. He was looking at a billionaire's private labor camp.

CHAPTER 98

G rady knuckled his eyes. How the fuck could he have been so stupid? And how the fuck could Minton do this? The same man who loved those birds, who sat calmly on his deck with his espresso and his tablet, and had Zoom meetings with the local Audubon Society? The man who'd given Grady a job and the chance to see this other world, a beautiful place Grady had never known existed, or could even have imagined?

How could that same man shit on all of it, then murder the same people he'd lured into building his fucking hideaway?

Raina, you were right, Grady thought bitterly. The aviary was a prison, and the 'ohana was a trap. No doubt Minton had planned to eventually kill him, too, when Grady became too suspicious, or interfered with Minton's plans for developing Hokuloa as his own private bolt-hole.

How long had Minton been doing this? The bodies in the gulch had been there long enough to decompose. It would have taken a lot of effort to drag them into the woods. So what had happened? If they had been people kidnapped by Minton, and not lost hikers, they might have tried to escape, gotten lost and died of exposure.

Minton would soon have figured out it was easier to use the boat and dump them in the ocean. Weight the bodies first, so they'd sink. Or he might not have bothered. If a body eventually washed up, would the police bother with a toxicology report? He wouldn't have to make it look like an accident; the island itself would take care of that. Same with the buried clothing: eaten away in weeks or months.

Synthetic fabrics would take longer, but then, who'd be looking for them? He could burn the shoes. The phones he'd keep as trophies, or so they'd never be found.

One of those phones could be Jessie's. The thought sickened him: that there could have been something of hers so close to him all this time, and he'd never known. He'd done nothing.

But he was here, now. She might be here, too, still alive. And that young man from the flyer was definitely here, and alive. The exhaustion he'd felt a short while ago burned away like butane. He sank to the ground beneath the koa tree to wait for nightfall.

CHAPTER 99

A s the sky darkened, he watched for activity below. A light went on in the back of the main house, but not in any of the bunga-lows. Could Jessie, or someone else, be imprisoned somewhere? Or she might be in the house right now, Grady thought, having a nice dinner with Minton and that other guy.

He shook his head—that was a fucked-up thing to even imagine, that she'd take off and never let Raina know. But Minton might have coerced her or abducted her. She'd have no phone, no internet access.

If she was still alive, Grady would find her.

She is still alive, he told himself.

He strained to hear music or voices but heard only the soft murmur of birds in the brief twilight. When he guessed an hour had passed since both men had entered the house, Grady ate his own dinner, the second-to-last pack of seitan chili. He watched the sky swiftly deepen from blue-gold to rose to deep violet. To the east, he caught a glimpse of Hokuloa Point through the trees. He'd barely noticed it earlier, but now the point dominated the horizon, just a few miles off.

The path he'd taken through the lava field led there, he realized. From Hokuloa Point, you'd be able to see not just the outlying islands but this entire coast, from the peninsula to where Li'ulā and the airport now stood. A thousand years ago, you could have watched for invaders from sea or land. Something nameless might have kept watch over the peninsula, but this would have been where Hokuloa's human sentinels stood guard.

He struggled to stay awake after eating. The pain in his ankle had ebbed. It was no longer swollen, just tender. He left the bandage off, gingerly slid his foot back into his boot. He leaned against the tree and shut his eyes for a moment.

His chin dropped against his chest and he jolted awake. How long had he been asleep? He fumbled for the binoculars to check if he'd missed something.

Inside the house, lights still glowed. The front door opened. Grady watched as Minton and the young man walked companionably across the grounds. The young man tossed back his head to gaze at the stars, swinging his arms like he was dancing.

Minton accompanied him to his bungalow. They halted, close enough that Grady might be able to hear them. He belly-crawled across the ground, froze when he sent a pebble bouncing down the slope. The young guy didn't notice, but Minton lifted his head to scan the dark hilltop where Grady lay.

"Brah!" Minton looked back at the younger man, who clasped Minton's upper arm. "Mahalo for dinner. For everything."

Minton smiled. "A pleasure, Cory."

Cory raised his hand in a loose shaka, walked unsteadily into the bungalow as Minton returned to his house.

Inside the bungalow, a light went on. Grady could see Cory moving around, a shadow behind the curtainless side window. Watching him made Grady feel like a creep, so he put the binoculars down. Within a few minutes, the bungalow went dark.

So did most of the lights in Minton's house, except for a single one upstairs. The light would be in Minton's bedroom, Grady thought. Black-glass windows or not, he'd have a view of the sea, Hokuloa Point, and the easternmost peninsula.

After a few minutes, that light went off as well. The compound dissolved into the darkness.

Grady crawled back to the koa, leaned against its massive trunk, and let his body go limp. He checked for his folded knife at his hip pocket, opened his pack, and, to calm his nerves, finished the tequila, as smoky as a firepit. He kept watch. The compound remained silent and still. At last he wrapped himself in the blanket and lay down, his head on his backpack.

Through the high canopy of koa, 'ohe and 'ōhi'a and fan palms, he glimpsed the stars in the eastern sky. The great Navigator's Triangle; to the north, Nā-hiku—Ursa Major, the Great Bear—and Hōkū-pa'a, the North Star. He followed the Great Bear's tail to find Hokulea, the Star of Gladness. And, spanning the sky in a sweeping curve from northeast to southwest, Laniākea, the ocean of stars reflecting the ocean below.

He had thought it would be impossible to sleep, until he started awake. The moon had risen, its light masking that of the stars. How long had he slept?

He rubbed his chin, taking a deep breath, and realized it had not been a sound that woke him but the rank scent of carrion and musk. He grabbed his knife as he bolted to his feet.

Moonlight shone through branches and palm fronds, but he saw nothing, only heard a low huffing sound, the crackle of a dead palm frond followed by a bird's agitated chirping in a nearby tree. Then silence.

CHAPTER 100

I t was still dark when he next woke, the sky tinged with pink and gray. On the horizon glowed Hokuloa—Venus as the morning star. He sat up groggily, lifted the binoculars to scan the grounds below. Everything seemed calm.

He set aside the binoculars. His mouth tasted of seitan and tequila and chili powder. He hadn't shaved for days. His hair felt greasy, his clothes were stiff with sweat and torn from his fall. Anyone seeing him now would think he, too, lived on the beach.

He forced down some granola, sipping a few mouthfuls of water. He checked his ankle: not too bad. He got his pack and found a spot near the koa where thick underbrush would screen him from anyone below. He settled in the ferns and waited.

Around him the forest awakened. Above the Pacific, a ridge of dark clouds burst into flame, scarlet and gold, like the sky was a flimsy curtain someone had torched. As the sun rose, the roof and sides of Minton's house looked as though they, too, had been set on fire.

A sudden sound came from above his head, a loud *clack*. He craned his neck as two large black birds soared from the forest, so close that he could hear their wings, a steady *whoosh* like a bellows. They circled before settling in a tall tree. One would clack or grunt, and the other would mimic its call, like they were having a conversation. They looked like crows, but there were no crows left in Hawai'i. So, mynah birds: an introduced species that had managed to intrude upon Minton's grim paradise.

Grady watched as another, very small bird landed on the ground barely an arm's length away. He could have touched it if he dared. Tawny brown with a white breast, it pecked at fallen leaves and dirt, oblivious to his presence. An 'elepaio. After a minute, it lifted its head to make its reverse-wolf-whistle cry, plucked a grub from the earth, and flew off into the treetops.

Grady sighed. He turned on his phone to check the time. Nearly seven o'clock. Still no signal. He pushed himself deeper into the ferns and continued to keep watch.

Half an hour might have passed before Minton stepped out onto his front porch, wearing the same sarong as when Grady had first met him. He stood, drinking espresso from a tiny white cup. He seemed to be listening to the black birds.

Minton shaded his eyes, staring up at the tree. One of the birds hopped from branch to branch, making its guttural cries. The other bird — its mate? — sat and preened, spreading its wing feathers like a magician displaying a deck of cards.

Grady focused the binoculars back on Minton. He watched the birds and smiled — really smiled, his eyes crinkling in delight. Grady had never seen him smile like that. He couldn't think of the last time he'd seen anyone smile like that. Not for months and months.

One of the black birds gave a sharp cry, flapped its wings, and took off, followed by the other. Minton turned and went back inside.

Grady remained where he was. A quarter hour passed before the door to the bungalow beneath him opened and Cory stepped out. He wore a green Kanaka Sun shirt and khakis, battered-looking Vans, sunglasses, and a gimme cap. He stood under the eaves, took out a vape pen, and had a quick hit, then strolled across the compound to knock on Minton's door.

Minton opened it. He'd changed into khaki pants, a long-sleeved T-shirt and sun hat, hiking sandals. He nodded at Cory, clapped a hand on his shoulder, and began to talk.

Grady held his breath, trying to hear what they were saying, but could only catch the word "back." Minton gestured at a storage shed, then the driveway. Cory nodded. Minton hurried down the steps and headed to the dock.

"Later," Cory yelled after him, and ambled toward the shed.

Grady lowered the binoculars. Minton was leaving, headed— where? For how long? Grady knew he had a powerboat—Raina had mentioned a bowrider. So maybe he was just going to get something from it, check the fuel level. In which case he'd return shortly.

A numb dread settled in Grady's chest. By his reckoning, the young man had been here for close to a month. Would that be too long for Minton? Did he burn through his victims the way Donny did cigarettes? Grady had gone stir-crazy during two weeks in quarantine—wouldn't this young guy be doing the same with Minton? Would he ask, or demand, to be taken back to town? Minton might not want to take a chance on a confrontation, especially one in which he might be overpowered. Better to get maybe a month out of a worker, then find another one.

Grady thought of Jessie. What about her? If she'd been here, Minton might already have killed her. The realization was like a fiery wall Grady couldn't get past, but now he forced himself to confront it.

If Jessie *had* been here—if she was dead—there would be some evidence somewhere. Grady hadn't found her clothing: obviously he hadn't searched the entire forest, but there might be something of hers in the compound. The young man with the tattoo might have seen her—their time here might have overlapped. If Grady could talk to him, he might learn something. He could convince the guy to help him overpower Wes—surely the two of them could take him on.

Or, even better, Grady could convince the guy to leave with him, hack their way back to civilization, call the police. If they couldn't find Jessie, they might at least bring back proof that Minton had killed her, along with all those others.

The roar of a powerboat's engine ripped through the tranquil morning. Grady sat up, fighting to remain calm. He waited until the sound diminished, until he couldn't hear it any longer. Waited a few more minutes to make sure Minton hadn't circled back. Then he grabbed his backpack, shoving the binoculars inside. He raked his fingers through his hair, pulled off his T-shirt and swiped it across his face, stuffed the soiled T-shirt into his pack and pulled on his sole remaining clean one.

He crawled out from the thicket, stepping into the shade of the koa and 'ohe grove. He watched as Cory went inside the storage shed. After a few minutes he emerged, toting a toolbox as he trudged across to the tree-shrouded driveway. Grady took a deep breath and made his way down the hillside.

CHAPTER 101

He approached Cory in the driveway. Despite the trees, it was hot: Cory had stripped off his shirt and tossed it on the ground beside the KTM bike. He glanced up when Grady was a few yards away and stared at him, puzzled but not alarmed.

"Hey," he said, straightening. "Howzit?"

Grady halted. He knew what he must look like. He also knew there was no way to do this except to just frigging do it.

"Listen," he said. "I, uh——"

"This bike, the alternator got a problem. My unka had the same one, same deal. Not sure can fix 'im, but." Cory shrugged, like Grady was the one who'd asked him to repair it. "Cannot help, I think. No can get parts, so what you going do? At least he got that." Cory cocked a thumb at the Tesla in the driveway. He opened the toolbox and removed a socket wrench.

"Yeah, sorry. I don't know about bikes." Grady stared at the KTM, wishing he could jump on it and hightail it out of here.

Cory adjusted his cap, which had a Seahawks logo. He appeared mildly stoned. "Where you came from, brah?"

Grady gestured at the forest behind them. No point in lying— where else could he have come from?

Cory frowned. "What, you came from the woods?"

He was a good head taller than Grady, his arms muscular and toned. He looked like an athlete. The missing-person flyer had said he was a lifeguard, and he moved in the loose-limbed way that surfers did, at ease on land or water. Grady could imagine him sitting in one of those tall chairs, chatting with girls on the beach. His dark eyes and wide mouth seemed accustomed to smiling.

He wasn't smiling now. He stared at Grady, then past him up the hillside, as though the koa and palm trees might be hiding someone else. He looked back at Grady. "Brah, you okay? You lost?"

"No, I just—"

"You look—I don't know. Kind of faded." Cory tilted his head, trying to get a bead on Grady. "You need help? Got some bad shrooms, like that? My friend just left, but he coming back in a hour. You can—"

"No," Grady broke in. "No, no, it's fine, I just, yeah. I got lost. Hiking."

"Hiking?" Cory laughed. "You never hike here, brah. Nobody hikes this side. Serious, where you came from? You friends with Wes? The boat left without you?"

"No."

Cory considered this. "No boat?"

"No, no boat. I told you—I hiked here."

"You hiked how?"

"I came across the lava field."

Again Cory laughed. But his eyes narrowed as he took in Grady's torn pants, the abrasions on his face, the Band-Aids peeling from his arm. "You shitting me?"

"No."

"No ways. You cannot."

"You can't," admitted Grady. "But I did."

He was scared Cory could hear his heart pounding, smell his fear, the way dogs can. An hour, Cory had said. Wes would be back in an hour. Grady tried to think rationally, do triage, like you did as an EMT. *Check for breathing, bleeding, broken bones.* What were his choices?

He couldn't run—he was too far done for that. And now, after just a few minutes talking to this guy, Grady knew there was no way in hell he could convince him that Wes was a murderer. He could tell Cory the truth about what he'd learned, but would Cory believe him?

No. If some sketchy guy appeared out of the woods the way he had, Grady wouldn't believe it either. If anything, Cory would think *he* was a murderer. He was fucked, and so was Cory.

"I get water. You like?"

Grady blinked, saw Cory's face creased in concern.

"You look thirsty, brah. Come, I get you something to drink."

Grady hesitated, then shook his head. "Thanks, I'm all set. I filled my bottles at a waterfall."

"What, you found one sacred pool, or what?"

"Yeah. Yeah, I guess."

"Not! No ways!" Cory laughed. "Brah, for real? No lie, I always wanted to see those. My auntie, she tell me stories since small kid time, and all I can think is, someday I going find where's that. One reason I came out here, Wes said he'd take me."

"Did he?"

"Not yet. He tell me he gotta take me out with him, otherwise I'd get lost on my own. I like go at sunrise, like Haleakalā. Unreal, so beautiful. That bone reef, too—we going out there when I pau this bike job."

He looked at Grady and laughed again, then cocked his head. "Eh, I think I know you, brah. You was sleeping on the beach, too, yeah? That was me all the way when I ran into Wes—I was living up north shore. I came over here last summer from Waikiki to work at the Royal Keawa. You know that one?"

Grady said nothing, and Cory went on.

"Yeah, I was lifeguard over there. I was on swim team in high school, thought maybe I'd train for the Olympics. But, you know, too much pakalōlō. So I go Waikiki—I was lifeguard at Queen Kapiʻolani beach. Then my friend tell come here, get better money at the Royal Keawa. So I come over here. Then the corona happens and no more work. I was staying with friends, but they all left, they get families. So I just live down the beach. Was fine, had pakalōlō, had surf. You surf, yeah? I surfed every day and then somebody had stole my board."

Cory shook his head like he still couldn't believe it. "The cops was coming for me, fucking irrahz. I keep moving, they keep coming. They no bother the people inside the big camps now 'cause they scared the corona, but if you sleeping all by yourself . . ."

He grimaced in disgust. "Couple weeks ago I meet Wes, he tell he need somebody for work on his land. So I come out here, help out. Then he tell I do good enough, so I can stay on. He needs a caretaker. He says he like give a hand up, not a handout."

"A caretaker." Grady felt like everything was happening in slow motion. "Here? It's a big place for just one person."

"Yeah, just me in the 'ohana and him in the big house."

Grady swallowed. "Have you—have you seen a girl here? A young woman, about my age?"

"No, brah. No girls." Cory shook his head as though this fact pained him.

"You've been here how long?"

"Maybe a month? Had one other guy when I started, from that camp by the airport. Young guy, he had quit, he never like the work—Wes, he works you hard. Pays you back—good food, but no beer, he's straight edge. No pakalōlō either, so that's on the DL. Anyways, Wes took him back in the boat."

Wes took him back in the boat. So fucking simple. Grady had been right, but now what good was being right? He forced himself to stare at Cory, to nod.

"Try wait little while," Cory was saying. "You can stay, too, I bet. You no mind work, yeah?"

Grady swallowed. "No, I don't mind work."

"Okay," said Cory, "you meet him when he gets back. Maybe a hour. He'll set you up—all the 'ohanas are empty, 'cept mine."

"Let me think about it, okay? But thanks." Grady smiled, hoping he didn't look as sick as he felt. "There a beach here?"

"Right there, brah," Cory said. "Past the first 'ohana, trail goes right down. Just be careful, yeah? Some steep, the trail. When Wes gets back, then we going out to that reef. I heard get beautiful fish out there, and bones. Pirates and shit. Tourist bones," he added with a grin. "Sharks, too. I hate sharks. Had one shark killed a windsurfer couple months ago."

Cory tossed the socket wrench from hand to hand, turning his attention back to the KTM. Grady remained where he was.

"You know, thanks for saying you'll introduce me to your boss, but I think I'll keep on hiking," Grady said slowly. "I've wanted to do this for a long time, see what it's like out here. Just, maybe don't mention it?" Cory looked up from the bike, and Grady added, "I don't want him to think I'm trespassing."

Cory shook his head. "No can trespass here. Hokuloa belongs to the people. Sacred land, 'āina. And Wes, he protects the 'āina, yeah? Get birds here that no more anyplace else. He's a real one. He see me living on the beach, he tell, 'You look lost, friend. Come with me, I can find a job for you.' He would do the same for you, garans. If I'm the caretaker, I know still get plenty work here for two guys." He shrugged. "But, you no like me say nothing, okay. You change your mind, you come back. Get plenty room. Promise, he's a good guy."

"Okay. Thanks, brah."

Grady collected himself, opened his backpack and took out one of the plastic bottles he'd filled at the waterfall.

"Here," said Grady. "This is from that sacred waterfall. When you go out snorkeling later by that reef, drink this instead of anything else. It'll keep you safe from the sharks."

He'd thought that Cory might laugh, but he took the bottle and bowed his head in thanks. "Mahalo. I'll save it for when I'm out there. For protection. Aloha."

"Aloha," replied Grady.

CHAPTER 102

He followed Cory's instructions to the beach trail, along a foot-worn path behind the first bungalow. The path cut through the vegetation, down a slope to a wedge of sugar-white sand bordered by boulders of black lava. Grady gazed longingly at tidal pools of aquamarine water winking in the sunlight. In another lifetime, he'd be there in a heartbeat.

Instead he cut through the woods. He could flee now and attempt to make his way back to Hokuloa Road by the way he'd come, but even under ideal conditions, he'd never be able to retrace his path. He couldn't imagine doing that, exhausted as he was, with hardly any supplies left. He'd come this far for a reason, even if it was a hopeless one. Still, for once, he'd see it through.

He climbed back up the hillside behind the compound and found a different vantage point from which to stand watch. He turned on his phone and stared at the EMERGENCY SOS button, tapped it. No signal. He prayed that Cory really wouldn't tell Minton—another long shot.

But if Cory could avoid drinking whatever Minton used to drug them, there was a chance he might be able to swim to safety. That kid 'Anuhe had almost made it. Cory was a lifeguard. He had a better chance of surviving this than Grady himself did.

He stared through the trees, watching Cory work on the bike. He didn't seem to be getting anywhere. That was one good thing— Minton couldn't hop on the KTM and blast through the forest looking for the intruder. Grady scoped out the bungalows, the toolshed and other outbuildings, the house. Cory had said it was just him and Wes living in the compound. No girls or women. If Jessie or anyone else was here, and alive, they'd be hidden away. Hard to imagine Cory wouldn't have caught on to that, but if Grady could search the grounds, he might be able to find something. And if he could get a phone signal, he could text Raina.

He flinched as the distant drone of the powerboat's engine cut through the air. He trained the binoculars on Cory. He'd turned from the bike to look toward the ocean, and was wiping his hands on a rag. The sound of the engine grew louder, then lower as the boat drew up to the dock, and finally fell silent.

Minton climbed up the metal steps. Cory called out, and Minton joined him. The two of them inspected the KTM. Minton shook his head as Cory lifted his hands in a gesture Grady recognized as the universal workman's signal for *It needs a replacement part*.

The two men stared at the bike in silence. Then Minton said something to Cory, who nodded. Minton turned and walked quickly to the house. Cory grabbed the toolbox and the water bottle Grady had given him, and returned to his bungalow. Five minutes later, he stepped back out, wearing a blue-and-white snorkeling shirt and board shorts, a set of flippers under one arm, the water bottle in his hand.

Minton met him at the top of the metal steps that led to the dock. He handed Cory a snorkeling mask and they proceeded down to the boat.

Grady watched until they were out of sight, feeling almost giddy with relief. He refused to imagine what would happen if Cory did tell Minton about seeing him, what would happen if Cory whipped out the magic water bottle and flat-out refused the drink Minton had slipped the roofie into.

Whatever transpired, he'd bought himself some time. Not much, if everything went tits up out there on the boat, but maybe an hour and a half if he was lucky—enough time to search the compound.

CHAPTER 103

He shoved the binoculars into his pack, shouldered it, and hurried downhill. He stopped behind Cory's bungalow, listening for the boat engine. He heard only the high whistles of birds, the wind in the palms.

He walked to the front of the bungalow and found the door unlocked. A small room held a twin bed, a table, and an armchair, a bureau with a glass tumbler and container of water on top, a battery-operated lamp. A tiny adjoining bathroom had only a composting toilet and some hooks for clothing. No running water. A faint earthy smell came from the composting toilet.

He yanked open bureau drawers to reveal clean socks, boxer shorts, a pair of khakis, and a Kanaka Sun T-shirt. Whatever clothes Cory had been wearing when he arrived here were gone. He looked under the bed—nothing—and hurried back outside. This bungalow, like the others, rested on concrete deck footings. So no foundation, no basement, no crawl space. Nowhere to stow a large suitcase, let alone a person or body.

He ran to the next bungalow. Here, too, the door was unlocked. Inside were the same few furnishings. There were no sheets or pillows on the bed. No clothes in the bureau drawers. But the earthy smell from the bathroom suggested the place had been occupied fairly recently, which would align with what Cory had told him about another person being here when he arrived.

The next bungalow was slightly larger than the others, with double beds and woven rugs on the wooden floors. Could Minton actually have guests stay here? In the fourth and last bungalow, a moldering folder sat on the bureau. It had an image of an 'i'iwi on the cover, above the words "Hokuloa Wilderness Foundation." The folder was empty, but it suggested someone from the organization had visited at some point. That or Minton had left it here and forgotten it.

Grady walked back outside, discouraged. He still heard nothing but birdsong and the wind, the steady sweep of waves on the shore below. He proceeded to quickly check the outbuildings tucked into the trees. Solar shed, a separate structure for the water pump and filtration system. A toolshed, better organized than Minton's garage. Another shed filled with boat-related stuff—plastic fuel containers, flippers and other snorkeling equipment, lightweight plastic containers and transparent seal-tight bags, a gallon of bleach and a large carton containing cotton rags.

But again, no hidden closets, no crawl space. No sign that anyone had ever been held captive here; no trace of blood or torn clothing. The bleach would take care of that, he thought grimly. He searched for a speargun or a boat hook, anything he could use as a weapon. Either Minton didn't have any or he kept them onboard his boat.

He left the shed and walked outside, even more discouraged. He paused, listening for the boat, then walked to where a patch of olomea grew at the edge of the trees. He stashed his backpack in the underbrush, keeping the binoculars. He made sure he had his knife and phone and ran to the house, stopping cold.

At the bottom of the porch steps, a large flat stone was set into the grass, about two feet square, dull red threaded with black. There was a carving in its center: a circle about a hand's width in diameter, surrounded by zigzag lines, a sun. The image seemed to glow faintly, as though a furnace burned deep in the ground beneath.

It was the same solar symbol Minton had used as the logo for his resort, Kanaka Sun. The glow came from a mineral—carnelian, perhaps—something hard enough that it hadn't shattered when the ancient artist had set stone tools to the ceiling of the chamber. Or when someone else, like Leonardo Sanchez, had attacked it with a jackhammer.

Grady stared at it in wonder, and also fury. How could Minton have done such a thing, with all his talk of the sacredness of the landscape here? In the chamber, the sun would have occupied its place in the carven sky map, a beacon or marker for anyone who knew how to read it. Here, it was just a curious piece of rock.

Grady's rage dissolved into another wave of grief. All this destruction and death, so that an ancient artifact could serve as a stepping-stone to a rich white man's house. He refused to lay a foot on it. He walked around the ki'i pōhaku, and climbed the steps to the porch.

CHAPTER 104

He looked for a hidden camera, knowing it was too late—any security system would have clocked him by now. Even if Minton had some way of monitoring a presence in the house, he was miles away at sea. Grady thought about what might be happening in the boat—Minton and Cory scuffling, or Cory drugged and pushed overboard, weighted down so he wouldn't be found.

Or maybe he'd overpowered Minton. Then Cory would be a hero, a role he was better suited for than Grady was. He placed his hand on the doorknob, turned it, and pushed the door open. No alarm went off. He stepped inside and froze.

It was like he stood within a shadowy prism, a kaleidoscopic dance of colors tinged to strange hues by the black-glass windows: indigo, royal purple, acid green; orange and molten crimson, turquoise and emerald, silver. Blinking, he tried to make sense of where he was. A room full of mirrors? A greenhouse? He shielded his eyes.

He'd entered a large room, its walls floor-to-ceiling dark windows, most looking out onto the ocean and sky. He took another step and felt like he was falling, like he was trapped in an onyx globe that might shatter at any second.

Fish, he realized as he focused on a pulsating umbrella, translucent pink with long tendrils streaming like violet hair. *They're all fish.*

The room was filled with aquariums, some rectangular and as large as the one on Hokuloa Road, others cylindrical and as tall as he was. They contained every kind of undersea animal—fish, jellyfish, coral and sea urchins, squid and octopuses, shrimp and starfish, eels and spiny lobsters, along with unrecognizable creatures that would be nightmarish if they didn't also resemble something from a candy store on Mars.

Slowly he crossed the room, walking over a labyrinth of electrical cords and plastic air-line tubing. There was no proper furniture except for a large console set against a windowless wall, tubing and cords snaking from it as though the entire room was on life support.

You couldn't hide a person here.

He made his way to the back wall, where he stared through the dark window at a deck with a teak table and chairs, a charcoal grill, shaded by the arching upper branches of trees that moved in the sea breeze. Below and a short distance away, at the top of the cliff, the metal stairway. Who needed clear windows when you could just step outside and have the Pacific directly below you?

The dock rocked as a swell rolled in. Farther out, whitecaps dotted the endless blue. A channel of darker water, almost violet, marked the dangerous current he'd been warned about. Grady squinted, trying to see a boat, but the chop and shifting play of sunlight made that impossible.

He made his way back through the room. It was an effort not to gaze inside each tank and marvel. Is that what Minton did with the people he took out to the reef, send them down to capture rare fish and other creatures? Then kill them?

He remembered what Minton had said when he first showed him the aviary.

There are not enough of them and too many of us.

He stopped when he reached the front door again. He'd been so bedazzled that he'd walked right past an open kitchen. He flung open cabinets, got on his knees to look under the sink for an adjoining crawl space, hurried through a pantry, a bathroom, a broom closet. All empty.

"Jessie?" he called out softly. "Jessie, are you here? I want to help you . . ."

Silence.

He raced up to the second floor, caught his breath on the landing.

"Jessie? Jessie!" He was shouting now, his voice filling the house. "Are you here? Is anyone here?"

There was no reply, no sound apart from his own footsteps and the wind rattling the window casements. He ran to a window in the hall, swept the binoculars across the horizon, blue as far as he could see. Raised his phone, dropped his arm. Still no boat. Still no cell signal.

He searched the second-floor rooms, feeling more and more panicked. Master bedroom and bath, two guest bedrooms, all the furniture and built-in bookshelves custom-made of golden-brown wood with a grain that felt like warm marble. Koa, a fortune's worth. Minton must have harvested it here.

In every room he knelt to peer under the bed: not even a stray shoe or flip-flop. He stood on the beds to see if there was any sign of a hidden door or panel in the ceiling, tapped the walls to listen for the telltale hollow sound of a passage or closet. He shouted Jessie's name, shouted for anyone to answer him. Nothing.

He rifled the clothes in a walk-in closet—Wes's clothes, sarongs with the Kanaka Sun logo, silk Hawai'ian shirts, hiking sandals and heavy hiking boots, scuffed and stained. Stacks of folded towels and sheets in the linen closet. In the bathroom, a stone-lined rain shower with a shelf of organic, low-phosphate soaps and shampoo.

But he saw no personal items whatsoever—no photos of friends or family, no artwork except for a few framed photographs of 'apapane and 'i'iwi, pictures Minton had surely taken himself. No paperback books or magazines, no electronic devices. Except for the clothing, it might have been one of those fancy hotel rooms he'd seen in magazine ads. Despairing, he walked back into the hall.

She wasn't here. No one was here. There was no sign that anyone ever had been, except for Minton, and there was barely evidence of that. He stood by the window, staring dully out at the ocean, then grabbed his binoculars.

A black fleck bobbed on the horizon. As he watched, it grew fractionally larger, until he could see clearly what it was.

"*Fuck.*"

He jumped back from the window, as though Minton might have seen him from that distance; grabbed his knife from his pocket. He was younger than Minton, but the older man was strong. And he hadn't been hiking through the wilderness for the last three days. Grady unfolded his knife and held it in front of him, tried to imagine plunging it into Minton's neck or chest, or . . . anywhere.

He couldn't do it. Couldn't picture it, couldn't see himself killing someone in cold blood. Even a murderer, even a serial killer.

He refolded the knife, pocketed it, and raced back downstairs, ran to a back window and peered out. Minton's boat was now the size of his pinkie nail.

Get a fucking grip! he imagined Donny yelling at him. *Don't be such a friggin' pussy! Use your fucking knife! You gonna let some rich asshole take you out like a trout in a barrel?*

Grady wiped sweat from his eyes. He could go outside and wait near the top of the metal stairs, find someplace to hide, jump Minton as he headed to the house. Slit his throat the way you do a deer's. Only Grady had never slit an animal's throat and had been sickened when he watched Zeke do it.

"Get a fucking grip," he whispered to himself, and started for the door.

He drew up short beside one of the aquariums. A fancy cylindrical one on a stand, like the tank back on Hokuloa Road. This one, too, was filled with wana, sea urchins, though only one kind: the delicately colored parasol urchins. They covered a large clump of coral, as innocent as undersea peonies.

He stationed himself a few feet from the wana's aquarium, near a window. Dark clouds had massed above the horizon, bruised purple and green. It was only midafternoon, but it looked like twilight. The sun had all but disappeared, and the heavy air crackled with electricity. The warm wind blew through the screened windows, ripe with a thick, green smell—decaying vegetation, kelp, a stink of rotting meat.

He watched as the boat drew closer, climbing each wave, then slamming down in the trough before the next wave flung it up again. He struggled to see if there were two people in the boat, or only one.

Within a few minutes, he knew the answer: one. The engine's roar dwindled as the boat approached the dock. A figure tossed a fender into the water, and then a line onto the metal platform. The engine cut off, the boat bobbed up and down as a man hopped easily onto the dock, tied off onto a cleat, and hurried toward the steps. Wes Minton.

CHAPTER 105

"**G**rady!" Minton shouted. "Grady, let's talk."

Grady edged behind the wana tank. Minton sounded calm, not out of breath. Grady swallowed, thinking of Cory. Minton had killed him—that was why he wasn't desperate. He probably kept a gun on the boat, in case anyone ever put up a fight.

"Grady!"

Through the front windows, Grady saw Minton pause in front of the porch before continuing across the grass. He started toward Cory's bungalow, abruptly turned as though thinking better of it, and walked quickly back toward the house.

Grady held his breath. Minton halted again, a few feet from the porch, beside the kiʻi pōhaku. He stepped onto the ancient carved stone, listening. A charcoal-gray cloud blotted out what remained of the sun. Grady could no longer hear the honeycreepers calling from the forest. One of the black birds clacked, but its mate made no response. From some impossible distance, a dog barked.

Minton shook himself, stepped off the kiʻi pōhaku and up the porch steps. The front door cracked an inch. Slowly, Minton stepped in. He wore a snorkeling shirt and diving gloves. No gun.

He glanced into the kitchen, leaving the door open behind him, and edged into the living room. As he did, a mountainous dark cloud slipped away from the sun. Light streamed through the doorway into the room, that charged, warning brilliance before a storm at sea. Sunlight exploded against the fish tanks, and instinctively Grady moved to shade his eyes.

"Grady." Minton's head whipped to stare at him. "Grady, god-damn it." His voice shook with anger and something else. The same disappointment and betrayal that Grady felt? "What are you doing here?"

As swiftly as it had come, the sunlight faded again.

"I walked here," he replied.

"That's what Cory told me. How?"

"Where's Cory?"

Wes shrugged. "Snorkeling. I left him at the reef, told him I'd pick him up later. How'd you get here, Grady?"

"The lava field."

"You crossed the lava field?" Minton's voice rose in disbelief. "How did you find the path?"

"I followed a dog."

"A dog?"

"A wild dog. Black and reddish. I've seen it before, at your house. I think it lives here, on the peninsula."

Outside, a bird trilled. Minton looked quickly at the door, then back at Grady.

"Where is she?" demanded Grady.

Minton frowned. "Who?"

"Jessica. She disappeared over a week ago."

"I don't know what you're talking about. There's no girl here." He looked genuinely puzzled.

"And Leonardo." Grady's voice shook. Could he be wrong? "Is he here? Did he bring her here with you?"

"Leonardo Sanchez? Is that who you mean?" Wes seemed even more taken aback. "I haven't seen him for months—before the lockdown. Why would he be here? Are you all right, Grady?"

Grady edged back as Wes walked toward the wana tank. "You look like you're in trouble, Grady. What happened to you?"

"Those people," Grady stammered. "You killed all those people. I found where you buried their clothes—there was a pair of women's shorts and a shirt."

Minton halted, resting his gloved hand on the side of the wana's aquarium. "She must have been a hiker. I found her body in the gulch."

"And you didn't tell anyone?"

"It was years ago. I have no issues with women. It's men who propagate like fruit flies. The virus—it's actually a good thing. You know that, right?"

He stared at Grady expectantly, then sighed, like Grady was a prized student who'd let him down. "*We're* the virus. We know that. Plagues are inevitable now—the ones that will kill us. I still have things to do—protect the refuges I've set up, create more..."

Minton glanced at the wana, motionless in their glass box. "I'm rethinking the future of this place. Hokuloa is mine, and I don't trust anyone else with it. Researchers, tourists, all those conservation people?" He shook his head adamantly. "Better that no one else ever comes here. I'll protect it. My 'apapane and 'i'iwi, my 'ō'ō...no one cares about them like I do. Why should our lives be privileged above theirs? Why should everything else disappear and we remain? Tell me that, Grady."

Without waiting for an answer, Minton plunged his gloved hand into the water to grab one of the parasol urchins, yanked his arm from the tank, and flung the sea urchin at Grady.

It struck his chest and fell to the floor, as Grady yelped and ducked behind the closest tank. Minton grabbed another urchin and threw it. This urchin splattered against the glass as Minton turned and bolted out the open door. Grady scrambled to his feet and stared at the shattered creatures on the floor, too appalled for a moment to give chase. Minton didn't give a fuck about protecting this place: he wanted it as his private kingdom, that was all.

Enraged, Grady grabbed the knife from his pocket, flicking it open. He ran for the door and down the steps after Minton, who'd nearly reached the Tesla. Grady stopped, panting in helpless fury as he watched Minton lunge for the car door. He'd never stop him now. Grady's hand dropped to his side, and he stiffened.

From the sky came a high-pitched, terrified cry: not a human's cry but a bird's. Immediately it fell silent, but within seconds another bird shrieked, a sound like nothing Grady had ever heard.

It came again, louder, followed by an even more piercing sound, and then another, and another, the shrill screams and hoarse croaking of creatures in pain. Grady hadn't known that birds could make such sounds, that their fear could be translated into this terrible chorus. He dropped the knife and clapped his hands to his ears, gazing at the sky, expecting to see a cloud of birds being chased by some winged predator.

He saw nothing. The trees had grown utterly still. Grady shook his head, trying to make sense of it, turned to see Minton stumbling away from the Tesla, back toward the house. He stopped by the kiʻi pōhaku and scanned the sky, his face a mask of fear and grief.

The cries of the birds grew deafening. Tears streaked Minton's face and he whirled in a frantic circle, searching for the cause of the birds' frenzied cries. Grady flung himself to the ground, watching in disbelief.

"Grady! Grady, please—"

Mist crept across the ground to where Minton stood, forming a shape that Grady recognized: at once coffin-like and resembling a dog that stood on its hind legs like a human. Grady dug his fingers into the earth, praying it wouldn't see him as Minton's pleas erupted into a scream. The mist grew thicker, hiding Minton until his shrieks were abruptly cut off.

For an instant the deafening clamor dissolved into silence: no birds, no insects, no wind, no waves. Then Minton screamed once more, a strangled howl followed by a snarl and a noise like a green branch snapping.

Minton's voice fell silent. Grady heard only the wet snuffling of a large animal and his own ragged breathing. In the rain forest, a bird gave a single loud croaking call, and was answered by the same cry.

CHAPTER 106

He didn't know how much time passed. Hours, it seemed. Stars glimmered in the sky. The moon had risen, sending bands of light across the ocean. The sound of crashing waves echoed his heartbeat, somehow strong and steady. As he got to his feet, a fresh wind carried the smell of the sea, of grass and ferns damp with night dew. On the shore below, black waves rose and fell, releasing clouds of white vapor.

Whatever terrible storm had passed through was gone. Grady turned on his phone's flashlight and walked across the lawn.

Minton's body lay a few yards from the top of the metal stairs. He was sprawled on his back, his face so badly mauled it resembled a bloodied jack-o'-lantern. One arm had been ripped from his shoulder and dragged to a clump of grass. His clothes were shredded so that Grady could see his chest, the clear imprints of teeth surrounding the open cavity where his organs had been. Mountain lions did that, tore open the soft bellies of their prey to devour their entrails.

These tooth marks were bigger and deeper than anything he'd ever seen, far bigger than a dog's or bear's or coyote's. The exposed rib cage glistened, the blood nearly black. Four ribs lay on the grass like a pile of sticks dropped beside a campfire.

Kaupe.

Grady covered his mouth, trying not to be sick. He turned and ran into the house, locking the door behind him. For a minute he stood there, gasping as he tried to process what he'd seen. Minton was dead, that was for sure. There was no way Grady could have killed him—he'd obviously been ripped apart by some animal—but Grady was a witness.

He knew from his EMT days what happened with an unattended death: the cops treated it as a crime scene until the cause could be determined by the medical examiner. Whoever had found the body was questioned, even an immediate family member in shock from grief.

Grady knew he'd be interrogated. Would the cops believe him? Arrest him? He couldn't run away—it was impossible to imagine he'd survive the wilderness a second time. He had to call 911, now; trust in his innocence, trust that for once the police would do the right thing. He'd tell them he came out here because he hadn't heard from his employer for a few days, and found him mauled by a wild animal.

But he had to find that spot where he could get cell reception. Where the fuck was it? He raced through the house, clutching his phone as he tried to find a signal. Minton had texted him in the past weeks, but from which room? Could he have done so from the woods?

He found the spot in a corner of the back deck, facing due east. One bar. He punched in 911 over and over, but the signal was too weak for the call to go through. He hit the EMERGENCY SOS button, then texted 911. He gave his location and a message saying that he'd come here and found his employer dead, attacked by a wild dog. Then he texted Raina.

i'm safe. wes dead. no jessie

He stared at the phone. *No Jessie.* That was one thing Minton hadn't been lying about. Grady was sure of it. Which meant she was somewhere else, dead and perhaps never to be found, he thought dully. Or maybe she was alive. He was too wrung out now to think about it. He waited for a reply to the texts he'd sent, to Raina and 911, but none came.

He went back inside, drained and numb. He surveyed the room with the aquariums, went into the kitchen and retrieved a spatula to pick up the two parasol urchins. One was crushed, the other partly intact. He hoped it would survive. He dropped both into the tank and watched as they drifted to the bottom, thinking again how Minton hadn't hesitated to use these endangered creatures as a means to kill him. Was that what had ultimately drawn Kaupe's rage and hunger? That Minton had not just trespassed upon its territory and vandalized it but destroyed the very things he'd sworn to protect?

He walked outside, to the ki'i pōhaku. Prints surrounded the carved stone—Minton's and those of a large animal—leaving a clear trail to where Minton's corpse had been dragged. Grady retrieved his backpack and went to the storage shed, where he grabbed some rags. He went to Cory's bungalow and wiped down anything he might have touched, returned to the house and did the same thing. He balled up the rags and shoved them in his pocket, and walked back onto the deck.

He stared down at the sea, listening to the waves but remembering the cries of unknown, suffering birds.

They say it sometimes imitates someone you love—to lure you.

Grady and Raina had heard human voices calling for help. Minton, like Grady, had heard his birds. Minton had claimed the role of guardian of Hokuloa and its imperiled creatures, yet he hadn't hesitated to use those fragile wana as weapons. And he was incapable of seeing that humans were animals, too, vulnerable and in need of protection.

Grady shivered. Minton had wanted to control Hokuloa, that was all. He had no qualms about disposing of anything, human or otherwise, that might prevent him from doing that.

Why had Kaupe shown Grady the way here? As a witness? As a warning? But then why had Kaupe never taken action before now, against Minton and the numberless people who had desecrated this island and all those others? Grady had no clue.

Why should everything else disappear and we remain? Tell me that, Grady.

He had no answer. His father had disappeared. His brother had done his best to make himself disappear. Grady would never have an answer.

From the underbrush came the whispery call of an 'anianiau, a tiny yellow bird that Grady had seen only once in the aviary. A moment later, a second 'anianiau answered, and then a third. Grady stared up at the darkening sky, the miles of unbroken, unspoiled forest that surrounded him, breathed in the subtle musky fragrance of the honeycreepers and felt the hairs on his neck rise—chickenskin, though not from fear but continuing amazement. He remembered Minton's words when he first showed Grady the aviary.

Can you imagine, coming to these islands twelve hundred years ago, and there were so many of those birds you were overwhelmed by their smell?

What would happen to this place if people learned that the man who'd paid for it was a serial killer? Scandal, lawsuits. The Hokuloa wilderness might be sold, or portions of it. Whatever foundations Minton had endowed would be dissolved, their reputations irrevocably tarnished. Without Minton's wealth, it would all disappear.

Or maybe not. From some distant part of the forest, a pueo hooted, and another answered. He listened, but they didn't call again. He turned and went inside to wait for the police. He would tell them some version of the truth, a truth that he hoped they'd believe, one that perhaps would keep this place safe.

CHAPTER 107

The police arrived about an hour later. They came by boat—two men and a woman, all in uniform, along with a detective in plain clothes and someone who was either from the hospital or the morgue. He was the only one wearing a mask.

Grady met them at the top of the metal stairs leading down to the dock. He didn't need to show them where the body was. It was the first thing they saw when they stepped onto the property, shining their flashlights through the trees and onto the ground in front of the house.

"I found him like that," he told the man who introduced himself as Detective Fairchild—the same guy Raina had pointed out to Grady at Kahawai Beach. "I hadn't heard from him for a few days and got worried, so I hiked out. I got here this afternoon, and after I checked the house, I found him lying there."

"Did he own a dog?"

"No, not that I know of."

"Do you?"

"No."

"Did you see the dog? Or some other wild animal?"

"No."

"Then why do you think it was a dog that killed him?"

"I don't know for sure. But I can't think what else could have."

The detective shone his flashlight on the ground. He crouched, staring at the body. "Well, it sure looks like some animal. Tell me again why you think it was a dog, if you didn't see one?"

"I did see one. But not here. Crossing the lava field."

The detective did a double take. "You crossed the lava field?"

Grady nodded. "There's no other way—I couldn't get hold of Minton, and I don't know the code to the security gate. I saw the dog in the lava field—that's how I found my way out. I was lost, I got disoriented, then I saw this dog, and it seemed to be on some kind of trail that led out of the lava field. So I followed it."

"You found a path through the lava field? Why didn't you drive?"

"I wasn't sure my truck could make it. I didn't want to get stranded—then I'd end up walking anyway."

Fairchild trained his flashlight on the Tesla. "Seems like he had no trouble getting out here."

"Wes has been coming here for years." Grady hoped the night would hide his anxiety over his lies and half-lies. "And that's one of those SUV Teslas. He knows the road. He's never had any problems, as far as I know. And . . ." He hesitated, then shrugged sheepishly. "The roads out here—they still freak me out." That, at least, was the truth.

The detective nodded, and stood as one of the other cops walked over. Her name tag read Emilia Aguillera. The detective cocked his head. "He says he got here by following an old road across the lava field. I've never heard of anyone who's even seen it."

Grady accompanied the detective around the grounds while the others took photos of Minton's corpse. After a while two of them went down to the boat, returning with a stretcher and body bag. Grady quickly averted his eyes as they gathered Minton's remains.

He tried desperately to think of a game plan. Should he tell Fairchild the truth—that Minton was a serial killer? Once that information was widely known, it would almost certainly compromise the future of the wilderness area, at least for the avian research facility funded by Minton. Would his fortune go to the families of the victims? Would the land be sold? Probably there'd be years of legal wrangling, not to mention an insane media circus. Grady had seen and read and listened to enough TV and news stories to know that

Hokuloa Point would become a magnet for tabloid sites, podcasters, murderabilia fans—every kind of crazy he could imagine, coming here in boats and helicopters, hiking through the forest, using drones to shoot footage of the compound and the surrounding woods. What would happen to the wild birds then, with their sanctuary disturbed and perhaps lost forever?

Yet if he said nothing, Minton's victims would remain among the missing. Their families would live with the torment of not knowing their fates. Would that be preferable to the knowledge that they'd been murdered?

The thoughts sickened him. He felt trapped by the realization that no matter what he did, there would be terrible consequences for others, humans and animals alike.

He wished he understood more—anything—about the Native people here: their involvement with the land and its legal status. He was a terrible liar, but if he stalled on telling the whole truth, he might confide in Dalita and Lorelei. Maybe they'd know someone who could help.

"Let's go inside," the detective said, interrupting his thoughts. "How long have you worked for Minton?"

"Only about three weeks. This is the first time I've been here," Grady said as he approached the steps of the main house with the detective and Aguillera. "I'm the caretaker at his place on Hokuloa Road. He spends most of his time here, I keep an eye on things there."

"Yes, the mysterious Mr. Minton." The detective stopped on the porch to gaze at the view. Even in the dark, it was spectacular.

"Can you believe this?" he said to Aguillera. "I wouldn't ever leave either. This is all a wildlife sanctuary. My wife's involved with the island Audubon Society—she said he arranged for it to be turned into a research station for bird scientists after he died. His house, too. I guess that's the one you live in," he added to Grady. "I think that's supposed to be their administrative quarters. I guess sooner rather than later, now."

Inside, Grady switched on the lights.

"Whew! This is quite a setup," the detective observed, walking around the aquariums. "If you weren't the caretaker here, who helped him out with it?"

Grady thought of Cory, ashamed and sickened that he hadn't done so before now. Could Cory possibly have survived? The police hadn't mentioned seeing a body in the water, or washed up onshore. Cory might still be alive. If so, and knowing Cory's distrust of the cops, would Cory want Grady to tell the police that he'd been here? Grady swallowed, finally said, "I don't know."

Fairchild raised an eyebrow. "Can anyone vouch for your where-abouts before you came here?"

Grady hesitated. "No."

Fairchild continued to stare at him, until Grady blurted, "Have they found Jessica Kiyoko? She's friends with a girl I know in town. I thought . . ." He realized he shouldn't finish that sentence.

"Not yet," said Aguillera, and she headed back to the boat.

The detective peered at Grady's face. "Do you want to see a doctor?"

"Uh, no, I'm okay."

But really, he wasn't. Perhaps Minton had deserved to die, though Grady had never believed he'd be able to kill him. Everything he'd ever known or learned, all his hours of EMT and wilderness training — it had all been designed to keep someone alive. Yet he still had some responsibility for Minton's death. Inadvertent, if Kaupe had used him as a lure or distraction so that he could kill him. But that didn't change the fact that Minton's corpse had lain a few yards away from where Grady stood now.

And Grady hadn't even accomplished what he'd set out to do — find Jessica. Once again, he'd failed.

"Grady?" He looked up to see the detective gazing at him. "Once we're back in town, do you have friends you can stay with?"

Grady stared at him. Wasn't he going to be arrested, or held for questioning? He shook his head, trying to process this. "Yeah, I have friends. But I'd just as soon go to where I've been staying on Hokuloa Road."

"Okay. We'll take you there, although we'll be here awhile. You sure you're okay? You must be exhausted."

"I'll be all right," he said, and ran his hands through his hair.

All he wanted was to get the hell away from Hokuloa Point. Drink himself into a stupor, forget everything that had happened here. Buy a ticket back home and sleep in his own bed in his childhood room and accept that he was never going to be anything but a carpenter doing day jobs for the rest of his life.

But then he looked out to where a frigate bird hovered above the cliffs in the moonlight, the long dark curve of the Hokuloa Peninsula like a great arm extending protectively from the lower slope of the volcano; the lava field and rain forest and gulches, all the untold things that flew and crawled and swam around them, seen and unseen. He'd never be able to forget this.

When the detective escorted him down to the boat, Grady found the others had gathered in the small cabin to radio in to the PD and morgue. The zippered body bag lay on a table like a cleaned fish. Grady left them and went to the stern. He watched the ocean, then lifted his head to see a brilliant golden orb shining above the eastern horizon. Hokuloa, the planet Venus in her aspect as the morning star. When he lowered his gaze, he saw its reflection in the dark water—an orange blur, seeming to bob up and down in the waves. He thought of the gumby suit, of Bree Farris's anguished expression when she confessed that she hadn't notified the authorities.

They would have been dead for a long time. It's better that no one ever found them.

He closed his eyes for a moment. When he opened them again, a cloud had moved across the horizon, and the morning star was gone.

CHAPTER 108

They finally arrived at Wes's place on Hokuloa Road, hours later. He was starting to feel almost delirious with exhaustion, the way he'd felt during his first jet-lagged days of quarantine. When the police car stopped at the security gate, Detective Fairchild turned to look at Grady in the back seat.

"You want me to drive you up?"

Grady shook his head. "Thanks, no. I could use the air."

Fairchild sighed. "Yeah, me too. This is what we call an unattended death," he said. "It looks pretty clear to me that your boss was attacked and killed by some animal out there at Hokuloa Point, but until the cause of death is determined, this remains an open investigation. Once the news breaks that Minton's dead, there's going to be a feeding frenzy for reporters all over the world. So for now we don't want any publicity, and I don't want you talking to anyone about any of this. *Anyone*. Do you understand?" Grady nodded. "There's a lot at stake here, for the island, for a lot of people. We'll contact you if and when the time comes that we need you to make a statement."

Grady got out of the car with his backpack, thanked Fairchild, and punched in the security code. The detective lifted a finger in a wave, then turned back onto Hokuloa Road toward town. Grady stood beside the gate and watched until the car was out of sight, wondering who those people were, the ones who had so much at stake.

CHAPTER 109

He texted Raina that he was home safe.

Omg sure you're ok

Yeah just beat

What about jessie???

He rubbed his head, feeling gutted by his failure, as he summoned the strength to compose a reply.

She wasn't there, he typed at last. Cops haven't found her. Too tired to talk, I'll call you later.

He turned off his phone, lay down on the couch, and fell into a sleep so profound that, when he woke, he thought he was back in Maine. Someone stood over him and he smiled, thinking it was his mom, but then Dalita enfolded him in a hug, brilliant sunlight streaming behind her.

"Dalita," he said thickly.

"Shh. I just heard what happened—friend of Lor's heard it on the scanner. Crazy story! I can't believe Wes is dead. Thank god you found him. Look, I'm not gonna stay—I just wanted to make sure you're all right. You should keep sleeping. I brought you this..." She pointed to a thirty rack of Pabst Blue Ribbon on the kitchen counter. "If you don't want to be alone, I can stick around."

He sat up groggily and ran his hands through his hair, felt grit and stubble when he touched his chin. He needed to shower.

He asked, "What time is it?"

"After four. You been asleep all day. I know, I kept trying to call."

"Four? In the afternoon?"

"You want me to stay?"

"No thanks. No offense," he added.

"That's okay. I want to hear about it, when you're ready to talk. They said you walked across the lava field. Is that true?" He nodded, and she shook her head. "You know you're gonna be on the news, yeah?"

"Oh fuck . . ."

"Come on! Richest guy in Hawai'i gets killed by a wild boar and his caretaker finds him? How is that not news?"

"A boar? It wasn't a boar. It was a wild dog. No, not a dog, it was—"

She pressed her hand gently across his mouth. "Don't. Better we don't talk about that, okay?"

She withdrew her hand, and Grady sighed wearily. He felt even more exhausted than when he'd gotten back here, if that was possible. "Right. Did Lor hear anything else on the scanner?"

"Just that Wes is dead and you found him. But I guarantee you, they'll be popping champagne at the Audubon Society."

She gave him the kind of look his mom used to when he stayed home sick from school. "You don't look too good. I'm gonna head back, but you need anything, just call me, yeah? I'll check with you tomorrow."

He stumbled from the couch to walk her out to her truck. "Thanks again," he said. "Lorelei's with the kids?"

"She wanted to come, but I claimed privilege. We'll do dinner as soon as you feel up to it."

She started to get into the truck, stopped. "Oh yeah, this is fucking weird. Jessica Kiyoko? That girl who disappeared, the one on the plane with you? They just found her."

Grady stared at her in horror. "Oh no . . ."

"No! I mean, they found her alive. Some hikers saw her staggering around in the forest. That night she disappeared? She says she was walking home when some dog attacked her—didn't attack her, it started chasing her. She ran and went into the park near the Quad—it abuts the Ounawai woods. She says she fell into a gulch and couldn't climb out. She's been there all this time. She says she hardly remembers anything, just that she stuck close to a waterfall. She's in the hospital. No one can see her because of COVID, they're not even going to let her parents come."

"Are you frigging kidding me?"

"No." Dalita gave him an odd look. "I thought you'd be happy. She'll probably want to tell you the details herself when you see her, so act surprised."

"I don't need to act," he said.

She laughed. "Well, there was our wild dog, anyway."

"When did they find her?"

"Yesterday afternoon, I read about it online before dinner. Her story's not getting so much attention because of Minton, but I bet she's okay with that—they're still going to charge her for violating quarantine. I'll talk to you tomorrow, okay? Get some more rest. Aloha."

He watched her drive off, feeling oddly numb. Shock, he realized—it would be a while before that wore off. Probably an even longer while before he could wrap his head around all that had happened. Maybe he never would, and he'd have to accept that.

He went back into the 'ohana and opened a beer. He texted his mother and Donny and Zeke, making a preemptive strike before the story hit the national news. He imagined the headlines.

BIRD-LOVING BILLIONAIRE MAULED BY MYSTERY BEAST?

Shit like that.

He finished the beer and called Raina. She didn't pick up, so he left a message. "Hey, Raina, it's Grady. Dalita just came by and told me about Jessica. I'm going back to sleep, but let me know if you want to talk and when you want to get together."

He waited awhile, drinking a second then a third beer to see if she replied. Finally he showered and went back to bed, and didn't wake till the following morning.

CHAPTER 110

Raina arrived the next day. He was reluctant to go into town, imagining TV cameras or police lying in wait for him. She let herself in at the security gate, pulled up in front of the house and jumped out, running over to hug him.

"Oh my god, Grady..."

He buried his face in her hair, held her close until she drew away, swiping her eyes with one hand. "Are you crying?" he asked.

"Almost. I did when I found out Jessie was okay."

"Have you seen her?"

"Only on FaceTime. They're keeping her in the hospital till tomorrow—they had to fully rehydrate her. She looked terrible."

Raina turned to stare at the screened upstairs windows of the aviary.

"I let them go," Grady said. "Before I headed out."

"I'm glad." She took his hand and squeezed it hard, then reached into the car for a paper bag. "I got some breakfast sandwiches at that food truck by Fitzie's."

Grady made coffee, and they sat outside the 'ohana to eat. For a while neither of them spoke. Finally Raina looked at him and asked, "Did you tell the police what you found? The drugs and phones, those clothes?"

He swallowed, remembering Bree Farris's story about the gumby suit, that smeared orange reflection of the morning star on the dark Pacific. "No. I didn't lie to them about anything. I just...didn't tell them."

"What *did* you tell them?"

"That I was worried about my boss and decided to hike out there to see if he was okay." He looked at Raina's face, mingled anger and disappointment, but also, maybe, relief. "Look, if everyone finds out what he was doing, what happens to the Hokuloa wilderness area? There'd be a million lawsuits. Reporters trying to crawl all over that place."

He clutched his head. "God, no matter what I do, it's wrong."

"What about those photos you said you took? Of . . . of what you found at Wes's place."

"I don't know. I need to think. Something I'm not doing a very good job of at the moment."

She reached over to take his hand. "How about you come to my place later and I make you dinner. I promise not to make you think about anything."

"That would be great," said Grady. Unexpectedly, he felt his heart open, like when he first saw the aviary. "I would love that."

CHAPTER 111

Two days later he went to Raina's apartment. Not for dinner but for lunch with her and Jessie, who'd been released from the hospital and was staying with Raina. He stopped at Mak Supe on the way. The same two sisters stood behind the register, wearing matching Wonder Woman masks. He nodded a greeting, and they responded cheerfully. He picked out a bottle of wine for Raina and Jessie, a six-pack of PBR for himself, and started to the register.

He stopped in front of the cooler holding clear plastic boxes of leis. He still didn't know what the deal was with those, but they were pretty, and for the moment, he had money in his account. He knew that wouldn't last—he no longer had a job—but he wanted to do something nice. He picked out two leis, one with plumeria blossoms, the other, small flowers like marigolds.

"Oh, someone's lucky," one of the girls behind the register sang, and he felt himself blush.

He felt nervous as he walked up to Raina's apartment door, balancing the wine, the beer, and the two boxes of leis. Nervous about seeing Jessie, after having projected so much on her, but even more nervous about seeing Raina. Something had shifted between them, and he didn't want to screw it up. He glanced down at the leis. Probably he shouldn't have bought them—it was too much, it would look like he was trying too hard.

But then the door opened and Raina stood there, grinning as she reached up to give him a quick hug. She pulled him inside, opening her arms in a *ta-da!* gesture. "Look who's here."

Jessie sat on the couch. She stood as he entered. She was thinner, her skin darker from the sun, and her round cheeks hollowed out. She wore sweatpants and a T-shirt he recognized as Raina's. Her oversized glasses perched on her nose, slightly askew.

"Hey," she said, smiling tentatively. "I remember you."

"Yeah, me too." He nodded and waited awkwardly, unsure how to proceed, then remembered his arms were full. He set down the beer and wine, handed one of the leis to Jessie and one to Raina. "These are for you."

Raina laughed, delighted. "Thank you!" She opened the box and held it out to Grady. "Can you put it on?"

He did, feeling all thumbs as he tried not to damage the plumeria blossoms. "How's that?"

Raina looked down at it, nodding as her fingers brushed a pink petal. "It's beautiful. No one's given me one in forever. Thank you, Grady."

He shrugged, hugely relieved and a little embarrassed, and turned to Jessie. She'd already slipped the lei around her neck.

"Thank you," she said, and lifted the flowers to her face. "They smell so good."

"You're welcome." He smiled, bent to pick up the six-pack. "Anyone want a beer? I brought wine, too."

"I'll open it."

Raina took the bottle and went into the kitchen. Grady slid out a PBR and set the six-pack on the coffee table. He popped the cap and took a long swallow. Alone with Jessie, his awkwardness returned. He didn't even know her, really—he'd learned more about her from reading news articles online, and from talking to Raina, than from their few minutes of conversation. "I'm glad you're okay," he finally said.

Jessie stared at him and laughed uneasily. "Me too. Here, sit . . ."

She scooched over on the couch and he sat. Her laughter put him at ease, as did Raina, who appeared holding two full wineglasses. She handed one to Jessie and plunked herself in the middle.

"To Jess," she said.

She clinked her glass against Jessie's, then Grady's beer bottle, and with a sigh leaned against him. He took another swallow of beer and looked at Jessie. "Do you feel like talking about it? What happened?"

Jessie nodded. "Yeah, sure. It's not like I haven't told it a million times already. So I left the bar a little while after Raina did and started walking back here. I crossed the parking lot to take a side road, because I was paranoid about the police seeing me breaking quarantine. There's a dirt path there that goes uphill toward the forest, and when I got near it, this dog appeared."

"What kind of dog?" asked Grady.

"Sort of like a German shepherd, only not as big. I couldn't see its color in the dark, but it looked mostly black. It had a curly tail. I turned and ran up the path. I screamed, but I guess no one heard me. It kept after me—it didn't bark, and luckily it never caught up with me, even though I fell a couple of times."

She adjusted her glasses with a frown. "And these got all bent up when I fell. I have to get them fixed when I get home. Anyway, I just kept running, and the next thing I know, I'm in the forest, and the dog is still after me. I don't know how long I ran before I tripped and slid down into a gulch. I landed on my phone and broke it, so I couldn't call or text. Every time I tried to climb out, the dog moved along the top of the gulch, watching me. The next thing I know it's the next morning. Or maybe it's the morning after that—I lost track of time. It was really weird, to tell you the truth." She sipped her wine, shook her head at the memory. "I actually don't remember much of it. Almost like I was dreaming or super-stoned the whole time. There was a little waterfall, so I had water, and I found some guavas that had rolled down into the gulch, and some liliko'i. I kept shouting for help, but I guess no one could hear me. I don't even remember how I climbed out of the gulch, except I had a nightmare that the dog was after me again and I tried to escape. That's when those hikers found me."

Grady listened in silence. He'd told Raina about seeing the dog in the lava field, but it didn't sound like she'd mentioned it to Jessie. He decided that, for now, he wouldn't either. "You're lucky you made it out," he said.

"I know. One of the doctors in the hospital said I might have had a dissociative fugue, when you don't remember anything. They thought I might have been assaulted, but they didn't find any evidence of that. I kept telling them about the dog, but they didn't believe me."

"We believe you," said Raina, and Grady nodded.

"Thanks." Jessie gave them a wan smile.

"What will you do now?"

"Go home for a while. I really need to see my parents—this has been so horrible for them." She seemed on the verge of tears. "The police didn't charge me with breaking quarantine, so that's one good thing. I'll come back in a couple of months, if Raina will put up with me."

"I think I can stand it." Raina slung her arm over Jessie's shoulder. "But we should celebrate, right? You're safe, Grady's safe—we're all here together. And I got fish tacos from Jess's favorite food truck."

Jessie nodded, lifting her wineglass. "Here's to fish tacos. And all of us." This time she really did smile. "Raina told me how hard you were trying to find me, everything you did. Thank you, Grady. I'm so glad I got to see you again."

Grady smiled. "Me too," he said.

CHAPTER 112

Days passed. The knot of guilt and grief inside his chest didn't loosen, but gradually he grew accustomed to it, the way he'd grown accustomed to his father's death. He wasn't sure how to handle his knowledge of Wes's killings. Send an anonymous letter? Wait and hope the police figured it out long after Grady had moved on? Live with this horrible feeling for the rest of his life? Who the fuck knew? He avoided going into Wes's house, and was relieved when he got a phone call from someone at the police department, telling him Wes's attorneys would be handling the Minton estate. Grady could stay there for the moment, but he needed to find somewhere else to live.

Still, one good thing he learned from Cousin Angelo.

"I saw a guy I know today," Angelo announced one night when they were eating chicken mochiko out on Raina's deck. "A lifeguard from the resort, nice kid. Cory Desoto. I felt bad 'cause he had nowhere to go when the resorts all shut down. I heard he was living on the beach for a while and I hadn't seen him, then last week I run into him at the beach. Different beach. He had some crazy-ass story, how someone pushed him from a boat out by the bone reefs and he swam back, slept on a beach and kept swimming the next day. I'm not surprised he made it back—he's a great swimmer, yeah? 'Cause he's a lifeguard!"

"Really?" Raina's eyes grew round. "That's amazing."

Grady swallowed his piece of chicken, reached for his beer. Sipped it as the others waited for his reaction. "That's wild," he said, choosing his next words carefully. "What about whoever did that to him? Pushed him out of the boat? Did he go to the cops about that?"

"Nah, brah, Cory would never go to the cops. Guy who pushed him coulda been a cop, yeah? Anyway, he's going back to Waikiki. Some hotels there, he's thinking they might open soon, he can find work better than here."

After dinner, Grady and Raina walked Angelo out to his car. After he drove off, they started back to the apartment building, but Raina stopped when they reached Grady's truck.

"Wait," she said, and pulled something from her pocket. "I keep forgetting. I got this for you."

She held up a bumper sticker emblazoned with a wave and the words EDDIE WOULD GO. She ran her palm across the bumper to clean it, then affixed it over the remnants of the old GO WIT AL decal.

"There," she said, straightening. She grinned and tapped his shoulder. "Now you won't look so much like a haole. Your truck won't, anyway."

He laughed. "Thanks," he said. He took her hand, and they walked back up to her apartment.

CHAPTER 113

 One morning two weeks later, he got a phone call from a number he didn't recognize. He didn't pick up, and his heart sank when he played back the voicemail message.

"Hi, this is Ailana Chang of the Hokuloa Wilderness Foundation. I'm calling for Grady Kendall. It's important that you get back to me as soon as possible."

Sighing, he set the phone down on the table. He stared at his breakfast, no longer hungry.

He knew that soon he'd have to find somewhere else to live, when the Hokuloa Wilderness Foundation took over Minton's house. He had thought it would take a lot longer for them to work out the details of Minton's estate. Grady had been eking out the money in his checking account—his only big purchase had been the firepit where he and Raina sat when she stayed overnight. Once or twice a week he and sometimes Raina had dinner with Dalita and her family, or he and Raina met up with Cousin Angelo. Grady had helped himself to whatever food staples remained in Minton's house. Gas for the truck was his biggest expense.

He had enough money to buy a plane ticket home, but much as he still missed Maine, the thought of returning filled him with something close to despair. Raina would never leave the island—she'd told him that when he carefully broached the topic.

But Grady would no longer fit in at home, any more than he fit in here. He would never be able to explain what this place was like to anyone in Maine. Even if he could, they would never understand. He didn't understand it himself.

He sat for a few minutes before deciding he might as well bite the bullet, and called Ailana Chang.

"Hey," he said, when a woman's voice answered. "This is Grady Kendall. I just got a call from this number."

"Grady, hi! Thank you so much for returning my call." She sounded older than he was, her voice smooth and confident. "I'm Ailana Chang. I'm going to be the head biologist out at the Hokuloa Point Wilderness Preserve—that's what we're calling it now. I'm also doubling as general dogsbody. We're still working out the details, but because of Wesley Minton's trust, there's enough money now for us to set up a permanent research station out there. And we're still figuring out what to do with all the marine life he had out there in those aquariums. We already have a few interns who'll be staying at the house at the point, along with me and the other team biologist, but we're looking for a caretaker. I read about you in *Island Pilot* and I understand you were Wes's caretaker?"

"Yeah," Grady replied, feeling as though he might not have awakened completely. "Yes, I was. Am. But at his house closer to town, not out there on the point."

"Right, yes, someone told me that. Anyway, we'll definitely need a caretaker, and you'll have your own bungalow."

"Yeah. Yes! I mean, yes, that would be great—I'd definitely be up for doing that."

"Are you sure? Do you want to think about it?"

"No," he said. "I actually haven't stopped thinking about it since I was out there. Can my girlfriend come visit when she wants?"

"Yeah, we can figure something out. Eventually we may be able to build bigger living quarters, maybe with a small school or something. Experiential-based learning for children of the team members. I know Wes had big plans for that land, with his luxury resort. We have big plans, too. Only different ones," she said, and laughed in delight.

CHAPTER 114

The following week, after a number of Zoom meetings, he finally met Ailana Chang in person, at the security gate that served as portal to the Hokuloa wilderness. For Grady, it was mostly a meet-and-greet before he relocated out here. Ailana had already started to move in. She told him she'd walk the few miles from the compound at the point to the entrance, then ride back with him in the truck. She climbed into the passenger seat, a tall brown woman with a ponytail and NO TMT cap. She wore broken-in hiking shoes and long khaki pants, a white shirt stained with sweat and dust, a face mask printed with sea turtles. Around her neck was a pair of binoculars that looked like the set he'd taken from Minton's house, and still had. From their Zoom meetings, Grady knew that she was thirty-three, and also that she was intimidatingly beautiful.

But he'd felt more at ease with her as they spoke about her research goals.

"I know Wes wanted to make use of that gene-splicing tech with the mosquitoes," she said during their first meeting. "But I think we need to establish what the bird population is out there—how many of them, which species, how healthy they are. I know Wes believed some extinct species survived there, but we'll need to do some taxonomic studies to determine if that's actually the case."

Grady shook his head. "I know there're some birds that no one thought were here. I heard 'anianiau—"

Ailana gave him a sharp look. "How do you know? They're endemic to Kaua'i. No one's ever seen them here."

"Wes had them in his aviary. And I heard them when I was out here. I think I heard ʻalalā, too—those Hawaiʻian crows."

"Huh." Ailana regarded him thoughtfully. "You actually know about this stuff."

"Some. I'm not a scientist, but I studied to be a wilderness guide. I always loved this kind of thing. And the birds here..." He gestured at the screen, smiling as though it were the forest he'd wandered out at Hokuloa Point. "They're amazing. They're not like anything else on earth. It would be an honor to work out there." That might've sounded hokey, but he meant it.

Ailana didn't seem to think it was hokey. She began emailing him articles about avian malaria and genetics, along with lists of building supplies they'd eventually need for constructing a lab. There would also be preparations for the kiʻi pōhaku to be relocated to its original setting, with a ceremony by the island's Native elders asking forgiveness.

"We're gonna work you hard," she'd said the last time they Zoomed. "I hope you're okay with that."

"I am," said Grady.

Now he put the truck into gear and they lurched forward on the rutted road.

"Whoa!" Ailana yelped, bracing herself on the dashboard. "I think the first thing we're gonna do is invest in a new truck for you. This is kind of a shit truck."

"Yeah, I know." Grady shrugged. "But it gets the job done."

"There are some electric pickups coming out—we can look into those."

"Wouldn't that be super-expensive?"

"Trust me, in ten years, everyone on the island will be driving one."

When they reached the compound, Ailana walked with him to one of the bigger bungalows. New sheets were folded and stacked on the bed. There were new towels in the bathroom.

"This will be your ʻohana when you move in next week. We donated all of Minton's stuff to Goodwill," Ailana explained. "Clean slate. We want the best people here to do research. Not that we're going to have any trouble. As soon as the island's Audubon Society sent out that press release about all the supposedly extinct species they think are here, I get a hundred emails every day, people sending me their CVs. Lot of serious birders out there," she added, "along with the ornithologists. When you're done unpacking, let's go have a drink on the porch. You've got to be tired after that drive." She rubbed her jaw, wincing. "Yeah, we're going to look into a new truck. The shocks on that one are shot."

He unpacked a few things he'd brought with him, then washed up and changed into clean clothes, combed his damp hair back with his fingers. He texted Raina a photo of the inside of the bungalow, and another of an 'i'iwi hovering above an 'ākala blossom.

> I'll be back tomorrow morning. Luxury accommodations here
> as soon as you can get out.

She texted back a string of hearts. gonna need a bigger bed

He laughed. He'd already broached the idea with Ailana of bringing Raina out here, too, when things started to settle down with the pandemic and the research station. If they wanted to have a school here, they'd need teachers and perhaps some teachers' aides. Raina would be great at that. They'd for sure want docents, once they started allowing people to visit. Ailana seemed open to the idea, even enthusiastic.

"I loved going to that aquarium when I was a girl! Yeah, let's talk about it when she comes to see you. We can't do anything till everyone gets a vaccine. But after that..." She grinned. "I love bringing the community into this. You protect a place like Hokuloa by sharing it, letting people see how special it is. We'll have to do that carefully, but it'll happen."

He texted a string of hearts back to Raina and walked across the long grass toward the main house, the sound of the wind fading into birdsong and rustling palm fronds. The sea wind felt fresh and cool, despite it being late afternoon. Yellow-gray birds arrowed overhead, and two larger birds carried on a raucous conversation from the upper branches of an avocado tree. Ailana walked out to meet him, her gaze fixed on the avocado tree. Her mask hung loosely around her neck above the binoculars.

"Do you see them?" She gestured at the avocado tree. "There are your 'alalā—Hawai'ian crows."

Grady watched the birds. "So they really aren't extinct."

"They are. Just not here. I've seen at least six nesting pairs, and that's just by the compound."

"That's insane."

"Right?" Like Grady, she appeared slightly bewildered. "That's not all. There are 'akialoa here—they look like the Kaua'i 'akialoa, but with darker plumage. The Kaua'i 'akialoa became extinct in 1965, and there's never been any record of one endemic to this island. There are other birds in the rain forest, too, that have supposedly gone extinct, finches and honeycreepers. Some species disappeared in the 1800s, some longer ago than that—we only know about them because amateur naturalists described them when the white people first invaded. It's like discovering dinosaurs in your backyard."

"How do you know they're in the forest?"

"Minton. He left a stack of notebooks this high," she said, gesturing, "where he recorded everything he saw here over the years. Mostly birds, but some species of land snails, too, and sphinx moths. He was an amazing amateur naturalist." She sighed. "I only talked to him on the phone a few times early in the year, but he knew my mother."

"Your mother?"

"Yes. We lived up there in his house, my mom and I—he bought it from her, I don't know, at least twenty years ago."

Grady stared at her. "You're that model's daughter? Maxine . . . ?"

"Maxine Kaiwi. Yeah. We only lived there a few years—after my parents divorced, my mother thought it was too isolated to be up there with just me. She thought there were spirits there. But I loved it—I mean, I *loved* it. I cried for weeks after we moved. Then when my mom died, I went to live with my father in Honolulu, but all I ever wanted to do was get back here. I got my undergrad at UCLA, then I went and did my PhD at Cornell, on contemporary waif biota and their impact on critically endangered kiwikiu on Maui. Being here now . . ." She turned in a circle, arms raised and head tipped back, an expression of delight on her face. "This is all I ever wanted."

They walked to the side of the house and onto the back deck. Grady sat as Ailana went into the kitchen, returning with a bottle of champagne and two wineglasses. "I saw you brought a couple cases of beer," she said, setting one of the glasses in front of him. "But I feel like celebrating. The interns arrive tomorrow, they've been in quarantine at a motel by the airport. After that we'll all be drinking cheap beer for a while."

She laughed, opened the bottle and poured some into their glasses, raised hers in a toast.

"To the 'akialoa."

Grady clinked his glass against hers. They sat on the same side of the table, a safe distance apart, and gazed out at the ocean, the waves crashing on the cliffs. Ailana removed her turtle-patterned mask and set the binoculars on top to keep it from blowing away.

"Look," she said, pointing to where a black shape broke the surface of the blue water. "Humpback."

"Wow," said Grady. "I've only ever seen minke whales, back in Maine."

They both sat and drank their champagne in silence. Finally, Ailana swept out her arm to indicate the ocean and distant islands. "If every single human being on this planet disappeared tomorrow, and this was all that was left, I would be totally okay with that."

"Yeah," he said at last, and nodded. "I would, too."

CHAPTER 115

A few days after he returned from the trip to Hokuloa Point, Raina helped him finish packing. "I'll see you once you're settled," she said as they stood beside the old pickup, now filled with cartons of supplies Ailana had ordered, along with his suitcase, a box of books from Minton's house, the firepit. "You think next Sunday?"

"Sooner," Grady replied, and kissed her.

That afternoon, he gave the firepit to Dalita and Lorelei, stopping by their house before he began the long drive to the point. "We'll never see you," Dalita complained. "It's a long trip, if they'd even let us in."

"They will." He helped her carry the firepit a safe distance from the play set they'd built earlier in the summer. "I told them it was a stipulation of my taking the job, that I could have friends visit. You can cram into one of the bungalows."

"Wow, listen to you! Mister Boss Man with the stipulations."

He laughed, then shook his head. "Thanks for all your help, Dalita—you and Lor both."

They made their goodbyes, and he drove on to Hokuloa Road, running over a mental list of what he'd do once he got back to the point. Unpack, catch up with reading an article Ailana had sent him on the relationship between birds and those odd bees he'd seen. Go through Minton's books to see what he had on designing a new, more efficient water catchment system. As Hale o Nalowale rose into sight, he saw the white-haired old man, who sat beside his shopping cart eating a mango. For the first time, Grady noticed that the shopping cart was jammed with paint cans.

On the plain behind him, Hale o Nalowale loomed above the dust and brown grass. The building had been painted over again, columns of old names and new ones covering the concrete walls beneath the words

NEVER FORGET THE MISSING
#ISLANDNALOWALE

Cory Desoto's name was gone from the list. So was Jessica Kiyoko's.

AUTHOR'S NOTE

The Hokuloa Peninsula is a fictional creation, as are all other locations in this novel.

In late 2021, the US Fish and Wildlife Service removed twenty-three species from the Federal Lists of Endangered and Threatened Wildlife and Plants due to extinction. Eleven of those species were found in Hawaiʻi, eight of them birds. Only seventeen forest bird species now survive in the Hawaiʻian archipelago. As of this writing, several of the endemic Hawaiʻian birds mentioned in *Hokuloa Road* are extinct or presumed extinct: Their survival in the story is a fictional construct. Visit https://www.federalregister.gov/documents/2021 /09/30/2021-21219/endangered-and-threatened-wildlife-and-plants -removal-of-23-extinct-species-from-the-lists-of for details.

The deadly parasol sea urchins in the book do not exist but were inspired by the flower sea urchin, *Toxopneustes pileolus*.

There is a wealth of information about Hawaiʻi available in print and online. For those interested in learning more about Hawaiʻi's language, culture, and spiritual practices, ulukau.org is an excellent starting point. For information on donating or volunteering to protect and restore Hawaiʻi's wild and culturally important spaces: Hawaiʻi Land Trust, https://hilt.squarespace.com. For information on endangered bird species on Maui, check out the Maui Forest Bird Recovery Project, https://mauiforestbirds.org.

ACKNOWLEDGMENTS

Many people helped me with researching and refining this novel: Any errors are my own and not theirs. My deepest thanks to all of the following:

Danielle Bukowski and Nell Pierce, my wonderful agents at Sterling Lord Literistic.

My editor, Helen O'Hare, who guided me through many (many) revisions with infinite patience. Thanks as well to Josh Kendall, Alyssa Persons, Gabrielle Leporati, and Betsy Uhrig at Mullholland Books, who helped bring this novel into the world. Dianna Stirpe did an extraordinary job copyediting the manuscript: I truly can't imagine what this novel would have been like without her insight and expertise.

The Eastern Frontier Foundation provided me with a writing residency, safe harbor, and much inspiring conversation with other artists.

I treasure several conversations with Susan Conley which inspired Grady as a protagonist.

Kristabelle Munson read numerous versions of this story from the get-go, sharing a profound knowledge and love of Maui's people, culture, spirituality, and history. I would never have finished this book without that support and encouragement.

Ellen Datlow, Callie Hand, Ben Holz, and Bill Sheehan all read early versions of this in manuscript and offered suggestions to improve it.

ACKNOWLEDGMENTS

Stephanie Keiko Kong taught me the nuances of Pidgin with humor, insight, and grace, sharing her delight in, and knowledge of, the language during a dark year.

Halena Kapuni-Reynolds critiqued an earlier version of this manuscript, sharing his great insight and knowledge of Hawai'i's culture and its spiritual practices.

Tony Pisculli's close edit and comments helped me immensely as I sought to fine-tune Grady's outsider perspective in Hawai'i.

Andy O'Brien was my go-to for Grady's Maine vocabulary: See NSW work by Andy and Hanji Chang at ochangcomics.com.

Tristan Grant advised me on WOW and additional Maine nomenclature.

Callie Hand and Ben Holz shared their 'ohana in Makawao, where much of this book was written. Julia and Frank Holz opened a portal to Kihei, and Julia spent many days with me hiking the area around Keone'ō'io and 'Āhihi-Kīna'u and exploring the lava fields.

Finally, all my love to John Clute, who explored the island with me, and each time showed me more.

ABOUT THE AUTHOR

Elizabeth Hand is the author of more than nineteen cross-genre novels and collections of short fiction, including *The Book of Lamps and Banners* and *Curious Toys*. Her work has received the Shirley Jackson Award (three times), the World Fantasy Award (four times), and the Nebula Award (twice), as well as the James M. Tiptree Jr. and Mythopoeic Society Awards. She's a longtime critic and contributor of essays for the *Washington Post,* the *Los Angeles Times, Salon, Boston Review,* and the *Village Voice,* among many others. She divides her time between the Maine coast and North London.

MULHOLLAND BOOKS

You won't be able to put down these Mulholland Books.

CHILD ZERO *by Chris Holm*

CONFIDENCE *by Denise Mina*

HOKULOA ROAD *by Elizabeth Hand*

THE DEVIL TAKES YOU HOME *by Gabino Iglesias*

BRIDGE *by Lauren Beukes*

Visit mulhollandbooks.com for
your daily suspense fix.